The Sun Chemist

'You didn't bring it,' was his gloomy greeting.

'No, well – '

'Okay, I heard. It's serious. You'll have dinner with me tonight. Today you will be busy. There are many things to find out.'

'Chemical things?' I said.

'What else?'

'But I'm no chemist. I haven't the faintest – '

'Persevere. They'll tell you. *I'll* tell you. Waste no time,' he said, and clicked off.

'Yes, well, our friend got it nearly right,' Julian said with satisfaction, coming in at that moment. 'I've just been speaking to Finster, who is handling the thing here. Mashed potato! It is a botanical species called *Ipomoea batatas*.'

'What's that?'

'Finster says it is in fact a kind of sweet potato.'

'Is he mashing it?'

'To tell the truth, I'm not absolutely on top line what he is doing with it. You're finding out, I understand.'

Lionel Davidson is a three-times winner of The Gold Dagger Award (for *The Night of Wenceslas*, *A Long Way to Shiloh* and *The Chelsea Murders*). His thrillers and adventure novels, most recently *Kolymsky Heights*, have won him enormous international acclaim. He has travelled widely, spent some time in Israel, but now lives in North London.

*Also by Lionel Davidson
and available in Mandarin*

A Long Way to Shiloh
The Chelsea Murders
The Rose of Tibet
The Night of Wenceslas
Smith's Gazelle
Making Good Again
Kolymsky Heights

Lionel Davidson

THE SUN CHEMIST

Mandarin

A Mandarin Paperback
THE SUN CHEMIST

First published in Great Britain 1976
by Jonathan Cape Ltd
This edition published 1995
by Mandarin Paperbacks
an imprint of Reed Consumer Books Ltd
Michelin House, 81 Fulham Road, London SW3 6RB
and Auckland, Melbourne, Singapore and Toronto

Copyright © L.D. Film Interests Ltd 1976
The author has asserted his moral rights

A CIP catalogue record for this title
is available from the British Library
ISBN 0 7493 1715 9

Printed and bound in Great Britain
by Cox & Wyman, Reading.

For Ralph and Stella R.

AUTHOR'S NOTE

Much of this story is fictitious; however, it is based on some substantial activities at Rehovot, so I hope that the 'real' people mentioned won't take amiss the things that they have been made to get up to. One further point: Mr Igor Druyanov did not edit volumes 15 and 16 of the Weizmann papers. At the time of writing, this task had not yet been allotted.

'You may have my rich brocades, my laces; take
each household key;
Ransack coffer, desk, bureau;
  Quiz the few poor treasures hid there, con
the letters kept by me.'

Thomas Hardy, *Friends Beyond*

1

I came in quietly, dabbing at the chill spots of rain on my forehead, and took my coat off and began sniffing. As I thought. At it again. I'd never actually caught her at it. I hung the coat up and padded silently down the carpeted corridor and got a fine full view of her through the open study door. She was standing by the window, the thing actually in her mouth, idly scratching some nether part as she looked out.

'Well, Ettie! Still here?'

'Christ!' She spun round, almost coughing it out. 'You come in like a cat!'

'Not finished yet?

'Just giving a last lick,' she said, flapping with the duster. 'I like you tidy in here.'

'Well, that's nice. Have a cigarette, Ettie.'

'I got one. Well, I borrowed one of yours, actually.'

'I see.'

'I run out of mine. Strong, aren't they? I couldn't smoke these all the time.'

'No, well, you don't actually have to, Ettie.'

'It's because I run out. What are the black things on the end for?'

'For Russians with black mouths.'

'Black hearts, more like.'

'Thanks very much.'

'Not yours. Not always. I'm nearly finished now.'

'Good. Did Hopcroft call?'

'No.'

'Or Caroline?'

'Nobody called.'

'Funny.'

'*And* I stayed in all the time, even when gasping for a drag,' she said, nodding at me, and drawing carefully at the one of my father's as she turned and flapped elsewhere in the room. I looked after her and then at the cigarette box she had left open on the desk. Three more gone. Not a tragedy: I never smoked them myself. Still, a principle was at stake. She was taking liberties. Everybody was taking liberties. Why no Hopcroft or Caroline? My stomach rumbled, as always before a journey. Too many things to see to. I sat down and took out a sheet of paper and attended to the first of them.

My sweet darling, Verochka, my joy,

There was no letter from you today, and for me this is a great deprivation. I hope that tomorrow there will be one, and I shall patiently await tomorrow. You ask me, little darling, to fondle you, if only by letter. Verunya, my dear, this is what I do in every word of mine, with every sound. But no such caresses can satisfy me. I hope, however . . .

There was a great deal more, and I toiled over it, conscious of Ettie still in the room, before steaming into the last paragraph.

You do know, don't you, that I think of you every second, that it is you I live, think and breathe. You are not going to be upset and cross but will write me nice tender letters and will love me dearly, kiss and caress me when I am with you, won't you, Verochka? Keep well, my joy, and write to me every day regularly, or I shall get very miserable. Love to my dearly beloved Verusenka.

Your
Chaimchik

'Funny writing that,' Ettie said.

She was behind me, looking over my shoulder.

'Yes. Was there something special you wanted, Ettie?'

'Well.' She seemed nervous, patting at her hair. 'What I was actually wondering,' she said, 'was if you could try a bit this month.'

'I see.'

I hadn't dated the letter, and did so. 'Pinsk, 27 August 1902.' Or was it 1903? I checked again. No, 1902 he'd written it.

'I mean, I don't want to press,' Ettie said, 'but you know. I wanted to catch you before you went.'

'I'm not going till tomorrow.'

'Before you went to the bank.'

'All right.' I'd already been. That's where I'd been to. There'd been endless delays about the tiny bit of foreign currency.

'It's this bleeding lockout that's coming up,' Ettie said. 'You know about that, don't you, a lockout. And you know who'll suffer.'

'The bleeding workers can safely be left to me, Ettie. I'm the expert there.'

'Well, if you're all right, I'll pop off now. You will try, won't you?'

'Yes,' I said, and drew another sheet of paper, frowning.

My dear Mr Motzkin,

Unfortunately I cannot come to you and am forced to contact you in writing. I am terribly hard up; I positively haven't a single pfennig to my name. The first is approaching, and I am unable to pay the landlady; I owe money to several persons who are causing me unbearable unpleasantness. I therefore beg you to let me have at least 30 marks without fail. This is the only source on which I can count. If you refuse, I shall find myself in a positively desperate situation. If I were able to find any other solution, I would have left you in peace, but I am in terrible straits and in fact depend entirely on you. I have nothing to pawn. My compasses have long been in the appointed place; and they are my only wealth. Forgive me for appealing to you.

Yours,

3

I'd heard Ettie in her pop-off routine during the course of this, changing her shoes and housedress, and various bangs to do with her two shopping bags and umbrella. But she'd let Caroline in before she went. I'd heard the doorbell.

'Caroline!'

'Yes.'

'What are you doing?'

'Just a tick.'

She came in like a long wet rat. She was carrying a pair of slacks and a woolly jumper.

'Been shopping?' I said.

'No, I haven't. I'm going to change into these. After a hot bath. It's absolutely pissing down out there,' she said crossly.

'You said you'd call.'

'I just jumped in a taxi. And lucky to get one.'

'Couldn't you have called from where you were?'

'I was at the Public Record Officc, and bloody shrivelled, I can tell you. They've got the heating turned down.'

'Where's Hopcroft?'

'Off to Swiss Cottage.'

'I thought you were going with him.'

'Well, I didn't. It was raining too hard. He took my umbrella. Just look at me. And I've got Willie tonight,' she said, and went.

I thought about this, and heard the bath running. Presently I got on with another letter.

Dear Verochka,

I have as a matter of fact decided not to write any more but to wait until you get around to sending me a Ietter, as incidentally you promised in your last postcard. Since my return from Vienna I have been writing regularly, either every day or every other day, but I haven't even received . . .

Acres more of well-merited complaint. I plodded on to the end.

There remains little to write about myself. My days and weeks are very monotonous, consisting entirely of laboratory work, and this is progressing very well. The end of the vacation is already approaching and people are gradually coming back. Perkin's assistant arrived the other day. His name is Pickles. It's four days since we began working together, and I am very pleased. In the first place there is a human being with whom one can exchange a few words during the day. Secondly, I can talk to him in English, which is extremely useful. By the time you come, I shall be able to converse almost freely . . .

Caroline was babbling from the bathroom. I signed and dated the letter, 'Manchester, 13 September 1904', and had a look at my watch. Half past two. What from Hopcroft?

I padded down the corridor.

'Caroline!'

'Yes.' She still had the water running.

'It's funny Hopcroft hasn't called. I've got to ring Connie.'

'I can't hear you.'

I went in. The untidy girl had dropped her clothes in a heap. She was lying back, smoking, a trickle of hot water still running.

'I said it's funny Hopcroft hasn't called.'

'Water in the lines. I did try to call you, actually. I couldn't get through. My goodness, this is the first time I've been warm today.'

'There's Connie to be considered. I've got to ring her, at Rehovot.'

'You've got your ticket, haven't you?'

'I haven't, darling, actually. Not the actual physical ticket. And I've got such a ton of things to get through.'

'If you could just dot this in the basin,' she said, giving me the cigarette. 'While at the same time screwing all notions that I will go and get your ticket. I'm not running about out there again.'

'Oh.' I tipped the ash off and gave her back the cigarette.

'Yes. I got a couple of jolly interesting things today, actually.'

'Did you, darling?'

'Quite fascinating. There's a Cabinet paper with Ramsay Mac laying off about Chaimchik. He made a tremendously strong impression on Ramsay Mac, you know.'

'Did he? How wonderful.'

'What is the big problem?'

'I have to tell Connie about Hopcroft. Whether he's got the thing or not.'

'He'll swim in, never fear. Literally. I got drenched.'

'What time did he go?'

'Well, I don't know. He was reading next to me. He had got on in some way to India Ofiice things – I don't know why. He drifts a lot. He's probably drifting about Swiss Cottage now. What time is it?'

'Gone half past two.'

'Well, he went before twelve. He'll be yarning to her. He yarns a lot, Hopcroft.' She sat up. 'Damn it. Could you take this a minute?'

I took the cigarette out of her mouth and gave her a towel for her hands.

'Why has Connie got to know now? Why can't you tell her when you see her tomorrow?'

'I don't know why. Some kind of tremendous flap has developed with Bergmann, in Jerusalem. She has to let *him* know. Perhaps he is going somewhcre.'

'Well, Hopcroft will appear. When he does, you can send him out for the ticket.' She was smiling at me.

'It's two hours on in Israel, you see. Half past four there. They knock off early.'

'They'll hang on. Might I ask you a personal question?'

'Ask.'

'What is it about small tits? I mean, I know you like extravagances. Whose is that jumper, incidentally?'

'I don't know.'

'Well, you have a high old time, don't you? *Re* modest

jobs, though, what is it?' She was looking down at her own. 'I know there's supposed to be *something* titillating, to coin a phrase. Only what?'

'What has Willie got to say?'

'Oh, come on. I can't ask him. As between friends. One never really learns when one needs to know.'

'Well, they're very pretty.'

'Do you think they appeal to queerish people?'

'Is Willie queerish?'

'There's such a whole range of things one never finds out. And it goes so fast. I mean, you find out at some stage, presumably. But it's later. You learn about everything too late. Saddening thought.'

'It's a thought of youth. You're in a stage of disquiet.'

'Am I?'

'Owing to youth. It is a stage of disquiet. And your work saddens you. The people one studies always end up dead and usually miserable, after their triumphs. We're analysts of tragedy, darling – at least the smack of it.'

'Yes. Your English is extraordinary, isn't it? Smack.'

'Thanks very much. And I'd love to know about Ramsay Mac and Chaimchik, and I'm sure you've spotted the absolutely relevant thing. You're a bright girl with a lovely brain and exactly right tits. They suit you, they really do. Only what it is, my stomach is turning over and over because of my journey, and I haven't packed or got my ticket, and Hopcroft hasn't phoned, and I have to ring Connie and don't know what to tell her. It's one of those fluid situations, you see. I don't like them.'

'Well, tell me what I can do apart from the ticket, which seems made for Hopcroft.'

'I don't know. His papers will have to be gone through, anyway, when he gets back, for queries.'

'I can go through them. I and my lovely brain,' Caroline said.

'You liked that, did you?'

'Mmm. Quite nice. I'd better get out, then, hadn't I, with this mountain of work.'

I moved over. 'Except you probably can't, damn it – I'll bet anything they turn out to be in Russian. Damn and blast everything. And I'm still wrestling with little Kaplan, in Manchester. I promised him those early letters.'

'I will wrestle with Kaplan, I,' she said, stepping from one steaming leg to the other.

'You cannot, idiot. As you know very well, they're in Russian, too. That's what Kaplan wanted. He didn't like the look of the published English. And I would have run out and got them copied myself if I hadn't worried that you or Hopcroft would ring, instead of slaving away by hand, which is the case you put me in!'

'Igor, darling, you're getting moany and foreign. So if you could just hand over some of your heavenly talc and fuck off.'

The telephone rang just at that moment, so I did, at the trot. Hopcroft.

'Hello.'

'Mr Igor Druyanov?'

Not Hopcroft. Long distance. 'Yes.'

'I have a personal call for you from Rehovot, Israel.

'Yes. All right.'

'Igor?'

'Connie, darling!'

'Well – this – is – amazing. I just this minute put in the call! I thought I would put it in and leave it standing. It is so late. You were going to call me It's amazing!' The ripe, slow, twangy cadences of Brooklyn came plangently over the line, with an undertow of Venezuela. I could see her standing there, the South American butterfly, dark eyes flashing in the animated face, in her room at the end of the corridor, in the glacial calm of the President's House, the nation's shrine.

'Well, you see – '

'Meyer is here. I am in Meyer's house He wants to say hello.'

I rapidly readjusted. Not in the nation's shrine. In Meyer's house. Next to Sir Isaac Wolfson's house. Natural pine, royal-blue carpets, splendour, many pictures; outside trees, the lovely landscaped harmony of the Institute.

'Igor, you son of a bitch.'

'Very nice of you to say so, Meyer.'

'Listen – Bergmann is on my ass. All kinds of geniuses are on it. How about getting off yours?'

'What's the trouble, Meyer?'

'Did you get them yet – those Vava papers?'

'Hopcroft is coming back with them now.'

'Who?'

'Hopcroft. A research assistant. He'll be phoning me. It's raining here, he probably can't get through.'

'What?'

Altogether too much to explain here to a man who'd just instantly got through from Israel. I saw his brows beetling: white brows, white mane, great squashed nose, tanned Red Indian face. He was seventy-nine and looked sixty, Hollywood tycoonish: Meyer Weisgal, idolater of Chaimchik, raiser of his Institute, guardian of the name.

'Everything's perfectly okay, Meyer. The problem is, Vava's daughter is in the process of moving. She's a paediatrician at University College Hospital and she's just left her husband and taken a flat in Swiss Cottage. There was some question whether the papers were there, you see, or at Wimbledon, where she lived with her husband.'

'Where?'

'Wimbledon. It's a place.'

'Sure. I know it. They play tennis there. Wimbledon.'

'That's it. Exactly.'

'You have the goddam papers or you don't?'

'Give Connie my love,' Caroline said from the doorway. She was in a towel.

9

'So I'll be seeing you, Meyer,' I said. 'And Caroline would like to give Connie her love.'

'Listen, Igor – bring that stuff, you hear? Connie, take this.'

'Igor.'

'Hello, Connie. Caroline sends her love. She's here.'

'Did she get engaged yet?'

'I don't think yet. Connie, what is this tremendous nonsense with Vava?'

'Oh, it's very involved. Do you have a batch of other queries with you?'

'A whole war full. It seems years ago.'

'So much has happened. Igor, listen – will you ring Dick Crossman and tell him he left his notebooks here? They are not lost. I have them. I will send them. Also Barney Litvinoff. Did you get that with Dick?'

'You are sending his notebooks. They are not lost.'

'Right. And with Barney they are going crazy in Jerusalem for his proofs of volume 5. He has them all, I don't know why. You couldn't get a set?'

'Not really, darling. I have to go and see my father.'

'Oh, well, so ring him. How are things there?'

'Very nasty. It's raining.'

'So you'll love it here. The oranges are out. I'll go out tonight and pick some for you. I will do it right now.'

'With orange blossom. *Shalom*, then, Connie.'

'*Shalom, shalom*, Igor. *L'hitraot.*'

L'hitraot. Till we meet again. The cadence seemed to carry its own delicious whiff of orange blossom. It was quite a shock to turn and see the long blonde figure in her towel.

'What did she say about me?'

'She asked if you were engaged yet. I said not quite.'

The corners of her mouth turned down. 'All that orange blossom. It's all right for some, isn't it? Pissy London.'

'You've got Willie tonight.

'Most true. Willie tonight.' She drifted off.

'Caroline.' I went and embraced her, in her towel. 'She said you were the most glamorous thing she could think of. She wished you were coming out, to give her a whiff of everything.'

'Really?'

'Really.'

She gave me a little kiss. 'Not just brainy, then, eh?'

The usual lightning transformation. I made an equally lightning one.

'I don't think there was any mention of brains. She regards you as madly sexy, and aristocratic, and everything that ladies would like to be. As most people do.'

'Do they, now?'

'As I understand it, with my limited grasp of these things.'

'In your builder-of-Socialism guise.'

'You will probably work a builder up, in your towel, with all my many things to see to.'

'You'd better see to them, then.'

She went off, in a cloud of my talc, well satisfied, and so did I; to the phone. I informed Mr Crossman of the missing notebooks, and Mr Litvinoff of the missing proofs, and put the phone down and looked at it for some time. It didn't do anything.

'Caroline.'

'In the kitchen.'

She was making herself something there. I wandered along.

'Don't you think it really is odd about Hopcroft? It's gone three. He can't be yarning all this time.'

'Vava's daughter isn't on the phone, is she?'

'Well, that's the point.'

She wasn't. She'd just moved in to Swiss Cottage and the phone wasn't connected yet. Her name was Olga Green, née Kutcholsky. The thing had blown up in the random way of many of the queries. Chaimchik had been writing to Fritz Haber, the Nobel Laureate in chemistry, and had mentioned Vava. The context was obviously scientific and not my preserve, but I had ringed the name all the same. No Vavas in our own biographical index, so I had sent it to Connie to see if they had anything on him in Rehovot. They hadn't, which made her conclude it must be something for Professor Bergmann in Jerusalem; which turned out to be correct. Bergmann was doing the scientific volume on Chaimchik, and all relevant papers had been transferred to his own files. From Bergmann, after a lengthy delay, had come a note to say that Vava was a Dr Vladimir Kutcholsky and that he had worked with one or other of the oil companies in London in the mid-1930s; and then another letter to say that there must have been correspondence between him and Chaimchik, and could we find out if any of it existed.

This was quite a routine thing to do, and Hopcroft had spent months on similar quests when we first started. My preserve was volumes 15 and 16 (1931–35, Chaimchik's period in the wilderness: a fruitful wilderness), and Hopcroft had turned up several previously unknown letters. Research is much a matter of one thing leading to another, and his drifting and yarning tendencies made him good at it.

He had gone to various oil companies and professional bodies, and had finally run Vava to earth, rather literally, in a ccmetery at Bushey, where he had been since 1962. His wife had predeceased him, and probate (as another line of research revealed) had been granted to a daughter, Olga, a doctor of medicine. Finding Olga had presented no difficulties, except that Hopcroft's moment of doing so had been unpropitious. She was separating from her husband, and conducting a piecemeal removal operation.

She confirmed the existence of correspondence between Chaimchik and her father, but couldn't immediately lay hands on it because it was in one of twenty or so brown-paper parcels either at Wimbledon or Swiss Cottage. Urged on by Rehovot, which after the original dilatoriness had suddenly become very urgent and demanding, I had spurred Hopcroft, who had spurred Olga. She had promised to have the stuff today, so that I could take it away with me. She'd taken off a few days, anyway, to complete her removal before Christmas.

This last reflection now provoked another.

I said, 'Do you know, it just occurred to me what Ettie was hinting about. She was hinting about Christmas. Another thing to be seen to!'

'Well, I'll see to that. Leave me a cheque.'

'I wish I didn't feel so terribly uneasy,' I said.

'It's probably the disquiet of youth.'

'I wish you'd save your *mots* for Willie.'

'Well, would you like to know something?' she said. She was looking down, slowly nibbling toasted cheese. 'To tell the truth, I'm a bit pissed off with Willie.'

'What's up with him?'

'Nothing. He's nice.'

'What's the matter, darling?'

'He's not madly there on top, you know.'

'I thought you were a bit off the brain.'

'In ladies.'

'What in God's name do you suppose has happened to Hopcroft?'

'Oh, well, bugger Hopcroft. I thought we were having an interesting talk,' she said.

'Caroline, what's up with you?'

'Well, what's up with you?'

Her normally pale cheeks had become pink and her eyes were gleaming a little. There were toast crumbs round her mouth, and she licked them off. The phone went while she was staring at me, and she said, 'Yes,' nodding, and went to answer it herself. The yes did not seem to be a response to the summoning phone, and I stared after her. What was it a response to? The idiot girl couldn't conceivably have taken a fancy to *me*? She'd just not ten minutes ago been conducting a perfectly normal conversation while in her

13

bath – or, rather, my bath. I'd given her my heavenly talc. I thought over this complication, and heard her mumbling away in the other room, and she called, 'Igor.'

She'd put the phone down and was staring at a bit of paper. 'Well, that was Hopcroft – or, rather, from Hopcroft. He's been knocked down.'

'Oh, my God! Is he hurt?'

'Well, he's in hospital. That was them. Not badly enough not to want to see you. In fact, he does want to see you.'

'Has he got the – ' I said, and bit off the uncharitable inquiry.

'I don't know what he's got. She said he's got contusions. The St Mary and St Joseph Hospital,' she said, reading

'Where the devil is that?'

'Around Swiss Cottage, apparently. I told you. He was probably just drifting about there . . . Well, look. I'll get on with the urgent things. What do you want me to do?'

'Oh, damn it, I don't know.' I was scrambling into my coat. 'I'm all in a flutter. I'd better get my ticket while I'm out.'

'What about Kaplan?'

'I've practically *done* Kaplan. You'll see what I've done. Send him the completed ones. Write a little covering note. Dear, oh, dear,' I said.

'Any calls to be made?'

'No. I don't know. Poor old Hopcroft.'

'Yes. In the midst of life, et cetera. He can't be all that bad, you idiot.'

'I'll see you in the morning, will I?'

'Yes,' she said.

'All right.' I hurried out, on the point of remembering to wish her an enjoyable evening, and then remembering not to, and got a cab outside, in Russell Square.

2

The St Mary and St Joseph was a snug small hospital, and Hopcroft had already established himself quite snugly in it. He was sitting up in bed in a small ward with three other men, all smiling as they listened to their headphones. Hopcroft was smiling himself, but not wearing headphones. He was wearing a pad of lint, like a little skullcap in his bushy hair, and he was smiling at a corpulent old lady with a dewlap who was not noticeably a nurse. She nodded and moved away as I approached, and Hopcroft said in an undertone, 'Nice old thing. She's a visitor. Her father was Skene, you know, the biographer of "the Liberator", O'Connell. She read Modern History herself under Namier at Manchester. Namier. Odd, isn't it?'

It was odd, but even odder (though I'd noted before his natural ability for the work) was the speed with which Hopcroft had extracted this information. Allowing time off for having his injuries dressed, and his clothes taken away, and for the insertion of himself into pyjamas, and into bed, he couldn't have had long with her.

I said, 'Hopcroft, what on earth happened to you?'

'It takes a bit of beating, doesn't it?' One lens of his spectacles was cracked and there was a small blue bruise on his forehead. His bushy little moustache put me again in mind of one of Wells's wistful counter-jumpers, some colleague of Kipps or Polly. He was an ageless twenty-four. 'I mean, the whole thing happened in a flash. There was nothing I could do.'

'Where did it happen?'

'Tancred Court. I was just going out. Didn't they tell you?' He seemed rather disappointed.

'They simply said you were knocked down.'

'And how. Whang. I went over like a tree. Incredible, really.'

'You were knocked down outside the block of flats?

'Not outside. I hadn't even got outside.'

'You were knocked down inside the block of flats?'

'Like a light. I mean, *boff*! I came down in the lift and this chap at the bottom said, "Can you give us a hand, Guv?" And I thought somebody had been taken ill or something, he looked so anxious. It's just at the back of the hall, there's a sort of recess, and there was another man there and he said, "Could you see your way to helping us out with a quid?" And I thought, Oh-oh. I mean. I'd got six quid in my wallet. I didn't want to sort of flash it. But at the same time it occurred to me, I'd been reading the paper in the tube, about people being laid off, these power cuts, and I thought. Well, *reason* with them, they might need a job, you know, sort of start a chat.'

Hopcroft had started a chat, and one of the men had hit him on the head.

'I mean – *boff*! I didn't even know what happened. I was just lying there. No wallet, no case – that smashing executive case of mine! I did notes on it, marvellous case, my mother gave me it. And I sort of staggered about, blood all down here, and the porter came out from somewhere, and that's it. I mean, you know, cool, eh? Broad daylight!'

'Fantastic!'

'Isn't it?' Hopcroft said, pleased at my reaction. 'Mugged in the middle of Swiss Cottage, at lunchtime. I'd not two minutes before been having a plate of soup with Olga – Doctor Green. She wanted to fry up a bit of veal, she was having some, but there was no phone, and I'd promised you, so I said, no, well, I'd better dash. And zap!'

'Did you – did you have anything in the case?' I said.

'Oh, well, crikey, yes. I found the agreement for his lease on the Featherstone Laboratory, 1931. That was yesterday's – I forgot to tell you about that. I got it from a solicitor in Gray's Inn. Copy of it. Quite interesting, too. I think he understated his expenses – you know, when he was going on about how modest the whole budget was, five hundred a year to cover the rent and salaries and so on. That would be a bit tricky. The rent was three hundred. Interesting point, eh? Though, of course, we can always get another copy, now we know where it is.'

'Yes. Anything else?'

'Something today. What was it? I had a bit of a clonk, you know.'

'Vava's papers?'

'Oh, yes. She hasn't got them.'

'*She hasn't got them?*'

'Not with her. I checked myself. It's a bit of a mess up there. It's this barmy way she's moving. There's one of the drivers at the hospital – University College – he's doing it for her. He keeps going there and back. There's apparently this one parcel with diplomas and so forth, birth certificates, that kind of thing. And she's got the letters in it. It's still at Wimbledon.'

'Oh.'

'That's what I wanted to tell you. Sorry to drag you out here.'

'Don't be silly, Hopcroft. I was worried about you.'

'It *was* a bit of a clonk,' he said, cautiously touching his skullcap. 'Thudding slightly. They insisted on keeping me in. We had the lot, you know – police, ambulance. The porter got them. Incredible, really. What else was there? There was something else, damn it.'

His eyes were crossing very slightly.

'I don't think you ought to be talking, Hopcroft.'

'That's all right. My mother will be here soon. Not much chance of getting that case back,' he said ruefully. 'Worth more than the six quid. My initials were on it. Rotters. Oh, yes. I know. Olga. She's sending you the stuff. I told her you were going to Israel and that they were mustard keen, so she's posting it. I said make it express, because of the Christmas mail and so forth, so you'll get it there. She's popping down the day after tomorrow; her husband won't be there.'

'The originals?'

'Oh, sure, the genuine thing.'

'You told her to make a copy.'

'Did I? Oh, crikey, I didn't. I don't think so. Oh, gosh, sorry.'

'It's all right. I'll go and see her myself.'

'Yes, well, you can't.' Hopcroft was looking very unhappy. 'She was going off after lunch to stay with this friend in Frognal. I'm terribly sorry. I don't know who the friend is.'

'She can't be reached anywhere?'

'Well, no. She's staying with her. She can't sort of stand being on her own. She's a bit cut up, just at the moment.'

'Could we perhaps get in touch with the husband? He might leave her a note.'

'Oh, she wouldn't like that.'

'What time is she going to Wimbledon, when she goes?'

'I don't know. I mean, there was no reason to ask her. Gosh, what an idiot I am.'

'Don't worry about it. It's a piece of luck she didn't have the papers. They'd have taken those as well.'

'Yes. They must have spotted me coming out of the bank. There's a Barclay's just below. I'd topped up a bit on my way in, got five quid out on my credit card. I mean, with that spiffy case and everything I might have looked a bit important. They probably hung around waiting for me to come down. There were people around when I went in, you see. I told the police that. They thought there was something in it. A bit cool, eh? Midday!'

'Lousy luck. I *am* sorry, old chap. Stop talking now, though.'

'It is thudding a bit,' he said on a fainter note, and looked slowly round as a simultaneous titter came from the three other occupants of the room. They were grinning at each other. A tiny batlike shrieking and a crackle of twigs were just audible from their headphones. 'Well, I think I will dry up,' he said. 'Have a good time in Israel, et cetera.'

'Thanks. Rest, Hopcroft,' I told him.

2

I was walking in Central Park South (this was the previous year, not long after my book on the 1930s had appeared) when from the opposite direction another figure came walking: a dapper small figure, white mane of hair, Red Indian face, hands clasped behind him. Our eyes locked some distance off, and he stopped as he came abreast and said, 'Hey – Igor Druyanov?'

'Yes.'

'Well, nice to see you, Igor.' He was giving me a most charming smile, and also his hand, which I shook. 'Isn't this the damnedest thing?' he said. 'I am Meyer Weisgal.'

'How are you, Mr Weisgal?' I was having my hand shaken a good deal lately by very affable once-met folk. I racked my brains.

'So what are you doing in New York, Igor? I saw you were at Harvard.'

'I'm doing a couple of lectures.'

'Well, it beats everything. Here I take a walk and turn over in my mind *The Betrayed Decade*, and who walks along? You know, you don't have to make things happen.' He was doing a kind of shuffle, salty eyes smiling up from under his brows. 'They just happen. They happened so often in my life!' (So they did. Interested readers may turn to his autobiography, *So Far*, published by Weidenfeld & Nicolson.) 'Quit worrying, we didn't meet yet,' he said. 'I am from the Weizmann Institute of Science, in Israel.'

'Ah.'

'It's a very good – even an excellent book.'

'Thank you very much.'

'I don't know if I would have passed the title. It takes the teeth out if you have to say it. I'm a good editor.' The salty eyes were still radiating away.

'You are – an editor at the Weizmann Institute?' I said in some confusion.

'Well, no, I'm not. I'm really the Chancellor there – whatever the hell that happens to be. Say, Igor, why don't you and I take a stroll?' He turned and we strolled back the way he had come.

'How's your father?' he said.

'Fine, thanks.'

'That's Maxim Druyanov, right?'

'Right.'

'What's he doing now?'

'He's lecturing at the School for Slavonic and East European Studies in London.'

'Do they guard him yet?'

'No, no. That was years ago.'

'Your mother is Jewish, right?'

'Perfectly right.'

'Well, hell. Goddam it,' he said. The accent was a rich mixture of Brooklyn, Russian, Yiddish. He told me why he thought we were so well met.

A large letters project was under way – the collected and annotated letters of Chaim Weizmann. An editorial committee had been set up some years before consisting of Lewis Namier, Isaiah Berlin, and Jacob Talmon, all very top-class; also R. H. S. Crossman, the British ex-statesman, who was doing the big biography of Weizmann.

Most of the volumes had been allocated and were being worked on by political specialists, but a certain hole had appeared for the years 1931–35, Weizmann's period out of office. For this correspondence, which apparently reflected well the *Zeitgeist* of that dismal era, it had not proved easy to think of the right editor. The appearance of *The Betrayed Decade*, with what was considered quite an intriguing name on it, might have solved one part of the problem.

'The other part is up to you. How about it, Igor?'

We were in his apartment by that time – a *pied-à-terre* just off Central Park South, which is where our stroll had led – and his wife, Shirley, was pouring coffee.

'Well. It's sudden, Meyer.' We were both now on first-name terms.

'It would be two volumes, of the greatest historical importance. It is kind of the prehistory of the State of Israel. He was in touch with almost everybody. Day after day, in a thousand ways, you see the moral collapse of Europe coming. You'd have running footnotes, a long introductory essay to each volume. It's yours, I see it, I have a feeling.'

His feeling was why I was now where I was, having mine.

It was the penthouse suite in the San Martin Clubhouse on the Weizmann Institute campus. Dignitaries usually got it. There weren't any at the moment, which accounted for my occupancy. The plane had been hours late – a bomb scare in London – so I wearily sat and admired the glory and had a drink with Connie.

More than ever, she reminded me of a small South American hummingbird – a confectioner's model, perhaps. She had very neat little legs and feet. Her eyelashes flickered. Her name was Nehama, but the nuns in the convent school in Maracaibo (where she had been born) had had some trouble with this, and asked what it meant. She had told them it was consolation in Hebrew, so they had renamed her Consuelo, shortened in class to Suelo. When the family had moved to New York, the teachers there had asked what Suelo meant, and she'd told them it could either be Nehama or Consuelo, and everyone had settled for Connie.

I said, 'So what is the panic with Vava?'

'Oh, you are too tired for these complications.'

'What is the complication?'

'Let me put it this way. *I* don't understand it, and I'm an expert. He was a cousin of Vera's, you know.'

'Vera Verochka. Vava was?'

'Your genius Hopcroft didn't find this out from Olga?'

'He didn't tell me. Perhaps it was his bang on the head.'

'Bergmann knew him in London in the Thirties. He'd forgotten about it. Vava came from Vera's hometown, Rostov. He didn't leave Russia till after the Revolution. Then he went to Germany, until the Hitler thing started, and Weizmann got him out. He was one of his refugees. He stayed with the Weizmanns for a short time and Chaim started him off with some work at the Featherstone Laboratory.'

'The Featherstone Laboratory.' Through the echoing longueurs of the day and of the jet, I remembered somebody telling me something about this laboratory. What?

'The Featherstone Laboratory in London. Weizmann's laboratory. The one he started when they threw him out of the presidency of the organization in 1931. When he returned to science.'

'Ye-es?'

'Well, that's it. So Vava stayed with them a short while, and then he got himself the job with the oil company, and found someplace to live, and they lived happy ever after, he and his wife and the little girl.'

'Olga.'

'Olga,' Connie said.

None of this seemed to answer the question, and I was too weary to grapple with it anyway, so I ate one of the oranges she'd picked for me, and listened while she told me what was going on at the Institute and who was still around. Most of the old faculty people were still around, the Sassoons, the Beylises; also a good egg from Harvard called Hammond L. Wyke.

I said, 'Anything further about his Nobel Prize?'

'Well, fingers are crossed. There is an upstart in Japan who has his backers. That Nobel committee – I would seek to influence them in subtle ways, like financial. The unworldly scientist says you can't. Then, Professor Tuomisalo of Finland is still with us.'

'The professor of higher mathematics.'

'That one. Well.' She yawned. 'Bat Yam is some kilometres away, with my bed in it. In the morning, you'll ring when you want to come to the House. Ze'ev will drive round and fetch you.'

I saw her down to her car and returned, dog-tired. It was very quiet; just the soft thud of the heavy-water plant from near the nuclear science complex a few hundred yards away. I stood at the open window and took in the scent of oranges from the dark. My eyes were jumping. I thought I saw something in rapid, jerky motion. It wasn't an animal, or a vehicle. It seemed to be a running man.

I watched the figure for some time, and went to bed, and tossed and turned there for hours, vaguely uneasy, sleepless.

2

Next morning, in the dead of winter, birds sang, sun glittered, trees shone with fruit, and God was back in business – all welcome after the London that Caroline had so pithily described. From the window I looked at the undulating grounds, magnificendy undulating away in all directions. Along the paths people were ambling on bikes between the temples of science discreetly embowered here and there – all very seemly and inspiriting.

I showered and shaved and topped off with a bit of the heavenly talc and descended for breakfast. There was only one other person in the restaurant, an Indian carefully feeding himself olives and cream cheese as he read the

Jerusalem *Post*. I filled up a tray, and bought a paper for myself and took it near the window.

Armies still locked together on the west bank of the Suez Canal; a very nice picture of Sheik Yamani, the Saudi Arabian Oil Minister, seraphically describing his regret at the unfortunate economic condition of West Europe; a mysterious shortage of rice among the wholesalers of Israel, portending an imminent rise in the price of the product.

'Excuse me. You are Mr Druyanov?'

The Indian was smiling tentatively down at me. Extended, he was a long, sinewy figure, slightly hunched.

'Yes.'

'Connie said you would be here today. We are good friends. Forgive me for intruding. I just wanted to say how much I admired your book. There were one or two things I would love to discuss with you, the role of Gandhi in 1939 – Oh, please don't let me disturb you.' We shook hands, I half on my feet, and a pickled cucumber fell on the floor. He shot after it like a python. 'There. I'm so sorry. I shouldn't eat it. Although the floor is very clean. Well, I don't want to disturb you. I am working here; we will meet again, I am sure.'

'I'll look forward to it.'

The first signs of trouble in Arcadia.

I finished breakfast and rang Connie, and a few minutes later was being driven by Ze'ev, the chauffeur, to the House. We went out of the Institute and turned left into the main road of Rehovot, and then left again and up the avenue for half a mile till we reached the gatehouse. This had been the guard post in the days when Chaimchik had been President of Israel. We sped through it and along the winding path between orange groves, to pull up in the drive outside the House.

The biggish white place sat like a swan in the beautiful morning. The semicircular green awning was down over the window of Chaimchik's old room, the wooden bird tray still attached to the balcony railing outside. He'd sat and fed the birds there while looking out to the Jerusalem hills, visible at this moment as a mauvish stain in the distance. I followed Ze'ev up the entrance steps and he unlocked the door.

'You remember the way up to Mr Meltzer?'

'Of course.'

The wide marble staircase spiralled up from the hall: a spacious hall, quite light, quite bright, quite stately. A certain glacial quality sat upon it, the product of much limed oak. Limed oak had been the thing in the London of 1937 when Verochka had superintended the building. She'd become something of a magpie at the time. The results of her raids upon Sotheby's and Christie's were all around: chests, ornaments, lamps, rugs. She'd long out-lived her lord; had slipped in her bath at the Dorchester on a visit to London at the age of eighty-five, and had returned in a coffin.

I went up the stairs and along the corridor to her old bedroom; it was now Julian Meltzer's office.

'Well. So they put a bomb on the plane for you,' he said.

Something about old Zionists kept them like Peter Pan. He was sixty-nine and looked ten years younger: big, bland, calm, all in order. Some way above his moustache a pair of innocent eyes cannily gazed.

'You didn't happen to bring a token from your old friend Fidel?'

I carefully opened my case and presented him with the token.

He looked at the little cabinet for a bit and his mouth opened. Then he opened the box and looked at the cigars.

'Oh, my word! I didn't mean it. Where did you get these?'

Caroline had got them. Her friend Willie was a gentle-man cigar merchant, also a wine merchant; his father, the Earl, was.

'Merry Chanukah, Julian.'

'And a merry Christmas to you. Igor, these must have cost a fortune.'

I agreed. 'Perfectly correct. As it happens, I have a rather extended little tab for you to sign. We can go into it later. What is the mystery with Vava?'

'Oh, well, Vava.' He was still looking at the cigars with some disbelief. 'I doubt if we'll see anything from Vava.' He very carefully put the cigars in a cupboard. There was another box of cigars in it, and a pile of books and files. 'Wait a minute. I don't think I ought to put these here, they aren't in tubes. Might take the smell.' He pondered a moment uncertainly. The cupboards had numerous fitted drawers. Verochka had kept her underwear here. As the correspondence showed, she had made very careful specifications for this range of cupboards. She'd driven the celebrated German architect Mendelsohn half mad. Verochka had become something of a madam as her Chaim-chik had risen in the world. 'I know.' He went to another cupboard at the far end of the room and lovingly enriched it with the precious casket. 'That chap wasn't attacked for his money. They were after the letters.'

'What chap? . . . *Hopcroft*?' I said, amazed.

'I'll smoke one of those tonight. My word, that's very handsome, Igor,' he said. 'Yes, we've been having some nonsense here. You haven't picked up any science from these letters?'

'I haven't got any scientific letters. Bergmann has them.'

'You'll pick up a bit.' An accent of somewhere – London, N.W., perhaps – slightly asserted itself. He'd come to Palestine in 1920, had been the *New York Times* correspondent for years, associated with Meyer for even longer. 'They have got keen here on Weizmann's acetone process,' he said. 'It cropped up when Bergmann was in America during the oil crisis. You can make petrol from it.'

'From acetone?'

'Vava turned it into ketones. Do you know about ketones?'

'No.'

'They put the kick into petrol. That's what that letter was. The one to Fritz Haber that you sent to Connie.'

I tried to remember the letter. It was in German. I couldn't remember a thing about it, except that the name Vava had cropped up, and I'd ringed it.

'So now they're all at it,' Julian said. 'You can make the stuff anywhere. All this crisis they're having in the West and Japan and everywhere, they don't need it. Any piddling little country can just make its own, and the Arabs can go back to being Arabs instead of the financiers of the world.'

'Are you serious?'

'Weizmann was, and he was a damned good chemist. He got blocked by the oil interests. He sent Churchill a stinker on the subject. They're digging all the stuff out of the files now. Your Vava letter started a few things.'

I stared at him. Churchill, oil interests, energy crisis.

'You see, Hopcroft was *mugged*,' I said. 'He had six pounds in his wallet, which they took from him. I saw him in hospital the day before yesterday.'

'Yes. Connie told me. Unlikely. Other stuff has gone missing, too, you see. Bergmann passed the word round in America. A chap got hit on the head in a place called Terre Haute, in Indiana. That's where Commercial Solvents was, the outfit that handled Weizmann's processes. This chap had picked up a pile of correspondence and two men came and took it off him while he was going to his car. He's dead. We only heard about it yesterday or I'd have warned you. We won't be seeing your papers.'

'But Hopcroft didn't have any,' I said.

'Well, they'll know that now. He was gabby, Hopcroft, wasn't he?'

'He *is* gabby,' I said. 'He's perfectly all right. I saw him.'

'That's all right, then.'

'Olga is going to *post* the papers. She said so. She is going to do it on Thursday.' I suddenly realized it *was* Thursday. She was popping down to Wimbledon today. Her husband wouldn't be there. It seemed suddenly a very long way away.

'Yes. Doubtful. Have a cup of coffee. Nellie!' he called.

Nellie came in. I'd heard her slowly typing next door. She was his secretary. She worked in what had been the nurse's room, next door to Chaimchik's room. She was a tiny, white-haired, lamblike creature, very gentle. 'Hello, Igor,' she said softly. 'I saw you flit by.'

'This man has brought me a present of cigars from his friend Castro,' Julian said. 'He deserves a cup of coffee.'

I heard Nellie clacking slowly and precisely down the marble staircase, and the coffee turned up presently. Later I went to see Connie along the corridor. All the files were in her room; she was the-main coordinator of research. Later still, I was working in Chiamchik's bedroom.

I state this because it happened in this order, but in fact I was thinking all the time of Olga, popping over to Wimbledon today, and of Hopcroft, nattering convivially in the St Mary and St Joseph, and of the unknown man in Terre Haute, Indiana, who was no longer in a position to be convivial. I was delving into the acetone process during this, and into a couple of other processes.

3

Chaim Weizmann was born in 1874 in Motol, a small village in Byelorussia, and as a boy moved with his family to Pinsk, a few miles away, which was bigger and even nastier. His father was a timber merchant, not prosperous, but he managed to put all of his large family through university. There was a rather sound family way of doing this. As each child completed university, he got a job and began contributing to the tuition fees of the next in line.

(Years later, while Chaimchik was pawning his compasses, or scraping a living with Verochka in Manchester, he still managed to send a pound or two a month to keep two sisters going in Switzerland.)

He soon got away from Pinsk and went to Germany to study chemistry, ultimately to the Technische Hochschule at Berlin Charlottenburg where he worked under the immediate direction of a Dr Bistrzycki. When Bistrzycki was called to a professorship at Fribourg in Switzerland in 1896. Weizmann followed him. He picked up his D.Sc. there in 1899, and went to the University of Geneva as a junior lecturer.

Dyestuff chemistry was much the thing at the time, and this is what he had been doing with Bistrzycki. He immediately began researching and publishing at a great rate. In a single year he produced three very extensive papers and took out four well documented patents. But he was busy in a bewildering number of directions.

Switzerland was at the time a hotbed of political activity. There were numerous groups of impassioned émigrés, mainly Russian, covering a wide spectrum of contrary opinion. There were simple Socialists, not so simple Socialists, Communists (including incipient Bolsheviks and Mensheviks), Anarchists, Bundists, Zionists. The wild object of many of them was to create a revolution in unchanging Russia, and of the last group to alter an equally unchanging situation, the dispersion of the Jews.

Zionism as a political movement was of later vintage than the others. Its basis was that the millions of Jews scattered about the world were not simply religious minorities in their different countries, as might be Protestants, Catholics, or Muslims, but a single people exiled from a particular land. The proposition was to repurchase the land, and the movement's organizer, a Viennese journalist called Theodor Herzl (whose dignified portrait today appears on Israli hundred-pound notes), in fact tried to do this by offering the Sultan of Turkey several million pounds for a 'charter' to it. The deal fell through, to the Sultan's regret, but there were very many alternative proposals, hotly contested by the impecunious polemicists and students who made up the active body.

Weizmann had been a Zionist for years, and in Switzerland found fertile ground and much unattached or even downright errant Jewish youth. He decided to collect what he could of it for Zionism, and with half a dozen friends arranged a meeting in the Russian library. This was a rash thing to do without securing the prior approval of G. V. Plekhanov, doyen of the squabbling émigré society and founder of Marxism in Russia. (In later life, Verochka recalled often seeing his two juniors Lenin and Trotsky meeting in a flat across the street.) Plekhanov's disapproval could virtually be guaranteed for interlopers to his scene, so that when the founding seven arrived at their venue they found, with no surprise, that all the furniture had been removed. They had the meeting, nonetheless, standing up, voted on a Hebrew name for themselves, *Ha-Shachar*, The Dawn, and then voted to call a mammoth conference to recruit membership.

This tremendous affair, addressed by representatives of all factions, lasted for three and a half days and ended at four in the morning with a great personal triumph for Weizmann – 118 new members – and a trembling confrontation with Plekhanov.

'What do you mean by bringing dissension into our ranks?' the offended Marxist demanded.

'Monsieur Plekhanov,' Weizmann grandly informed him, 'you are not the Czar!'

Apart from these heated public affairs, the young experimenter was having a couple of private ones. He was living with a young lady, Sophia Getzova, to whom he was engaged, and carrying on with another, Vera Khatzmann, a medical student from Rostov-on-Don. By about 1904 things began to get on top of him, and he decided to narrow his activities to the scientific and try his luck elsewhere.

His fancy fell on Manchester, centre of the British textile industry, which had an excellent university department of organic chemistry presided over by the distinguished Professor Perkin. Perkin's father, many years before, had made his name in the field of dyestuff chemistry by synthesizing aniline blue (thus heralding in the 'mauve decade') – a fact that Weizmann thought might dispose him in favour of another dyestuff chemist. But Perkin greatly took to the animated young Russian anyway. In an affable conversation in German (Weizmann as yet had no English), he pointed out that while no staff jobs were open at the moment, he could offer him the use of a little basement laboratory at a nominal sum of six pounds, with the services of a lab boy thrown in. Weizmann accepted, and while Perkin went off on vacation – it was the summer of 1904 – installed himself in the empty university.

By the time Perkin returned, he had quite a lot of English. He had learned it from the chemistry department stores book, the Bible, and the purchased works of Macaulay and Gladstone; and also – as he wrote to his sweet darling, the joy from Rostov-on-Don – from conversations with a young demonstrator of Perkin's who had arrived back from vacation. With this young man he instituted a series of experiments, so that when Perkin took up his chair again, much refreshed by his holiday, Weizmann was able to show him quite a lot. By the winter he was on the staff, with students of his own.

He couldn't, however, stay away from Zionism. Pogroms in Russia brought a mass protest rally in Manchester, which the young Russian was asked to address. At the rally was the prospective Liberal candidate for the constituency, a Mr W. S. Churchill, keeping his eye on the electorate. He couldn't understand a word of Weizmann's fiery oration in Yiddish, but was much impressed by the effect on the audience, and made haste to wring the orator's hand and to hint that he could be of great service in swaying the Jewish vote. Weizmann declined: he said he was interested only in Zionist issues. Anyway, the January, 1906, elections were at hand, with other politicians astir. Contesting them was the Prime Minister himself, Mr Balfour, also with a Manchester constituency. Came January and Mr Balfour, and Mr Balfour's agent, who thought he ought to have fifteen minutes with the intriguing young man who knew so much about Russia and the state of the Jews there. The fifteen minutes stretched to an hour and a quarter, and ended with both men knowing rather more about the state of everything.

He was determined to stick to science, however, and he did. He brought over Miss Vera Khatzmann, his Verochka, married her, and slogged on with his chemistry. An interesting new problem had appeared. The world's supply of rubber was unequal to the demand: a task for the synthetic chemist. Perkin interested himself, and put teams on it, including Weizmann's.

Chaimchik's approach was novel. He had become interested in fermentation. Verochka's sister had married a scientist who lived in Paris on the Left Bank. The Weizmanns visited from time to time, and Chaimchik picked up a freelance assignment that involved work at the Pasteur Institute, kingdom of the great fermenter himself.

The basis of fermentation was that micro-organisms, bacteria, could by creating a ferment in one substance change it into another. He looked up the literature and found that the essential substance of rubber was the five-carbon compound isoprene. Further study showed that a Russian called Winogradsky had recently observed a five-carbon compound in nature. It could be isolated by fermenting sugar with certain bacteria to produce a volatile compound exhibiting the odor of fusel oil.

Weizmann repeated the experiment in Manchester, and found that Winogradsky had got it wrong. The substance produced, though smelling of fusel oil, was something else. It was not a five-carbon molecule, either. It was a four-carbon one, and it was butyl alcohol. He was a very dogged experimenter, and he tried it many times with a variety of bacteria. It always turned out the same, but in the end he got more butyl alcohol.

Professor Perkin, to whom he showed the results, permitted himself one of his rare puns. He said, 'Your butyl alcohol is a very futile alcohol,' and advised him to pour it down the sink. Chaimchik didn't do this. He kept on refining the product with a variety of treatments. He got a very large yield of butyl alcohol and smaller quantities of other substances, including methyl alcohol and acetone, the latter about 30 per cent of the total.

He kept on doing this, and the First World War broke out, and a new problem asserted itself. It impinged on Manchester in the form of a Dr Rintoul, from the Scottish branch of the Nobel explosives firm, whose problem was most acute. His firm was supplying the British fleet with cordite for its large naval guns. Strategic considerations made it imperative that the location of these guns should be concealed from the enemy. The solution was to propel the shells by smokeless gunpowder, made possible by the chemical solvent acetone, previously, but no longer, obtainable in generous supply from the forests of Europe as a by-product of charcoal. Not all the forests of Britain could supply the present need for acetone. Was there some other method of producing it?

'Walk this way, Dr Rintoul,' said Dr Weizmann, and showed him a method.

Dr Rintoul made haste to the telephone, and the night train from Scotland brought the managing director of Nobel's, together with several of the senior scientific staff. They went carefully through Chaimchik's lab books and repeated his experiments: acetone in abundance. Terms were stated for this valuable patent, to which Chaimchik and the university readily agreed. And then occurred a strange accident. The Nobel works blew up. They were unable to take up the patent. The problem was no less urgent for the accident, and Chaimchik, placed in charge of it, was sent by express train to London and ushered into the office of the First Lord of the Admiralty. He found the First Lord of the Admiralty was Mr W. S. Churchill, last encountered wringing his hand while trying to get him to nobble the Jewish vote in Manchester.

The two men got on famously, and Churchill asked him what he required. Weizmann replied that existing fermentation plants were largely operated by distillers of whisky and gin. Churchill told him to take his pick, and he picked the Nicolson gin distillery in Bow, which was immediately sequestered for his use.

For the next two years he took on a most daunting, almost mind-boggling task, the one-man creation of a completely new industry: industrial fermentation. The government built him a factory and took over the largest distilleries in the country. He himself took over the laboratory of the Lister Institute in Chelsea, to train teams of chemists to go out and operate the plants.

The process depended on a bacterium that he had isolated and in countless experiments improved, *Clostridium acetobutylicum weizmann*. It worked on starch-containing products, and the method he had perfected demanded large quantities of maize. When U-boat warfare interrupted overseas supplies, he switched to horse chestnuts in Britain, and the process crossed the Atlantic to be employed on Canadian maize. A plant was taken over in Toronto, and soon turning out acetone; and when the United States entered the war, the process was also adopted there, at two big distilleries in Terre Haute, Indiana. His operations had spread to Asia before the war ended; but by that time he had transferred his energies.

While he had been keeping the Navy's guns firing, the Army's were blowing the Turks out of their old Ottoman Empire, which included Palestine. The wartime coalition government was headed by Lloyd George, very keen on his Old Testament, and the Foreign Secretary was Mr A. J. Balfour, whose mind had been so enlarged on the Jewish question in 1906. Weizmann became most tremendously busy. He had never ceased to be active in Zionism, had attended all the big pre-war European conferences. But now the war had cut off the European societies, and from being a well-fancied middleweight in the movement he had become its senior statesman. Much negotiation brought about the Balfour Declaration, which declared: 'His Majesty's Government view with favour the establishment of a Jewish National Home in Palestine'; and while his ancient sparring partners Lenin and Trotsky were raising hell making their incredible dream come true in Russia, Chaimchik sped off to Palestine to attend to his.

He found fighting still going on, but lost no time in getting down to his first scheme, a project planned more than half his life, the laying of a cornerstone for a Hebrew University in Jerusalem. He invited the victorious General Allenby to the ceremony, and, recalling the prophetic utterance that the Word should go forth from Jerusalem, Allenby was both happy and moved. Gunfire could still be heard rolling in the Jerusalem hills while the future centre of learning was founded, and everybody was very moved.

But things were moving everywhere, and in a variety of directions. On the scientific front, acetone was phasing out, and was anyway being produced as a by-product of the rising petroleum industry. Keeping pace with the petroleum industry was the rising automobile industry. The automobiles needed painting, and mass-production methods required fast-drying varnishes. The best solvent was found to come from Chaimchik's butyl alcohol, which Professor Perkin had advised him to pour down the sink – still obtainable and in large quantities, by his patent method.

He let his patent agents attend to that one, together with Commercial Solvents, and threw himself into politics.

He was the leader of world Zionism, the builder-up of the national home, the settler of the people in it, the raiser of the money to do the job. The university was his pet project and he raised that. For the next thirteen years, almost every minute was accounted for. He travelled, exhorted, pleaded, presided; and in 1931, thoroughly exhausted, found himself kicked out of the job owing to factional differences.

I was sitting in his chair and staring out at his grave as I pondered this, his presence strong in the room, so that when the hand fell on my shoulder I silently rose and almost went through the ceiling.

'Igor, we are going down to lunch now,' Connie said. 'And Meyer wants you to call him afterwards. He didn't want you disturbed while you were reading.'

4

'Mashed potato – wonderful!' Dan said.

Mealtimes were rather Old World at the House; time had stood still since Verochka's death. Luncheon was *served* (although served now in the morning room behind the kitchen), and it was served by Verochka's old housekeeper, Batya, still part of the establishment.

It was served to the archival staff, Julian magisterially at the head of the table. He sat with so grave a mien I'd half expected him, when I'd first eaten here, to break into grace. He didn't quite do that. He robustly dealt with what was before him.

'It *is* nice,' he said judicially.

'It's delicious,' Dan said. 'Well, you live in style here. Very high off the hog, if the allusion gives no offence to the lady in the kosher kitchen.'

His name was Dan Navon, and he'd published a best-selling book about Israel the year before. We'd overlapped for a few weeks on the American newspaper lists. He was now doing some work on the connections between Herzl–Weizmann–Ben-Gurion, counterpart of the Abraham–Moses–Joshua triumvirate of earlier history, and he was doing it in Connie's room, which was why I was in Chaimchik's.

'Mashed potato is the stuff,' he said decisively. 'That's right, Igor?'

'Quite right,' I said absently.

'You will give us salvation through mashed potato.'

'Will I?'

'So Vava will.'

'How do you mean?'

'Mashed potato. His stuff. He made the petrol from it.'

'What's the joke?' Julian said.

'Not mine. Michael Sassoon's. I had dinner with him yesterday,' Dan said. 'He'd got it from Bergmann. The Vava papers revolve around mashed potato.'

He had a long bony face and an engaging smile; also, behind his glasses, a very intelligent pair of eyes that missed little. His corn-crake voice quite often came out with peculiar deadpan jokes, though.

'They do, eh? Well for your information, old friend,' Julian said, 'there aren't any Vava papers. There's just a single letter *mentioning* Vava, in 1933.'

'From the single letter mentioning Vava in 1933, Professor Bergmann has made a deduction. He is an investigator with the brain of one of the great detectives. From this one mention it was at once obvious to him that Vava had made a super petrol with an octane number of 150, and he made it from mashed potato.'

'Why mashed?' Julian said humorously.

'Vava mashed it. I don't know why,' Dan said simply. 'Perhaps you have to.'

The conversation moved on from mashed potato, but not very far, and when the meal was over and Dan announced he wouldn't be coming back in the afternoon, I followed Connie ruminatively up to her room.

'Was that serious about mashed potato?' she said.

'I don't know what's serious today, Connie,' I said, and had a look at my watch. Two o'clock. Twelve in England. Worth a try. I picked up the phone and in about half a minute Caroline said breathlessly, 'Hello.'

I suddenly understood how Connie had felt the other day. 'Hello, Caroline.'

'*Igor?*'

'Yes, darling. Have you been ringing Olga?'

'I gave her a buzz earlier. There was no answer. I came back to start again. What's up?'

'Well, when you get her,' I said, 'tell her to leave the letters there.'

'You don't want them copied?'

'I don't want her to do anything with them. She can leave them, for the time being.'

'I see. I think,' she said. 'Igor, is everything all right?'

'Well, it isn't bad, really. It's quite nice,' I said.

There was a slightly breathy pause. 'I just got in,' she said. 'I could hear the damned thing. What are you talking about – you don't want the letters copied and you don't want them sent?'

'That's right. How's everything there?'

'Well, how do you expect it is? It's pissing. How's orange-blossom land?'

'It's turned a bit grey and chilly now,' I said, staring out at the marvellous day. 'Well, then.'

'Just a minute, for heaven's sake. You do realize, don't you, that she might easily have popped down this morning?'

'I did realize that.'

'Or that if she's there this very minute she might not answer the phone, because she knows nobody will be ringing her at Wimbledon.'

'That crossed my mind, too.'

'Has anything cropped up?'

'It isn't really as urgent as it was.'

'I see. That's why you're ringing me, is it?'

'What would you like me to bring you?'

'I've just been seeing Hopcroft,' she said. 'He's yarning away, perfectly all right, only his eyes keep crossing. Would you like me to go to Wimbledon and tell her all this – I mean, on the off chance of her being there?'

'No, I wouldn't. Don't do that, Caroline.'

'Igor, are the Russian secret police after you or something?'

'That's it, darling. Connie says there are some stunning caftans around. Would you like one?'

'Well, I'd love one . . . When are you coming back?'

'The twenty-ninth or thirtieth. If you do manage to contact Olga, could you call me?'

'Because it is so unurgent. I do see,' she said.

'Reverse the charge, of course. If not, Happy Christmas.'

'Quite.' She hung up right away.

I pondered this a moment, and jiggled the phone rest and got Meyer.

'You didn't bring it,' was his gloomy greeting.

'No, well –'

'Okay, I heard. It's serious. You'll have dinner with me tonight. Today you will be busy. There are many things to find out.'

'Chemical things?' I said.

'What else?'

'But I'm no chemist. I haven't the faintest –'

'Persevere. They'll tell you. *I'll* tell you. Waste no time,' he said, and clicked off.

'Yes, well, our friend got it nearly right,' Julian said with satisfaction, coming in at that moment. 'I've just been speaking to Finster, who is handling the thing here. Mashed potato! It is a botanical species called *Ipomoea batatas*.'

'What's that?'

'Finster says it is in fact a kind of sweet potato.'

'Is he mashing it?'

'To tell the truth, I'm not absolutely on top line what he is doing with it. You're finding out, I understand.'

'Am I?'

'Meyer said so. Finster works for Beylis at the Daniel Sieff. Ze'ev will take you. Ze'ev!' he yelled from the doorway.

A response came from below.

3

'It is really a very simple problem of carbon chemistry,' Dr Finster said. 'There's little of what you would call higher interest any more. It's work, after all, from fifty years.'

He didn't look very pleased with it himself; he was wearing a pullover instead of a lab coat, perhaps as a mark of displeasure. Some hint of the reason for it had been given me by Professor Beylis, on whom I'd looked in first. The Weizmann Institute is a very high-class institute, and like its peers, the Rockefeller, Princeton, MIT, and so forth, is interested in distant advance on the frontiers of knowledge. The hall of fame and the name of Nobel hang in the air. In this climate, teasing out some further application of an ancient process long chewed over by commercial chemists was like asking for improvements to soap powder: very small potatoes.

I was in Weizmann's old lab; he'd worked here a bit soon after it was put up in the Thirties. It was now Professor Sprinzak's lab, and he'd ushered me over to the corner where Dr Finster was muttering at a small fermenter. There was that unsettling smell of a strong gas leak and of chemicals that had always instilled such dread on entering the school laboratory. The place had a cluttered, old-fashioned look: shelves crammed with jars, benches with retorts and Bunsen burners; numerous experiments seemed to be under way.

I sat on a high stool and looked at disaffected Dr Finster and his fermenter. It was a cylindrical affair of stainless steel, electrically heated. Tubes and retorts issued from it

to a glass jar. In the cylinder was Dan's mashed potato –
'We first must make a mash of our raw starting material'
– and in the jar what seemed to be a lot of water.

'That's it, is it?' I said.

'Yes. This is the product of fermentation.'

He inclined the jar towards me and took the top off.
Rather a pleasing and wholesome fragrance came out of
the jar, not immediately placeable but strangely familiar,
all the same. It didn't smell at all of potatoes. I looked
more closely at the absolutely anonymous liquid. Was this
the secret stuff of life? He had been talking rather a lot
about life forms.

'Does fusel oil smell like this?' I said.

Dr Finster placed his own nose over the jar. It was a
powerful and useful-looking organ, and the end of it
quivered delicately as he made his observation.

'Yes. Very like. By no means unlike fusel oil. However,
it is not fusel oil.'

'No.' I could imagine Winogradsky's nostrils fluting
excitedly over it seventy years ago, and Weizmann's, more
critically and subtly, a few years later. 'What happens to it
now?' I said.

'What happens to it is whatever one wants to happen. It
is a very basic substance,' Dr Finster said wearily. 'I will
explain again.'

I listened with more determination this time.

Organic chemistry was the chemistry of living or once-
living forms. It was largely the chemistry of carbon. The
carbon came in some way from the sun, and growing
vegetable matter synthesized it into starch, sugar, and
other substances. Animals ate the vegetables, and people
ate animals, together with vegetables. But whether they
were eating it or wearing it, making furniture out of it or
burning it, they were utilizing the energy originally supplied by the sun, and thus participating in the carbon cycle.

Vegetable matter that had in some way got out of the
cycle by escaping contemporary use had become fossilized.

It was recoverable in the form of coal, shale, peat, oil, and so on, and the solar energy in it was also recoverable, by scientific means. The simplest scientific means, as in the case of coal, was to put a match to it; it would then release, in the form of heat and light, some part of the original far more lavish solar contribution. This was a crude means of conversion, and Dr Finster said so.

'However, if we are to regard this as fuel,' he said, giving the jar a little shake, 'all we have done is to accelerate the natural process. We have taken vegetable material and allowed certain bacteria to break it down into alcohols and other substances. This certainly is what nature has done to make oil. But in nature it has occurred over millions of years, while here we have done it in hours.'

'And this is what Weizmann has done?' I said, falling easily into his preferred perfect tense.

'Yes. He has done it with maize. He isolated certain bacteria – in fact, certain *Clostridia* – that he observed with the maize. And he has set them to work, by making a fermentation, to digest the starch in the maize.'

'I thought he got acetone out of it.'

'Here also we have acetone, and other substances.'

'And what has Vava done?'

'He has worked with *Ipomoea batatas*.'

'I see,' I said. I couldn't think of anything else to say. Dr Finster looked at me. He looked as if he would like to help, but didn't know how.

'As between Vava's batatas and Weizmann's maize,' I said, is there much difference, Doctor Finster?'

'With the result? There are differences. I have not found the great differences that Vava has told him.'

'How do we know what Vava told him?'

'Ah!' Dr Finster went to a box file, lying on its side. There was an open lab book inside, with a ball-point pen in it. He removed this and took out a paper lying underneath. It was a photostat, which I remembered as soon as

I saw it, of the letter to Fritz Haber that I had sent Connie months ago. There was only page 2 of the letter. Haber had been having difficulty settling his affairs in Germany. The government had imposed a levy on all Jews leaving the country. He had earlier pointed out to Weizmann that scientists who had gone to Turkey had been released from payment of this levy on the intervention of the Turkish government, with whom Germany was on friendly terms. Weizmann had not got anywhere with Ramsay Mac-Donald on this question, but he had written to the great Rutherford at Cambridge (where Haber had been invited) to use his scientific influence. He was telling Haber this. Then he went on to various gossipy items. The ringed paragraph was in the middle of the page.

Was den guten Vava betrifft, er ist unverbesserlich. Er hat mit mir letztens an der Protein Frage . . .

'You read German?' Dr Finster asked.
'Yes.'

As to the good Vava, he is of course incorrigible. He has been working with me lately on the protein question, but has been waylaid by more basic interests. He has discovered a variety of *Ipomoea batatas* together with a paying guest which will give it, as he has written to me by every post, an octane number of 150. This will hasten to its destined place the food in question, but the unfortunates who eat it will not come back for more!

'This is all!' I said.
 'Yes.'
 'What is the "paying guest"?'
 'A bacterium, evidently. This is Bergmann's understanding.'
 'And you are working with this bacterium?'
 'No. How can we know what Vava has worked with?'

'Ah.' Light began to dawn. 'Or the variety of – *batatas*?'

'We are working here with the common *Ipomoea batatas*.' Full daylight set in.

'You are not getting an octane number of 150,' I said.

'Nothing like it.'

'If you had Vava's batatas and also his bacterium, you might get an octane number of 150?'

'But this is what he is saying!'

'Yes.'

It had taken some time to get there. As Meyer had said, with chemical things you had to persevere.

2

The Chancellor was exceptionally natty that night, the host to a select small gathering. He had got the Sassoons and the Wykes, and also, to balance numbers, Professor Marta Tuomisalo (Shirley remembering that we had got on well together during my last visit). Conversation with this professor of advanced mathematics had at first been difficult, with much confusing talk of parameters, until I had observed, with reciprocated approval, that she had got a very fine pair of her own. Our intercourse had extended after that, and had been consummated last June at the Galei Kinneret Hotel in Tiberias. We shook hands very cordially and I inquired after her husband and two fine boys. Marta returned my kindly greeting and said that all was well at Helsinki.

Felicia Sassoon watched this with an observant eye and gave me a kiss. She worked in the Institute's administration. 'Well, Igor, how are things in your village?' Her husband, Michael, was smiling behind her, and we shook hands. His short-back-and-sides gave his head the rather endearingly English look of a promising Oxford undergraduate of a previous generation, which he had been. He was now a rather senior professor on the campus.

'Igor!' Marie-Louise Wyke enclosed me in a warm embrace. Her slightly sodden appearance was unearned because she didn't drink a drop. Her husband, the prospective Nobel Prize winner, helped in this equation, and he threw a bearlike arm round me, the other holding his glass, while greeting me in Russian. He had spent a year in Moscow and liked to air his bits of the tongue.

All of this was very convivial and a happy party ensued.

After it, Meyer took me to one side. 'What is this son of a bitch of yours gabbing all over London? Doesn't he know what the oil interests are doing to us?'

'What are the oil interests doing to us?'

'My God, we have here a clear breakthrough. Oil can be available to any country that wants it! Cheaply. Cheaper than those bastards are blackmailing everybody into paying. We have something of inestimable advantage to the world. We will not take from them a cent! We will freely make available the knowledge. It is what the Chief would want!' He always referred to Weizmann as 'the Chief.'

'Meyer, old friend,' I said. He had drunk very abstemiously but I had not. 'We have not got the knowledge. Nor had the Chief. He did not understand the knowledge. He thought Vava was making some new kind of laxative.'

'He did not. He dictated many memos. Didn't you speak to Bergmann yet?'

'I didn't yet.'

'You'll speak to him!' he said grimly. 'If your son of a bitch had only – '

'But, Meyer, I'm no scientist – '

'Scientists we have! It isn't science. It's a needle in a haystack they're looking for. Igor, I tell you, it's something tremendous. At the end he foresaw what would come with the Arabs here. He foresaw the opening up of their oil fields, which they didn't have at the time. Their asses were hanging out at the time. He wrote the most prophetic memo to Churchill. But this is old history.'

He'd been moving to the telephone, and suddenly stopped. 'Goddam it. He left today for the States, Bergmann. This is why we needed – So it will have to be Weiss.' He paused uncertainly. 'He goes to bed early, Weiss. He is kind of an old seventy. Even yet not seventy. Give me Weiss,' he said into the phone. He did his little shuffle while waiting, looking up at me from his eyebrows. 'What did you arrange for tomorrow?'

'I didn't arrange anything for tomorrow.'

'Weiss? Well, hello, for God's sake. It's Meyer. I have here Igor Druyanov, who wants to come and see you in Jerusalem tomorrow . . . *Druyanov*. The son. With regard to Vava Kutcholsky. Wake up there, Weiss, you're getting old or something? Of course the ketones. Exactly. So when? I'll ask him . . . Can you make it by eleven?' he said to me.

'I don't know. I suppose so.'

'Eleven is perfect. Very good. In the laboratory. So go to bed Weiss. You sound tired.'

'You are seeing Weiss at eleven tomorrow,' he said to me.

There was some confusion at the car, which Felicia tried to sort out, unsuccessfully. They were picking somebody up somewhere.

'He can walk Marta back to the Lunenfeld-Kunin.'

'Why should they walk back when we're going that way?' Michael said.

Marta had got in the back during this. 'So perhaps we will meet again,' she said to me brightly, winding down the window, 'during your stay?'

'That would be lovely. We must do it.'

Good nights rang out cheerily. I walked back to the San Martin.

Caroline hadn't rung back.

Next day I got the lot.

3

One of the stranger aspects of the discussion with Weiss was that he later supplied me with a transcript of it. I hadn't noticed a tape recorder in the room, and there'd been no one else there. He'd suffered a lot, of course, from misrepresentation, had Weiss, and I suppose old habits die hard.

I'd seen photos of him as a young man, Weizmann's young man, confident, febrile, brilliant, with a certain impatient pazazz to him. The pale triangular face was wasted now – fires banked. It had taken time to find him. Unlike Rehovot, which as a research institute had only a few graduate students, Jerusalem's was a great teaching university, and most of its undergraduates were still in the Army. The huge stony campus seemed empty, just a few people drifting in and out of the buildings. But I'd followed my nose, and smelled the unsettling smells, and found people drifting aimlessly about the chemistry department, too, and at length found his office.

Weiss had spent much of his life in Bergmann's shadow, had been involved in the tremendous conflicts that had broken out in the late 1940s between the President and Bergmann, until then the heir apparent at Rehovot.

The subject of the conflicts was enshrined in a correspondence, not for publication, and under most severe restraint, anyway. I'd had a good look at it, of course, before coming to see him. I wondered if he knew of the existence of this correspondence, and after one look decided that he did, and moreover that he very likely knew of the existence of everything.

He was a small, hunched, elegant composition in greys and blacks, and he looked at me most suspiciously as he shook my hand and seated me. But in a couple of minutes he'd crisply put into perspective all of Finster's plodding science.

*

Yes, it's finished, kaput, the world of cheap energy, of cheap everything. Very good. We can make a better world, stabler. The importance isn't the power. There'll be nuclear power, perhaps other kinds. The importance is the chemicals. Almost everything comes now from the petrochemical industry – our food, medicine, clothing, a hundred things – which is insane. Overnight we see the world held to ransom and prices quadruple. Why should we put up with it?

I'd tried to stem the tide, but it had rolled on.

We have to stop living on our capital. This is what we are doing. The oil, the coal – it's *capital*. We have to live on our income, because nature every year is making inexhaustible supplies of the same substance. Technologically we are still at the stage of hunting-man. We hunt for the energy when we should be breeding it. You ask why we don't?

I hadn't. I'd said, 'Very clear, most lucid, Professor. But with regard to Vava –'

Because always the oil companies oppose us. The thing to understand is that a viable fermentation process would shift influence from the oil belts of the world to the starch belts – a factor of huge significance. The requirements are of climate only, not geological accident. Further, an incalculable gain, you solve the world's food problem. All the infrastructure, the irrigation, has to go in first. Today, half Africa can drop dead, and the world will give sympathy. Let them keep it! Africa will feed itself – and all of us. You ask where the capital is to come from?

I'd asked nothing at all. The brilliant young man with the pazazz was staring uncannily at me through the wasted face.

*

I can tell you. For anything offering the same convenience of processing as oil – which coal and shale do not – gigantic sums are available. Those in at the birth of the petrochemical industry know this. So many things had to happen together there, so many discoveries, with simply massive industrial development. Compared with that, this is child's play. All the development has been done. It's simply a matter of replacing your source material. Instead of getting it from a hole in the ground or the sea, you grow it. At a time of cheap oil there was no incentive. But now? All that stops us is a technicality. The established processes of fermentation are too slow and the yield too low. What another investigator has found, however –

('Vava?' I'd said. And he had acknowledged with a wintry smile: 'Vava.')

What another investigator has found is that existing yields from fermentation may perhaps be doubled, and the time halved, by working with a particular strain of bacterium on certain materials. However, at the present time we have no knowledge of his bacterium or his materials. This briefly is the background to the problem.

Well, we'd got to it, and I briefly celebrated, and said, 'As you know, Professor, all I can do is concentrate on Vava. What can you tell me about him?'

'Professor Bergmann, I think, has already told you.' The scientific ice pack now broken, the wintry sun was more in evidence. 'He was simply a colleague of ours in London, in 1933.'

'He worked at the Featherstone Laboratory?'

'He hardly worked there. He popped in and out. What do you know of the Featherstone Laboratory?' The smile was now quite mellow.

'An address on a letter-heading.'

'The Featherstone Laboratory – it was like something

from Dickens. We had there – Weizmann had rented – as I remember, the second and fourth floors. Somebody else was on the first and the third. All day we ran up and down the stairs. It was something unbelievable. It was in a tiny side street off Holborn. The place doesn't exist any more. I made once a sentimental journey to have a look. Nothing. It was bombed out of existence early in the war. All the day, up and down we ran. A very dark staircase. It corresponded to none of the safety conditions written into the law for such premises. Yet we did some work there.'

They certainly had. They had done much of the basic work on which the petrochemical industry, which he was now lamenting, rested: petroleum-cracking, aromatics analysis. I mentioned the fact.

'I see you have read something of this. Yes, we made certain investigations which entered the literature. Shell took over the processes. Old history,' he said. He was now smiling most genially.

'Not a very elaborate laboratory, I believe.'

'Elaborate?' I saw all his teeth. 'No. You may say so. We had no spectroscope or physical apparatus. However, there were friends in various quarters. What was required was available. Yes, we did some work in the Featherstone Laboratory.'

'And Vava helped.'

'Vava?' The teeth vanished. 'Vava was not engaged in these things. He was occupied with a different problem, protein. He came and went. It was a matter of weeks only. He was living with the Weizmanns at the time. Then Weizmann got him a job – through the good offices of Lord Melchett, as I remember, who was at that time the chairman of ICI.'

'It's strange that there's no correspondence on file between Vava and Weizmann.'

'As I have explained, they were living together at the time. Why should they correspond?'

'Weizmann says he heard from him by every post.'

'Well, I'm no expert on correspondence. However, when Bergmann received your letter he had the files searched. And it turned out from late material, which neither of us had looked at, that Weizmann did indeed recall the work with Vava.'

He pressed a buzzer on his desk, and a secretary appeared.

'Give me the late Weizmann material . . . You will see,' he said to me, 'it's something in the nature of – meditations. It didn't seem to us of the first importance. Of course, when the oil embargo blew up, Bergmann telephoned from America for the transcript. You will see the relevant papers. And inquiries were made there also. Commercial Solvents had a lot of his papers. Ah!'

The girl had come back with the material. It was a collection of Xeroxes in a box file: typewritten notes and memos. They were all dated, some very fragmentary, a mere two or three sentences.

'He was almost blind at this time, and very ill, of course,' Weiss said.

'Comatose, I'd heard.'

'It wasn't a coma. He simply stayed in bed. Sometimes he got up. I was not seeing him then, of course.'

'No.'

He looked at me, but didn't say anything. I was glancing over the papers.

'Towards the end it is quite mixed,' he said.

It was mixed. One short memorandum in 1952 contained three observations: one on the economy of Egypt, a suggested experiment with saline water, and a complaint about some roughness in one of his slippers.

'A secretary took dictation when required.' He saw me smiling slightly and said abruptly, 'He was a great man.'

'Yes.'

'A very great man.' Again he opened his mouth and closed it.

'Can I take this?'

'Of course. It has been prepared for you.' He paused, staring at me for a moment with a rather odd scowl (which only later struck me as embarrassment), and then took out of a drawer a copy of *The Betrayed Decade*, which he asked me to sign.

What with this, and the fate of the world, and of the chaps in the starch belts, now in some way in my hands, I felt somewhat flummoxed on the way back to Rehovot.

4

I read conscientiously through the memoranda in the afternoon. There was something rather strange in doing it in the room where it had been dictated twenty-odd years ago. The bed, where he had lain, was a couple of feet to my right. I was seated in the chair in which when 'sometimes he got up' he had sat. His grave was in easy eyeshot in the grass below. All this was disturbing. The notes themselves were disturbing, a fine mind become trivial, occasionally pettish; here and there a shaft of light, but not very often.

It was a somewhat uneasy mixture of scientific thinking and rambling reflection. For one whole week, evidently, he had been much concerned with a famine in India: something every day about his protein process and a mode by which the waste from molasses could instantly be converted on a large scale to feed millions of the starving. There was a good deal of random invective about uncaring multinational companies, particularly oil companies. Inserted in all this was much bickering about the political direction of Israel, together with his own creature comforts. He seemed to have become very faddish about his food; every word taken down. I wondered where the original notebooks were that had contained this dictation and listened for Connie, but I couldn't hear her.

'Would you like a cup of tea, Igor?'

Nellie had come silently in, and I started. I had been gazing broodingly at the grave below.

'I'd love one, Nellie.'

'We'll all be going in about half an hour. Of course, you can stay on if you want, but they shut the gate at the gatehouse, so you can't get out that way.'

'No, I'll be ready when everyone is.'

I got up and stretched my legs and walked about the room. It was an elegant room. Verochka had promised him somewhere in the correspondence how he'd find it. He'd found it complete, his pyjamas ready for him under the coverlet, his first sight of it. He'd been terribly busy rushing about the world at the time, of course, so she had superintended the whole thing: stylish light stripy curtains, the same material on the bedcover and on the dressing-table stool. All chosen with much love and care and her madamish sense of the highest English style for her lord in this Levantine place. She hadn't really much liked Palestine, still less Israel; had never learned Hebrew; couldn't speak Yiddish. It was Chaimchik's favourite language: all of his affectionate nature and warmth and humour came out in it. A strange partnership.

Every item, she had chosen and placed. His bed against the wall, a most elegant bed, single; it was in some smooth light wood like pale ebony, head and foot ceremonially curved with a suggestion of Egypt and also Empire; Napoleon in Egypt. Beside the bed, a small commode with a silver candlesnuffer and a clock (stopped at 6 a.m., when he died), and also his prayer book, placed slightly askew as he had laid it down, yellowish pages open at the place.

Next to the commode, and in the big semicircular bay where he had fed the birds, the large dark-oak refectory table at which I had been working. It was scattered with his knickknacks: photos, a barometer, a desk calendar, bits and pieces. Everything kept exactly as it was: his clothes in the cupboards, his soap and toothbrush in the adjoining bathroom basin (even his sleeping pills and stomach tablets in the cabinet) and a towel left ready for him on the towel-warmer in the small room off the bathroom.

55

There was a door out to the landing, but because he hadn't left the room for months it had been kept locked, and still was; one entered through Nellie's room, which had been his nurse's room. Nellie now entered through it, with a cup of tea, and I silently drank it.

2

For his sabbatical, Ham Wyke had swapped houses with a man across the courtyard from Meyer. They had made me welcome at Harvard, the Wykes. He was a large, almost elephantine man surprisingly fast on his feet at ball games, and with a capacity for going still as a waxwork, mouth open, when working on a problem. Despite his eminence (the anticipated Prize was for his massive work on cancer research) he was a simple soul, with a taste for practical jokes. He was also the only scientist who'd ever been able to explain to me in simple terms what he was working at.

A particular hazard in going to dinner with them was Marie-Louise's tendency to buttonhole me on the state of her two stable worries: Ham's 'drink problem,' and those connected with their dropout son Rod, now 'into the drug scene'. Fortunately, people were expected in for drinks later, which fussed her, so the expected consultation didn't take place. I took the opportunity to have one with her husband instead.

'Is there still anything in fermentation, Ham?'

'Well, it's old-fashioned, of course.'

'But can it work?'

'You can make anything work. The heat engine works. Do you realize our whole civilization still operates on the heat engine – since the day that Scotchman watched the kettle boil? It's a kind of lunatic obsession. Every advance in science and technology has been ingeniously brought into line to improve the damned thing!'

'You mean old-fashioned-superseded?'

'Just old-fashioned. Known. All done. It wouldn't excite anyone here.'

'It doesn't excite Finster.'

'Exactly. It's only fiddling now, getting your coordinates right, the optimum material, the optimum bug.'

'It couldn't be done on a computer these days?'

'How? Too many variables.'

'But if it's a question of finding a lot of starch – '

'Well, it isn't. At least, I would think not. You'd need to find something with exactly the right qualities, then just the bug to turn it on. A number of things must be critically right.'

'It would need an accident, you think?'

'Probably. It's like Ziegler – you know about him?'

'No.'

'Recent history. He was working there in Germany. He was doing something with ethylene, in an autoclave. One day he suddenly found this filmy kind of scum building up; he couldn't understand it. So he looked at it, and it occurred to him that the technicians hadn't cleaned up properly from the last experiment, so he put up a notice in their place to find out who the hell was supposed to have. And naturally nobody showed up. They thought they'd get fired. So he offered a reward, something like that, and a guy came up finally and told him what the last experiment was, and that is the story of polyethylene. They gave him the Nobel Prize for it – Ziegler, not the technician.'

'Is it true?'

'Perfectly. That's how it was. Of course, he had put in something like half a lifetime figuring what the hell to do with ethylene. But that's how it happened. Accident.'

'If this particular accident worked – the sweet potatoes – could it threaten the oil business?'

'How would it? It is their business.'

'They wouldn't have an interest in suppressing it?'

'How do you suppress knowledge of this sort? It's general knowledge, surely.'

I saw what Connie had meant about the unworldly scientist.

'They might prefer the general knowledge to go no further?'

He thought about it. 'I don't see that. They would surely want to get in on the act.'

'Hello!'

The first after-dinner guest had arrived. With a lowering of spirits I saw it was Dr Patel, my Indian admirer.

'How terribly nice to see you. I won't say it's an accident,' he said.

'Ram has been wanting to meet you,' Marie-Louise said. 'I'm not going to of offer you a drink, Ram.'

'You may do so, my dear. I will have a glass of orange juice. Fresh, mind. I'll have none of your canned.'

Close behind him came the Horowitzes, from practically next door – Professor Nathan Horowitz, Vice-President of the Institute – and after them the Selas, and further couples. Apart from Patel, they were all Israelis, and after a while as the place filled up I saw that Connie was there, too, and I moved over to her.

'Igor, why do you run from Doctor Patel?'

'I don't like him.'

'That's very unpleasant. He is a sweet person, apart from being brilliant and good. You won't have such a fan. People are delighted to have him in Rehovot. Where is your Finnish friend?'

'I don't think they've invited her.'

'Maybe they did, and she knew how unpleasant you were.'

'Has she some other special friend since I was here?'

'I don't like these questions. Ask her yourself. Igor, you've been drinking. I don't like you at all.'

'You see, it's a sad life, Connie. I sat in Chaimchik's room and read over his last memoranda.'

'In that case, you can have a drink. Life is sad,' she said as we had one, 'but – I have to say it – your reaction is childish. The Israelis here are putting on a show for you. Life at the present is not just sad but tragic, and I don't even know how to explain it. How can a person like you not see this?'

'Connie, have you been having one?'

'Well, I did have one, but it isn't that. People come here and they have only read about it in the newspaper. A most tremendous tragedy has happened here. Two and a half thousand young men were killed in a fortnight – can you imagine! And people try to carry on, and you tell me life is sad because you sat in Chaimchik's room, an old man of seventy-eight, at the end of his life. And I know what you mean – but still. Oh, well, it's sad,' she said.

'Did I give offence in some way?'

'I am the one giving the offence. But at least – realize things are not normal. I should not be saying this. I want to say it to everybody, but it's wrong. Really, I don't know why I'm saying it to you.'

I knew why she was saying it. The sense of enormity had hit me often enough. But with me, my family, these figures were so trivial, the disillusion so slight. I said, 'Connie, it's a world of terrible mistakes and accidents. I don't know why you feel this way particularly, I mean just particularly tonight. But if you do, I'm sorry. And I'll be terribly nice to Doctor Patel if it will help.'

I was smiling at her, so she smiled back, and presently I did go and have a chat with Patel. It was a lengthy chat, I remember, but the strange thing was that I couldn't recall any of it later, though I tried.

I had a further Scotch or two with Ham after the throng had gone, and woke with a headache.

It was a day of headaches, anyway.

3

There was a very peculiar memo of Chaimchik's that I pored over. He had evidently not been having a good day either. It was November 7, 1952, and the memo went on, with spaces, over several pages. It seemed to have started early, because there was something about his breakfast, and the next item was immediately about Vava.

I particularly want those appointed to superintend the matter [next words missed] my absolute conviction that Kutcholsky's contribution is a major break-through, the equal if not more [CLOSTRIDIA?]. My excuse must be that at the time we were not investigating such questions, and after much harassment I needed the rest, although I admit it to be no excuse and a demonstration of blindness. In which connection it is ironic that in my present blindness I am able . . .

He appeared to have lost the track here, and he said his mouth was furred. There was some trouble with his teeth. After a space, Vava returned.

As I have written [?] Kutcholsky with his large amounts of carotene and other substances [?] naturally several difficulties. But it is necessary to work with and not against nature, and in fact it gives us the key, even the trigger, to tremendously increased yields, which we have found in the work with Ketone Bill. We have produced a most elegant reaction, certainly with a very large conversion to methyl. He has the lab books himself. There can be no doubt that with the methyl already present together with the carotene that it is the answer to the problem.

Such [catalysis?] taken with his halving of the time of fermentation will double the yield and provide a ketonic product of extreme concentration making immediately available to Israel a complete high-octane fuel.

In this connection, the findings with the saline water are of the utmost significance. This drain [strain?] extensively in the Negev with minimum cultivation at no cost to us in potable water or otherwise cultivable land.

The benefits only begin here. For half my life I have found all contests with the oil companies to have a predetermined end in the question of an alternative supply of raw materials. Here for the first time a determined attempt may be made, a working model for the world. Our teams of workers can make the poorest areas of Africa and Asia independent of oil wells.

The next decade will show not only great increase in production from Arab oil-fields and those still to be found, but explosive advance in the field of petro-chemicals. It is possible to visualize a situation where the economies of even the developed countries may be dependent in a large degree on Arab oil, a situation with grave consequences for us. To my suggestion with regard to Egypt, I add . . .

A page or two of political reflection followed, very disjointed, with some further trouble about his teeth, and then a single cryptic paragraph.

I have been thinking. Perhaps the Bradford people will be able to let us know. I will think again later. That German would make a cat laugh. Never mind, he will prove the best internationalist of us all. It's a funny world. We will celebrate the holiness of the day.

There was no more that day, except some tantrum to do with his food.. He'd had a sudden desire for chutney, and then wouldn't take it; his every remark by now was being noted, the end near. The following evening. November 8th, he went into a coma, and he died at six on the morning of the ninth. I could imagine the nurse, listening to his breathing, running in at the door. Nellie now trotted through it.

'Mr Weisgal would like to talk to you, Igor. He is on the phone to Mr Meltzer now.'

I went through to Julian's room, and after a moment or two was handed the phone.

'Igor? Weiss tells me he explained to you.'

'Well, yes, he did. He explained a bit, Meyer.'

My head was throbbing evilly. 'I am just going through some papers he gave me.'

'He has a further point. He asks where Vava got these potatoes in the first place, how he even came to deal with such things. That's very interesting, eh?'

'Well, it is,' I said, 'I suppose, in a way.'

'It raises the question of locating Vava's other correspondence – not just with Weizmann. Weiss says he had many friends in London. What I am thinking, this Joe of yours there, he could initiate some work in that direction.'

'He's in hospital just now.'

'So give him a call.'

'Yes, all right, Meyer.' Lying in bed, with his eyes crossing, would not, it suddenly occurred to me, greatly interfere with Meyer's own telephone activity.

'What is it? You have some problem?'

'Weizmann's last memo. It's very fragmentary and complicated.'

'Yes?'

'Well, that's the problem. I'm thinking about it.'

'Can I help?'

'It's the last week of his life. He is saying strange, disjointed things. I don't understand them.'

He was silent a moment. 'So maybe I can. Come over here. That guy will bring you.'

I put the papers together, and Ze'ev ran me there.

It was really a very beautiful house. The contrast between its impatient occupant and the building's own unhurried harmony, the natural wood and stone and the several dozen fine pictures, was very striking; not more so, of course, than the many striking contrasts in the character of the occupant, whose taste it faithfully reflected. He had a splendid study in it, but his preferred place of work was a collapsible card table on the landing. There was a phone on this table, and another on a chair alongside. I took the phone off the chair and sat down. He was in a dressing gown of subdued blue stripes; natty as ever.

'*Nu?*'

I showed him the long last memo, and he put his glasses on and carefully read it.

'What prescience, eh?' he said admiringly at last. 'Twenty-odd years ago, he saw this coming. Who else did? "Where the economies of even the developed countries may be dependent in a large degree on Arab oil." I tell you!'

'Yes. I don't understand about the people in Bradford.' I read it over his shoulder.

I have been thinking. Perhaps the Bradford people will be able to let us know. I will think again later. That German would make a cat laugh. Never mind, he will prove the best internationalist of us all. It's a funny world. We will celebrate the holiness of the day.

'Well, you recognize the last sentence,' he said.

'I don't.'

'*Goy.* It's from the Yom Kippur service. It's the last thing he read. *Unctanah tokef kedushat hayom*, et cetera. He had his prayer book there. Probably he looked at it just then. Yom Kippur. When this last war broke out. It's a strange thing, isn't it?' His battered face was creased in a most solemn expression.

'Yes. The German who made the cat laugh couldn't be Vava, could it?'

'How could it? Vava was not a German. He wouldn't think of him as a German.'

'Haber or Willstätter, perhaps?'

'Certainly not. He had the greatest respect for them.'

'Hmm.'

'It's a problem. Bradford people. Was he ever in Bradford?'

'Well, Meyer, I am sort of asking you.'

He took his glasses off, and put them on again, and read the whole thing through once more.

63

'Bradford is a place in Yorkshire, England, right?'

'Right.'

'A textile place. I don't recall anything from Bradford. Who the hell do we know in Bradford?'

He was looking at me, so I shook my head. I didn't know a soul in Bradford.

He put his glasses on and off a couple of times and looked in frustration at the transcript. 'This is ridiculous,' he said. 'Who the hell took it down?'

'Well, I thought I'd ask you that, too.'

'Some goddam stenographer took it down, it's obvious.' He picked up the phone. 'Give me Julian Meltzer.'

He had a somewhat inconclusive chat with Julian. Julian didn't know who'd taken it down either. It was established that the dictation books ought to be around somewhere, though. A whirlwind round of phone calls revealed that several of them were in the basement of the Wix Library; and about five minutes later, so was I.

The Wix Library was another magnificent building; I picked my way down to the basement and found Dan in it.

He said, 'Cassius hath a lean and hungry look; he thinks too much . . . Mashed potato, Igor?'

'Mashed potato.'

'That's the stuff.'

These were the main Weizmann archives, embracing some scores of bays of shelving. In the House there were only typed copies of the outgoing letters, translated from Russian, Hebrew, Yiddish, French, or German where necessary. Here were the originals, incoming and outgoing, plus everything else relating to the great man: photographs, certificates, drafts, invitations, telegrams, minutes, cuttings – every memento of his life, stacked in box files, shelf upon shelf. I'd done some work here, but it was an oppressive place to work in; the ceiling was low and the air heavy in the strongroom.

Alizia, the librarian, expected me, but the notice had been short and she was somewhat flustered.

'These are from 1952, Mr Druyanov. Would you like to check that everything is here?'

'I wouldn't know what to check. I will take your word for it, Alizia.' This statement was the more heartfelt because a quick glance at the books showed they were all in shorthand.

'If you would just sign here.'

I signed, and on the off chance paused at Dan's desk.

'Dan, can you do shorthand?'

'A little ... Hmm. Pitman I will tell you something disheartening, Igor.'

'What's that?'

'They do Gregg in Israel.'

This turned out to be correct. But by the afternoon, Connie had organized a Pitman person.

There was a small gathering at my place in the evening, including Professor Tuomisalo. I was rather ashamed of my question to Connie.

'We haven't really met much, Marta.'

'Well. You will be spending some time here.' Discreet as ever. I found myself overstimulated again by the very cool mixture of brain and propriety and sexuality.

'You are marvellously tanned, Marta.'

'I take fruit back to my apartment at lunchtime and sun on the balcony. The winter sun is very special.'

'Is the work working out?'

'Of course. I told you. There's a tiny group of us, and two happen to be at Rehovot. It's really a most blissful situation.'

I had seen the two, who gave no problems. Her English was excellent. So was her Russian. Everything about her was by no means ordinary. She was nine years older than I, which I had felt once or twice was in a way a pity, apart from other considerations, which were that she was well contented with her lot. She was charmingly ignorant of various areas of knowledge in which I was informed; which worked both ways, except that she was incapable of explaining hers. In other areas, of course, we suited, and she smiled calmly at me. 'Is your life going very nicely in London?'

'The life of a bachelor is always strange.'

'Are you thinking soon of normalizing it?'

'Well, I'm getting old.'

'It's everybody's problem. Don't worry, Igor.'

'I'm not worrying. How do you like my penthouse?' I said. 'My very private penthouse.'

She had a look around it. 'It is very nice. Mr Deutsch at the desk below, who is always at the desk below, is a good friend of mine.'

'I see. And all your good friends will still be at the Lunenfeld-Kunin, will they?'

'Oh, yes, we're all good friends there.'

I recalled her room at the Lunenfeld-Kunin. She was very family-minded. Her bullet-headed father kept an eye on proceedings; also her mother, and her husband and two sturdy lads: photos all about. All the people who had been there with me had inspected these domestic treasures: I had never been in a position to inspect them alone. Discretion, circumspection, propriety.

'Well, we must try and see a little more of Israel while I'm here.'

'That would be very nice. Where would you recommend, Michael?' she said to Michael Sassoon, who had at that moment amiably joined us. 'Igor would like to see something of Israel while he is here.'

'December, hmm. The Dead Sea, I should think. Somewhere down low, you see. Tiberias is low, but chancy. You can get a lot of rain at this season.'

'I've been to Tiberias. That was June.'

'June, ah. It can heat up considerably in Tiberias in June.'

66

It had heated up considerably in Tiberias in June, as the faintest glance from Marta acknowledged.

'How are the sweet potatoes doing?' he said.

'Not much at the moment.'

'Is your research man all right?'

'Well, he's hard-headed,' I said. I couldn't remember telling him about Hopcroft. News circulated at Rehovot.

While I pondered this, he began talking about some work in his department. 'Mechanochemistry. It comes out of polyelectrolytes and irreversible thermodynamics,' he said.

'Ah, does it?'

'Oh, yes. Polymer research, basically – membranes, that kind of thing. Quite fascinating.'

'What does it do?'

'What does it *do*?' He frowned. This was always the sticking point here, of course. Surprisingly, it did something useful. It promised, in some distant future, to provide an alternative to the heat engine by duplicating the action of muscle. Muscle apparently expanded or retracted in response to the effcct of certain body acids.

'Happens when you lift your hand or scratch your nose, or whatever. Quite fast, you see – no intermediate processes.'

Muscle cord was being made out of various polymers, and the acids from something else, and the membranes that would admit one kind or the other from some other material.

'You mean it works?' I said.

'Oh, yes. It's primitive. The models just turn little wheels and lift weights, and so on. The interest is with the polymers, you see.'

Others had joined the group, and in a way that I did not quite mark it became a discussion of biological membrane and the brain. Marta had become quite animated during this, in connection with some apparent rate of energy conversion that did not accord with her advanced standards, and an interested small party was arranged to go and view the experiments right away, except, as a phone call established, the man in whose demesne it lay was out, so it was decided to do it tomorrow. Vava's batatas and the economic plight of the world were happily lost sight of. The only thing settled, really, in a little tête-à-tête, was a weekend twosome to the Dead Sea.

4

One of the problems with research is to know what to look for. Too little material leads to groping and stress; too much to drifting – Hopcroft's complaint. Here there was far too much. It was necessary to write myself a short list and then check with experts that it was the right list, and then put somebody on to keeping to it. Sitting in Chaimchik's chair, and gazing out the window to the position he occupied in the grass below, I tapped pencil against teeth and reviewed the situation.

It was twenty-one years ago that he had been placed in position below, and the situation I was reviewing was almost exactly twenty-one years before that. What we had was a fine upstanding figure, in his prime, distinguished, full of life and vigour indeed as remote from the moulder-ing remains in the ground as I now was.

The House that now sat like a museum all around me was still in the future; as was the stripy material for Verochka's eye so delightedly to light on – where? At Harrod's? No Institute. No Israel. The 2,500 young participants in the tragedy referred to by Connie not yet born; few of their parents born. Chaimchik was beavering away in London and elsewhere to make the national home that they would be born in.

Of the period of his life between 1931 and 1935, I now knew more than anyone – more than Bergmann, who had lived and worked with him; more than Weisgal, who had laughed so often with him. Day by day, month by month, from the records of this prodigious witness, I knew the onset of every chill and bowel irregularity, every sleepless night, every little affair (though not as much as I wished: Verochka had spent a year ahead of me at the files, at about the time that I was seven). I knew what he said in public and wrote in private. I knew what he had thought, and bought, and had seen and done; could visualize the excellent, intelligent man, trim beard, knowledgeable sardonic eyes, delightful smile.

Of course with all this, it goes without saying, I knew practically nothing – little more in any sensible way than he could know, presented with my catalogued particulars, of the person who would one day have to dress him in footnotes and exhibit him. Still, I knew something. I knew that at the time he had underestimated – rather patronized – mysterious Vava. Between us, we might yet do more for him than ungrateful Israel.

In 1931, thoroughly exhausted after thirteen years of political struggle, he had found himself kicked out of the leadership of world Zionism, owing to factional differences. He was fifty-seven, and he didn't know what to do. An early thought, naturally, was to return to science, but science had rolled on. Was he still up to it?

At this time, Professor Richard Willstätter, Nobel Laureate, first director of the massive Kaiser Wilhelm Institute in Germany, and perhaps the greatest chemist in the world, came to London to address the Royal Society and to receive its Gold Medal. Weizmann asked his advice. The Laureate sternly catechized him, told him he would still do, and graciously undertook to collaborate with him by mail on a small piece of research to do with protein, Willstätter's own subject.

Not very encouraged (and he had lately suffered some further discouragement), he went to see his old patent agent, who occupied rooms in an ancient house in Featherstone Buildings, and without much cheer took rooms there himself, which he equipped as a laboratory.

The source of the further discouragement was particularly galling. He was still the president of the Hebrew University in Jerusalem, which he had founded, and which incorporated in its many resolutions a most glowing one looking forward to the day when he would go and work there. He had been privately critical of recent academic standards at this university, but at the prompting of Einstein from Princeton he wrote to them saying that the day had now come and that he would be grateful if a small laboratory and some assistance could be placed at his disposal. He was most abruptly and coldly turned down, on the grounds that no funds were available.

Since whatever funds were available had come largely from his efforts (and because, despite being out of office, he was about to embark on a wearisome tour to collect further funds for practically bankrupt Palestine, and the extra few hundred would scarcely rock the boat, particularly in view of his scientific reputation, which was thus being meanly devalued along with his political one), this rankled.

'If anything at the university can be said to be "academic,"' he wrote to the American banker Felix Warburg, 'it is this resolution ... I am now running a lab myself here in London. It is quite a modest installation, but it answers the purpose. The total budget of this place, including the salary of my assistants and all that is necessary for somewhat advanced work, is £500 a year.' He added that he wanted to work half the time in Palestine, 'but should I succeed in this, I shall not be establishing myself within the precincts of the University of Jerusalem.'

The first part of this paragraph, with its caustic disdain for ingrates who denied him £500 a year, perhaps explained the slight discrepancy deduced by Hopcroft from the rent agreement; and the second part, perhaps, the reason why the Weizmann Institute was now at Rehovot and not at Jerusalem.

Anyway, here he was, at the 'Featherstone Laboratory', as his new letter-heading grandly announced, returned from the gruelling tour that kept Palestine afloat for another year, and ready for business himself. Willstätter kept his word, and the correspondence began to flow. In little time, his fertile and optimistic brain working again, the small piece of research became a wide field. The Great Depression had begun, and his irrepressible humanism led him to conceive an ambitious scheme for feeding the poor of the world with a protein food made from waste matter for practically nothing. He quite soon came up against the 'uncaring international companies', who naturally enough didn't stand to make much out of it themselves, but he persevered. Further storm clouds were building, anyway. In Germany, they were accompanied by storm troopers and Adolf Hitler.

Aflame again with his scientific work, he resisted the fray as long as he could (replying to urgent demands from the hero-worshiping young labour leader Ben-Gurion in Palestine that he was engaged on work of 'momentous importance' for the world and that he had 'no right to jeopardize such a situation for the sake of a problematic and unattractive political victory'). But he couldn't stay away from the refugee problem. He was still the most prominent Jew in the world. Very soon he was chairman of various refugee committees, and very soon after refugee scientists were crowding in on him.

Early in 1933, a telegram from Berlin warmly recommended a young scientist just dismissed from the Dahlem Institute, Dr Ernst David Bergmann, and Weizmann took him in. Others followed. Then something else happened in 1933. A friend from Manchester days, Israel Sieff, one of the heads of the Marks & Spencer firm, came to see him. His young son Daniel, seventeen years old, had just died; he asked Weizmann's advice on a suitable memorial.

They walked ruminatively in Hyde Park, and Weizmann gave his advice. Daniel had been reading science. Weizmann thought a small research institute, bearing his name, might be the best memorial, in Palestine. He didn't think Jerusalem was the place for it. He thought a village called Rehovot was: it was then known as 'the gateway to the desert', and the Jewish Agency was running a small agricultural station there. Such an institute, apart from perpetuating the boy's name, would serve a multiple function. It would give employment to scientists now being thrown out of Germany, who might themselves be able to give employment to other thousands. The desert had to be pushed back; science had to explore the country's resources and make opportunities. The small barren land was the only hope for millions now trapped in increasingly hostile Europe.

The bereaved father agreed and plans were drawn up for the Daniel Sieff Research Institute. Not long after, Weizmann was able to suggest a scientific director for it: he was greatly taken not only by young Bergmann's scientific ability but also by his executive capacity. Also agreed, and the Institute thudded ahead, to be opened the following year, 1934. Weizmann got Willstätter – still in grave communication about protein – to come and do the job. But alas, it wasn't the old Willstätter. The great scientist was soon to be flung out himself. Weizmann prevailed on him to continue his work in Palestine, but he died first, broken-hearted, in a rented room in Switzerland. The great Fritz Haber, too: despite comings and goings and to-ings and fro-ings, no journey's end at Cambridge for him. He also died in humiliation. Weizmann had invited him to Palestine, too – but only his magnificent library ever arrived.

And that was it: the idyll in Featherstone Buildings over, the situation far too menacing for him to be kept out of the leadership. He was co-opted back to it, and from then on it was Zionist politics, and my period was over.

Four years, 1931–35: a fertile wilderness, as I'd observed before. He'd painfully found his way back to science, characteristically lighted on a problem of immense concern to humanity, but hadn't time to finish it (hence millions dead of starvation who might have lived), made the early laboratory steps with his assistants in laying the foundations of the petrochemical industry, taken a leading part in the resettlement of refugees, kept shaky Palestine afloat for a bit longer, and raised in it the small but promising Daniel Sieff Research Institute, germ for the present splendour.

Not a bad wilderness.

Somewhere in this wilderness had been sown another seed, overlooked at the time, whose memory had come back to plague him, in this room, twenty-one years ago, between fiddling with his teeth and his slippers and his diet.

This was the context, and I pencilled my short list:

> Desert reclamation – batatas
> Saline irrigation – batatas
> Protein – batatas
> Bradford – all correspondence

The German who made the cat laugh was rather a worry. I couldn't think of anything for him.

5

'What is really very odd,' I said to Connie (to whom I gave the list), 'is that there shouldn't be *anything* about Vava in the files. I mean, it's odd, isn't it?'

'Well, we know we are missing many letters.'

'Not in the 1930s. From the early 1900s, yes.'

This was true. Almost all his early Manchester letters were missing (apart from those to Verochka); all the letters to his family in Pinsk were missing – they'd had no reason to keep them, hadn't realized young Chaimchik was to be the future Moses. 'No, we're pretty complete on the 1930s, apart from a few love letters and the like,' I said. 'Yet, here's Vava, a relative of Verochka, wanting to get out of Germany. He must have written to them about that, at least.'

'Perhaps to Verochka.'

True enough. Verochka hadn't been such a careful keeper of other correspondence. 'Still,' I said.

'What are you hinting, Igor?'

'Well, letters were going back and forth between them about batatas if nothing else. Where are the copies?'

'Everything scientific went to Jerusalem.'

'Exactly. And stayed there. Then poor Hopcroft gets hit on the head in London, and this chap comes to a sticky end in America, and all of a sudden there aren't any Vava letters in Jerusalem.'

'We don't know that there ever were.'

'But there ought to have been, if they existed at all. And

we know that they did exist. Olga has the originals – had them. Where are the copies?'

'Igor, you surely don't mean –'

'I mean we ought to keep things here in future. Something funny could be –'

'In Jerusalem?' Connie said, wide-eyed.

Before looking wide-eyed at me, she had thrown a similar look, of the warning type, towards the other person in the room. This was a rather severe-faced young person, the Pitman expert, who was now also looking wide-eyed at me. Security, like charity, evidently began at home.

I said, 'Well, Margalit,' and walked over to her. 'How's it coming?'

'So far, it's coming well,' she said, collecting herself. 'I don't find differences. It's a correct transcript.'

I looked over her shoulder. She was writing it out by hand. Her handwriting was rather spiky and not easy to follow, but some differences hit the eye right away.

'Why are you breaking up the paragraphs in that way?'

'You said to copy as it's in the book.'

'In the book it's not joined in paragraphs as in the transcript?'

'No, there are spaces – pauses. The sense is joined together, of course. A good secretary would naturally join together in this way.'

'I see.' Implied was that she was herself a secretary of this type. Miss Knowall. Not bright. I became at once interested. Caroline was too bright. Marta was bright, too, of course, but in a different way – perhaps owing to Finland and thinking in numbers.

'Where the words are crossed out,' she said, 'you want me to put in those words and then cross them out again?'

'Exactly. Every mark you see there, I want transcribed.'

'Good. So I am doing this.'

She conscientiously got on with it while I looked over her shoulder. Connie went out of the room, anxiously studying my list. A rather pleasant smell of soap came up off the young expert's neck. Her nail-varnished fingers moved swiftly and gracefully. The severity, which had to do with her high Slavic cheekbones, didn't seem to extend below her neck. The continuation of her, in fact, was in no way restrained. As I made this observation, I was suddenly aware that she knew I'd made it, and at the identical moment; the familiar, but encouraging lightning female reflex. She made no adjustment to the general state of affairs.

I saw she'd left a two line space and was writing:

NEW PAGE:
Yes, start again. It is cold in here. Which indeed we have found in the work with Ketone Bill.

I said, 'Margalit, there's a bit at the end about a German. I wonder if you could find it. Right at the very end.'

She leafed over a few pages, managing to do it in a way that quite confirmed my observation, and pored over the last page.

'Yes, here.' Her nicest fingernail was describing an elegant circle around a few lines of hieroglyphs.

'What does it say?'

'It says – ' she compared with the transcript. 'It says what it says here.'

'Nothing more?'

She checked again. I noticed a few words of English written sideways in the margin and screwed my head round to see. SUPPER – NO CHUTNEY. This was crossed out, too. There were several crossing-outs.

She seemed to misconstrue my head-screwing and sat up a bit straighter. 'No. That's all. It's a good clear shorthand. Of course, the spacing is a little different. This last line – it was said after the rest. "We will celebrate the holiness of the day." Actually, this is a quotation,' she said.

'Of course. From the Yom Kippur service.'

A keener look set in above the cheekbones. 'You know this?'

'I know a lot of things, Margalit,' I said, and smiled at her. 'Why is the chutney in the margin?'

'Chutney? Ah. There was a previous mention.' She skimmed back a page. 'Yes, Chut-ney. Well, it is spelled out also,' she said, just as I saw it was. Another crossing-out. It had been ringed as well, apparently as a reminder. It said, GREENYARD'S PICKLES — CHUTNEY, with a couple of squiggles in front of it.

'What does the shorthand say?'

'It says the same. It says, "He wishes for GREENYARD'S PICKLES — CHUTNEY."'

'Igor!' I'd heard sounds off from the direction of Julian's room, and Connie now ran from there. 'Meyer is on the phone with Julian. Will you speak with him?'

I gave the expert a little nod, and she gave me a little nod back; both nods quite interested and noted for future reference; and I trotted back along the corridor with Connie, and received the phone.

'Yes, Meyer.'

'What is this goddam nonsense?'

'Which goddam nonsense?'

'In Bergmann's department there is a *spy*?'

'I said no such thing. Letters are missing that I think should not be missing. People drift in and out there, I saw myself.'

'We shouldn't tell them about all this?'

'About all what?'

'I hear you have worked out a clever list of questions.'

'Well, there's enough to occupy people here for the moment.'

'I think it's a piece of goddam nonsense.'

'Fine. Tell them, then, Meyer. I've got enough to attend to on my own. To tell the truth, I'm a bit cheesed off Vava. I've got Hopcroft going cross-eyed in London. I'm sorry I ever heard of Vava, I really am.'

'Nu, meshugganeh,' he said in a more muted tone. 'So come and have dinner with me tonight.'

'I can't have dinner with you tonight.'

'For lunch I'm busy. See me at three.'

'At three I am going to see a muscle machine.'

'So you'll see it another time.'

'Goodbye, Meyer.'

'Wait. What? Igor?'

'Meyer, you'll do exactly what you want. Get everybody busy in Jerusalem.'

'What are you doing tomorrow?'

'I am going to the Dead Sea tomorrow.'

'What is this, a paid vacation?'

'With many grateful thanks to you.'

'Well. Listen. Until you can spare me a moment in that busy life, do it your way.'

'Fine.'

'But I never heard such goddam nonsense.'

Julian and Connie were looking quizzically at me as I hung up. 'Well, damn it, Julian, I don't know,' I said. 'What do you think?'

'I think it *is* a bit funny,' he said neutrally.

'Do they eat much chutney in Israel?'

'Chutney?'

'He seems to have been screaming for it, for his supper. That last memo.'

'Oh, that. The Greenyard's. Well, that would have been Mrs Weizmann. She kept rather an English table, you know, Robertson's jam and Tiptree marmalade, and the old Earl Grey. I expect there was H.P. sauce and Colman's mustard, as well.'

'Was he in the habit of giving his dinner orders to the secretary?'

'You see, Mrs Weizmann wanted to know every word he said then. He wasn't easy to understand, he was having trouble with his teeth, and she couldn't hear too well herself. She was deaf in one ear, you know – blast from a flying bomb outside the Dorchester during the war.'

'Igor, this is a most tremendous amount of work,' Connie said, flapping the list. 'Which is the most urgent?'

'Well, it all is, Connie. I suppose Bradford would be easiest, wouldn't it?'

'Well, if it is just letters *to* Bradford. But I mean, my goodness, this is years and years of letters. There are *thousands* of letters. I guess we would have to start, what – 1933 and work right on to 1952?'

'Oh, yes. But you've got the subject index.'

'We have the subject index, which is fine if the whole letter is about Bradford or *to* someone in Bradford. But if it's just a stray reference to some personality in Bradford, it is not going to show up in the index. And all these batatas Well, I just don't know what we are going to do with the batatas!' she said, with a glint of panic. 'I mean, desert reclamation, okay. Saline irrigation, okay. Protein, okay. All these things are certainly in the index. But who can know if it's batatas?'

'Bergmann and Weiss weren't here in 1952, were they?' I said.

'No. Beylis was, though,' Julian said. 'Do you want me to fix up a meeting?'

'Thanks. What I think for the meantime, Connie,' I said, 'is press on with Bradford.'

'Okay. I'm glad, anyway,' she said as we left the room, 'that you remembered you couldn't have dinner with Meyer tonight.'

'What delights have you got in store?'

'That's a good question. You'll see. Where in God's name is Bradford, anyway?'

'Everybody knows that,' I said. But apparently everybody didn't; and it also turned out to be a good question.

2

The muscle machine was a great disappointment. From the reference to the lifting of hands and the scratching of noses, I'd expected something brisker than the rather surly contraption that rumbled wheels and raised weights after ponderous pauses.

I masked my disappointment while the others fiddled with the machine, and presently, with Ham Wyke and Marta and the dreaded Dr Patel, who had joined the party, I followed Michael Sassoon on a tour of the building. He'd told me that a few Soviet immigrants were there, and thought they might like a chat in Russian. It seemed impolite to refuse, though I impatiently awaited a chat with Professor Beylis on questions relating to batatas.

The tour was rendered less useful still by the fact that the Soviet scientists were not only trying to forget Russia, but didn't want to talk Russian. Ham began using his stumbling Russian on a youngish physicist who had come from Kiev University, which Ham had visited during his stay, trying to establish with him the name of a well-known immunologist on the campus. The fellow couldn't remember the name and said so, rather reluctantly, *'K'to onbil? Patom skarzhu,'* and they were still trying names on each other when I left.

I caught Beylis signing letters and looking at his watch. But he made a phone call when he saw me and told someone he would be late.

'Batatas,' he said. 'Yes, there was a bit of work done, I can just about remember it.' He made a note. 'I'll get on to the plant genetics people.'

Plant genetics. Another one for the list. I made a note, too. 'Was this in Weizmann's day?'

'Oh, yes. In his last days, in fact. It didn't go far. Sweet potatoes aren't eaten here much.'

'It wasn't for petrol?'

'Nothing to do with petrol. For the desert, actually. A

saline water test, if I remember aright. Batatas will grow under poor conditions, you see. It's a climbing plant, *Ipomoca*, the same family as convolvulus and morning-glory. The edible varieties are able to convert low-grade materials, saline water, into a lot of starchy tuber. That was the interest for Weizmann. The desert stimulated him. Of course, it did everybody. They were quite stirring days.'

'It couldn't have been for his protein idea?'

'It wasn't for any particular idea. People were just growing things,' he said. He was looking at me quite kindly and helpfully. 'The land had been bare for a long time. Hills were being reafforested, swamps drained. It *is* quite stimulating to have a land of your own. I don't think there was more to it than that.'

There obviously had been more to it than that. Little Miss Margalit hadn't finished the memorandum, however, and she needed the Xerox for comparison, so I had nothing to show.

'Anyway, we'll see,' he said. 'Finster is carrying on with the work.'

'With the ordinary kind of batatas.'

'It's all we have.'

'Wouldn't the plant genetics people have any others?'

'Not specimens. The plant doesn't come true from seed, and they wouldn't have kept tubers after the work was dropped. They'd just have records of crosses, sports, et cetera.'

'What crosses, sports?' I said.

'If you want new strains, you cross-fertilize, or watch out for mutations – sports. It's a slow business, and the roots don't keep. In countries where they grow this thing – the West Indies, Africa, et cetera – they do it with bits of tuber or cuttings. You have to keep growing them on to keep them in cultivation. They wouldn't have done that after the research was called off.'

'Why would it have been called off?' I said.

'Well, there was a host of pressing problems, you know.

People were pouring in by every ship, from camps in Europe and elsewhere, the Arab lands. The country was really very primitive. People were living in tents. They had to be fed and clothed, somehow taught a common language. Quite a lot of confusion, as you can imagine. I expect the sweet potato was just quietly dropped.'

'Without his knowledge?'

'Oh, he'd lost interest by then.'

'By when?'

'The period we are talking of – his last days.'

I felt my brain beginning to unhinge slightly. An unaccustomed mass of lore had been thrust into it lately. As soon as I grappled with one lot, it was dislocated by another. Weizmann had lost interest in the sweet potato in his last days? But he'd surely exhibited the most violent interest in it, and *on* his last day; and not from a bucolic desire to 'grow things' but to make petrol.

'I mean, he specifically says so,' I said. 'It's almost his last coherent thought.'

Beylis sat and rubbed his nose and looked at me.

'Hmm,' he said thoughtfully. 'Well, I didn't know about the date. It might explain certain contradictions. We are having trouble with Vava.' He rubbed his noise a bit more. 'You see, from the note to Fritz Haber, which is all we have, Weizmann doesn't seem to be taking the work seriously. If Vava had achieved real results, I don't see how he could fail to be interested. He was, after all, a classic innovator himself in the field of fermentation. Yet he is laughing at it. Why?'

'It doesn't work?'

'I don't know. It looks as if we never will. But there certainly is something a bit odd about Vava. What he has apparently done is three things: he has found a particular plant, and a particular bacterium, then a method of converting the result into something much better.'

'Is that difficult?'

'The speed is. *Just* the plant, just the bacterium, just the method – all in a few weeks. Each of them can take years.'

'Do you mean he couldn't have done it?'

'He could – given a series of very happy accidents and uncommon intuition. But Vava wasn't famous for his intuition. He was not one of the great lights of science, you know.'

'Are you saying he invented the whole thing?'

'I'm saying he wasn't noted for his intuition. On the other hand, Weizmann was. You see?'

'Ah.' He was smiling at me rather sagely as he said this, and nodding, so I nodded back. 'No,' I said.

'Well.' He rubbed his nose again. 'If you're right about the date, it might explain a couple of things. You see, at the time of the saline water tests he was absolutely not interested in petrol. I mean, this I can tell you. I remember it. Not a flicker of interest. He'd been through the petrol thing. He did manage to make it, incidentally – and very expensively, I may say. Nothing in it. But if *after* the tests he suddenly recalled Vava again, and in a context of sweet potatoes and petrol, and with an apology, so to speak, for having laughed at him, it does seem to indicate he'd thought of something new.'

'Obviously. It's what he's saying.'

'Mmm. Well. Could be,' Beylis said. 'It's a fact that problems ticked on in his mind for years. He kept returning to them, like a dog to a bone. He was a very dogged man.'

'Yes.'

'As well as being intuitive. Things often happened to him like that. Suddenly he would know something. He was very much of a piece – in his political work as well. But I'm afraid this doesn't help you much.'

I had an odd feeling – no doubt to do with his remarks on intuition – that it did. Something had happened to me today. Something had started to tick, and I couldn't think what it was.

It continued ticking after I'd left him, though.

3

I took a taxi to Connie's at seven, and brooded all the way. It was a long way. Bat Yam was below Jaffa on the coast, a newish town. It was apartment land, the streets canyons of tall blocks. I thought of the ships disgorging their occupants a generation ago, and of the encampments of tents, and of the problems they'd had to deal with then; and of the kind that they could now apply their minds to. Not so long ago, a generation. Just time enough to change from being objects of the world's sympathy into the villains of the piece. Well, hardly a novel transformation for the people hereabout.

I alighted in Balfour Street, still brooding, and went upstairs to Connie's apartment. Three people were there already, including Marta: one of Connie's promised delights. Not a word from her during our inspection of the muscle machine that she would be a participant in the evening's revels. She'd apparently gone home with Connie in the car. Some other people turned up while we were having a drink, and Marta said to me, 'What's the matter with you?'

'I need a weekend off.'

'How is the car situation?'

'Settled.' I was borrowing Ham's. 'We could have lunch either at Jerusalem or Zohar.' We were going to Zohar. There was a quite good hotel there. Friday was half-day, which gave one Friday night and Saturday night; drive back Sunday morning.

'Have you booked?'

'Two rooms,' I said.

'We can have lunch in one of them.'

During the course of the evening, Connie said, 'Is something the matter, Igor?'

'Fatigue.'

'We won't make it late.'

We didn't. At twelve, it broke up, and I took a taxi back alone. Marta was sleeping at Connie's.

I didn't have a very good night, still brooding; I rose early, went below, and saw Dr Patel again. It was a very strange thing. At whatever time I descended, Dr Patel was there: going in to breakfast, or at it, or just leaving. This time it was absurdly early. The restaurant wasn't even open. The girls were still laying out the trays of victuals. He was standing by Mr Deutsch's desk with an envelope in his hands while Mr Deutsch, back turned, was placing mail into the slots.

'Ah, here is Mr Druyanov. It is for you, Mr Druyanov,' Mr Deutsch said, turning.

Dr Patel gave me the envelope somewhat hurriedly. 'I was expecting an express from London myself,' he said.

I looked at it, and saw the express stamps, and turned it over and looked again. It was a manila envelope and on the back it said. 'From Dr O. Kutcholsky-Green, 32 Tancred Court, London, N.W.3.' Dr Patel was looking at me as I opened it and drew out the contents. I didn't draw them fully out. I just saw, in the sheaf of papers, the familiar signature 'Ch. Weizmann,' and stuffed everything back again, and went out of the swing doors, at the trot. It was a lovely morning. Dew was glistening on the grass as I panted across the drive, and across the main avenue, and into the courtyard. I heard my breath singing out as I pounded on the door.

'Mr Weisgal, please,' I said politely when it opened.

'Mr Weisgal?' was the hushed response. 'He's in bed.'

'Well, get him out of it,' I said, and to make sure I ran in and up the Chancellor's stairs, crying, 'Hello! Hello! Wake up, Meyer. Wakey-wakey, then. I am the sweet-potato man.'

6

Friday turned out to be not a half-day but a completely whole one, and night, very confused. I had breakfast with Meyer, who, after a somewhat startled and dishevelled wakening, spent some minutes in his bathroom to emerge suitably robed, spruce as ever. We gravely took our places at the card table and he put his glasses on.

There were eighteen sheets in the envelope, air-mail paper, written on both sides, except for a single sheet from Weizmann headed 'Sanatorio Stefania, Merano, Italia', and dated September 6, 1933. The correspondence comprised seven long letters from Vava; Weizmann had written his replies in the margins and in any available spaces on the back. Weizmann had been holidaying in Italy, and Vava had been hounding him there. It occurred to me that this might have been why he hadn't given the matter due attention. I suddenly remembered this holiday, and the reason for Weizmann's remark in his last memorandum that 'after much harassment I needed the rest.'

Meyer was going very carefully over each sheet of the correspondence, his hands trembling slightly, looking very senatorial in his robe and every inch the Chancellor of a great Institute, except that he spoiled it at the end by saying, 'Shit! Every word in Russian.'

'Yes.'

'Well, we have to get – Hey! You read Russian, don't you?'

'Naturally.'

'*Nu*, cluck. *Read!*'

I didn't read very far.

I said, 'It's in Russian, Meyer, but it's also in science.' It certainly was. It was all solid carbon business, generously illuminated with little drawings of poly-sided figures representing atoms, and rows and rows of equations and formulas. After the briefest of salutations, the letters became immediately incomprehensible. The only intelligible contributions were Weizmann's, quite spry and funny. In one of them he cracked the joke he had made to Haber; it was strange to see the original of it here, just as it had occurred to him, in his rather curly cursive Russian. I recognized his new fountain pen, and remembered where he'd got it, and wondered if Verochka had found out; and then realized that of course she had. Whatever I now knew, she had known before me, at about the time that I was seven.

All this had put me in something of a tizzy, and I saw that my own hands were shaking.

Meyer was on the phone. He said, 'Nathan? I am terribly sorry to disturb you. Could you have breakfast with me?'

Nathan apparently said he couldn't. It was Professor Nathan Horowitz, Vice-President of the Institute.

'Nathan, would I dream of disturbing you this time of the morning if it wasn't something of the greatest urgency? I have Druyanov here. He has the papers of Vava, the original papers. He this minute ran into my bedroom with them . . . So good. Very good.'

We sat and had coffee and oranges and toast. Shirley, alarmed by these movements, and hearing that Horowitz was coming, tried to get him to go to the breakfast room. He wouldn't move from the card table. He pored hungrily over the letters.

Horowitz also had a light breakfast at the card table when he arrived. I began reading the correspondence to him in English, pointing out the place as I went along, but after some minutes he said, 'Meyer, this is too specialized.

Who is doing the work at the moment? It's Finster, isn't it? Finster has to see it.'

Meyer's hands were already on the phone.

'Wait. Think a moment,' Horowitz said, smiling. 'He doesn't live in the Institute. He has an apartment in Rehovot.'

But Meyer wasn't calling Finster. He was calling his chauffeur. 'You know Dr Finster? You know where Dr Finster lives?' There was a tone almost of menace in his voice. 'Go and get him. Go this second. Bring him safely to my house. I am waiting.'

He put the phone down and stared at me rather superstitiously. 'How come it arrives here just like this, today? You know, I had a feeling. Something told me today something will happen. Right there in bed, I had this feeling.' He looked full into Horowitz's face with the same staring look.

I was looking at the envelope. It was postmarked 'Frognal, 0900, Dec. 18'. That was the day I'd left. Hopcroft had been hit on the head the previous day. This was surely very peculiar. She hadn't had the papers when Hopcroft saw her. By express post the following morning, they were in the mail. I laboriously worked this out. She had been going to stay with a friend at Frognal after Hopcroft had left. She had been going to Wimbledon two days later. Well, evidently she'd changed her mind. Perhaps she had prevailed on the friend to go down to Wimbledon with her that very day, perhaps in the evening. Perhaps she had discovered her husband would be out. Perhaps the friend had gone alone. Whatever it was, she must have got the letters the same day that Hopcroft had been bashed, and before he'd had time to yarn his story to half the world. This certainly was a stroke of luck.

Horowitz was looking at his watch and rising.

'Nathan, what are you doing?' Meyer said.

'I don't think I can be of use here, Meyer.'

'Don't think of leaving me!' Meyer said. 'Do you realize

what we have here? The fate of the world, the fate of *Israel* could depend on it,' he said, stressing the greater enormity.

'I am aware of the importance, but – '

'We have to decide where to keep this!'

'Well, you'll have it copied, and distributed to those concerned, and the originals can – '

'You are joking! Nathan, do you know the heartaches we have had with these papers? He – this one – *Igor* – he doesn't think we should even show them to Jerusalem! You don't know what has been happening. Give Nathan another cup of coffee,' he called to Shirley. 'Nathan, sit down.'

He started telling him some of my fears, and with such dramatic force that it didn't occur to me for a little while that they were now groundless. No papers were missing from Jerusalem. Jerusalem had never had the papers. The economical duo had been writing to each other on the same bits of paper. There weren't any copies; nothing for the files at all; there never had been. None of this put Meyer off. He'd had all night to think about it, and now had plenty of fears of his own. He was still cataloging them when Dr Finster appeared, looking very alarmed.

'Sit down, have coffee, Finster,' Meyer said.

'Meyer, are you mad?' Shirley said. 'You can't all sit and have breakfast at the card table.'

'Give him coffee!' Meyer said. 'Finster, you don't read Russian?'

'Russian?' Finster said, in astonishment. 'No, I have never undertaken studies in – '

'So it's no time to learn,' Meyer said. 'Go over it with him, Igor. Take toast, Finster.'

Dr Finster obediently took toast, pausing between crunches to catch what I was saying. His eyes roamed over the pages. He made no comment whatever.

'Finster, you're following?' Meyer said, watching his rather immobile face in an agony of suspense.

'It makes sense to you?'

'Of course. Dr Kutcholsky is here preparing from his bacterium – '

'That's good, Finster. Don't tell me. Keep going.'

We kept going. Horowitz phoned his secretary a couple of times. Finster had two cups of coffee and two slices of toast and an orange. He checked me with a grave finger from time to time and slowly studied the formulas. I read him Weizmann's comments, too. Something like a smile crossed his face at one of them.

'Yes. Well. Not bad,' he said at the end.

'What do you mean not bad?' Meyer almost snarled.

'Logical. It corresponds with my results. Of course he achieved far better. When we get his bacterium – '

'We can get his *bacterium*?'

'Why not?' Dr Finster said, taken aback by the vehemence.

'He gives the *name* of that bacterium?'

'He gives a number. The prefix I recognize to be one of the Pasteur Institute's. This evidently is where he must have got it. He has applied some novel treatments – '

'Where does he give the number?' Meyer said.

Finster searched around a little, and with my assistance found it. Meyer removed the sheet and put it in his pocket. He gave his nose a rather decisive wipe as he did this. 'Good. So now his new potato. What about it?'

'Which potato?'

Meyer picked up an orange, and I thought was going to throw it at him, but he just held it in both hands, apparently for illustrative purposes. 'The sweet potato. Vava's sweet potato. The *new* potato,' he said.

'There is no new potato.'

'What are you talking about, Finster?' Meyer said.

Finster looked from him to Horowitz, who was not looking very happy, and back again. 'Unless it has been read out wrongly – as we have all just heard, what Dr Kutcholsky is proposing is the specifications for a potato.'

'Specifications?'

'It is a hypothetical potato.'

'It is, eh?' Meyer said. 'Hypothetical. I see.'

'For which he specifies certain qualities. From these qualities he makes calculations, based upon the performance of his bacterium, and projects a very superior octane number. It is a question of genetic manipulation. Starting with the particular family of batatas that he mentions, he is proposing – '

'He mentions a particular *family* of batatas?'

'Yes. What he proposes – '

'Where is that goddam family?'

The same performance took place with the papers. 'And he says what you have to do with it?' Meyer said.

'Yes. However, as Weizmann points out, the difficulties raised by the increased quantities of methane to be expected with the carotene – '

'Where does he point this out?'

'On the same sheet that you have placed in your pocket,' Dr Finster said.

I was remembering the difficulties pointed out by Weizmann about the carotene and the methane. I was remembering them from the memorandum. Except that in the memorandum, they had not seemed difficulties. Had they?

'Good. So how long will it take to get this potato?'

'Which potato?'

'The hypothetical potato,' Meyer said, quite softly.

'Ah. I cannot help you. This is for a plant geneticist. I am a research chemist, 'Dr Finster said.

'Okay, Finster. Very good. Have a cup of coffee.'

'No. I have now had my breakfast. But l will be greatly interested to duplicate his experiments with the bacterium. I would like at the earliest opportunity to obtain this bacterium.'

'Which bacterium?' Meyer said. He was smiling at him.

'The one from the Pasteur Institute.'

'It's a good idea. Obtain it, Finster.'

'You have the code number in your pocket.'

'Are you telling me you can't remember that number?'

'I am afraid . . . numbers,' Dr Finster said, somewhat embarrassed.

'Well, that's nice. That's okay. Don't you worry about it, Finster, we'll get it. Thanks a lot. I'm really obliged. Nice of you to come and see me.'

Horowitz tried to go out with Finster, but Meyer rose in his gown.

'One moment, Nathan!' he said.

2

A small programme was arranged before Horowitz went. He had a word himself with the man in charge of plant genetics. He copied the Pasteur Institute number of the bacterium on a bit of paper and took it back to his office. Meyer rang for a small photocopier to be sent round from the Stone Administration Building, with somebody to work it. He had three copies made of the documents, and two of the copies, together with the originals, went in his safe. He got me to point out what was already being called the 'security stuff' and he cut these out of the third copy with a pair of nail scissors. Then he gave me this copy.

'What's this for?'

'Translate it.'

'Oh, come on, Meyer, you've got scientific translators. This is beyond me.'

'Finster understood every word. Also this is now a small circle. For better or worse,' he said solemnly, 'you are a part of it. Also we need action. It's a short day. People have to go.'

'I have to go.' I suddenly saw with astonishment and alarm that it was half past eleven. 'I have to go in half an hour,' I said. I'd totally forgotten the weekend of illicit bliss. At least, it wasn't so very illicit for me: It was illicit for Marta. The well adjusted person had a good six months of appetites that needed satisfying. Illicit or not, there was no doubt that she was now buzzing through her morning in high expectation of some very active bliss.

'What, going in half an hour?' Meyer said. The phone rang and he picked it up, still scowling at me. 'Yes, Nathan. Wonderful. Very good.' He spoke energetically for a minute or two, and put the phone down with satisfaction. 'Well, things are moving. He talked with Paris. The bacterium will be on the first plane Sunday. He has organized a conference with the geniuses from the plant genetics for tomorrow – Shabbat! He needs the translation by then.'

'But I'm going away for the weekend!'

'Are you a madman, what? A whole world is waiting out there. They are waiting for us.' He pointed out the window to where they all were.

Ten minutes later, I phoned one of them from the House, and explained about the weekend.

'Oh, it's too bad. It really is,' she said tightly. 'At the last moment!'

'I know. It's awful.'

'You mean you will be working the whole weekend?'

'Well, I don't know. Well, no, I can't. Well, God knows, it's a terrible lot of work,' I said with mild panic.

'Igor, if only I could help – maybe with the typing or something?' Connie was calling sympathetically.

'You have some people with you?' Marta said tensely on the phone.

'Yes. Yes, I have.' Miss Knowall was with me, too. I could smell her soap as she bent over my desk and numbered the pages of the typed transcript, which she'd omitted to do before. She was doing this in a very unrestrained way. A tremendous lack of restraint was about six inches from my distracted eyeballs.

'Well, will you be going for lunch to the San Martin?' Marta said.

'No, I'll just be having a sandwich here.'

I could hear her breathing quietly with annoyance.

'I will call you later, then,' she said.

'Yes. In the afternoon.'

'I mean, I am not such a wonderful typist,' Connie said as I put the phone down. 'But it will need typing, won't it?'

'I don't even know how I'm going to *write* it in the time. There are eighteen – there are *thirty-six* pages here.'

'Well. If it could be dictated,' Margalit said. 'I mean, I don't like to work Friday afternoon, but if it is so urgent . . .'

I looked at her. 'I think that's – I'll let you know in a few minutes, Margalit.'

I went along to Julian's room and phoned Meyer from there.

'Is she on the staff?' he said when I'd explained.

'No, Connie brought her in. She's the Pitman expert.'

'Is it so much to do by hand?'

'It's thirty-six pages.'

'It's full of pictures, the pages.'

'Well, I can't draw the pictures.'

'So what is she – an artist? Leave the pictures, *meshugganeh*. Also the sums. Put numbers on these things and leave spaces. Leave big spaces. They can be copied. My secretary can fiddle with this. All you have to do is the bits between.'

'It took a solid hour reading those bits between.'

He clucked a little. 'Don't exaggerate. Half the time he sat there and thought. I watched him.'

'It's a minimum ten minutes a page, Meyer, by hand.'

'So it's six or seven hours. What of it? With a rest in between, it's nothing. What do you want with her? Send her home. Write clearly,' he was saying as I slammed the phone.

'Well, that's terribly nice of you, Margalit,' I said, in Connie's room, where she now was, 'but I've just checked and I don't have to do it all. I can manage.'

'Igor, is this the secret service?' Connie said when she'd gone.

'Meyer has suddenly got very security-minded.'

'*I'm* not supposed to know?'

'Don't be ridiculous, darling. Do you think we could try the typing, if I read it out slowly?'

'Well, of course. Look, if you would just kind of arrange yourself, I will run and get sandwiches while I can.'

She ran and did this and I kind of arranged myself.

We plodded away in the otherwise silent House till about three o'clock, when Marta turned up, and we took a break. She'd walked through the Institute grounds. The House itself, in its ten acres of woodland, was outside the Institute property but the whole area was part of the Weizmann Memorial Foundation. By car, you could only approach the House by the side road and the gatekeeper's lodge. There was no resident gatekeeper any more, and the big solid-panelled steel gate was locked after office hours. Connie had a key to this gate, so she'd been able to leave her car in the drive.

To get to the House through the Institute meant a longish walk. The main Institute avenue ran for three-quarters of a mile. At the end of it was a broad marble-paved plaza commemorating the Holocaust; and beyond that a little lane which led to the House. It led to it via the grave.

The doorbell sounded only in the domestic quarters below and we hadn't heard it, so Marta hallooed a bit in the garden, and I went down and let her in. She hadn't seen the place before, so I showed her round while Connie went and made a cup of tea. She did this rather silently: we'd had words just before. The correspondence was very difficult, and the wastepaper basket was filling up. I'd fumbled my way through the correspondence with Finster, but it was much trickier putting it into coherent sentences. It didn't have to be a literary masterpiece, as Connie had

95

pointed out, but I couldn't have it in gibberish, and the strain was telling. So I wasn't all that pleased to see the lady with whom I was supposed to be in bed at the moment, and who evidently still had some sense of rebuff, not lessened by her hallooing below. She didn't obviously show it. But restlessness had brought her on the nice long walk, and there was a certain steely edge to our greeting.

Shutters were down everywhere and keys turned in locks. It wasn't looking very cheerful; it was rather dim and chill. The central heating had been removed on Verochka's death. We tramped drearily round. Big dim salon, big dim library all dim, cold, desolate as charity. Pictures, sculpture, bric-à-brac, all chosen in their day; signed portraits of the long-dead great. The couple it had all belonged to were lying in the grass outside. I wished Marta would run away; and Connie, too. I felt nervy and harassed; something was wrong; the translation was wrong. It wasn't only the translation that was wrong. Something was wrong.

'Where is it you work?'

'Up here.'

Up the echoing marble stairs. Verochka's old bedroom. The nurse's room. Chaimchik's room.

'I've been working here.'

'Snug.'

I suddenly realized, with distinct unease, that her eyes had paused on the bed. They paused only fractionally.

'Will we have it in the kitchen?' Connie shouted up. 'Or will I bring it?'

'I'll come and get it.'

'It's all right.'

Clack-clack, clack-clack, came her feet up the stairs.

How to get rid of them both? Something was wrong. I remembered the identical feeling, at the age of thirteen, being whisked out of a room with a Christmas tree in it, in Stockholm. I'd experienced it since, but never so strongly. Down below in the library I'd noticed a tray set with drinks; the bottles had been there since 1966, untouched, as Verochka had left them. I thought I would go and have one of those just as soon as these two females were out of the House. I seemed to need a drink. It also seemed to be important that I should be in the place alone.

'Here we are,' Connie said.

We all sat and had a friendly cup of tea around the kerosene stove in her room. Both ladies were in a state of concealed ill temper with me. We had rather a jolly talk, and at about a quarter to four I said, 'You know, Connie, I can't think of doing any more now. I'll have a go later.'

'Can you do it at the San Martin?'

'I don't think I can.' We'd been consulting files as I'd worked; Weizmann's replies contained references. 'I thought I'd have a rest and come back here.'

'How would you get in?'

'I was wondering if you could lend me your key.'

'Well, I would. I mean, I am not supposed to – but of course we can get you a key from the key security on Sunday. I mean, you can have my key with pleasure, but how are you going to get here?'

'I'll walk, or borrow a bike from Ham.'

'Well, okay. If that's what you want. I mean, we could still do some more.'

'I am going now,' Marta said. 'I only came for the walk.'

'No, I'm tired. I want to stop.'

Connie ran us back, dropping Marta first, and we all parted still in a state of friendly ill humour. I went upstairs to my penthouse, stretched out on the bed, and fell fast asleep for about an hour and a half. Then I rang Ham up, and borrowed his bike, and pedalled back.

3

It was after six and pitch black when I got there. I left the bike in a patch of bushes in the grounds, kept a careful eye open for the grave, which I skirted, and after a few minutes stopped and tried to divine where the devil they'd put the House. It was so dark, the big white place was quite indistinguishable in the trees. I'd only done this once before, in daylight. It was bewilderingly different at night. I began to pick my way to where it ought to be, and presently found the three flights of rock steps up from the sunken lawn. After a couple of minutes I found the front drive. Front steps. Front door. I spent a few seconds feeling it for the lock, and then a few more feeling the wall inside for a switch.

It was certainly no more cheerful than in the afternoon – less, in fact. A skull-like sheen shone off the limed oak. A bronze head of Chaimchik observed me coldly. I shut the door and stood there a few moments after the disorienting experience outside. Well, I had the place to myself, at least.

I unlocked the library and switched on the light and made for the drinks tray. Sandeman's sherry. Gordon's gin, Old Taylor bourbon, all reasonably full. There was something slightly sacrilegious, not to say necromantic, in calling on these old spirits. Still, my need was greater than the museum's. I poured a spot of Old Taylor and cautiously sampled it. Nothing amiss. The years in the bottle since 1966 hadn't affected it, except for the better. I went to the kitchen, put a drop of water in, and took it upstairs with me.

A rather desperate chill had settled on Chaimchik's room, so I shifted the kerosene heater from Connie's, lit it, and walked about, sipping, till the room warmed up. I had a look at little Miss Margalit's transcript as I did this. She had done a good job. She had put herself out. She had written in all the things in the margin, and the various things between the lines. She had indicated where there had been a new shorthand page, and had numbered both her pages and the shorthand ones accordingly. She had also very carefully written all the words that had been crossed out, and had then crossed them out again. A very faint whiff of her soap seemed to come off the pages. There were numerous domestic odds and ends not in the Xerox: orders that had been ticked off or crossed out. He'd had a fancy for pickled cucumbers and olives; he was rather insistent that his milk should be fresh. Well, the flavour, at least, had come through in the Xerox. These were only grace notes, after all. There were some rather more mystifying items. 'CROMER-LE-POLYTH?' LE-ROY-PARMA?' 'COONE FIRTH?'

The room wasn't warm enough to work in yet, but the Old Taylor was doing a good job, so I went below and poured another. The library looked much less unfriendly now, a tribute to Old Taylor. It was a big room, forty-five feet by fifteen. Sofas and easy chairs were grouped around the fireplace; the remaining acres scattered with cabinets, chests, tables.

For privacy, Mendelsohn had put no windows in the outside wall, but instead a series of glass portholes to admit light, well above eye level. The inner wall was well-windowed (though curtained now) and looked out to the swimming pool. At the opposite side of the pool was the salon, which also looked out to it. In front of the pool was the vine-clad patio where the old man had drunk endless glasses of tea on his good days: Panama hat, dark glasses, shifting himself from one seat to another. A restless man. He hadn't paused long anywhere between Motol and here.

The library portholes were above the bookshelves (limed oak, of course): the whole wall clad with books. One large section consisted of his old chemical library. Above the fireplace was the Oswald Birley portrait of him, which Verochka had greatly liked. She'd made Birley change the cheekbones, but she'd thought it the best likeness of him. I went and had a look at it, and wondered why. It caught the slightly Mongolian look, Lenin-like, but warmer; there was presence, authority, aloofness. The lurky humour of the photos wasn't there; the Yiddish element. Well, it just hadn't been her element.

Old Taylor and I drifted about for a while, glancing at the framed photos on tables and cabinets. Love from everybody: the Queen of the Belgians, Einstein, Churchill, Lloyd George, Smuts, Balfour, Truman. The great enchanter had enchanted them all. An extraordinary life: rather a magical and miraculous life, which had found him always waiting and receptive. Then the dreary end. Well, it was as I'd told Caroline! I poured another draught of ancient Old Taylor and took it upstairs. Time for work.

I picked up where Connie had left off, writing very clearly as instructed, and trying it out on other bits of paper first. I did this for about an hour, and then paused, wondering what it was that was so wrong. I'd had the sense of unease for hours; had had it yesterday. Not evidently from these scientific mysteries, which were well beyond me, anyway. Some overall thing was wrong; something that I'd come across and not digested. To do with the last memorandum, but not only that. What had bothered him so on his last coherent day? Or, more to the point, what bothered me about what had bothered him? There was a desperate feeling in the memorandum that he was not being understood.

It was nearly eight o'clock. A good three hours' work lay ahead translating the nattering that had gone to and fro between London and the Sanatorio Stefania in 1933. I would have to get some dinner. I certainly didn't fancy negotiating the woodlands again for it. It was a question of seeing what was in the fridge below.

I went down and found some sliced smoked turkey, and cut a bit of loaf and made sandwiches. While I was at it, I put the kettle on as well. I walked about with my cold collation on a plate; unlocked the salon and had a little tramp in there.

It was bigger than the library: an extra bay for the fireplace corner. The whole area was spread in most stately array, with the acquisitions of the magpie who'd popped so often into Christie's and Sotheby's. In a far corner, somewhat dwarfed, was a grand piano, in the favoured and ubiquitous limed oak. Pictures everywhere, a couple of Utrillos, a Laura Knight, a Rubens; a T'ang horse, Japanese ceramics; marvellous silk rugs on the floor.

All a long way from the days when he'd pawned his compasses and dreaded the landlady. I remembered the early tender letters between them. They'd sent each other little bits of money to bail the other out of some emergency. She'd had her ways, had often taxed him with not loving her enough. He'd driven himself silly saying he did, that he longed for her, that it was rainy and foggy in Manchester and everybody half daft and they had no cafés or argument. He was slogging doggedly away at his chemistry and trying to talk English to Perkin's assistant and aching for her. If only they could be married, how they would comfort each other!

There was a photo of her, evidently from the early 1930s: a three-quarter portrait, soft dreamy focus; more than a touch of Sybil Thorndike, or some great European diva. There was a tiny remote smile on her face as she looked out of the photo, as though waiting for something. For what? For the slippery bathtub that also waited in the Dorchester?

All these were very melancholy reflections and I gladly responded to the summoning whistle of the kettle from the kitchen.

I took the coffee back to Chaimchik's room; but still couldn't settle. His towel waited on the towel-warmer off the bathroom. His suits waited in the wardrobe. I opened his dressing-table drawer. Two very large sets of teeth were in a bag; unusually long palate. Were these the ones that had given him all the trouble? Or were they now out in the garden with him, and these an earlier source of irritation? There was a collapsed rubber bladder. Something for taking his own blood pressure?

This wouldn't do, of course. There was work to be done. But instead I sat on his bed and put down the coffee and picked up the shorthand notebooks, and felt over the pages, the pencil indentations. Taken down right here. He had been where I now was, his head a foot or two away: pointed beard, yellowish sick face, vehement, his teeth in, or out, telling her things. Trying to get her to understand. What?

None of it, as turned out from little Miss Margalit's more exact transcript, was really coherent; sometimes there was just a single phrase on a page, indicating that he had dozed off or dried up. The earlier Miss Knowall hadn't, evidently, known what to make of it, though she'd strung it all together. My Miss Knowall had set the phrases down as they came.

As I have written [?] Kutcholsky with his large amounts of carotene and other subs stances [?] naturally several difficulties. But it is necessary to work with and not against nature, and in fact it gives us the key, even the trigger, to tremendously increased yields.

NEW PAGE:

Yes, start again. It is cold in here.

Which indeed we have found in the work with Ketone Bill.

Put on [SCARS?] scarves you.

We have produced a most elegant reaction.

Please see that the milk is always fresh. Yesterday's milk may be used for puddings if tasted first. For cereals or coffee use only today's. It does not taste like milk, anyway, the rascals are watering it.

He wishes for GREENYARD'S PICKLES — CHUTNEY.

NEW PAGE:

Start. Where have you been?

Vivat [?] We have had

Nurse, I am busy. What do I want with it? Of course I don't want it. Idiots.

So write.

Certainly a very large conversion to methyl. He has the lab books himself. You will get the book for me.

I will rest a little and tell you.

NEW PAGE:

There can be no doubt that with the methyl already present together with the carotene that it is the answer to the problem. There is no doubt. Later I will tell you. You will get me it. I have told you.

CROMER-LE-POYTH? LE-ROY-PARMA? COONE FIRTH?

Tell Nurse the teeth.

NEW PAGE:

Such [catalysis?] taken with his halving of the time of fermentation will double the yield and provide a ketonic product of extreme concentration making immediately available to Israel a complete high-octane fuel.

After this, several paragraphs quite coherent and in no way different from what we had; and then the very trying last paragraph, also not much different, but apparently containing a few more home truths that had not found their way into the other transcript. The spacing different, too, of course.

NEW PAGE:

I have been thinking. Of course, idiot. Write down.

Perhaps the Bradford people will be able to let us know.

I will think again later.

NEW PAGE:

Write.

What? What is it with these lunatics? How many times?

That German would make a cat laugh. Never mind, he will prove the best internationalist of us all.

NEW PAGE:

It's a funny world.

We will celebrate the holiness of the day.

Well, that was it, and I could see right away the answer to one of the problems and experienced a certain lightening of heart. But there was really no time to go into it now. The translation had to be ready by the morning, so I buckled to, and managed to finish a little before midnight. I took the things I'd used down to the kitchen and washed them up. There were a few carrots in the vegetable rack. I munched a couple to help with the night vision, as I went round switching everything off and relocking doors, and then took to the woods again.

The bike was where I'd left it. I pedalled back to the San Martin, let myself in, and took my room key. There was a note in the slot: Professor Tuomisalo had phoned me at half past nine. She hadn't left a message.

7

Professor Horowitz had organized Dr Finster as well as the plant geneticists, and the conference took place in the plant genetics laboratory. Numerous plants were diligently growing in the greenhouses outside, and I could see that the windows had steamed up there. It had suddenly grown very chilly. The sky was grey and lowering.

Copies had been made of my translated document (all the diagrams and formulas separately copied and inserted), and the geneticists now had the parts of it that concerned them. Meyer had asked me to attend to explain anything that was not clear. I sat and watched them read slowly through.

It didn't seem to be a very conclusive conference, but as soon as it was established that there was nothing for me to explain, I left. Just before I did this, one of the 'geniuses' had been telling Meyer that it might be possible to get something approaching the hypothetical potato in four or five growing seasons, but another had been saying that maybe it mightn't. The reasons for this seemed to be that all the work done on improving the sweet potato, in those areas where they liked it, had been done to enhance flavour and appearance (qualities in which the hypothetical one would evidently be very short) and that it would therefore be necessary to start from scratch to find quite different parentage. To find this *parentage* might take four or five growing seasons. Meyer was looking rather anguished as I left.

Dr Patel was outside. He was peering into the misted-over greenhouses.

'Do you know, I have never had a look at what they are doing here,' he said. 'Some day I must. My word, it has become quite chilly.' So it had, and he was wearing a muffler. 'What about a good cup of hot coffee?'

'Well, I'd love one, but I'm actually in a terrific hurry. Work to do.'

'Work to do. A terrific hurry. On the Sabbath Day?' he said gaily. 'Where are you working – at the Weizmann House?'

'Yes.'

'Well, I've never had a look at that, either. We could take a brisk walk together. I promise not to get in the way of the work!'

'I'm going by bike.'

'Ah. Oh, well. Another time.'

I began to trot, to emphasize the hurry, and picked up the bike from outside the San Martin and pedalled away on it, with a jolly wave to him. There'd been no need to return the bike to Ham. I had told him I wouldn't be able to take advantage of the offered car, so he had gone off in it with Marie-Louise to Jerusalem. And I wasn't actually in such a terrific hurry. I'd wanted to phone Marta first. She had been at breakfast when I'd called earlier. This now meant using the complicated after-hours telephone system at the House, which I didn't understand. I wondered if I shouldn't look in first to the Lunenfeld-Kunin, but a few spots of rain now began to fall, and the sky was distinctly menacing, so I pedalled on.

There was hardly anyone about. The grounds were open to the public on Saturday and were normally thronged with ambling Israeli family groups. These were not normal times. With the Army still called up, nobody was making pleasure trips, and the sky was unpropitious, anyway. The first thunderclaps began to roll as I arrived at the House.

They were rolling in profusion, accompanied by the most fantastic electrical displays and a cataract of rain, as I went briskly upstairs rubbing my hands. A dark chill had settled everywhere and there was a faint reek of kerosene from the stove I'd used to late the night before. The rain thrashed and pelleted against the windows as if the place were under machine-gun attack; wind howling; the sound level quite extraordinary. I'd been in Israel the previous year, in late October. On a heavy, humid day, still summer, there had come suddenly a single puff of wind from nowhere; a giant belch. The leaves fell all at once off the trees, the sky opened, the dry dusty streets began to run like rivers: autumn had come. Not hard to believe the Biblical accounts of creation in this abrupt part of the world.

I was humming 'The Ride of the Valkyries' as I hurried into Chaimchik's room and switched on the light. No light came. Hmm. Lights very often didn't come on when lightning began to crackle in Israel. I lit the kerosene stove. That didn't come on, either, and I looked at it rather superstitiously, until a moment's reflection suggested that the kerosene must have run out. The thing had been stinking rather in the latter reaches of the night. Where the devil was the kerosene? And how to fill the thing, if found? No time for these technical complexities. My teeth were chattering. I might even have been gibbering as I sprang about in the unearthly din looking for another heater.

Nellie had a neat little electric heater. Jolly good, and I gratefully switched it on, and after a moment received the message, but swore all the same. I ran into Julian's room. He had quite a nice setup of built-in heaters, all electrical. I scampered up the stairs to the turret room, the lair of Harold Blumberg, Julian's deputy. It was not, now, unlike the lair of Frankenstein, grimacing and leering in blinking violet light. Through the window I saw the rain bouncing off the flat roof. Harold had a couple of stylish little two-bar electric heaters set in the wall.

I ran in mild panic about the detonating house. I found a kerosene heater in the kitchen and ran back upstairs with it, lit it, and then ran down again, picked up Old Taylor and a glass, and rejoined the heater.

I regained my spirits in about five minutes, at much the same time that the sun came serenely out on a balmy, glistening world faintly steaming. Well, not bad for starters. It wasn't quite eleven o'clock. The telephone began to ring somewhere. I chased it all over the House, picking up phones. For some reason, the voice came out of the receiver in Harold's room. It was Connie's.

'Igor? They told me you weren't at the San Martin. Are you still working at it?'

I brought her up to date on batatas, and said, 'Connie, how do I make a call from this House?'

She gave me detailed instructions about switches and buttons. 'Do you want help, Igor? Do you want me to do anything?'

'Well. I'd like his diaries.'

'They are in folders – the photostats are – on the bottom shelf on the left as you come in my room. Are you in my room?'

'No, I'm in Harold's room.'

'What are you doing in Harold's room?'

'It's the only room the phone answers in, Connie. It's a very funny house, this.'

'Which diaries?'

'For 1933.'

'Why 1933?'

'The batatas. I don't think he was only doing it with Vava. I was looking at the memorandum again. It isn't what it seems, Connie. The paragraphs are run together, but they weren't really. He is referring to two different pieces of work. He talks about something they did with a catalyst. There is no mention of a catalyst in the correspondence with Vava.'

'Are you sure?'

'Certain. It doesn't come up at all. He was doing it with somebody else.'

'So why the diaries?'

'There might be some mention. I mean, if it was all done at the same time, he could have been in correspondence with somebody in the same way as with Vava. They could both have been writing away on the same bit of paper, and there'd be no copy. I thought perhaps he might have made a note, some stray mention in his diary. It's this funny German, you see, the one that made the cat laugh. It might be with him, mightn't it?'

'Well, it might. Certainly. Igor, shall I come down there?'

'Of course not, darling. It's just that I didn't sleep well, It's been on my mind.'

'There's also the correspondence for 1933 – something could have been overlooked there.'

'That was on my mind, too.'

'Except, in 1933 there were many Germans.'

'I know. Okay, then, Connie.'

I'd put the phone down before I realized I hadn't made a note about the buttons and switches. I pressed one or two experimentally, and then remembered she'd said something about Nellie's room, so l went and examined them there and pressed some more. All the phones started to ring again. I hared up to Harold's room, wildly helloing. Dead. Connie's, Nellie's, Julian's, everybody else's – nothing. They stopped after a while, and I realized that not only couldn't I receive a call but I couldn't make one, either. Awkward. Marta would be rather miffed by this time. Still, I *had* called her, and left my name. She would realize something must have cropped up.

I was by now in Connie's room, so I had a look at the bottom shelf on the left, and saw the folders, 'DIARIES'. I ran along them to the one I wanted, and slid it out.

Being the twenty-fourth year of the
Reign of His Majesty King George V
(acccssion, May 6, 1910).

I buzzed rapidly through to late summer and early
autumn. 'Sept. 1st, Zermatt – Hotel Seiler.' 'Sept. 5th,
Merano – Sanatorio Stefania.' 'Sept. 21st, Paris – Hotel
Plaza-Athénée.' 'Sept. 25th, London – home.' Not many
days later he was in Paris again; and then Brussels – Hotel
Astoria. 'Oct. 9th – dinner, King & Queen at Palace.' High
Life. Not very high in detail, though; not the faintest
mention of catalysts, or batatas, or anything beyond
appointments and visits. It would have to be the correspondence, then.

I lugged it out, boxes of it, and took it through to
Chaimchik's room. When had Vava entered his life,
anyway? Weiss had said they'd worked together for only a
few weeks, so it couldn't have been much before that
September. Hadn't he mentioned something about it in the
letter to Fritz Haber? I quickly located the letter. October
2nd: 'As to the good Vava, he is of course incorrigible. He
has been working with me lately – ' Lately. How recently
was lately?

Well, his holiday that year had begun in August. Plenty
of references to it here. They'd toured about first in a car
that had kept breaking down. So he'd gone away in
August, and had left Vava work to do, which probably
meant Vava had turned up in July, perhaps June. I played
safe and started with May.

I'd read for about twenty minutes, barely covering the
first week of May, before it occurred to me that I was
going at it the wrong way. The other process, the one with
the catalyst, must have followed Vava, and not preceded
him. Vava, after all, had initiated the work with the batatas
– clear enough from the stuff I'd translated yesterday.

After Vava, then. This, of course, was very dreary, and brought us back to square 1. I'd already made a list of all the correspondence to be looked into after Vava. There was twenty years of it. Except ... if Weizmann had bracketed the two things together in his mind, must they not have occurred in some sort of proximity?

The correspondence with Vava had finished when he'd left the Stefania. He'd got back to London September 25th. On to September 25th.

A positive deluge of letters on his return. Several dozen relating to German and refugee questions. Protein. Plans to visit Palestine, where the outer shell of the Daniel Sieff Institute was nearing completion. Personal letters arising out of the holiday. One to the Humber Company, complaining about the car.

Dear Sir,

I trust you will forgive me asking your personal attention to the following matter. Shortly before leaving England for a motoring tour on the Continent, I bought a new Humber car (at a cost of £750), in which I and my party set out from Calais early in August intending to proceed by leisurely stages to Portugal and then back through France to Switzerland. I had been careful to enquire in buying the car as to its capabilities in such matters as hill-climbing, number of passengers and amounts of luggage ...

I plodded on through the first week of October, on to the second. One to his wife from the Astoria in Brussels: 'Last night I dined with the King and Queen, who expressed their regret that you were not there.' One reigning monarch to another. Where had vanished his little Verochka, his Verunya, his Vemsenka, darling and joy? Stately relations.

The sky had blackened again, and an air of doom settled on the place. It was a fact that I hadn't slept much. My eyes were jumping. I leaned my elbows on the table, covered my eyes, and felt them hot and throbbing. This certainly wasn't a quick Saturday-morning job in which a bit of inspiration, a bit of luck might bring results. With this man's lively and broad-ranging mind and his universe of connections, 'proximity' to the Vava problem could mean anything. He'd carried problems in his mind for years; as Beylis had said, had returned to them like a dog to a bone. The following year, 1934, was one of his heaviest years of correspondence. I could remember the figure from the rough notes I'd made for my introductory essay. He'd written 1,083 letters in that year, many of them four- or five-pagers.

I tried to visualize him at the time, but I couldn't; couldn't at all see the 'I' of I and My Party, Motoring on the Continent, Proceeding by Leisurely Stages, Accepting Royal Regrets. All I could see was a yellowish sick old man, pointed beard, cooped up in this room, vehemently trying to tell somebody something; within hours, really, of the most leisurely stage of all.

I opened my eyes and blinked. The grave was giving up its dead! A white-shrouded figure materialized vertically above it, as the Last Trump sounded. A second, and clarifying, blink revealed Marta, straightening up from reading the inscription. The long roll of thunder was still unrolling. She was in a long white mac, startling in the gun-metal light. She saw me peering, and waved, and I waved back and ran down to let her in. The sky had divided instantly at Heaven's command and she had caught a little of it even before reaching the door. She was panting slightly.

'Hello,' she said brightly; relations evidently still somewhat metallic.

'The telephones don't work here,' I said energetically. 'I hope you got my earlier message.'

'Oh, yes. I thought you might try again. I called you at the San Martin and they said you'd gone out.'

'Yes, well, you see –'

'Still busily at work?'

'It's other work. I was working till midnight on the translation. And then I couldn't sleep. This is related to it, but it's not really – '

'Is Connie helping you?'

'No, no. I'm alone. I could stop now. It isn't going anywhere. If I could have used this damned phone – '

'Is it too late for the Dead Sea now?'

'Ham took the car, you see.'

'Ah. Of course that is the only transport in the Land of Israel.'

'Well, it might be today. It's Shabbat, no buses. And it would be very difficult to get anything else, because of the war. Well, you know that, Marta. Anyway, we couldn't get back easily.'

'I wouldn't for the world want to disturb you.'

This was all very ridiculous, and the door was still open, so I closed it and kissed her.

She was far, temperamentally, from those who kept things going; but she was now somewhat wound up and feeling herself absurd, so her face was hard and her coat of mail very severe. It was a wet-look garment, quite genuinely so at the moment, as was her brainy head. She took the coat off after a minute, put it on a chair, and recovered herself.

'Well,' she said returning, and began to get some value out of her parameters. As was soon obvious, she got more than I did, my mind still on 1933. Still, *toujours la politesse*. Still enclinched, I unbuttoned her blouse, and attended to her skirt, which she stepped out of. I took the blouse off myself, also her brassière, which left her rather incongruously in a pair of tights. We must have made a rather regal pair ascending the marble staircase; I carried her discarded clothing.

'I think you could skip various things just for now. Only just for now,' she said not long after. 'Oh, my God! Oh, darling. Oh!'

'Well,' I said presently.

'I'm afraid I haven't been cutting such a dignified figure recently.'

'Not in the most recent moments.'

'I mean, it was unfair. I'm quite controlled normally, as you know . . . I have had a celibate six months.'

'I didn't know they were giving medals for that kind of thing at the College of the Sacred Heart these days.'

'I was never a collegiate there. But you know I don't go in for things on the campus. You know that about me, don't you?'

'Of course I do.'

'I didn't sleep terribly well either . . . This pillow's a bit low.'

I went and had a look in the cupboards and found more.

'It's a tiny bed.' She had closed up to the wall to make room.

'For one.'

'Do you suppose I am the first woman in it?'

'I'm certain of it.'

'Would he mind us using it?'

> 'No more need we corn and clothing, feel of old
>   terrestrial stress; . . .
> Fear of death has even bygone us – death gave all
>   that we possess.'

'What's that?'

'That's Hardy.'

'Who's Hardy?'

'An English poet, ignorant Finn.'

She was looking calmly at me, flecked grey eyes, slightly turned-up nose, broad cheeks. There was no appearance here of one of the brains of the world, but it was there. I ran a finger over the somewhat Eskimo cheeks: a very ethnic and Northern person.

'You won't have been so celibate, I take it?' she said as I did this.

'Should I have been?'

'I don't know. Anybody much?'

'Not much.'

'Who is Caroline?'

'A young historian. She works with me.'

'How young?'

'Twenty-three. She is going to be married. To an Honourable,' I said.

'What an Honourable?'

'In this case he's the younger son of an Earl.'

'You've picked up a great deal of English lore and learning. Is she a Lady?'

'Small "L". Why these questions?'

'Connie said she was in love with you.'

'Connie said that?' I tried to remember the occasions when they'd met. Connie had been in England the previous year. Caroline had been going with Willie then.

'M'hmm. What is she like?'

'Caroline? Well,' I said, thinking over this piece of information. 'She's tallish and thin. Fair.'

'Nice-looking?'

'Not ill-looking. English-looking.' I tried to think what she looked like. I could barely recall her.

'Nothing like me?'

I was abstractedly making a ring round her breast as I made this effort at recall, and now looked at it. It was a large, firm breast, moving up and down in a warm and attractive manner.

'Nothing at all,' I said.

'That's all right. *I* love you, anyway,' she said.

'Do you?'

'Yes. I'd like you for weekends. And my husband and family. Now that would be an impossible thing, wouldn't it? Have you finished that cigarette?'

'Yes.' I put it out.

'How do you feel?'

'How do you feel?' I said.

'I feel six months is half a year, which is a lot in terrestrial terms. You can tell me more of that poem later. Just now you can think of other things.'

2

The joint lack of sleep took a somewhat unromantic toll and after a while we both had some. The kerosene stove was out when I woke up, and some time later she said, 'You've got a cold bottom.'

'It's numb.' I'd wondered when she'd notice.

'Well, let's get under.'

'Are we going to stay here into the evening?'

'What else do you want to do?'

'Aren't you hungry?'

'Oh, you Russian.'

'Well, the carbon cycle has to be kept going. You know all about that, don't you?'

'I thought you were eating here.'

'I think I must have eaten it all. I don't know what I'm going to tell them.'

'We'll go and find something.'

We found the rest of the cold smoked turkey and bread, and some cheese, and coffee, and took it all back to bed.

'Meat and milk products. Not a kosher mix,' she said.

'You've heard that, have you?'

'You learn such things here. Do you *feel* Jewish?'

'I don't feel anything – not Russian, not English, not anything. My mother apparently now does. She's got a rabbi.'

'In an English village?' she asked.

'He comes. He's terrified of my father.'

'Do you remember all that, when he defected?'

'Of course.'

'I was at Stockholm at the time, postgraduate,' she said.

'It was a most tremendous story, naturally. How old were you?'

'Thirteen.'

'Mmm. I suppose I seem old to you, don't I?' For some reason we were now talking in Russian.

'As the hills.'

'I expect that's true . . . What happened?'

'There was a Christmas party, for the diplomatic children, in the British Ambassador's place. There'd been something that year. Macmillan and a man called Selwyn Lloyd had gone to Moscow, and there was an Anglo-Soviet trade pact, so *we* were allowed to go, too, which of course normally we wouldn't have been. I remember we were snowballing in the garden, and we were called in to get our presents from the Christmas tree. I'd seen my father just a bit earlier. He'd come along with his driver. But I never got my present, though the tree was there. I was just rushed through into another room. My mother had gone in to have tea some time before. And my father had gone to look at some pictures. The whole thing was fixed. Anyway, that was it. He'd sweated on it, to get us all together, you see, which was very difficult to do. And we all flew off the same evening.'

'Were you glad?'

'Glad? I was infuriated. I wouldn't talk to him for weeks.'

'Why?'

'I wouldn't talk to my mother, either. I knew she was in it with him. They were both traitors.'

'Did you feel that?'

'I was absolutely inflamed. They couldn't do anything with me. I was a young builder of Socialism, you know.'

'In the Komsomol?'

'To my lasting regret, I wasn't. I was a Young Octobrist. We were actually just going to start a group of Young Pioneers, but we hadn't yet. I was to be the brigade leader. The Komsomol was the All-Union Leninist Communist

League of Youth, and you couldn't be that kind of youth till you were fourteen. I'd been writing away to Moscow to establish this cadre of Pioneers, and I'd got a most encouraging response. There were quite a lot of us there in Stockholm. It was important for some sort of intelligence reason. That's why it wasn't so awful my father having the job.'

'Was it such an awful job?'

'Well, damn it, he'd been a Deputy Prime Minister, with Molotov. He was a Molotov man. Then Molotov was disgraced and sent off on his rotten job to Mongolia, to get him out of the way. We'd had quite a tricky time in Moscow ourselves, though of course I didn't know it. But my father had worked with Khrushchev, you see, quite an old hatchet man of his in the south, and he sort of weathered the storm, and they gave him this job in Stockholm. Of course, he was sold out then – but it never occurred to them he would run. Nobody had, in his position. I mean, they were quite a dedicated gang.'

'Is he not?'

'Well, he is, but rather old-style.'

'Did he do the terrible things they say?'

'I'm afraid he did. I think so.'

'The collectivizations and so on.'

'He's writing a book – whether of explanation or expiation, I'm not sure.'

'And were you very distressed?'

'You see, in Moscow I'd actually been a Pioneer. You stopped being a Young Octobrist when you were about ten. That's about what they were in Stockholm. Maybe they didn't let them take the older children with them as a general rule, I don't know. Anyway, all these terrible little Comrades were Young Octobrists, and there weren't any Pioneers. Oh, yes, my ultimate dream was the Komsomol. I wanted to devote my whole life and go there.'

'Go where?'

'To Komsomolsk.'

'It's a place?'

'Oh, my word, I can tell you everything about it. I can *recite* it. It stands on the left bank of the River Amur, well over a hundred miles from Khabarovsk. There was a tiny village called Permskoye, and the Komsomol took it over in 1932 and built a town there. I used to receive the most regular and up-to-date information, all pamphlets, all booklets, and I cut everything out of the children's newspaper. Do you know, by the time my dream was shattered, it was the third largest town in the Soviet Far East. There were almost two hundred thousand Komsomolniks there, all connected to everywhere else by Trans-Siberian Railway, a section of which they'd laid themselves. What do you think of that? *And* fifty schools and a couple of polytechnics, and factories galore, heavy engineering, et cetera. All built by the young builders, you see.'

'Well, this is a surprise, Igor.'

'You don't see me as a young builder.'

'I don't. I didn't know any of this. So when did you learn it was not paradise?'

'Oh, well. Gradually. A series of shocks. It was a question of what to believe. It sets you looking into things, you see. History and such.'

'Ah.'

'We could have a most enormous chat about mathematics now, if you like, and what they are. What are they?'

'Oh, Igor, this is too hard. You wouldn't understand.'

'All right.'

'Don't be offended. It's just – look.' She suddenly made an energetic reach over me and, still bending over, used my writing materials on the desk. 'What's this?' she said.

$$E = mc^2$$

'Einstein's equation, isn't it?'

'Oh, well, thank goodness. Well, that's a relief.' She gave me a kiss.

'What about it?'

'It's – music, that's all. It's like asking someone to explain music to a deaf person. It isn't as explainable as your things, Igor. It's appallingly difficult, it really is, but – well. You know what music and mathematics have in common?'

'The initial?' I said attentively.

'They resolve things. They make order. They do it with economy and elegance. In this equation – look at the beautiful thing – he makes an equivalence of energy and mass.'

'A mass of what?'

'Mass as space-time.'

'Oh.'

'You see. I did very little teaching; I'm terrible at it. *Please* don't ask me to explain. But look at the sheer stark loveliness; and the grace and fun. Libraries, universes of thought in that delicious equation.' She was looking very fondly at it herself. 'You know what composer this reminds me of?'

There was here a need to walk with extreme caution. As one who was totally tone deaf, I knew the indignation aroused by a careless attribution. It was almost an imputation against the other's task and personality. The fond look could easily portend thoughts of home.

'Sibelius,' I said.

'Oh, my God.' She threw the paper down and also herself, quite coldly, away from me.

'I was teasing. Idiot,' I said, and leaned over her.

Who, for God's sake? Not evidently the moody and melodious Finn. Beethoven? A bit noisy and obvious. Bach? Plenty of mathematics there, except I couldn't actually recall anyone saying he was all that funny. There was only one name that seemed to give no offence.

'Mozart,' I said softly into her ear.

'Darling.'

Thank God for Mozart, whom we celebrated for a

while, after which, with something apparently ticked off in her mind about me, she was disposed to enlarge in a less inhibited way about her own mysteries: Mozart, music, and mathematics.

'The great equations have this air of profundity with wit, just like him. It's a pity you can't play them.'

'Well, it is.'

'It's grace; there's no other word. You know when I heard that gorgeous bit of sublime nonsense for the first time, I shivered.'

'Mozart?'

'Einstein.'

'Why nonsense?'

'Well not nonsense. The brevity says nonsense. Of course it isn't. It makes everything else nonsense. Your father starving off those millions of peasants. All those insane little men running about in your book, fixing everything. Just to fix something true! To get down in a few symbols so much truth, with wit and urbanity, as he did.'

'Einstein?'

'Mozart.'

This was very diffficult. 'Who first taught you that equation?' I said.

She'd been looking upward, but she turned so suddenly that our noses touched. She said with surprise, 'Well, I should know that. Who was he? I'll tell you in a minute.' We'd been talking Russian, so he said this in Russian. '*K'to onbil? Patom skarzhu.*'

We were so close I couldn't see her. I raised myself and stared down.

'Koivisto!' she said up at me triumphantly.

'Oh, my God!'

'Professor Koivisto. Professor Nestor Koivisto.'

'Well, of course! That's it. It must be!' I said.

'You know him?' she said, amazed. 'What on earth's the matter?'

I had sprung out of bed. I was sitting in Chaimchik's chair, racing through the pages of the memorandum.

Of course. Here it was. It had bothered me for days; had started ticking in my brain since the young man from Kiev had first said it, after I'd seen the muscle machine.

'*K'to onbil? Patom skarzhu,*' he had said.

She had just said it again. Here it was in the memo. That's where it had first struck me, oddly placed.

Not taken down correctly, of course. The secretary had misheard the muttered Russian exclamation, had tried to make sense of it as an English phrase.

'Ketone Bill. Put on [scars?] scarves you.'

'*K'to onbil? Patom skarzhu.*'

'Who was he? I'll tell you in a minute.'

I read rapidly through the paragraph, heart racing.

NEW PAGE:

Yes, start again. It is cold in here. Which indeed we have found in the work with – who was he? I'll tell you in a minute. We have produced a most elegant reaction.

He'd forgotten the name of the man with whom he had produced the elegant reaction. I'd been right. It was another piece of work. It had nothing to do with Vava. He'd said he would tell her later. Had he? Where?

NEW PAGE:

Start. Where have you been?

Vivat [?] We have had

Nurse, I am busy. What do I want with it? Of course I don't want it. Idiots. So write.

Certainly a very large conversion to methyl. He has the lab books himself. You will get the book for me.

I will rest a little and tell you.

There can be no doubt that with the methyl already present together with the carotene that it is the answer to the problem. There is no doubt. Later I will tell you. You will get me it. I have told you.

CROMER-LE-POYTH? LE-ROY-PARMA? COONE FIRTH?

Tell Nurse the teeth.

'Igor, what on earth is the matter?'
She had got up and was standing behind me, shivering and rubbing herself in the chilly room.
'It's difficult to – Just a minute, Marta,' I said, frantically going from one page to another.
'We'll freeze here. Isn't there another heater?'
'There's an electric one next door, in Nellie's room.'
The heater materialized presently. A couple of dressing gowns did, too. I'd switched on the desk lamp, so she drew the curtains. I was hardly aware of any of this.
'"Later I will tell you . . . I have told you."'
He'd told her or he hadn't told her? Which? I turned pages.

NEW PAGE:

I have been thinking. Of course, idiot. Write down.

Perhaps the Bradford people will be able to let us know.

I will think again later

NEW PAGE:

Write.

What? What is it with these lunatics? How many times? That German would make a cat laugh. Never mind, he will prove the best internationalist of us all.

NEW PAGE:

It's a funny world.

We will celebrate the holiness of the day.

What the devil?

He'd said he would tell her. Then he'd said he had told her. Was something missing, something she hadn't heard, or had misheard? She had evidently taken down every word uttered, whether she had understood it or not. Here it was, immaculately transcribed by my Miss Knowall. He had certainly told her something. And it was here somewhere. Where?

'Igor, can I help in some way? What is it?'

I looked at her dazedly. She was in one of Chaimuhik's dressing gowns. So was I. This didn't seem quite right. A rather enormous number of things at the moment didn't seem right.

'Do you know anything about chemistry, Marta?'

'Not very much.'

'Look at this.'

She read it, frowning.

'There doesn't seem to be much chemistry.'

'Does any of it make sense to you?'

'Not more than it says. I don't understand it.'

I stared at it again, trying to will the meaning out of it.

'What's Cromer-le-Poyth?' Marta said.

'He apparently didn't have his teeth in.'

'Oh. What? Poys? Cromer-le-Poys? Is it a place?'

'He seems to think he is telling her a name.'

'Le-Roy-Parma. Coone Firth – Firs?'

All the phones began to ring. We ran into Nellie's room. The mathematician applied herself to the buttons. Unbelievably, a voice said, 'Have you been working there all day?' The voice was Ham's.

'Hello, Ham. Yes.'

'Well, come and have a drink.'

I looked at my watch. In some way it had become 7 p.m.

'Did we have a day!' he said. 'We have got tickets for the Midnight Mass, in Bethlehem. For you, too. For Monday.'

'Monday?'

'Christmas Eve. What in God's name are you still doing there? Do you have the bike?'

'Yes, I've got it.'

'Well, come on over. Drinks waiting.'

This sounded like a good idea. It sounded like an excellent idea. I wondered what Ham could add to this.

'I will call Marta,' he said while I thought this.

'I will call Marta.'

'She'll need picking up, if she's in.'

'I'll pick her up. I'll give her a ride on the bike,' I said; which I did, and presently Saturday passed, the Sabbath. By Jewish tradition it had started the night before, dusk to dusk. Before then, the grand design had been laid out, and rest and contemplation were decreed for one day to follow.

Something very like that seemed to have been happening here. A design of some sort had evidently been laid out. One way or another, throughout the long Sabbath, I had been contemplating it.

8

The three tickets for the Midnight Mass were increased to four to include Marta – this was accomplished on the day itself, Monday – but on the Saturday night we discussed Chaimchik's last memo. The starting point for Ham's own entry to the hall of fame had been, oddly enough, an early observation of Weizmann's in the field of coal-tar chemistry.

In the far-off days when dyestuffs had been the thing, Weizmann and some assistants had systematically examined derivatives of coal tar, which later had been found to be cancer-producing. In investigating why this should be so, Ham had made his important discoveries about the nature of cancer cells. He had started with something totally different – such is the orderly march of science – while engaged on tar-sand research for an oil company.

It didn't help much with Weizmann's later brainstorms about petrol or Vava; but still, Ham knew the subject, and told me what he knew. He didn't think that Cromer-le-Poyth(s), Le-Roy-Parma, or Coone Firth(s) were place names; they seemed to ring a distant bell with him, but he couldn't think why. He also pointed out that the Bradford (which Connie and her assistants had been slaving away at) need not be Bradford, England. There were numerous Bradfords in America, the land where Weizmann's processes had been most thoroughly exploited.

On his hosts' bookshelves we found an atlas and gazetteer and tracked down a long run of Bradfords in Arkansas, Illinois, Maine, and so on. There were ten, all told, in the USA.

All this was naturally very uplifting. I made an unsteady journey back to the San Martin. Ham wasn't very steady, either, after the evening of discussion and refreshment. Marie-Louise ran Marta home.

I called Weiss next morning in Jerusalem.

It was his problem, damn it. He had been there at the Featherstone Laboratory while Vava had diverged and Chaimchik had proceeded in leisurely stages.

'Cromer-le-what?' he said.

'Poyth. But I think it's Poys.'

'Cromer-le-Poys. It's familiar. Well, I will make a note. They can look. Cromer-le-Poys.'

'The next is Le-Roy-Parma.'

'Ah, yes. That's different. He was a chemist.'

'Who was?'

He spelled it. It came out as Leroy Palmer. 'An American chemist. He did various things.'

'Did Weizmann work with him?'

'I shouldn't think so. No, no. Tsk!' he said.

'Well, why is he talking about him?'

'Where is he talking about him?'

'In his last memorandum.'

'He discusses Palmer in his last memorandum? I didn't observe it. Well, we'll see. What else?'

Coone Firth drew a blank, and I paused before the next, wondering how to put it. 'Could there be,' I said, 'any kind of process involving' – I stumbled over 'chutney' and decided against it 'the name Greenyard?'

'Greenyar, certainly.'

'Eh?'

'It's a well-known process. What of it?'

'How would you spell that?' I said uncertainly.

'How to spell it? G-r-i-g-n-a-r-d. Grignard. What is the mystery?'

'What does it do?' I said.

127

'It's a catalytic reaction.'

'It is?'

'Mr Druyanov, if you will tell me what you require – How do you come to the Grignard reaction?' he said sharply.

'Well.' I was in such a spin I couldn't recall for a moment how I had come on it. 'It was the chutney in the margin,' I said.

'Chutney?'

'There was a confusion with the name. They thought it was – Professor, did Weizmann do any work with the Grignard reaction?'

'A great deal. I did some with him. So did Bergmann.'

'When?'

'When? I can't give the exact date. Look up his published papers – from, let's say, 1934, 1935. A great deal.'

'Why?'

He spoke to somebody else. He said 'Excuse me' into the phone in between. Presently he came back very briskly. 'Mr Druyanov, I have a tight schedule this morning. If you could give my secretary a list of your queries.'

'I'll ring back. I'm not sure of them myself at the moment.'

'Very good.' He hung up right away.

I put the phone down and looked across at Connie. I was in her room. Connie was looking back at me.

'It isn't chutney, it's a reaction,' I said.

'I see.'

'There are ten Bradfords in America.'

'Well. That's a lot, isn't it?'

'Leroy Palmer isn't a place. It's an American chemist he never worked with.'

'Would you like a cup of coffee?'

'Yes. Yes, I'll have a cup of coffee, Connie. Have we got his list of published papers?'

'Oh, yes, we've got those.'

'Can I see the ones from 1934 onwards?'

'Of course you can, Igor. You just sit there.'

Dan came in while I was sitting there.

'Hello. Have you usurped me?'

'No. I'm just sort of sitting here, Dan. I'll go away if you like.'

'It's nothing, just a quick reference. Sit. What's the matter, Igor?'

'Well. Dan. A lot of names have suddenly flooded in on me that I've never heard before.'

'Ah, footnotes. Dreadful things. They can be a real snare. The danger is not to get lost. You can spend weeks chasing a promising footnote. Is it something I would know?'

'Oh, no,' I said sadly. 'Nothing to do with the triumvirate. It's an American chemist that nobody ever heard of who was in some way involved with him.'

'Mashed potato?'

'I think so.'

'Who was he?'

'Leroy Palmer.'

'Ah, the writer.'

'What writer, Dan?'

'A writer. He wrote.'

'What?'

'Books. *A* book, at least. It's in the library below.'

'How do you know?'

'How do I know? I don't know. I saw it. My eye lit on it. It's an improbable name. Did they say, "We must call this lovely little cherub Leroy?" . . . I think it's somewhere on the left,' he said as I went down.

I pattered down the stairs, unlocked the library, moved to the left. On the left was the chemical library. There was a matched set of volumes: The American Chemical Library. Leroy Palmer. *The Chromolipoids*. (Cromer-le-Poyth?) I drew it out and opened it. The title page read:

The Chromolipoids
Carotinoids and Related Pigments

I skimmed quickly through the chapter headings. 'Carotene.' Oh, my God, it was all happening a bit fast.

I took the volume upstairs, and met Connie coming down with a cup of coffee.

'Oh, I just took this up. I am just bringing it down. Where are you going to be?'

'In Cromer-le-Poyth,' I said, and showed her the volume.

Wc went slowly back upstairs together.

The shock waves rippled out from there. I had a look at his list of published papers from 1934 onward. There was suddenly, in 1935, a very large number to do with the Grignard reaction.

I had a rapid shuffle through the correspondence for the period.

Yes. It had started the year before. From the Featherstone Laboratory, September 7, 1934, to the Mallinckroot Chemical Works, St Louis, Missouri, USA. He wanted at their earliest convenience 100 grams of specially purified magnesium metal for the purpose of making a Grignard reaction.

Other orders followed. I followed the other orders, and soon got lost, and recalled Dan's warning.

Stop. Think. Define.

Up in his room, there was no doubt he'd had a big idea for solving Vava's difficulty by means of carotene and the Grignard reaction. Carotene was evidently a basic substance and posed no problems. But what the devil was the Grignard reaction?

2

'The Grignard reaction?' Emanuel Beylis said, rather startled. He'd just returned from a lecture, to find me impatiently waiting. 'But how have you come to this, Igor?'

Never mind how the devil I'd come to it! I wanted to say, 'My eye lit on it.' Or, 'While in bed with Professor Tuomisalo, my attention was directed to . . .' Far too many people were asking how I'd come on things. I didn't know how I'd come on them. I didn't know what they were.

'References,' I said briefly. 'What *is* it?'

'It's a mode of catalysis. Grignard employed magnesium.'

He did, eh?

'What did he do with it?' I said.

I couldn't follow what he did with it, but he told me exactly what catalysis was.

'If you want to transform one substance into another, you can employ a catalyst – some other substance – to help. You carry out the work in the presence of this other substance, the catalyst. The catalyst itself isn't changed or consumed, but the other materials are.'

'Yes. Emanuel – suppse I have this big jar of sweet-potato juice and I want to make it into really super petrol, do I just wave my magnesium catalyst over it, like Grignard?'

'That sort of thing, yes. Of course, there's a bit more to it. We'll say we decide to do something with your butanol, yes? That would be one of the important products of your fermentation. Finster is getting a big reading in it, as a matter of fact. Well, you could heat butanol with critical quantities of, say, magnesium oxide, and get something else – yes, you could.'

'What would be so critical about it?'

He laughed. 'Well, everything. What degree of heat? How many times? What proportion of magnesium? There are hundreds of variables. That's the trick, you see.'

'Ah.'

'So now you can tell me,' he said kindly, 'how you have come to the Grignard reaction.'

I told him about Weizmann's papers on it, and of Leroy Palmer and carotene, which baffled him rather.

'Palmer on carotene. Very odd.'

'Why?'

'Old-fashioned. The authority on carotene is Coone.'

'Spell that,' I said sinkingly.

'K-u-h-n. Kuhn.'

'You'd go to Coone Firth, would you?' I said.

'To Kuhn first, certainly,' he said, looking at me rather queerly.

'Yeth.' Obviouth enough, without your teeth in. 'Weizmann would have had Kuhn, would he?'

'Without any question. We must have the stuff here somewhere. Kuhn was Willstätter's assistant, you know. Later on he became director of the Max Planck Institute. He is *the* authority on carotene. He got the Nobel Prize for it.'

It was strange how everyone around Chaimchik seemed to come in for this Prize. It seemed to me I was doing quite enough to get in line myself.

Emanuel was still looking at me rather strangely. 'I am not clear where the carotene comes in,' he said.

'It doesn't make sense?'

'Not with Weizmann's Grignard stuff.'

'He seemed to think it did.'

'Well, if you can get his published papers for the period, we can look at them together, perhaps see something.'

I had the list of published papers with me, and produced them immediately. He was rather taken aback at this ready delivery. But he courteously dived in.

When he'd finished, he said, 'Well, there is certainly a lot of Grignard. I see phthalic anhydride, ethyl . . . I don't know what you expected of the carotene.'

'It couldn't have anything to do with it?'

'Nothing.'

'What can he have meant?'

'You must have misread it. Or someone did.'

'Doesn't it make *any* sense?'

'The Grinard does. I've told you. It's a catalytic process

that he might easily have used to improve a fermented product. But carotene? There's no connection.'

'But – he goes on about it in the memorandum. He asked for this book about it. I am sure he did.'

'Well, I don't know what to say. Carotene is a pigment. It makes carrots the colour they are.'

'Does it make sweet potatoes the colour they are?'

'Those with orange flesh, yes. It does.'

'Well, that's the connection.'

He was smiling at me. 'Igor – suppose you found in the notes of a chocolate manufacturer some mention of boot-laces. It doesn't mean he is trying to make chocolate out of bootlaces. He is simply worried for some reason about his bootlaces. I couldn't tell you why.'

'Still, there could be a connection.'

'We have no department of psychiatry.' He was smiling. 'All I can tell you is that Grignard and carotene definitely do not tango.'

So. A slight reversal of the situation. Grignard was all right. No nonsense out of him. But what can have gone on in the smiling land of carotene?

3

Meyer rang up. He said, 'Okay, well, we got it.'

'Well, that's marvellous, Meyer. I'm terribly glad.' I couldn't think what he was talking about.

'We sent a driver to the airport. It came in on the plane from Paris. Right away I took the label off. It's in the safe. They are working with it now, in a plain test tube. What did you find out yet?'

What had I found out yet? Was it only yesterday morning we'd sat together with the geneticists while I'd looked out at the steamed-over greenhouses?

'Not much. I am just sort of reading away, Meyer.'

'What is this with Grignard?'

'Now, how have you come to Grignard?' I said, getting in the way of it.

'I spoke with Weiss. What's the matter there? You sound sleepy. Wake up.' There was something rather brisk in his voice.

'I have been working all hours. But yet I have nothing to tell you.'

'You don't, eh? So I'll tell you something.' Definitely a brisk tone. Rather a gleeful tone. 'You know this bunch of African states that has nothing else to do but break off relations with Israel? They drop in the streets from starvation. But we are their only problem.'

'Yes?'

'You know we had many missions with them, teaching, helping?'

'Yes?'

'Many of them *agricultural* missions?'

'So?'

'What do they just love to eat out there?'

'Oh.'

'Aha. You woke up. If you can spare a moment in that busy life and be in the plant genetics laboratory sometime like about ten to three, you will find me there, and others there, including a young man just newly back in Israel. He has come back from Africa, Igor. They didn't want any more relations with him. He was growing for them like fifty thousand different kinds of sweet potato to see which one they liked the best. Do you know what this nice young man just happened to find among his fifty thousand?'

'Okay, ten to three, Meyer.'

'Keep reading, Igor.'

The young man newly returned from Africa was not noticeably a son of the soil. He was a slim shy young man with slipping spectacles and a number of sores on his head. They were painted bright violet: a casualty of the bush. I wondered what they'd made of him out there. He seemed to have liked them himself, and shyly said so. He peered up to make a comment from time to time while reading from his folio of handwritten pages. They were his field records. He had some other records that had been made by others of his team, nutritional and analytical ones.

Though shy, there was not much stopping him. He just nodded at interruptions and kept going: stubborn. In his stubborn way, he seemed to have got through a mountain of work. He said his soil tests had shown the local varieties of sweet potato to be not the most suitable. He had introduced others and he had also done some large-scale seeding. (This was Meyer's fifty thousand: he had raised fifty thousand seedlings.) He had selected a few hundred with promising tubers and had sent them for analysis. From these he had reselected and cross-fertilized. He had spent years at it in the bush.

He was unhappy at having to leave, and looked forward to going back. He had brought cuttings of the most promising of his parent plants, to keep them in cultivation. Among them was one with an analysis that Vava had fantasized about while Chaimchik was having his trouble with the Humber. It wasn't a very appetizing variety. The enormous knobbly thing apparently cracked as soon as it was dug up, and went bad: it was also very bitter and almost blood-red and strongly aperient. But it was a demon in poor soil, and this vitality promised wonders in genetic lines.

Meyer sat and smiled beatifically as the young man told of his work and of this particular beauty.

'Very nice, Uri,' he said at the end. 'It's a pleasure to listen to you.'

Uri had brought several of his cuttings and they were in shallow seed trays, labelled and waxed. They were just little slices of tuber. The particular one was like a piece of putrescent liver. A tiny waxy pimple, like a wart, glistened on it: the growing point. I looked at the wart. Given the laws of genetics, and also the facts of life, it did not seem strange that the fate of continents might be decided by what could come out of this wart.

Meyer was looking at it, too. His face was wreathed in the kind of smile associated with the season and its patron saint.

'It makes you feel good just to look at that cute little thing,' he said. 'Doesn't it?'

Sunday, December 23rd, that was.

I was going to be up half the following night in Bethlehem, so I went to bed early. There were two phone calls first. One was from Meyer, still full of good cheer. 'Is that baby going to change a few things out here!' he said gleefully.

I hadn't told him of the carotene complications yet, and he didn't seem to have got the message from his other sources. There was no point in alloying such pure and quite delightful pleasure.

'Yes,' I said.

'Listen, I was just talking with New York.'

'I thought it was to be kept confidential.'

'Not about this, for God's sake. God forbid!' he said, shocked. 'Of course confidential. It was other matters. When are you going back?'

'The twenty-ninth or thirtieth.'

'The twenty-ninth is Saturday – very restricted flights. I don't want to push you – I mean, don't hurry your work here. But Kammermann will be in London the twenty-eighth.'

Kammermann. Weizmann's confidant of the 1930s. 'I didn't know he was alive.'

'He's *just* alive. He's been a recluse for years. They are sending him to Switzerland. He will be in London a day and a night. A specialist is seeing him. He will be at Brown's Hotel.'

'You want me to see him?'

'Well, he will see *you*, which is something. He doesn't see people. He was interested in your book. I just spoke with his doctor, Brodie.'

'All right. Can he remember anything?'

'Who knows? But he undoubtedly has political papers. He didn't answer our letters. It would be nice to have the papers.'

'Okay, Meyer.'

The other call I made myself. I knew Caroline would be at her parents' place tonight. She was going to Hampshire to Willie's tomorrow; she was staying there the whole week and not coming back till the following Monday, the thirty-first, so I wouldn't see her till then. I hadn't liked the way we'd signed off on the phone. Also, of course, she didn't know of the parcel from Olga.

'Hello, Caroline,' I said wben I got through.

'What's the trouble?' she said loweringly.

'No trouble. Good news. Vava's letters turned up.'

'Yes, she told me she'd sent them.'

'Oh, you spoke to her?'

'I went to see her, with Hopcroft. She phoned him. She got them the day Hopcroft had his accident. Her friend went down and got them.'

'I thought that. Well, that's good, and anyway they're here and all's well. Are you packing up and so on?'

'Yes, I'm packed. What are you doing?'

'I'm going to Midnight Mass tomorrow in Bethlehem.'

'Well. All in the family, I suppose, isn't it?'

'Quite. Would you like to give my mother a ring and tell her that? She might be tickled.'

'All right. Anything else to tell her, like when you're coming back?'

'Yes – Thursday, the twenty-seventh.'

'Oh. I thought you said the twenty-ninth or thirtieth.'

'Meyer wants me to see an old personage who is passing through London on Friday. So I'm coming Thursday.'

'Oh, you want me to make arrangements.'

'No. I only rang to say hello. It was nice of you to go and see Olga. What's she like?'

'Odd.'

There was really nothing much doing with her; monosyllabic, situation distinctly strained. This was a pity. She'd been a good assistant, Caroline.

'Well, it was only hello,' I said.

'All right. Hello. Happy Christmas,' she said rather grudgingly.

I repeated the salutation and hung up, brooding.

Not a good idea.

4

On Monday I dropped Vava and got back to volume 15. Connie had set matters in hand and there were answers to my large pile of queries. A lot of work had been done in the archives, but I still had to go there myself for some hours in the morning.

Everything with Weizmann's own autograph was kept in plastic envelopes and had to be examined there. He'd had a habit of adding handwritten PS's and comments in the margin that hadn't got back to the carbon copies.

To his ladyloves, often the only source for his private views on factional disputes, he had confided stray comments of political importance. All to be explained in footnotes. Verochka had shown admirable detachment here. Obviously, she hadn't liked what she had read. But her sharp eye had seen what might later be needed. Hard to tell, of course, what she *had* destroyed.

His attachments were well signalled, the customary overture 'Dear Friend' accelerating rapidly over a couple of weeks to steamier terms. A consistent pattern in the content, too: a paragraph of endearments abruptly followed by several much longer ones, stiff with political views. He had simply needed somebody: opposite gender, young. Not to be seen in the Birley portrait, but you could just spot it in the photos. There was a look, a certain mercurial flicker that had never apparently left him. Until the bleak end. Almost everything had left him in the end. The man who had written 1,083 letters in 1934 had written three in 1952. Of course he had written something else in 1952, but I put this severely out of mind and attended to the enthusiasms of a livelier decade.

5

I thought the best thing to do about sweet potatoes was to write a report for Meyer, and let him worry about it. I would outline the problem, of which he was at the moment unaware, and present my conclusions. The snag was that I didn't have any. I wasn't even certain that I knew the problem. The whole thing was very unpromising, and my silence led Ham to inquire what was eating me. We were making a slow pilgrimage to Bethlehem; numbers of others were doing the same. I was seated next to him, and Marta and Marie-Louise were in the rear.

'It's carotene,' I said.

'What about it?'

'It can't have anything to do with petrol.'

'Perfectly correct.'

'Weizmann thought it did.'

'You can't be right all the time,' Ham said.

'If he'd thought about it for twenty years, you'd think he might have half a chance, wouldn't you?'

'Tell Uncle.'

I told Uncle. He swore a bit from time to time – not at the problem, but at other pilgrims, many on donkeys. We were part of a straggling procession. Bethlehem is not much above ten minutes out of Jerusalem; it had taken us nearly an hour already. It was still quite early, just after ten, but we had to find our alloted parking place. A sticker on the window gave its number.

You couldn't bring a car into town without a sticker, and you couldn't get in at all without a ticket. We were stopped frequently at roadblocks by young soldiers with automatic weapons. They gave us quite jovial Christmas greetings, however, and the nearer we got the more evident the festive spirit became.

Little stars were twinkling, in the approved manner, like diamonds in the sky, and a glow was radiating from the little town on its holiest night. It came from the television lighting that ashenly illuminated the scene like a piece of flashlit police evidence. The Church of the Nativity was on high ground, and our parking place on rather low ground, which meant a long trudge up.

I didn't know how much Ham had caught of my problem amid the confusion. The trouble was that the problem had rarely remained the same for more than a couple of hours. It had kept subtly changing itself. Originally it had been the simple one of obtaining Vava's papers, but then it had become the more complicated one of obtaining his bacterium and his sweet potato as well. All of these had been posers in their hour, but at least they had been understandable posers. The carotene and the Grignard were something else, and because I wasn't a scientist I didn't know how to explain them. I simply knew that they would become problems because Chaimchik had said so; at least, I thought he had said so, which was another problem.

It was true that experts on the various problems were to hand, but to get proper answers you had to feed experts proper questions. It suddenly struck me that I had presented no single expert with the whole problem. I had gone running to separate ones with separate bits of it. This was because the problem itself had been revealed in piecemeal form.

Weiss, when primed, had unscrambled Greenyard into a

reaction and Le-Roy-Parma into a chemist; Dan had directed me to where he lived in Cromer-le-Poyth; and Beylis had explained that he could have had nothing to do with Grignard. Except wait a minute – no, he hadn't. He'd said carotene could have had nothing to do with the papers I'd shown him.

Could there be some other papers?

No, there couldn't. Expert Weiss had directed me to the papers. He had known everything that Weizmann had done with the Grignard reaction from the mid-Thirties onward. And Weizmann had published nothing for thirteen or fourteen years before then, which took us back to the Twenties or earlier. Which wouldn't work, because there'd been no Grignard until the Thirties. Or had there?

This reflection was so novel that I stopped short, and Ham walked on a few paces, and the women, following behind, bumped into me. We had trudged up the hill and were crossing Manger Square. It was thronged with pilgrims, all looking, in the blinding chalky light, like characters from an early flickering movie.

Jesus freaks abounded, the younger ones, from affluent lands, sitting on the ground and begging. Numerous old Arabs were going about selling felafel and shashlik, and younger ones were having a marvellous time feeling the girls. There were thousands of girls to feel. A troupe of young Franciscan monks, brown-habited, cruised with their guitars, bizarrely singing 'Jingle Bells'. A grotesque scene, stranger by far than the remote one it was celebrating; a Bartholomew Fair. To add to the madness, peals of bells continuously clanged.

I was rooted to the spot and gazing about, bedazzled.

'What's up?' Ham said.

'When did Grignard react?'

'What's that?' He was shouting and cupping his ear. We had begun to move again, pushed from the rear. I yelled my question again.

'Grignard? His catalytic reaction? I don't know. The turn of the century, I think. Why?'

'Oh, my God!' I said.

It was a proper thing to say. We were ducking into the entrance of His earliest standing church. Inside was a Roman temple. The normal entrance had been bricked up at some time in antiquity to prevent the entrance of horsemen and camels. Numerous legends had developed about the need to be as a little child before one could get into the place. It was built over a cave in the rocky hillside, the presumed site of the Birth. The Emperor Constantine, in a rash of enthusiasm, and at the behest of his newly converted mother, Helena, had built the first one, but Justinian had pulled it down and built this one. He had done it by the year 537, and this was it: a Roman temple, soberly designed for the exercise of a cult – in this case the cult of Christ, and therefore quirkily constructed in the form of a cross to conform to faddish new Christian modes.

It was a handsome building, designed by a sound temple man, but constructed, for reasons of economy, out of local materials; four rows of tremendous Corinthian columns, ten in each row, of pink Bethlehem marble supported the roof. It was already nearly six hundred years old when the stupefied Crusaders, coming from places with hardly any buildings to speak of, had first cast awed eyes on it. Generations of acolytes had been swinging censers through it ever since, which accounted for the exceedingly strange smell – the earliest sort of Christian smell.

We made our way to where the Western Christmas was being celebrated and found the church already crowded; it was after eleven. It held about a thousand, standing, which is what everybody was doing, shuffling and snuffling in heavy clothing in the chill.

The big white church was sumptuously decorated: pictures, statuettes, flowers. Red curtains hung on windows and doors. The white-and-gilt altar shone triumphantly.

Six long candles, in enormous virginal candlesticks, flanked the cross, interspersed with vases of gladioli. A picture of the mother of Christ hung from the gallery, above which the gilded organ pipes thrummed sonorously. Candelabra hung from ceilings and walls; the place was a blaze of colour and light, added to by the television arc lamps.

The Latin Patriarch was performing an office before the altar while the priests sang Jesus Redemptor. Then the Patriarch recited the lesson; and then everyone was singing again in Latin.

I was experiencing some confusion. Grignard had reacted at the turn of the century? I was not perfectly clear which century I was in. Rather too many appeared to be in evidence round here. In some bemusement I gazed at the gorgeous antique vestments of the Patriarch; he was just departing to change into some other vestments. I had seen a photo of him, in the afternoon paper, arriving at the church. He'd arrived in his Mercedes, which had struck me as odd at the time – a grander mode of arrival surely than that of the pregnant lady who now gazed calmly down at him from below the organ pipes. There was a faint smile on her face, not unlike that of Verochka in the photograph, as though waiting for something to happen.

Suddenly it happened. A voice sang:

> '*Dominus dixit ad me:*
> *Filius meus es tu,*
> *Ego hodie genui te.*'

> *The Lord said to Me:*
> *Thou art my Son,*
> *I have begotten Thee this day.*

It was midnight. The Midnight Mass could begin; which, with the return of the Patriarch, even more gorgeously attired, and to a perfectly glorious Gregorian chant, it did. In a moment, the chant was drowned by a wild clanging of bells and a thrilling peal from the organ, which had practically every hair on my head standing up. The miracle had occurred. He had been born.

Simultaneously, a semicircle of words lit up in blue above the organ pipes: GLORIA IN EXCELSIS DEO; and a Star of David flashed alight in electric bulbs overhead. The Star of David? A second blink showed that it was not. It was another six-pointed star, a representation of the one that had directed the Magi to this place. At the identical moment, it seemed to have directed me to one. I was still prickling all over with the miracle; and I got it then, or perhaps a moment later, when the procession of priests passed. Words were entwined in the embroidered hems of their silk garments, and I screwed my head sideways to read the words and, as I did so, recalled an earlier occasion when I had screwed my head sideways to read words.

The Gloria was succeeded by the Alleluia and the Gospel and the Credo; and then the Sanctus and the Benedictus and the Agnus Dei – marvellous all of them, not much marred by the Patriarch passing by with a doll in his arms.

'Why are you smiling?' Marta said to me.

'The miracle.'

'You don't believe in miracles.'

'I do.'

The Patriarch went below to put the doll back in the cave while Lauds went on. They went on for a long time. It was after two when we streamed out.

'What was the problem with carotene?' Ham said, yawning, as we went down the hill.

'You can't get chutney out of it.'

'So?'

'You get something else.'

'Okay, I'll buy it. What?'

'God knows,' I said happily, which was true enough. I didn't, anyway. I thought I might, though, after a bit of a nap. It looked as if I'd only have a bit of one. Lots to do on Christmas Day, and tidings of joy for some, I shouldn't wonder.

9

I skipped breakfast and just had a cup of coffee while waiting for Ze'ev to pick me up. I'd rung Beylis as soon as I'd got up, but he was in the shower and I couldn't be bothered to wait. I was aflame with my idea and wanted to check it immediately.

'SUPPER – NO CHUTNEY' were the words in the margin; but in the body of the thing it had said something else. It had said, 'He wishes for GREENYARD'S PICKLES – CHUTNEY.' Well, he hadn't. That was obvious. She had heard him say Grignard, and assumed it to be chutney; as I'd assumed the Star of Bethlehem to be the Star of David. But she had hung on to her assumption for rather longer.

Christmas Day was a workday at the Institute, and also at the House. Connie called down the stairs as soon as I arrived.

'Igor – is that you?'

'Yes.'

'Professor Beylis on the phone. You called him?'

'Coming.'

I raced up the stairs and took the phone in her room.

'Emanuel?'

'Yes.'

'Rejoice, Emanuel!' I commanded.

'I am always ready,' he said equably. 'About what should I rejoice?'

'In the glory and mystery of carotene.'

'I rejoice in it.'

'When did Weizmann work with it?'

'Did I say that he did?'

'*I* am saying that he did.'

'Oh, it's a quiz. Let me think.'

'When would he have had occasion?'

'Well, as I've told you, the authority is Kuhn, and Kuhn came to it through vitamins while working with Willstätter on protein, so –'

'But we found nothing then. When else?'

'There is an else, is there?'

'There must be an else. It isn't a quiz, Emanuel. I need to know when he *could* have worked on it.'

'Well, carotene is a pigment. Colouring matter,' he said slowly. 'But that would have been very early on.'

'It could have been very early on.'

'In that case, perhaps ... his dyestuff work. I don't know.'

'When did his dyestuff work go on till?'

'Oh, about 1910.'

'And when did it start?'

'That's how he did start.'

'What – the turn of the century?'

'That sort of period.'

Ten years, then. 'Where did he do most of it?' I said.

'In Manchester. He did dozens of papers there.'

'What's that – 1904?'

'Yes. About then.'

Six years. 'Could he have known about Grignard then?'

'Oh, dear. Are we still with Grignard?'

'Could he?'

'Grignard, 1904? Yes. He could.'

'What could he have done with Grignard then?'

'Oh, now really, Igor, I can't do it off the top of my head. If you've got the papers there – have you got the papers there?'

'They will be here. I think so.'

'So go through them. It'll tell you – if you see the word "magnesium" somewhere, give me a ring. It might be an odd word with things in front or behind. Don't worry about that. Just look for the magnesium.'

'All right,' I said, and put the phone down. I seemed to be panting slightly.

Connie was looking at me queerly.

'What is all this?' she said.

'I want his published papers up to 1910.'

She got them for me. 'Igor, sit down. For God's sake, what is it?'

I couldn't tell her what it was. I didn't know. I took the papers from her, several sheets of them. The list started in 1899 with a paper in German. I went carefully with my finger down the first page and stopped.

'Organomagnesiumbromides.'

It was at the end of a line, and I went to the beginning.

The Action of Anhydrides of Organomagnesiumbromides.
Samuel Shrowder PICKLES and Charles WEIZMANN.
Proc. Chem. Soc., 1904, 20201. Chem. Zentr., 1905, I, 236.

'Oh, my God!' I said.

'*What?*' Connie said, in something of a frenzy.

'He wanted Pickles.'

'What pickles?'

'Samuel Shrowder Pickles.'

'What? *What?*' On her neat little legs she was now jumping.

'He didn't want chutney.'

'You know he didn't. He wanted Grignard.'

'He wanted *Pickles*. He wanted the Grignard he'd *done* with Pickles.'

'Igor, what are you *talking* about?'

'Oh, dear. Oh, dear me!' I said, suddenly shocked. I'd just remembered something else, something absolutely incredible. I said, 'Connie, we've got volume 3 of the published letters, haven't we?'

Connie silently picked the volume off a shelf and gave me it, and I opened to the index. Pickles, S. S. page 342.

I turned to page 342.

Manchester, 13 September 1904

Dear Verochka

I have as a matter of fact decided not to write any more but to wait until you get around to sending me a letter, as incidentally you promised in your last postcard. Since my return from Vienna I have been writing regularly, either every day or every other day . . .

I looked up at Connie with staring eyes. I'd read this letter even before I'd left London. I'd not only read it, I'd written it, in Russian, for little Kaplan in Manchester.

There remains little to write about myself. My days and weeks are very monotonous, consisting entirely of laboratory work, and this is progressing very well. The end of the vacation is already approaching and people are gradually coming back. Perkin's assistant arrived the other day. His name is Pickles. It's four days since we began working together, and I am very pleased. In the first place there is a human being with whom one can exchange a few words during the day. Secondly, I can talk to him in English, which is extremely useful . . .

Connie read to the end, and looked at me. From my jumbled remarks, and from the letter, she had evidently made some kind of assessment. She reached for a packet of cigarettes, gave me one and herself one, and lit them.

'Have we got anything on him?' I said.

'I doubt it.' We were still staring at each other, and for some reason talking in hushed voices. 'I mean, why would we? Is that all he did with him?'

I looked at the list again. There was another paper with Pickles.

Halogen Derivatives of Naphthacenquinone.
Samuel Shrowder PICKLES and Charles WEIZMANN.
Proc. Chem. Soc., 1904, 20220. Chem. Zentr., 1905, I, 364.

That was all. He'd done a couple of papers with Perkin's assistant.

'Well, I'll see. Maybe – There's a pile of old correspondence somewhere. It's from when the researchers were looking into sources. They made a general inquiry for letters in Manchester. It was sometime like the early 1960s.'

'Where is it?'

'Well, let me think. There is old stuff in that storeroom next to Harold upstairs. I will look into it.'

While she did, I looked into something else. I had an elusive impression: some other thing I'd read about Pickles, somewhere, at some time. Where? I hunted the shelves for Weizmann's own autobiographical notes, found a copy, dog-eared, no index. I thumbed through his Manchester days, his first days at the university, with the place almost to himself. Yes.

With this complete absence of distraction my work progressed rather well, and when Professor Perkin returned about six or seven weeks after our first interview, I was glad to have something to show him. He seemed pleased and was most encouraging. I had as my assistant a young demonstrator by the name of Pickles, a Lancashire boy with a massive North Country accent. He was an extremely likeable fellow, whose only defect was his illusion that he could speak German.

Connie returned just in time to see my expression. She didn't say anything, but read where my finger was still placed. She didn't say anything then, either.

'Do you think his German would make a cat laugh?' I said.

'Well, I – I guess so.'

'It's him, Connie.'

'But — we have been searching Bradford. This is Manchester.'

'Connie, it's him. I know it.'

'Igor, stop shaking. Sit down. I'm having the storeroom cleared. If there's anything there, we will soon know it. I will get you coffee.'

While she did it, I phoned Emanuel. He took down the details and said he'd call me back. Then I went to Chaimchik's room and concentrated on the memorandum.

There was not now such an enormous area to concentrate on. With so many of the missing details supplied, the thing was beginning to read like a scenario, almost a comedy of errors. By only a small exercise of the imagination, it was possible to insert the stage directions.

He'd started off in fine style, pointing out that Vava's apparent or projected difficulties with carotene could be turned to good account, could even become the 'trigger to tremendously increased yields'; but almost immediately had run into the snarl-up with Grignard and Pickles.

No doubt confused by his grumbling over the milk, Miss Knowall had assumed he was still issuing general food directions. He had triumphantly remembered Grignard and Pickles, and she had triumphantly translated it into a short order evidently for immediate execution.

NEW PAGE:

(*Flourishes; summonses; enter Secretary.*)

Start. Where have you been?
(*She'd been to see Nurse.*)

We have had —
(*Enter Nurse on cue.*)

Nurse, I am busy.
(*Smiling Nurse archly dangles chutney before fractious Patient.*)

What do I want with it? Of course I don't want it. Idiots.
(*Secretary throws look at Nurse; Nurse throws bigger one at Secretary, and exits.*)

So write . . . Certainly a very large conversion to methyl. He has the lab books himself. You will get the book for me . . . I will rest a little and tell you.
(*Confusion on part of Secretary. Has dreaded short order been mooted again? Exit Secretary, scratching head with pencil.*)

NEW PAGE:

(*Flourishes; summonses; enter Secretary.*)

There can be no doubt that with the methyl already present together with the carotene that it is the answer to the problem. There is no doubt. Later I will tell you . . . You will get me it . . . I have told you.
Secretary's eyes roll; head swims; tremulous enquiry session produces quick flurry of capitals: CROMER-LE-POYTH, LE-ROY-PARMA, COONE FIRTH

Tell Nurse the teeth.
(*Exit Secretary, not knowing whether on knee or elbow, and returns with Nurse, who supplies, or makes adjustments to, Teeth; after which several coherent paragraphs.*)

NEW PAGE:

(*Enter Secretary.*)

I have been thinking.
(*Secretary studies Patient; enquires if thought to any purpose.*)

Of course, idiot. Write down.
(*Irascibility indicates further exchanges as to short order: petrified Secretary doesn't know whether to write it down or not; doesn't; awaits enlightenment.*)

Perhaps the Bradford people will be able to let us know . . . I will think again later.
(*Further musing as to present location of short order emboldens Secretary to further attempt; exits.*)

(*Enter Secretary, nervously.*)

Write.
(*Enter Nurse, also nervously, with pot of authentic Green-yard's to tempt capricious palate.*)

What? What is it with these lunatics? How many times?
(*Exit Nurse, throwing huge look at Secretary, who writes quick marginal note banning all short orders, and stoically disregards further requests. Maddened Patient retires into reverie.*)

That German would make a cat laugh. Never mind, he will prove the best internationalist of us all.

Well, that must have been the way of it, and I was still musing when Connie came in with a dusty box file. It was marked 'Manchester', and in it was a bulging mass of papers.

The Manchester period had proved a knotty one for the researchers. With almost nine years of letters missing, a special effort had been thrown in. There were dozens of interviews with people who'd known him (including little Kaplan), recollections of old students. He'd shifted lodgings a good deal in his early days, and attics and cellars had been scoured with a little but not much result. A Professor G. N. Burckhardt, senior tutor of the university's organic chemistry department, had undertaken to check all university documents, and a lengthy correspondence had followed.

The chemistry department had been known as Owens College in Weizmann's day, and there were various abstracts from annual college reports in which his name figured (as Dr Charles Weizmann, his *nom de guerre* at the university). Burckhardt had also, from other records, compiled his own list of all those who must have worked with him. Several question-and-answer letters showed him digging up further particulars on specific people, with whom the researchers had then established their own communications. But nobody had raised any queries about Pickles. He was there, however, modestly, in the middle of a list, unticked, unringed, unqueried.

PICKLES, S. S. B. 15 Apr. 1878. 1st Class Hons. Chemistry, Man U. 1903. M.Sc. 1906. D.Sc. 1908. Research assist. Prof. Perkin. Subsequent Career: Research Chemist to Spencer Moulton & Co., Bradford-on-Avon, Wilts. D. 12 Feb. 1962

'Bradford, *Wilts*?' Connie said.
'It's another county, Wiltshire.'
'Oh, well. That makes twelve of them.'
'Yes.'
'D. 1962.'
'Quite.' As with Vava.
We looked silently at the spare obituary, and I thought again of the empty university in the summer of 1904, and the pair of them working away in the basement, Chaimchik trying out his English, and the likeable fellow his German. How differently their subsequent careers had gone: one embarking on the fierce tide that had carried him to a state funeral and the grassy plot below, the other on the quieter waters of the Avon to Spencer Moulton & Co. – and perhaps a grassy plot in Wilts.
Connie's phone rang. She answered it and called me. Emanuel's voice at the other end was rather subdued.
'Well, nothing doing,' he said.
'No carotene?'
'Not a trace.'
'And the other paper?'
'Quite impossible.'
'But there must be something – '
'I agree,' he said. Definitely something strange in his voice. I said, 'What is it?'
'Finster has found something. Something very odd.'

The three of us examined it. The fermented liquid wasn't the colourless stuff I'd seen before, and it didn't smell as nice. It looked like a jar of cider, and it smelled rank.

'What's wrong?' I said.

'This is not so easy to say,' Finster said.

'Hasn't it produced what you thought?'

'Far more than we thought!'

The bacterium from Paris was a later generation of the one used by Vava, but anything its ancestor could do it could do better. It had practically torn the soul out of the potato. It had done it at ferocious speed, and had even tried to come back for more. ('Traces of secondary fermentation' was Finster's explanation of the phenomenon.) In the process it had produced several unwanted and at the moment inexplicable properties, which had actually brought an abrupt shift downward in the octane number. With Vava's batatas the shift would occur on a massive scale.

I watched the puzzled frowns of the scientists in a mood of some serenity. On every point where it had been possible to check, Chaimchik had come up trumps. He'd said there was correspondence with Vava, and despite a baffling lack of copies, correspondence there had been. He had said the process depended on two stages. Evidently it did. He had foretold a problem with carotene. One had just surfaced. And he'd also said that the problem carried its own solution.

That looked like the next, and last, operation.

I sat with Beylis a bit later while he pored over the work of Kuhn. He impatiently flipped papers aside after reading, and I glanced at them.

Investigations into the Structure of Long-Chain Compounds Containing Conjugate Double Bonds: The Polyenes and

Diphenylpolyenes Connected with the Chemical Nature of Carotenoids.

Heavy stuff, Kuhn.

All the same, the phrases that made any sense made cheering sense rather than otherwise. As he had got older and investigated his subject more deeply, Kuhn had come to the conclusion that he knew practically nothing about it. The honest man had said so:

> The fat-soluble yellow colouring materials, so widely spread through nature, and with a role evidently vital . . . A universality which seems to bespeak some basic but as yet unknown significance . . .

Strange stuff, the stuff in carrots that helped you see in the dark; and more of it about, evidently, than folks knew.

Meyer slammed his phone down and looked at me. He'd scowled horribly to hear of such long-chain compounds containing conjugate double bonds.

'What the hell was that?' he said.

'Well, you insisted on hearing. They don't understand it.'

'Do *you* understand it?'

'No, I don't understand it.'

'So who understands it?'

'Nobody. That's the point. They're all dead,' I said. 'Kuhn's dead. He spent a lifetime trying to understand it. Vava's dead. He never began to. Weizmann's dead. He'd *just* begun to. And Pickles is dead. He wasn't even aware of it. But the answers are in his lab books.'

'Lab books,' Meyer said, grasping at something concrete. 'Where are they?'

'Perhaps the Bradford people will be able to let us know.'

He looked at me sharply.

'I will think again later,' I quoted further.

I couldn't tell if he knew I was quoting. I couldn't tell if he knew he was doing it himself when after a moment or two he spoke. He spoke briefly and meditatively. 'It's a funny world,' he said with a sigh.

I did think later. I thought for most of the night. It was a noisy night. A man called Dr Foka Hirsch was having a Christmas party. He had it at his country home at Caesarea. Foka Hirsch was a bachelor, a rich elderly bachelor, the local agent for Vickers Armstrong, and he liked to keep in touch with the scientific establishment. I'd been to his parties before. I wasn't a very convivial guest at this one.

I tied things up next day, and went back the one after. I made my farewells the evening before and spent half an hour with Meyer: He told me the young man from Africa was confident of the virility of his plant and knew it would respond to forcing. He anticipated taking ten cuttings from it within three months, and ten from each of these within another three. By next winter, he thought he would have several thousand for planting out.

We had a drink on this, and then I went to Jaffa and had another with Connie and Marta. We dined at Jaffa, and afterwards I bought a caftan. Connie ran Marta back first (a fond but decorous farewell), then she ran me back.

It was December 18th that I had arrived in Israel, and the twenty-seventh that I left. In the air it suddenly struck me that last week I'd never heard of Vava's batatas, or ketones, or the Grignard reaction. If I was on the way now to becoming a world expert, it was only because there weren't any others. It was in some ways a disturbing thought. The man next to me was reading a newspaper. The headline said, 'ARABS WARN: NO INTERFERENCE'. Definitely disturbing.

3

The early-afternoon plane turned out, in the normal way, to be a late-afternoon one. It was nearly ten o'clock before I debouched wearily from the taxi in Russell Square. I went up to my seventh-floor eyrie, trudged along the corridor, put my key in the door, and paused. Someone was inside.

My thoughts flew immediately to St Mary and St Joseph and to Terre Haute. I left the key in the lock and very carefully put my bags down. The memorandum and my notes were in the small executive case. At the end of the corridor was the fire cupboard, with its cylinders, buckets, and hose. I padded down to it, placed the case in conceal-ment, and returned.

Having done this, it occurred to me that with or without the case, eyes could still be made to cross. I cleared my throat, coughed, and, with my heart unpleasantly pound-ing, unlocked the door and, leaving it open, went inside. All the lights were on. The sound was coming from the kitchen, and I went there, my bag at the ready.

She was just shutting the fridge door, having evidently got some ice for a long gin and tonic. She was in a dressing gown.

'Caroline?' I said.

'Hello.'

'What are you doing here?'

'Oh, well.' She'd had a bath, and also washed her hair. It was clinging damply to her head, giving her a rather furtive, not to say guttersnipe, look. She was looking guilty, anyway. She licked her lips. 'I thought you'd put it off till tomorrow. It got late. I thought you weren't coming.'

'Aren't you supposed to be at Willie's?'

'Things got difficult at Willie's.'

'But – '

'I gave Antonia my flat, over Christmas. She's got her bloke there.'

'Oh. But won't your parents – '

'Well, I can't go there. I'm at Willie's.'

'I see. Yes. I see,' I said.

'You can put your case down now,' she said. 'You're there. How was orange-blossom land?' She was recovering herself, and I saw that the guilt and resentment very probably had as their source the fact that she was drunk.

'Hang on a minute,' I said, and put down my case. I retraced my steps, and returned with the other, cautiously thinking over the matter.

'Something wrong with the flight?' she said.

'Yes. Delays.'

'Do you want anything to eat?'

'Not really.'

'Well, now.'

'I brought you a caftan.'

'That's nice.' She was looking definitely stoned.

'How many have you had?' I said.

'Several. How many would you like?'

'I'll have one, just for now.'

She got it while I took my coat off. 'Go and have a wash,' she said as I did this. 'You look horrible. Saturnine.'

I went and had a wash, still working the matter out. A logistical problem had to be worked out.

The drink was awaiting my return: a whisky with water.

'And stop looking so bloody worried, as well as saturnine,' she said. 'You appeared as what I would describe as thunderstruck on arrival.'

'I didn't know it would be you.'

'Who did you – Oh.' She became alert. 'Have you gone and made an assignation?'

'No. You silly cow,' I said irritably.

'Well, that's all right, then. Silly cow, eh?' She seemed rather pleased with this. 'Go on. Abuse me. Feel free. On the other hand, a scheduled arrival would have presented you with a composed person, respectably seeking a night's shelter. A proper request, understandable situation. Is how it seemed to me, on giving it thought, which I did, after checking flight times. However . . . usual balls-up.' She took an enormous glug at her drink.

I sat down and took one at mine. We watched each other. 'How was it?' she said.

'Busy. How was yours?'

'Fucking awful.'

'I'm sorry.'

'So kind. I'd curtsy if I wasn't sure to fall over. You'd be surprised at how much kindness there is in the world. Do you know what I was doing while you were watching by night? I was wrapping little bloody gifts for about two million old ladies. You wouldn't credit the number of old ladies they keep alive round there. They all live in these little homes, and they smile like this, and you smile back, and – oh, yes, we had the *waits*. Have your English studies led to waits?'

'Waits?'

'Carol singers. You've got to be extra jolly with them; times have changed, unlike old ladies. "Had to reach down for that one, Charlie, bottom of the barrel, ha-ha, ho-ho – " Ch-rist! And Mama shows you how to do everything, and Papa so affable, and everybody so – bloody – unremittingly – kind.'

'You're not marrying the family, Caroline.'

'I have special news for you, Igor, Tovarich. I am not marrying any bloody one of them.'

'You just left?'

'In fact, yes. I rang Antonia, and she rang me back.'

'Hmm.'

'Not good, eh? I wasn't there four days,' she said wonderingly. 'Well, it's a pity.'

'Isn't it? How was Connie?'

'Fine. Love, et cetera.'

'Did Mr Meltzer like his cigars?'

'Oh, yes.'

'Did Mr Weisgal like your work?'

'I think so.'

'Do you like me?'

'Yes.'

A slight pause set in.

'Was the Vava nonsense solved?' she asked.

'Partially.'

'More letters around?'

'I'll have to explain later. I'm tired.'

'Go to bed.'

'I will presently. It's been a long day.'

'For me, too. I'm exhausted. Mentally exhausted.'

'How's Hopcroft?' I asked.

'Sparkling. I bought him a new case. He hasn't got it yet. They're doing his initials.'

'That was nice, Caroline.'

'I am nice.'

'Were you nice enough to ring my mother?'

'Oh, yes. Without response. An unresponsive family, yours.'

'Oh.' I'd forgotten. Just in the same moment I remembered. I'd looked in on my father in the last scrambled hours before Israel. He'd told me there was some trouble at their country house, the central heating, the double glazing. They'd gone away for Christmas, too. I remembered him huddled over the electric fire in his Gower Street flat, studying his memoirs. He was stuck somewhere, 1935. A whole weight of things suddenly came back on me, and I finished off my drink rather suddenly.

'Want another?'

'Well . . .'

'I'm having one.' She swallowed hers in an enormous gulp and took both glasses. I looked after her uneasily. Definitely some difficulties ahead.

'To set your mind at rest,' she said, returning with the glasses, 'you will be sleeping in your bed.'

'What are you going to do?'

'I will be sleeping in it, too.'

'Oh.'

'I'm certainly not sleeping on the bloody sofa.'

'Well, in that case – '

'And nor are you. It's an enormous bed. I won't rape you. You silly cow,' she said. 'Are you sure you don't want something to eat?'

'No.'

'Well, gobble that off, and let's get there. I'm dead.'

In the bedroom she took off her dressing gown and found she didn't have anything on underneath. With notions of propriety she stumbled about, swearing a little, and unpacked a nightie. I brushed my teeth and got into my pyjamas, then into bed.

'Good night,' she said.

'Good night.' I switched the light off.

'I'm sorry about this,' she said after a while.

'Go to sleep.'

'No, but damn it, it's awful. I didn't mean this at all. I was just feeling rather desperate, and now it's got worse. Say something like "Good night, Caroline, darling," and it would be better.'

'Good night, Caroline, darling.'

'You could throw in a hug while you're at it, just to show you're not in a raving bloody temper.'

I threw her one, and also a kiss.

'That's all right, then. Good night, Igor,' she said, and tried to throw a quick one in herself as I moved away, and missed.

Whether from the drink taken or the exhaustion mentioned, she went off to sleep almost immediately. When I woke in the night, I found her still sleeping, quite neatly, on her own side. She wasn't there in the morning. It was quite late. I heard her in the bathroom.

I lay quietly listening, and filled my eyes with grey London skies, and heard the buses passing below. A world away, under blue skies, a white house sat, armies were locked, Finster fermented, and part of the carbon cycle was having its shiny wart forced into life. All a long way away, that freewheeling lunacy. But in the grey North other kinds hadn't stopped. From the bathroom a bump sounded, and an expletive rang. This was the kind that called for immediate attention.

10

'Carry on about carotene,' Caroline said.

She was sitting in the caftan. She'd taken a couple of Alka-Seltzers but still looked slightly stunned.

'Are you taking all this in?' I said.

'Everything is going in. There is nothing I'm not experiencing this morning.'

'Because I couldn't bear to tell it again.'

'Well, all this energy is going round on a – or, rather, in a cycle, and if you know how to you can plug in on it with sweet potatoes.'

'Among other things,' I said.

'Quite. But what is so sweet about this potato is it grows in useless sorts of places, particularly where millions of poor people are starving away. All you have to have is this bug that eats it, because nobody else will, and it turns it into petrol.'

'Ketones.'

'Exactly. And they've cleverly found all this, except it also makes a lot of rubbish that's hard to get rid of, including something I'm not clear on – carotene, which at one and the same time is useless but also terribly useful in solving everybody's problems.'

'Well. Very good,' I said; which it surprisingly was. She was clumsy this morning, and banging herself, but seemed in good order aloft. 'I don't understand the carotene, either, but few people do, if any. The theory seems to be that it's not so much the carotene as the *presence* of the carotene.' This seemed mad even as I said it. 'Anyway, for what it's worth, find a suitable catalyst – Do you know about catalysts?'

'They change things.'

'Exactly. Find one of those and it changes this stuff – transforms it, you see; converts it; sort of triggers it, like – well, I don't know.'

'An atom bomb.'

'Yes. You're bright this morning.'

'Well, I know about those. I've got one of those.' She was holding her head. 'They do trigger away.'

'So that where you get the carotene with methyl – or is it ethyl? – this whole transformation scene takes place. All the stuff that you don't want turns into the stuff that you do want.'

'The Pickles Effect.'

'Yes.'

'And that's it, is it? Or is there more?'

'That's it. Doesn't it seem strange enough?'

She considered a moment. 'It will do. It will seem stranger, that is. Everything seems strange now. You do. Your face is quite abnormal. Your teeth flash when you trigger away, did you realize?'

'No.' I looked at her. The face that had seemed so unmemorable was really quite memorable; slightly lop-sided and pale like a slice of moon, and of lunar humour; eyes a bit flat and dead at the moment, but evidently in good working order.

'Oh, God. Are you going to say something pissy about my face?'

'A bit hung over. Nothing terrible.'

'Some leftover of Dracula's.'

'Well, I wasn't really . . .' The chubbier and altogether merrier face of Sheik Yamani caught my eye, in the newspaper on which the percolator was resting. Seraphic as ever, he was somewhere else, still hilariously regretting. A wave of something suddenly hit me. The incredible series of events that had brought this son of the sands, like an imp from a bottle, from desert wastes to the ingenious cities of the West was surely more and not less fantastic than anything in Chaimchik's memo.

Yet the intuitive man had foreseen it, had clearly vizualized the situation at a time when, as Meyer said, 'their asses were hanging out'. He had worked out the alternative, scientifically, logically, and left time to work its madness for the necessary emergency.

I had the strangest feeling that I was reading the thing in a history of the period: 'The grave economic crises of the Seventies, and the reliance of the industrialized nations on a stable source of . . .'

I shook my head sharply.

'Oh, don't do that,' Caroline said.

Her flat eyes were still gazing at me, narrowed with pain.

'It can all happen, Caroline!'

'Any bloody thing can happen. But just don't do that again. You didn't bring an orange, did you?'

'I did, actually. Well, mandarins.' Connie had plucked them, leaves attached, while I bade Marta farewell not many hours ago. They were still buried in my bag.

'Oh, well, my God, mandarins! How I need a mandarin!'

I got her one, and she sniffed the leaves, and popped the peel, and crooned over it, holding it in both hands, like a holy chalice.

I saw Kammermann at four, a tiny corpse-like figure of over ninety. It scarcely seemed worth shunting him to Switzerland. Still, he'd always hung on, had Kammermann, a close and cautious man, which had been his value to Chaimchik as a confidant. He'd hung on to his upper storey, too, rather remarkably, and remembered quite a lot. But the only real interest in him was his papers.

I managed to win cautious assent to Rehovot having them 'in due time'. But he wouldn't actually sign anything to say so. Still, as a parting look confirmed, the time couldn't be long delayed, so I left Brown's not dissatisfied. The papers were from the early Thirties, and therefore my papers; not a wasted journey, like his. Except could his journey be said to be wasted if on the way he'd met me? There was a random quality to life that it was tempting to see as its chief quality, unless one bumped into men like Chaimchik. Would a speeded-up version of his life not show the random events forming a pattern, if one were in a pattern-making mood?

2

'How long has Antonia got your flat?'

'Till Monday.' It was now Friday night, and we were having a meal out. 'Why?'

'Because my father's is only round the corner. Nobody in it.'

'I'd bloody freeze there, wouldn't I?'

'I was thinking I could do it.'

'Ah, my leprosy. I see.'

'I was thinking of old Ettie.'

'Well, bugger old Ettie. Oh. *Compromising* me, you mean!'

'Well – '

'Why is it, I wonder, that I am surrounded by such gallant chaps? I scarcely slept with Willie, you know.'

'No good?'

'Well. He had trauma on the few occasions. I wonder what it is about me?' she said curiously.

'Perhaps he thought you were too nice.'

'Too nice for what? And what can you mean about Ettie? She won't turn up till Monday. What *is* it about everything? I never seem to find out. There's Antonia having a wild time with practically – Well, I wouldn't like that. But I'm normal. Aren't I?'

'Your chaps seem bent on marriage.'

'Well, that's true. But why should it put people off having a try? I mean, they have. I'm not vestal. Wrong ones, though, in general – either terrible drips or gallants.'

'Perhaps your definitions are too strict. All gallants, all drips? Nothing in between?'

'You mean my beady and selective eye puts them off?'

I groaned inwardly. 'Oh, look, Caroline – '

'Yes, I know, all right. It's a bloody bore, isn't it? Well, if you want to go to your father's, you can.'

'Not if you'd feel insulted. But it's odd sleeping with a girl without having relations. And our relations are terribly good already,' I added quickly, 'and individual and rare, and it would be a crime to spoil all that for something not so individual or rare, which it would – however madly desirable the notion certainly is,' I said, to keep her end up. 'And you know I'm a bit of a trifler in that direction – you've pointed it out.'

'Hmm. Well. I do see that,' she said reflectively, and had a sip of wine. 'It isn't that you've got another occupant lined up for trifling with, is it, in one or other of these beds?'

'I've told you not.'

'That's all right, then. I only want to lie out in one. On the other hand, I'm not going to chase you out of yours. I could go to a hotel, I suppose, if it came to the point.'

This seemed a reasonable point to get to, but I said, 'Don't be silly, Caroline.'

'All right. Well, subdue the beast and keep us rare and individual. I'll have to do something about Willie, damn it. That wasn't good. He'll be ringing up Antonia – perhaps my parents. I'd better phone him, and also get off a fast letter.'

'Do you want to do all that now?'

'No. What I wouldn't mind doing now is watching a picture. I feel like slouching somewhere and not thinking too hard.'

We went and slouched at the pictures and returned to Russell Square and I pensively opened the door.

'It's a bit late for ringing people up, isn't it?' she said.

'It is a bit.'

'Oh, well. Beddy-byes. Are you coming?'

'Shortly.'

'Oh, look, you'll make me feel most hideously self-conscious. Don't skulk about somewhere while I'm getting undressed. You've seen as much of my physique as is possible without instruments. If we're going to keep it free and easy . . .'

'All right.'

We went into the bedroom and undressed.

'No books here,' she said chattily. 'Don't you read in bed?'

'Not much. Ettie removes them.'

'Strange. I keep piles . . . Do you have a bath at night?' she asked from the bathroom.

'No. Do I seem to need one?'

'Simple interest.'

We smoked a cigarette, sitting up in bed, and she gnawed a nail and worried about Willie. 'It is bloody awful, isn't it? I feel terrible.'

'Well, it's done now.'

'He'll feel such an idiot. And he's a nice bloke. He really is. I got the whole boiling at once, Christmas and everything. Just wasn't for me. Gosh, it's ghastly, isn't it? I wasn't there four days. I hadn't even arrived, last week at this time. What were you doing last week, this time?'

What had I been doing, last week at this time? Friday night. I had commenced my long Sabbath. I'd patrolled the haunted House with Old Taylor. About now, I'd been sitting by the kerosene stove in Chaimchik's room, feeling the indentations in the notebooks and poring over little Miss Margalit's transcript . . . CROMER-LE-POYTH, LE-ROY-PARMA, COONE FIRTH. Only a week ago?

She quietly listened as I told her.

'Can't you wangle me a trip next time.'

'I'll try.'

'All right. I'm going down now. Good night.'

'Good night.' I put the light off.

'You can fling in a quick cuddle.'

I flung one in.

'Also one of your lighter kisses, accompanied by a "Good night, Caroline, darling."'

'Not too drunk to remember?'

'Oh, no. I threw you a light one, too, I recall. Lips smacked air.' She smacked them again. 'You can have them now,' she said, and placed them on my cheek. She placed them quite lightly, but she left them there, and presently made small movements with them.

'It's the small of my back that neels rubbing,' she said drowsily.

I rubbed it, for some time.

'Why have you stopped?'

'I thought you were asleep.'

'Not yet. Beautifully soothing. Carry on till the first snore.'

I carried on.

'Nightie not in your way, is it?' she said.

There was no answer to this, so I silently raised it, and continued rubbing – evidently too beautifully.

'Yes, well,' she said, rather more alertly, 'this thing will very likely strangle me in the night. Hang on.' She wriggled away, and came back, without it.

Oh, well.

'You're not roasting in that great uniform?' she said.

'They're normal pyjamas.'

'My goodness, you're buttoned up to the chin. Almost to the ears. You're like a Red Guard,' she said. 'You'll incinerate. Very unhealthy.' She undid a button, and then another, and slipped her hand in.

'That's much better, isn't it?'

'Yes.'

'Of course it is.' She snuggled herself back in place. 'Well, it's more or less totally delicious,' she said. 'Carry on, then.'

The first snore seemed evidently now well at bay. After a while she said in my ear, 'Beast subdued?'

'Trying.'

'Beasts have to be subdued.'

'I know.'

'Nature ordains.'

'Quite.'

'Wisely providing the means.'

Well, people couldn't be expected to keep their word about bed, and as Chaimchik had said, contests against determined forces had a predetermined end. But I was struck by her single-minded cunning, and she mistook the pause for dim-wittedness.

'What I was thinking was that if that were a rightful object of the evening, the means of subjugation are close at hand, if you had another hand, and where the hell is it?'

I produced the other hand.

'Exactly. You gormless, half-witted, imbecilic – oh, God, darling.'

The normal developments ensued, not too expertly at first but improving in the course of the evening's objects, and satisfyingly enough, but I thought sadly I'd probably lost free and hoydenish Caroline, innocent swearing companion, and only gained a lover.

3

Saturday rolled on (in much the same rolling way as last Saturday, it occurred to me during the course of it) and so did Sunday. Monday brought Ettie and Hopcroft, the latter bushy and sparkling as ever. 'Welcome home, and all well round at the old brain box, then?' he said.

'Fine. You look restored to manly vigour, Hopcroft.'

'Oh, sure. Glad to get the papers and so on and so forth, were they?'

'Very. It was nice of Olga to send them.'

'I knew she would. She's a good old horse. I rang her up over Christmas, incidentally. She's still a bit cut up. Continuing ructions on the marital front. That old man of hers – mad as a hatter.'

'What's up with him?'

'Bonkers. He rang her up Christmas Eve, raving that she'd wrecked the joint, out of spite. You know – Merry Christmas, you fiend.'

'Wrecked the joint?'

'Wimbledon. He'd had a break-in, apparently, and jumped to the conclusion she was behind it.'

'I see,' I said. 'When was this?'

'He wasn't sure. He'd been away and popped back for something and found the place in this state of chaos, drawers out, papers everywhere. He rang her up, frothing.'

'Was anything taken?'

'Well, he didn't know what she had taken, you see. He thought she'd just gone on the rampage. Screaming that he was going to put the police on to her, and on to that driver of hers. All very upsetting for the poor old thing. I think it would be quite a nice idea if you went to see her, really. I mean, she has been jumping about rather for us.'

'Yes, I was thinking that.' I had been, but I now thought of it a good deal more seriously. The thick-ear, not to say cross-eye, aspects of the sweet-potato question had tended to recede over the past couple of days, and now came on again, very strongly. There was the question of what to tell Hopcroft, anyway. His yarning tendencies made particular disclosures unwise; on the other hand, with lab books to be pursued and eye-crossers still operating, non-disclosure was still less wise.

'She's not actually on top line yet, anyway,' he said

while I paused, 'as Caroline might have told you. Oh, she won't have blown in yet, will she? She's in Hampshire.'

She'd actually not long before blown out, to attend to her flat. 'She mentioned on the phone that she'd found her a bit odd,' I said.

'Ah. Odd? Hmm. A touch fey, I would say. Not a jot of harm in her. Verochka was actually a relation of hers, you know.'

'So I learned at Rehovot.'

'I meant to tell you that day at the hospital. I knew there was something. Well, back to the old routine, I suppose.' He was ruefully emptying a battered old briefcase.

'I wouldn't mind popping down to Swiss Cottage this morning,' I said.

'Ah, well, she isn't there. At this friend's, you see, at Frognal. I expect she's gone back to work, anyway. Want me to give her a tinkle?'

Hopcroft gave a couple of tinkles, to Frognal and to University College Hospital, the latter more extended and producing some exclamations.

'Well, I'm blowed. Hang on just a tick, Olga . . . She'll be home this afternoon about three,' he said to me. 'Like to go then?'

'Yes.'

'Three is fine, Olga. Sure. I understand. What an absolute swine . . . Well, I never,' he said, replacing the phone. 'That chap is genuine nut-house material.'

'Which chap?'

'Her husband. Green. He's gone and done *her* place. She got back last night and found it a shambles. What a damned shame. She'd just got it sorted out. Rotter.'

'Is she sure he did it?'

'Well, crikey! Papers like confetti everywhere. Paying her back, you see. She's got the police coming round. They told her to leave everything as it was. She was apologizing for things being topsy-turvy again. Sweet old thing, really.'

'Hmm.' It seemed fortunate indeed that she'd got the papers off in time.

'Do you want me to carry on as usual, or is there anything fresh to attend to?'

'There might be,' I said.

'I expect you want to get sorted out a bit first.'

'That's it.' It was a long shot, but it seemed as well to get Olga sorted out first.

We got there before three, and Hopcroft had a little yarn with the porter, proudly showing me the recess where he had received his boff and gone over whang. Olga was on the third floor, and a detective was just leaving as we arrived. He gave us rather a keen look, and Hopcroft said, 'Quite all right. Friends of the family.' He tried to start a conversation with the detective, but the man was not communicative and went; I was shaking hands with Olga. She was a large sloppy woman in a huge knitted costume and amber beads, no trace of the family connection with Verochka showing.

'Well, it is a most malicious thing,' she said, in some bewilderment. 'To use a professional!'

'He used a professional?' Hopcroft said indignantly.

'The detective said the door had been professionally forced. Oh, to think!' There was a just discernible German accent, and the oddness showed up in a slight jerkiness, or perhaps mistiming, of gesture. She stared around at the confusion like a great tragic clown. The place certainly was a mess. Books had been tumbled off shelves, drawers hung open, papers scattered everywhere; the glass of some pictures was broken.

'Well, if we just turn to,' Hopcroft said, 'we'll have this lot back in a jiffy. It's okay to do it now, is it?'

'What can it matter? In the face of such malice,' Olga said. 'He knows how to hurt me – oh, yes, he knows. The photo with my father!' She had bent and was now clutching one, in a broken frame. I had a look at Vava with some interest. He was seated in a beach chair with a child of six or seven, presumably Olga, on his knee. The crowded background indicated a portion of the Baltic coast in the late 1920s. The child seemed to have been arrested in the act of picking her nose, and Vava in the act of restraining her. The photograph had been taken a moment too early.

In persona, Vava seemed not unlike Ollie Hardy, the fat one of Laurel and Hardy – same little moustache, same plump chops and twinkling comicality. There was a look of the tenderest affection on his face as he strove to redirect finger from nose. I could see the charm of such a photo, but it was an odd one, surely, to frame and exhibit. Perhaps it was the only one of Vava, or perhaps in the very mistiming it had caught some essential quality of his, of them both, perceived and appreciated by Olga. There was certainly cause for celebration in her own unpredictable timing in the matter of the papers.

Hopcroft had turned to meanwhile, and I gave him a hand; in a jiffy, as he'd said, the place was returning to rights, and Olga was inquiring if anyone would like soup. She had left the hospital without her lunch to meet the detective.

'Always ready for a spot of soup,' Hopcroft said, giving me a nudge. ('Lonely old thing,' he muttered in my ear.) We all had a spot.

While having it, I thanked Olga for the letters and enlarged on their importance in the general picture of the thirties, which seemed to please her.

'Is there any other correspondence, or lab books, that kind of thing?' I said.

'With Weizmann?'

'With anybody. I was wondering if the name Pickles meant anything to you.'

'Pickles. Should it?'

'Your father might have mentioned him, or there might have been correspondence.'

'Pickles. I don't remember. I could get in touch with the

oil companies he worked for. That I could certainly do,'
Olga said.

'No, no, quite unnecessary! It wasn't anything like that,'
I said, putting an immediate stopper on this one. 'I simply
wondered if *you* had anything.'

But she hadn't, and the long shot had been tried.

'Who's Pickles?' Hopcroft said as we left.

I waited till he was on the seventh floor in Russell Square,
with a glass in his hand, before I told him. He seemed
stunned when I'd finished; particularly by the fate of the
man in Terre Haute.

'I mean, crikey!' he said.

'Quite.'

'These chaps following *me*!'

'Not the same ones, Hopcroft. Couldn't be.'

'But how could they have known what I was looking
for, if I didn't?'

'Evidently from America! Have another drink.'

He had one.

'Olga's flat *not* done by her husband,' he said, bewil-
dered, the parts slowly assembling in his mind.

'Doubtful.'

'And ditto Wimbledon. Not just burgled.'

'It doesn't look like it, does it?'

'Oh, well, damn it. I mean, it makes you think.'

'Still, all's well now. The papers are safe.'

'Yes, well, I just hope they know it. It gets dark a bit
early now, doesn't it?' he said, peering out of the window.

'It's all over, Hopcroft. Cheer up.'

'Yes, but do *they* know it's over?' His bushy little
moustache was bristling and his eyes sparkling. The second
drink had stirred him. 'A chap is surely entitled to take
thought if he has to creep about not knowing who is going
to boff him next. I mean, I understand about Pickles and
starving chaps and the fate of the world, et cetera, but how
about things like police protection?'

'You can't have police following you about all over, Hopcroft. You wouldn't even want it, would you?'

'Well, there are certain obvious attractions if one is being followed at all, in knowing the chap in the rear is a policeman who is there to stop some other chap nipping in and giving one a boff. I mean, the thing is self-evident, isn't it?'

'Nobody's *going* to do it, Hopcroft. There's no reason, as I've tried to – '

'Oh, quite. I don't want to be awkward. But there was no reason before. I mean, in point of fact. I wasn't carrying the papers. *Only they didn't know it,*' he said significantly. 'Result, among other things, I couldn't see straight for a week. If I make my point. I'll have just one more, if I may. Small one.'

I poured us both one. 'Well, the reason for that was,' I said, 'that none of us knew what – '

'Yes, well, with respect,' he said, 'I doubt if reason comes in it too much. As such. These were definitely not reasonable chaps. I mean, you couldn't reason with them. I don't want to labour the point, but it was a case of whang. Whoever set them on to me – you know, field of communications not strong. In fact, weak as arseholes. I mean, they might just get into the way of following me about and hitting me whenever they see me. They definitely need switching off, these chaps,' he said urgently.

'All right, fair enough.'

'Exactly!'

'You think we ought to hold off a bit?' I said.

'No question. Also the word passed, in no uncertain terms, that no further papers are available. Case absolutely beyond hope. No point.'

'Well, I suppose I could ring up Israel.'

'If that is the quickest way. You certainly could.'

'All right.' I went to the phone and dialled international. 'What we want,' I said, recapping, 'is the information disseminated that Rehovot now has the papers.'

'All of them. None more going. All got.'

'To all interested parties in America.'

'Every man jack. I mean, ideally I would like every sodding soul in America to know it,' he said passionately. He was pouring himself another drink.

I gave Meyer's number, but this time there would be a delay of an hour. It didn't look to me as if Hopcroft was going to get through the hour. He had become rather attached to my bottle, between peering out of the window. He was stretching his legs now, to peer more closely.

'I'll tell them all that, then,' I said. 'It's been rather a trying day, Hopcroft. Why don't you take a taxi home? At the old firm's expense, of course.'

'That's very handsome. Streets still quite busy,' he said, looking out.

'Of course. It's only six o'clock.'

'Not quite as busy as normally, perhaps.'

'I'll come down with you, take a breath of fresh air,' I said.

We rode down in the lift and paced a little outside, waiting for a taxi. One came and Caroline stepped out.

'Well, hello, there. How was everything?' Hopcroft said amiably.

Caroline sniffed. 'It seems to have been fine,' she said.

'Jolly good. You won't forget any of that?' Hopcroft said, stepping in.

'Rest assured.'

'Right. Crikey!' he said, subsiding inside.

'What was that?' Caroline said as the taxi took off.

'Oh, well. Things happened today.'

'Did they?' she said. They'd happened to her, too. She had decided to go and see Willie. She'd told him what she had to tell him. She was giggling a bit in the lift, but crying when we got in the flat.

4

Hopcroft started work on Pickles without enthusiasm. He had been keeping what he described as a 'low profile.' There were certain difficulties with Pickles that there hadn't been with Vava. With Vava there had been an exchange of correspondence at a time when Weizmann was famous and it was natural that correspondence should be preserved. Here there were only lab books, and probably not even in Weizmann's writing, since in 1904 he couldn't write English.

Further, the experiments noted in the lab books had appeared to have so little practical importance that they had never been published. It was understandable that Pickles should keep them for a while – but for a lifetime? Even if he had, out of sentimental attachment, would his survivors have retained the same attachment? They were old notebooks, among perhaps dozens, scores of notebooks, now seventy years old. If it had been a long shot with Olga, this seemed an even longer one.

But yet – and here it was a question of faith – Weizmann had said that Pickles had them. He had said so in 1952. He had known about Bradford, which seemed to argue some contact. If there had been contact, and with Weizmann the luminary in the world that he had become, might the family not have retained these mementoes of an illustrious connection?

It was all very iffy, but a lot of things were.

We'd discussed all this, and Hopcroft had made somewhat gloomy preparations. He didn't want any letters written off to Bradford in case we got one back with a firm's name and address printed on it, and somebody else saw it. He had become preternaturally nervous about anyone knowing what he was doing. He'd looked up Bradford-on-Avon.

'Population 7,800,' he said.

'That sounds a copeable small place.'

'One extra would tend to show up in it, wouldn't he?' He carefully checked the area. 'Half an hour from Bath ... Bath, population 84,900. Yes, well, I know where I shall be. No need to get in touch,' he said on parting.

He hadn't been in touch himself, and he returned looking not much more cheerful.

The Pickles family had hailed from Lancashire, and he hadn't raised much in Wiltshire; still, he'd raised something. The family didn't have the lab books, but there was a recollection of them. This was because Pickles had apparently many years before given them away, to a young student or a colleague, and at some subsequent time had tried to get them back, unsuccessfully, which had rankled.

'Do we know who he gave them to?'

'Absolutely not. Vanished into a limbo.'

'But it must have been someone interested in the work. Or someone he was very fond of. He surely wouldn't have given anyone else collector's pieces after Weizmann became famous. When was it?'

'That's it, you see. Nearest estimate – donkey's years.'

'Well, as work it could have had interest only around the time it was done – not even ten years later. Dyestuffs had moved on. All that work was finished.'

'Totally. Stone cold. Dead as a doornail.'

'But if he was annoyed at not getting the books back, doesn't that imply that he knew they were around? Which presumably was after Weizmann was famous. Not make sense?'

'Yes, well,' Hopcroft blurted, 'if the thing makes such splendid sense, and there's suffering humanity, and the world economy, and geniuses in Israel, wouldn't you say a chap was entitled to a bit of help – say a small team of assistants, well-muscled?'

'Oh, come on, Hopcroft. Who is to connect Pickles with anything? Nobody could. And it wouldn't help them if they did. The thing is meaningless in itself.'

'Yes, well, that might be,' Hopcroft said, 'and I'd be just

as reasonable if I were you. But I'm not. I'm me, the one they are following. I mean, I can't help it. I felt it again today, coming in.'

'Not people following you again, Hopcroft!'

'All right, laugh. So would I, loud and long, I assure you hee-hee, ha-ha. Only I've also worked this thing out, quite painstakingly, and it by no means fails to make sense, the idea of being followed. They followed me that day, didn't they? I'd picked Caroline up, and off we popped to the Public Record Office. They couldn't have known I was going there. I'd been buzzing around Gray's Inn the previous day. So they followed me from *here*, because they know I work here, to the PRO, and from there to Olga's, and when I came out they boffed me. That is the point that keeps recurring, you see. Follow Hopcroft.'

'Well, damn it – '

'Oh, yes, I know. I assure you!' Hopcroft said. 'I have had ample time to think over every angle of this, which is one of the effects of a good boff. I can see it your way. The thing is a piece of tremendous nonsense. Chap's frightened of his own shadow. A little trundle round Bradford-on-Avon – what is there to it? Particularly as everyone knows all the papers are in Israel. No more to be found. It's all dropped now. Except it isn't, is it? There are more papers to be found, and we are trying to find them.'

'Yes, but they can't possibly – '

'So that looking at it from their point of view, whoever they happen to be – which is another point, you see. I am a chap who likes to know. Part of my nature. Very worrying not to know who these other chaps are, particularly if they are inclined to give one a boff from time to time. So, viewing it from their position, I should take into account that old Hopcroft might still be at it, snuffling around in his usual pertinacious manner, whatever might have been put about to the contrary. I mean, I would definitely think that. Either the question is of importance or it isn't. If it is, no stone unturned, et cetera, and Hopcroft is definitely the horse to watch.'

'All right. I respect your view. But, laying that on one side, what's your reading of Pickles?'

It was now quite obvious that he had one. He really was very good at this. The lively and practical curiosity that had taken him to Gray's Inn was a useful illustration of it.

I was not wrong. He'd pondered the information I'd brought from Israel. It seemed to him that if Pickles had got his doctorate in 1908, he would have had his own pupils soon after, and that what one needed was a list of these pupils. The period was remote, but if records were still available for Weizmann's pupils they ought to be for Pickles's.

He thought that a period of ten years from Pickles's doctorate would be a practical one, which gave one a frame of 1908-18. In the latter part of this period, Weizmann was already well known in scientific circles, which narrowed the frame still further, because he agreed that after that point Pickles was unlikely to have parted with the books.

'You feel someone does have this stuff?' I said.

'I do, really. Yes. I do.'

'How about a drink, Hopcroft?'

Hopcroft looked at me nervously.

'You wouldn't take advantage of a chap. I mean, I've spoken freely.'

'Of course I wouldn't.'

Hopcroft went to Manchester on a Sunday, when he thought he wouldn't be so keenly watched. He didn't want to go from home, in case anyone was watching there. He and I spent the morning together, strolling and keeping our eyes open. He picked up a taxi in busy Trafalgar Square, which took him to one that Caroline had been holding for him at Marylebone. This one took him to

Euston, with his train ticket in his pocket and only minutes to spare before the train left.

He was away for almost a week, and again he didn't keep in touch. He discovered that Professor Burckhardt, previous source of the university information, had retired, but Hopcroft had gone direct to the sources, anyway. He had checked all the records of Owens College from 1908 and had noted the name of everyone with whom Pickles had worked. He had followed up these names, and in contacts with university staff and relatives had finally discovered to whom Pickles had given the lab books. He had given them to an undergraduate called John Hobhouse Bottomley. He had this name written on a piece of paper, together with a number.

'Well, damn it, you're a hero, Hopcroft. Really. Is that his phone number?'

'No, it's his war grave number.'

John Hobhouse Bottomley had been killed on April 22, 1915, in the second battle of Ypres. He had been a volunteer, aged twenty.

'Oh, well, that's . . . Who got his effects?'

A young woman called Nancy Greatorex had got them – at least his diaries and notebooks. His parents had tried to get them back. Miss Greatorex had refused.

'What happened to her?'

'I don't know,' Hopcroft said.

'You mean she's dead?'

'Not under that name. Not in this country.'

'Did she marry?'

'Again, no record, if so.'

'You mean, she's still around?'

'I don't know,' Hopcroft said mulishly.

'Hopcroft – you've gone so far – '

'I just can't go any further,' he said. 'Honestly, I'm absolutely knackered.' He was certainly looking it. 'You'd be surprised how everybody jumps on to Weizmann up there. I mean, get anywhere near the subject, and they know. It's uncanny. I – well, I'm sorry. You may say it's nerves, but – '

'Hopcroft, I know money wouldn't influence you, and we haven't much further to go, but if it would help – '

'No, it wouldn't, and that's it. There's only a few more months, after all, and you can't say I haven't done my bit. It was a good effort, though I say it. And I wouldn't have mentioned it, but I did actually get this splendid offer some time back, from the Churchill papers, and they still want me.'

'I see.'

'I would have slogged on. It's interesting, and useful, but I can't take any more of this, and I doubt if you've got a right to ask me – I mean, knowing how I feel on the boffing question. I'm sorry to be saying this,' he said awkwardly.

'Well, no, I understand,' I said drearily, and wondered what the devil was to be done now.

'Of course, I'll write every scrap of everything I've found. You'll be in exactly the same position.'

'There's no replacing you, Hopcroft.'

'Well, it's nice of you to say so. I mean, crikey,' Hopcroft said.

True enough, though: no replacing that good horse. I was next to useless at it myself, so I racked my brains; but it still took time before I hit on the obvious solution.

11

The world-wide recession was well into its stride by this time as the shortage of oil and the high price of it began to work its wonders. The roaring inflation had brought about a sort of incomprehending global pandemonium – much in keeping with Islamic fantasy, with its emphasis on the mutability of things and delight in mischievous imps, and beggars become kings, and worlds turned topsy-turvy.

With ornate arabesques, the oil suppliers had decreed which countries might overflow with oil, and which not, according to the language of love; and on the high seas rerouted tankers described even fancier arabesques as the oil companies translated the message into other languages. In the end, everybody spoke the same language, and nobody overflowed, and everybody was cut, but those with the least money were cut the most.

The price of the stuff was now a hundred times what it cost to produce, and those transformed by impishness to kings had become very kingish, almost spurning trade. As an earlier member of the troupe, similarly lit up, had put it:

> I wonder often what the Vintners buy
> one half so precious as the stuff they sell.

Which was a sound question, for there was nothing so precious as the new stuff they were selling, and they couldn't begin to spend the billions they said it was worth. It was as if by cosmic freak they now controlled all the air in the world, and it was hardly worth their while to let others breathe. Those with money to pay could choke a little easier, but it was hard luck on the beggar lands, among whom they had previously been counted, for the most they could offer in the way of help was to lend their old friends the money, at special rates, to buy at the new prices. They couldn't let them have it at the old prices, because this would place too great a temptation on old friends to get into the act themselves. They advised them, and they advised everybody, not to squander the stuff, because it was obviously much too precious to squander.

The imp had been let out of the bottle, and mischief was abroad.

But other bottles, other imps.

Kaplan had come to England with his parents at the age of sixteen in 1906. His father had been a well-to-do textile merchant in Russia. Weizmann had been invited down to dinner within a couple of months of their arrival in Manchester, and he became at once for young Kaplan a lifelong interest. Weizmann had then been a bachelor. His left hand was in a glove at the time, the result of a recent accident in the laboratory, and he had worn a rather threadbare but elegant suit with a waistcoat that had an unusual number of buttons.

Kaplan had recalled all this in perfect detail when he'd told me about it sixty-seven years later. I'd met him the previous year, when Julian Meltzer, to whom he had been writing, had kindly unloaded him on to me. He was a spry eighty-three; a little hunchback with a curly old-fashioned bowler and an expression of Mr Punch. He had travelled to London for the express purpose of examining the young man who had been given the grave responsibility of handling Weizmann's papers of the 1930s, and also to have a good chat in Russian. He remembered Wiezmann's Russian well, and all his little nuances in it; this had caused him to query certain points in the English translation, and it had caused me to send him copies of the Russian originals.

For the communications that now began with Kaplan, some elaboration was required.

Hopcroft's fears, when I thought seriously about them, seemed by no means out-of-the-way. It was almost a certainty that he had been watched, and only due to Olga's erratic arrangements that he had been attacked at the wrong time. The burglaries at Wimbledon and Swiss Cottage had soon followed, although not soon enough; all the same, there had been intelligence behind them.

His reasoning that the operation wouldn't so soon be called off seemed also correct. Either Rehovot had the papers or it hadn't. If it hadn't there were good grounds for continuing to watch my flat. If it had, there were less obvious but still good grounds. For a variety of reasons, Rehovot might engage in a correspondence about the papers. It seemed to me that I had better do something about this; so I destroyed everything relating to Vava and Pickles, and asked Rehovot not to write to me about them any more.

Kaplan was another matter. It seemed best not to put anything in writing to him, either. But I did send him off a first long letter of explanation.

I told him Rehovot had heard of the existence of some lab books done by Weizmann with Pickles, and I explained about Bottomley and Miss Greatorex. I urged the need for discretion on the grounds of conflicting claims for the books (which was true enough). I said that Rehovot, to complete its records, would be happy to purchase them, or to give whatever recognition seemed appropriate if sentiment proved an obstacle. And I asked him not to write back but to ring.

To my astonishment and delight, within twenty-four hours he did – almost stammering with excitement. He said that he recalled Pickles perfectly. He had met him first at a picnic in 1907, with Weizmann and Verochka and some other people. He remembered that Verochka had been pregnant at the time. They had all gone back to the Weizmanns' house in Birchfield Road for supper – which Weizmann had bought on the way back: fish and chips.

He had known several other members of the Pickles family, in a long life of local affairs, and he also had a distant recollection of the Bottomleys, but he couldn't think why. He thought they had been an unfortunate family. But he would certainly find out, and immediately.

This was very cheering, and he was as good as his word. A few days later he rang with a complete rundown on Bottomley's short-lived romance with Nancy Greatorex. The couple had met in Brackpool in August, 1914, and had become informally engaged before Botttomley had volunteered in February, 1915. She had lived in Bolton but had been studying at a teacher-training college in Manchester. He had been shipped out to France and killed almost immediately in April of the same year. They had known each other barely nine months.

Kaplan had learned this from Bottomley's youngest sister, a Mrs Mellish, the only surviving member of the family. And he had been quite right about the family's misfortunes. Three sons had fallen in the Great War, and the father had gassed himself. Mrs Mellish could barely remember Nancy Greatorex (she had been a child of eight when John – or Jack, as he was-known in the family – had been killed); but she could recall her sense of awe that Jack's sweetheart was going to be a teacher.

Jack had been the apple of the family's eye, a clever boy who had kept winning scholarships. He had been something of a favourite with Pickles. She remembered the tremendous occasion when Dr and Mrs Pickles had once come to tea; she hadn't been able to open her mouth with staring at him, and he had given her sixpence. She didn't know anything about lab books, but she recalled a dramatic family occasion when everyone had helped Mrs

Bottomley compose a letter 'from a broken-hearted mother' to the Greatorex family in Bolton to try to persuade Nancy to return Jack's papers (diaries and poetry, she thought), which was considered proper, particularly as she had never 'worn his ring'. She didn't know what had happened to Nancy, except that she had become a teacher and had taught in Manchester.

'But don't you worry about any of that,' Kaplan told me vigorously. 'I shall be on to her. I've got a line out to the educational authorities now.'

He was having a perfectly marvellous time, only too delighted that he could still be of service to the shade of Weizmann.

'Do you think that she's still – still around, Mr Kaplan?' I asked hesitantly. He had told me she had been nineteen at the time of her understanding with Bottomley, which would make her now a rising seventy-eight. But I'd just remembered that he was eighty-three himself.

'Still around – why ever not?' he said.

There was a pronounced Lancashire flavour to his Russian, which we were talking, and a certain lip-smacking as he savoured again his translation of English plebeian nuance: she had never 'worn his ring'.

'I shall turn that young woman up. Never fear,' he said.

It was March by this time, and Meyer had taken to ringing me up every weekend for encouraging talks on the state of the batatas (cuttings taken weeks before and all growing vigorously). There was scarcely a stable government left in the world. Prices were going up so fast my mother came anxiously to town to do some shopping. On the infrequent occasions when she did this, she stayed overnight at Gower Street. Caroline hadn't met her yet, so I took her to tea there.

My father was coughing over one of his black-tipped cigarettes as I unlocked the door of his little flat (he had always scrupulously refused to accept a key to mine), and he was sitting rather close to the small electric fire. 'What – already teatime? Then everything stops,' he said, and took his cigarette out of his mouth and kissed me. Then he kissed Caroline.

He had a silk muffler tucked into his dressing gown. With his ruddy broad cheeks and sparse slicked-back hair he did indeed look the distinguished butcher of repute. A desk lamp was burning over his typescript.

'How goes the work?' Caroline said, smiling at him.

'It goes.' He didn't want to discuss it.

I said, 'Where is Mama?'

'Resting. You can get her up now.'

'Darling, in here,' my mother called at the same moment.

I went into the bedroom and found her lying under the covers. She was fully dressed, with her fur coat on. 'Come and kiss me. This hideous little place is an icebox,' she said.

We had a minute or two of her own heating and glazing problems while she stroked my face and smoothed my hair. She was his second wife, still in her middle-fifties, much younger than he, a member of his old secretariat, a great beauty in her day. She was still very striking, classical centre-parting, olive skin, luminous eyes. Even before her devotion to the rabbi, she had shown signs of becoming rather holy.

They were enormously different in temperament: despite her dramatic appearance, she was the passive and conservative body, while he, despite his, which was solid and stocky and wrapped in a baleful irony, was the romantic. He was a product of a romantic period, as he'd told me. He wasn't so much irritated by my mother's new interest in her religion as wryly amused. He knew his Bible well (from pre-Revolutionary school days), and she didn't (from post-Revolutionary ones), and he derived much satisfaction from easily confounding her.

She got up after a while and we had tea, and later a spot

of the yellowish vodka my father fancied, and he enlarged a little on his historical difficulties. He was still rather stuck on 1935, a slight case of fixation. It had been one of his big years, of course. The assassination of Kirov the previous December, and the subsequent trials over the next couple of years, had resulted in almost everyone in sight being shot: Zinoviev, Kamenev, Tukhachevsky, Bukharin, Rykov. In the emptying rrmament, Molotov had put him up for a key foreign policy speech at the 7th Comintern Congress: Popular Front. Standing stormy ovation; Stalin nodding and clapping for two minutes; Comrade Druyanov had arrived.

Caroline had always been fascinated by him and could hang on his words for hours, which didn't, I saw, endear her to my mother. I'd spotted right away that she hadn't taken to her. It wasn't a great success, the tea party, but in the course of it I asked her for her little devotional book – I knew she never went to bed without it – and hunted through for an English translation of the familiar words. Yes, here they were: 'We will celebrate the holiness of the day . . .' I read on:

. . . for it is one of awe and terror. Thou alone art judge and arbiter; thou writest down and settest the seal, thou recordest and tellest; thou rememberest the things forgotten. Thou unfoldest the records, and the deeds therein inscribed proclaim themselves . . .

Well, remembering the forgotten, recording and telling . . . Quite a basic Jewish preoccupation. The thousand-a-year letter man had certainly helped in the good work.

The room was thick with the tangy smoke (my mother on the black-tipped cigarettes, too) and I sat on the sofa, while the talk went on round me, and looked into the electric fire and saw quite a different room, with a green canopy, and heard the breathing stop and the nurse run in again. His prayer book was askew on the bedside table where he had put it before lying back for the last time. In that brooding period before the engulfing darkness, had he foreseen, apart from new worlds of petrochemicals and chaos, somebody like me remembering things forgotten, recording and telling; might his last reading have constituted a final hint to the judge and arbiter?

It was rather an encouraging prayer in such a random world, and I read it again.

Back at the ranch, things were much less encouraging. Kaplan hadn't rung for a few days, so I rang him, to learn from a great-niece that he was 'very poorly'. He had been to Bolton, without his umbrella.

'Oh, I'm sorry about that. When will he – '

'Doctor says we mustn't let him up for a couple of weeks.'

A couple of weeks ... with batatas growing furiously, and a world growing madder!

Could he use the phone? I asked. No, he couldn't: there wasn't one in his room. Could he write to me, then, or dictate a letter? She said she'd see about that.

I put the phone down with some gloom, and almost immediately it rang, and nemesis was there, speaking vigorously from Rehovot. Why wasn't I getting off my goddam ass? I wanted to explain that the trouble wasn't with my ass. It had been with Hopcroft's, and now seemed to have shifted to Kaplan's. But I couldn't do this. Nobody knew about Kaplan; not even Caroline knew. This seemed much the safest, allowing him to work in isolation, in no way connected with me, which was why I didn't intend going to see him.

I still couldn't tell if I was being watched.

As it turned out, there were also a few other things I couldn't tell about at that time.

I merely got cautiously on with my work, and while I did it, another government or two collapsed, and the odd riot erupted here and there. But that was in 1974, and I was safely back in the chamber of horrors of 1934.

3

Kaplan was still too poorly a couple of days later to speak to me, but the great-niece had something useful to offer.

'I know he is worrying about you, Mr Druyanov,' she said.

'Does he say why?'

'Isn't it Miss Greatorex's pension?'

'What is?'

'That is worrying you. If she is getting it.'

'Ah. Yes,' I said. Kaplan, like Sherlock Holmes, evidently had his methods.

'Well, she is. He said so when he came back.'

'Well, that's very good,' I said. A moment's reflection showed that it was; very good. Miss Greatorex; pension; still getting it.

'He was making further inquiries, knowing your concern, and then this happened. I'll let you know when he can write, though.'

He was able to write – or, rather, dictate – a couple of days after. I told her not to send the letter to my address but care of the central post office in Trafalgar Square, and next day I went to get it. I made a leisurely journey via the bookshops of Charing Cross Road, and bought a couple of stamps before producing my passport at the post office.

The letter was there; a rather guarded letter, dictated in English.

From the education authorities in Manchester, he'd learned that Miss Greatorex had retired in 1956, at the age of sixty; they had lost track of her when she dropped out of an old teachers' circle not long after. Taking another tack, he'd contacted the local office of the Ministry of Social Security to ensure that her pension was being duly paid; which he was sure I'd be very glad to know was the case, but owing to a certain officiousness they wouldn't say where.

Through contacts in Bolton he had found the family of a second cousin of Miss Greatorex's, with whom she had lived in retirement. He had been to see the family and had learned that on the death of the second cousin, and not wishing to be a burden to the children, Miss Greatorex had decided to remove to Manchester to be nearer old friends.

The family in Bolton, although fondly attached to the old lady, had not been in touch with her since 1969, when an exchange of Christmas cards had ceased. This had coincided with a decision of the old lady's to convert a 'little bit of money she had on one side' into a life annuity for herself. With this annuity, she had removed to a private 'retirement home'.

From the proprietor of her last address he had gathered that the old lady was rather 'short' in her ways and not reliable in the matter of correspondence, but from *all* contacts he had gained the impression that her recollections of Mr Bottomley were still green, as were all *mementoes of him*, and that she was *hot on pickles*. I could almost hear him smacking his lips as he'd told his amanuensis to underline the relevant phrases.

Before being forcibly put to bed he had apparently written to her at the retirement home, and though he didn't expect an answer, he would go there as soon as he was 'up to snuff'.

I read the letter in a telephone box in the post office, and I carefully tore it into tiny pieces, below the level of the glass window. I felt a fool doing this, but I burned the pieces when I got home.

Kaplan was no sooner out of bed than he was up to snuff, and on the phone again.

He had been to the retirement home, a place called

Barraclough House, and had found the old lady very short in her ways.

'I don't think she is quite mad,' he said, 'but it's a fine line – very fine, you know, in these cases.'

The case seemed to be that Bottomley had been a genius, and some annotations he had made in the lab books had the effect of altering the whole scope and dimensions of science. Unscrupulous people had tried to lay hands on them before, for purposes either of financial gain or scientific renown – apparently a reference to the Bottomley family and Dr Pickles – and she had known how to deal with them.

'But didn't you explain – '

'Of course I did. I told her everything about the Institute.' She apparently wanted to check his credentials before seeing him again, and he thought I had better write to her immediately on Institute notepaper. 'Sign yourself as the official representative, you know. She won't reply but I'll go and see her again right away.'

I wrote the letter, and told Kaplan, and two days later he rang me again, in rather a lather. She wanted to see me herself. She wanted to see me tomorrow. He had tried to get the appointment delayed, but owing to some reason to do with a lawyer, it would have to be tomorrow.

'You mean a lawyer will be there?' I said.

'It's hard to talk to her, you know. Very short. She talks over you. But she was impressed by your name. She knows all about your father. I think something will be doing. But I have to tell her, you know. Would there be any special difficulty in it?'

I was trying to think of the difficulties. If I got the lab books, I didn't want to return with them to the flat. I would have to take them immediately to Israel. It was because Olga had, without reason, acted so fast that we had got the letters. Speed was the thing.

'No. No special difficulty,' I said slowly.

'Good. Very good. Take the train, my boy. It's hard for me to get to the airport. There's a good one at ten-thirty, nonstop, gets you in well before one. I'll meet it.'

'Oh, that isn't – We could surely meet – '

'No, I'll do it. Don't hold me back now. I think something will be doing! I must get on to her. Ten-thirty, mind. Yes.'

Yes. In some confusion I flew down seven floors, and out to the travel agent, and booked a train return to Manchester and an air return to Israel and flew back again and rang Connie. I didn't tell her much. I told her I'd located the lab books, and might be seeing her the day after tomorrow. If I didn't ring her, I wouldn't have them.

4

It was raining in Manchester, and Kaplan was looking by no means up to snuff. He was in galoshes and an enormous overcoat and looked like a little question mark under his baggy old umbrella. Despite the curly bowler, I scarcely recognized him; there was a beaky strained look about the Mr Punch face.

'I'm sorry to bring you out in this, Mr Kaplan.'

'I'll survive.'

He was looking none too sure of this, however, so we went into the warmth of a buffet and had a brandy, which did him good. He grew discursive about the Bottomley-Greatorex situation. Thousands of young women had never married after the enormous casualty rate of the first war, and Miss Greatorex had been one of them. Many had developed delusions, and he had been warned in Bolton about Miss Greatorex's. The family knew all about the 'silly old cat's' treasures

'What exactly is Rehovot's interest?' he said.

'Weizmann's first work in England, you know,' I said, nodding easily.

'There is some genuine value in it, is there?'

'Oh, I think so, Mr Kaplan – historically. I'm sure you'll get a letter of appreciation from Mr Weisgal.'

'Well, that would be nice. Hmm. But I have been thinking, you know. I have been wondering about these books.'

'Oh yes,' I said cheerfully, in some dismay.

'I mean, if they are of genuine value ... The President of the State is a professor there, isn't he?'

'President Katzir? Yes, he is.'

'I mean, if they are of genuine value.'

'Oh. A letter from him, you mean?'

'That would be something, wouldn't it?'

'Well, I could try.'

'I mean, if they are of genuine value,' Mr Kaplan said earnestly.

He primed me further in the taxi on how to cope with Miss Greatorex. She hadn't apparently taken to him, but he thought she was still susceptible to younger male charms. She had delved a good deal into the connection with my father. 'Knows all about the Popular Front – from her active days, you see. Nineteen-thirties, hiking clubs, workers' educational weekends. A bit weak on Israel, but kibbutz all to the good. Tractors, oranges,' he said vaguely.

Barraclough House was an old Victorian pile, lurking in shrubbery, not so very far from the university. The lab books hadn't wandered far since written. Weizmann, passing with brisk tread (and Kaplan pointed out that he probably would have passed this way), might easily have cast eyes on this old magnate's mansion. It would have looked to him somewhat newer and more stately than the white House at Rehovot now looked to me.

There was a determinedly cheerful air about the place, and we were conducted briskly enough to Miss Greatorex's room along a creaky corridor. She looked to me absolutely normal, younger than her years, despite a thatch of rather wild white hair and somewhat startling eyes, enlarged by her glasses. She was slim, a bit above average height, neatly turned out, rather 'refined' Northern accent: a retired teacher.

'But you haven't come just to see me, have you, Mr Druyanov?' she said after some minutes. 'You'll forgive my pronunciation, I'm sure. How do you say it again?'

'Dru-*ya*-nov.'

'Dru-*ya*-nov. I love to hear it properly pronounced. I have such respect for your father, Mr Druyanov, for all of your great people, of course ... What exactly are your intentions with regard to Mr Bottomley's work?'

I explained about the publications programme.

'Yes, I understand that. But you do know that Mr Bottomley made rather great changes to the scientific theories?'

'That naturally adds to the interest.'

'I mean, it hasn't been unknown for the work of great men to be appropriated – I don't cast the slightest aspersion on you, Mr Druyanov,' she said, with a swift look at Kaplan. 'There, I've got it wrong again, I know you'll forgive me. Please say it once more.'

'Druy*a*nov.'

'Yes.' She was glowing at me with her magnified eyes. 'It's lovely. It really is. You won't take amiss what I'm saying?'

'I'm not sure I understand it.'

'No, well – from your background,' she said, with another glance at poor Kaplan. 'It's simply that – It's Mr Bottomley's work, you see. It's a *trust*. It would be published exactly as it is, without alteration?'

'Nothing at all will be published without your permission, Miss Greatorex.'

'To me, a sacred trust.'

'I can give you my word.'

'Well, I do think that would dispose of the problem.'

'Well, that's wonderful,' I said; which it certainly was. 'Perhaps I could see the books.'

'I shan't lose a minute. I shall go and see Mr Hinchcliffe right away.'

'Mr Hinchliffe?'

'My lawyer. They are in his keeping.'

'Oh. When could we – '

'Well, I *did* actually have a word with him about it,' she said, glowing at me. 'I was sure with your background, everything would be all right, Mr Druyanov. Dru*ya*nov?'

'Yes.'

'I was sure of it. He can start tomorrow.'

'Tomorrow,' I said dismally.

'And have something prepared by next Tuesday, I am certain.'

'Next Tuesday.'

'So if we could meet again on Wednesday?'

'Wednesday.' My life seemed to be drifting past.

'Easter in between, you see.'

So it was; Easter. The world had swung and the season of redemption was at hand. Christmas I'd been in the Holy Land last.

Kaplan had kept the cab, and we shambled back to it under his umbrella.

'I'm sorry about that,' he said. 'I was certain she'd got the books there. I didn't understand about the lawyer. Another journey for you.'

'It's all right,' I said, wondering how the devil to manage it. I'd left the flat early in the morning and had taken rather a spin around London, by various means of transport, to shake off any possible pursuit. The prospect of having to do it again was not so very promising.

Kaplan had now begun to sneeze rather a lot, and it seemed best to get him home as soon as possible, so we went there first. The great-niece opened the door, and with a single exclamation of 'Oh, Uncle!' pulled him inside.

'We haven't yet made arrangements,' he said to me weakly.

'I think you'd better get to bed now.'

'Immediately,' the great-niece said. She was stripping his coat off him.

'Look, come upstairs with me and have – '

'Goodbye, Mr Druyanov,' the great-niece said rather grimly.

Kaplan was in something of a half nelson, and I couldn't quite shake his hand, so I shook his sleeve, nodded encouragingly, and trotted back through the rain to the taxi.

On the return journey I thought up a story for Caroline, but she wasn't there when I got back, and she didn't ring all evening, so it wasn't necessary. It wasn't necessary to ring Connie now, either.

5

I thought hard that evening. It seemed to me that if surveillance was going on, I could expect some action now after my disappearance. Except that after Hopcroft's disappearances, to Bradford-on-Avon and Manchester, there hadn't been any action. This was strange, when I considered it.

He had received attention just once – when he was definitely expected to have papers on him. He hadn't had the papers, and the places where the papers might have been had then received their due of attention. Didn't this show rather expert intelligence?

It was true that Hopcroft had yarned a good deal before his attack, and not much after it: still he *had* disappeared on a couple of occasions, and might have found further papers. Why hadn't further attention been paid to him, or to my flat where the papers might have been? Well, there hadn't been any further papers. But whoever knew that had known a lot. It showed intelligence of an even more disturbingly accurate nature.

There was another factor. On the first occasion, I'd been

on the point of going to Israel. The idea seemed to have been to prevent my taking the papers with me. It was obviously a first-class idea not to let anyone know I was going to Israel now, and an even better one not to tell anybody anything. There was evidence here of the Hopcroft syndrome; and as I thought this I recalled another aspect of it. He had thought himself safe enough when innocently employed going there and back to the Public Record Office. My thoughts were tending in the same direction.

There were, independently, good and practical reasons for this. Volume 15 was almost complete; just a bit of polishing to do and a few footnotes, scattered through the book, to be written. Some would have to be done at the PRO, anyway, and it would establish a useful pattern of daily activity. I would be tailed there and tailed back (if I was being tailed at all), and while I was away the flat was available for leisurely inspection – if it was thought worth inspecting.

I thought it might be. For there were differences between Hopcroft's disappearances and mine. Despite all precautions, he hadn't enjoyed the same degree of secrecy. I had known where he was going and with what result, and so had Caroline – perhaps even Ettie, and others. One way or another, there had been a leak of information. This time there couldn't be, because nobody had any to leak.

Good reasons, all these, to continue not letting the left hand know what the right was doing.

Thursday morning brought Caroline and Ettie.

'What happened to you yesterday?' Caroline said.

'Nonsenses.'

'Oh?'

She waited a moment to see if any amplification was coming her way, and when none did turned away.

'I was at my parents' last night,' she said.

'Oh, yes.'

'Their phone was out of order.'

'Ah.'

Over a cup of coffee I assembled volume 15 into my executive case. We went silently to the PRO together.

It was after three when we got back, and in response to a drumming noise from the bedroom, Caroline let Ettie out of the wardrobe. She was tied up inside with a gag in her mouth. She was quite eloquent when it was taken out. She had opened the door to two men with balaclava helmets over their faces. They had put her in the wardrobe right away, but she had heard another arrive later. It was probably this other who had gone so professionally through my study. Every paper in it had been turned over, and most left on the floor.

When Ettie had recovered herself, she discovered that four pounds were missing from her purse. This was so improbable on a Thursday that she had a hard job keeping a straight face, but I gave her the four pounds, all the same, to the approval of the police who were there by then.

It wasn't much, to learn I'd been right. But it was a disconcerting thing to learn.

Caroline and I spent a dismal Easter weekend together. I didn't know what to say to her. I wished she'd go away. She might have been at her parents'. The phone might have been out of order. But I'd been remembering other things. She'd been going with Hopcroft that day to Swiss Cottage; and she hadn't gone. And she'd returned early from Willie's when she knew I was returning early. There were good reasons for all these things, and she'd told me them. I still wished she'd go away.

We'd had a row after returning from my parents. She had been curious, even before this, about the progress with Pickles and carotene, but I'd been able to put her off easily enough. Emboldened by her introduction to the family circle, she had become more curious, and I'd had to put her off more roughly — more roughly than I intended, which was a pity.

But the whole thing was a pity. As I'd foreseen, she wasn't much good at trifling, had been much better as a friend than as a lover. She was a bright girl, Caroline, but I wondered what else she was bright at.

We went to the PRO again on Tuesday; and in the evening I ran over the plan for the following day. Kaplan was still unwell, so I knew I'd be doing it alone. I went over every detail in my mind. Caroline slept restlessly on beside me.

'What Hopcroft forgot,' I said, skimming through volume 15 after breakfast, 'was the lease on Featherstone Buildings.'

'Do you need it?'

'I do really. You couldn't slip over to the lawyers this morning?'

'Where are they?'

'I've got the address,' I said.

Caroline slipped off to Gray's Inn, and I slipped off to the PRO. A few minutes afterwards, I slipped off to the lavatory, accompanied by volume 15. The emergency exit, beyond the toilets, was unlocked. As I'd discovered last week, it led out to Clifford's Inn. Clifford's Inn led out to Fetter Lane, and Fetter Lane to Fleet Street.

A man was just alighting from a cab outside the *Guardian*, and I got in.

'Airport,' I said.

12

Miss Greatorex was glad I was alone, and she had already told me so when I had phoned her from the airport. Her hair wasn't quite so wild and she'd actually got a touch of lipstick on. Her hands, which had been somewhat papery and rustling on our first meeting, were now much softer and rather tacky: she'd been refurbishing them with hand cream. She hung on to mine for a few moments. 'You couldn't know it, but you gave me such a turn when you first came in that door, Mr Druyanov. Shall I tell you why?'

'Please.'

Still retaining one of my hands, she turned and took an oval frame from a shelf and silently gave me it. Something very like a human greyhound looked out of it. A flat Army cap was jammed on one end, and some distance away, beyond an immensely long nose, thin lips were bared at the other. It was signed 'Now and Ever – Jack.'

'Mr Bottomley?' I said reverently.

'The spitting image.' Her magnified eyes were moist, and it took a moment or two to realize that the likeness referred to was not between Jack and his photo, which was natural enough, but between Jack and me, which was ridiculous. I suddenly recalled Caroline's description of me as saturnine. Something would have to be done about this, if necessary by surgery. I realized I was shaking my head in unconscious rebuttal, and altered the motion to a slow nod. Miss Greatroex's head was corkscrewing in a similar manner; she was swallowing hard.

'And now the most precious mementoes that I have of him,' she said. She had taken the photo and replaced it on the shelf. Next to it, I now saw, was an old green box file secured by a band of bloomer elastic. 'Would you like to see them now?' she said.

My nod became a good deal more emphatic.

'His poems.'

'Oh.'

'Do sit.'

We both sat, on a settee, and she slipped off the elastic. A faint musty smell, compounded of camphor and lavender, wafted of Jack's verse. A heavy spring held down a tremendous amount of it, written in brownish ink. The top one ran.

> Shall I compare thee to a summer's day?
> Thou art more lovely and more temperate.

'That's actually one of Shakespeare's,' she said.

'Ah.'

'He wrote down things that he thought might – you know – apply to me. But he composed in that manner himself. His own lines were very, very Shakespearean, very similar.'

So they were; the odd word changed here and there. His more personalized verse, though still in Shakespearean vein, had a homelier tramp. One began rhetorically:

> Shall I confess where lies my dearest fancy?
> 'Tis in the face belonging to our Nancy.

As poem followed poem, I began to wonder, rather uneasily, what she was playing at. She had referred only to 'the papers' on the phone – and rather playfully, at that. Was she having me on? Kaplan had had his troubles with her in the matter of the lab books. Everyone had had troubles with her in this connection. Was this a bit of

fancy foreplay to soften the final congé? I was wondering
also what time the shops and the library closed, and how
much the taxi was ticking up. I'd picked up the taxi at the
airport, and we'd gone for a preliminary tour. We had
visited the nearest library and the shopping centre and the
post office. All in order there.

I snickered away respectfully at some gayer examples of
Bottomley's fancy, and glanced surreptitiously at my
watch. She caught me at it.

'We have a little time yet,' she said gently. 'I knew you'd
want to see them, but of course they mustn't leave my
hands. I thought we could have a peep before Matron
came.'

'Matron?'

'You see,' she said with concern, 'I don't want you to
think I am being obstructive, Mr Druyanov – There, I've
got it wrong again. Please say it once more.'

'Druyanov,' I said in anguish.

'Lovely. I've always thought it a lovely language, Russian. I used to have a record once – oh, years ago – of
"The Volga Boatman". They only had to say "Put that
record on and watch her cry," and I did. It tugged at my
heart. You'll know it, I expect, Mr Druyanov?'

'Very well,' I said, and almost felt a snatch of the
desperate song rise to my lips. 'In what sense obstructive?'
I said.

'I want Matron to witness that I don't mean to mislead
you. She'll be here at four.'

Bottomley's verse, increasingly lugubrious, hardly sped
the time; but sharp on four, Matron appeared, and was
introduced. She was a rather jolly small woman. 'Well,
love. What would you like me to do?'

'You know all about it, Dolly, but I have to say it again
while you're both here. Mr Hinchliffe said so.'

The lawyer had apparently told her that though she was
entitled to hang on to the books as a right of gift, she was

not entitled to authorize publication. This lay in the power of the copyright holders, and she was not one of them.

I said, 'Oh, but I'm sure – '

'Yes, I know. *I'm* not the one being obstructive. It's them, you see. They wouldn't want all their theories changed, would they?'

'No, of course not. But – '

'They wouldn't *let* you print Mr Bottomley's amendments. And from my point of view, it's a trust, a sacred trust.'

It took a minute or two to see what she was getting at. Her point was that if the work was published at all, equal credit had to be given to Bottomley. It couldn't be published, and no part of it could be published, unless all Bottomley's amendments were also published.

It was because of this unconventional condition that Hinchliffe had suggested that she come to a separate agreement with me. As she turned back from getting the document, I saw that held in her other hand was a small brown paper parcel, sealed with red wax, and my heart almost missed a beat. She'd got them, then. I was getting them! With all the talk of obstruction and advance apologies for misleading, I'd already given them up, I'd seen myself lurking about London for weeks, no longer safe even at the PRO.

'Before you sign, Mr Druyanov,' Miss Greatorex said seriously, 'I think you had better look at the books and see the full extent of the amendments.'

I could scarcely wait to get my hands on them. I broke the seal and opened the parcel. Two exercise books in buff covers with the printed black shield of Owens College. The first one started unequivocally:

10 September 1904

C. Weizmann & S. Pickles.
   It is hoped to study the analogous reaction of succinic anhydride and of aliphatic Grignard compounds.

Squarish writing, evidently Pickles's. As page followed numbered page, each day's work methodically dated, I spotted bits of Weizmann's curly Russian, and in the same pen poly-sided figures and equations. There was much crossing out. Another hand, large and loopy, conveyed Bottomley's amendments, fortunately in pencil. There were plenty of them. He agreed, disagreed, spotted flaws, quoted other authorities, with all the confidence of a second-year student and ten or eleven years' hindsight.

Pages and pages of gibberish:

... the condensation of pthalic anhydride & naphthylmagnesium bromide leading to *ortho*-(1-naphthyl)-benzoic acid (CII) cyclized to , 2-benzanthraquinone (CIII).

In the middle of a page, suddenly, standing on its own, a bald paragraph:

Yesterday's reaction showed conversion of a greatly increased order, believed due to contamination of retort IV by $C_{40}H_{56}$, which will be investigated.

There was an asterisk here and a figure 17. Page 17 bore another asterisk on a paragraph mid-page.

The contamination of retort IV noted earlier has proved to be of small quantities of $C_{40}H_{56}$ (carotene) and further investigations will be conducted.

There was a pencilled note, not Bottomley's, which said:
Book 2, p. 6.
I turned to Book 2, p. 6. There it was:

27 September 1904
It is hoped to investigate the effects of $C_{40}H_{56}$ with Grignard reagents.

Pages and pages of the investigation followed.

Without knowing it, I'd been holding my breath, and it came out then as a rather soft and lingering sigh. Journey's end, appropriately enough in a retirement home. I remembered that it had started with a view of the grave, myself seated in Weizmann's room, racking my brains over the highly opaque directions to the goal: Cromer-le-Poyth, Le-Roy-Parma, Coone Firth, people in Bradford, the old Greenyard's.

'We have produced,' he had written, 'a most elegant reaction ... which will provide a ketonic product of extreme concentration. He has the lab books himself.'

Well, I had them now. And Rehovot had the sweet potato and the bacterium. Full House. Jackpot.

'Yes, in both books,' Miss Greatorex said, watching me flip rapidly there and back as I sighed between the pair of them. 'Very extensive amendments, as you can see. I am not a scientist, of course, but I remember him saying, as clearly as yesterday, that they made tremendous differences to the theories.'

She was rather tense, and the magnified eyes bore a pleading look. The moment of truth was approaching for something she'd had to take on trust for the greater part of her life. Bottomley's beautiful poetry was one thing; his scientific genius quite another. She had delivered it into my hands.

It suddenly struck me that the dab of lipstick and the hand cream were not entirely for my benefit. Something of a sacramental nature was taking place, another evidence of phantom Jack being exhibited and bidden farewell. Who else, apart from the surviving sister and the man who kept the numbers of the war graves, knew that he had so much as existed? She was certainly very wrought up. The earlier corkscrewing motion of her face and the devotional session with the poems fell into place.

'I hope I am doing the right thing,' she said.

'I'm certain you are, Miss Greatorex.'

'Dr Pickles *did* think highly of him.'

'His favourite pupil.'

'And you do agree with the conditions? Read them before signing. I did explain fairly, Dolly, didn't I?'

Dolly told her how fair she'd been while I read through the nonsense; and a couple of minutes later we'd all signed. Just a few minutes afterwards I was back in the taxi, and so were the lab books. Everything had to go like clockwork now.

2

First stop, Marks & Spencer: hand grip. The hand grip needed to be bulky and well filled, which was a good idea anyway. I hadn't been able to bring anything with me from home. Pyjamas, underwear, slacks, shirt, razor, toothbrush. From the stationer's I bought a couple of large manila envelopes. Then we went to the library.

I was so long inside that the driver came and peered suspiciously to see what the devil I was up to. I was feeding change into the copying machine. There were thirty-four filled pages in one notebook, twenty-two in the other. The copy sheet size could cope with three but not quite four pages at a time. This was far too much of a fiddle, and I was copying a double page on each sheet. The sheets went into one envelope and the lab books into the other, which I gummed and addressed, 'Meyer W. Weisgal, Esq., The Chancellor, Weizmann Institute of Science, Rehovot, Israel.'

'Post office,' I said emerging.

'Got your stamps?' He was looking at the bulky handful.

'It needs registering.'

'Registering? You'll stand there forever. You said you hadn't booked your flight back.'

'I haven't.'

'Well, you won't get one if you hang about there. The

business chaps queue up early for a standby to London. You'll have to take the train.'

Oh, no, I wouldn't. No trains in the plan. The plan called for my sleeping near London airport tonight, with minimum movement away from it.

'Is there a post office at the airport?' I said.

'Not for registering. Not tonight.'

The morning, then; at London airport.

'All right. Skip the post office,' I said.

But uneasiness gnawed as we moved. A change of plan; a small one, true, and it could go off as easily from London as from Manchester. All the same, the plan had said Manchester. And I had two copies now. I hadn't planned to spend the night with even one.

By a quarter to nine I was back in London, and in the international building.

I passed the baggage office, followed the arrows to the toilets, and locked myself in a lavatory where some transferal operations took place. The copy sheets were going with me to Israel, and would be spending the night in the baggage office with my grip. This left the envelope with the original lab books: they couldn't go in the grip. They had to be posted off before I reclaimed the grip in the morning. The essence of the thing was speed, as shown in the case of Olga. The things had to be separated. I didn't intend walking about the airport with both in the morning.

I cursed silently and put the lab books in the executive case, together with volume 15, added toothbrush, razor, and pyjamas, and locked it. I hung grimly on to it as I returned to the baggage office. I deposited the grip, saw it labelled and lodged in anonymity among dozens of identical Marks & Spencer grips, and carefully pocketed the ticket. Stage 1 over.

Flight reservations next. El-Al fully booked, as I'd foreseen, but others free and willing. I slotted in to an 11 a.m. flight, was told to report by nine-thirty, and that was stage 2 over. All that remained was to put myself away for the night.

There was a mob at the hotel desk. The overworked clerks were explaining that a lot of Easter traffic was still about. Ten minutes of waiting, the lab books smouldering in my case, revealed that the Easter traffic was infesting every bed around London airport; people were being booked into central London. I heard a couple of them booked into the Russell Hotel in Russell Square, and another couple into the Imperial Hotel in Russell Square, and turned away.

I'd thought of something else while waiting, probably the best in the circumstances. No watchful eyes to worry about while booking in, or at breakfast, or while booking out. I found a taxi and told the driver Gower Street.

The curtains were drawn, and I saw that he must have left at night-time. I closed the door behind me, and looked round the Spartan little place. Something about its early-Victorian plainness appealed to him; also, of course, its proximity to the School for Slavonic and East European Studies. I had a look in the bedroom to see that the curtains were drawn there, too. Then I double-locked the door and left the key in, so that nobody could surprise me – not that it was likely. He wasn't due back himself till after the weekend, and he complained often at the lack of service; the place was unkempt and rather dirty.

I'd barely eaten anything all day, but I wasn't hungry or even tired. I felt simply flat. I put the case down, sat myself down, and looked at it. It didn't seem surprising to me now, or even odd, that I'd got the stuff. A Lancashire lad had found his dearest fancy in the face belonging to old Nancy, and the world could start to change now. The moment should have been large and exhilarating, but it wasn't. I probably needed a drink.

The floorboards creaked as I crossed the room to get one. I found I was tiptoeing, and realized I'd been doing it since entering the flat. Not a soul in the world knew I was here. This was obviously a fine thing, but there was nobody to tell. I seemed to have stepped sideways out of the human race, and wouldn't be reappearing in it again till the morning.

I'd promised to give the clerk at flight reservations the phone number, and I was actually dialling when I thought again, and stopped. Why do it?

Connie was a different matter, a world away, so, phone in hand, I called her at home. Again one of those bewildering immediate connections.

'Igor – darling – you – sound – so – close! Where are you?' There was a crowd in the background.

'In London.'

'Is it – is it okay ? '

'Yes, it's okay.'

'You mean, you got it ? '

'Yes.'

'Oh, my God. What time do you get in?'

I told her and heard her repeating it. 'You mean it's really all there? '

'Yes,' I said. 'I think so.' I was almost whispering. It seemed half the world must hear the howling at the other end.

'It is too fantastic! You remember how we sat and read through those papers and found Pickles?'

'Yes, yes,' I whispered. 'I remember it all, Connie. Good night.'

'Wait. Listen, Igor. Where are you?'

'I'm here, you know, getting ready.'

'Caroline is okay?'

'Fine, fine.'

'It's really incredible – just two days ago they started work with that bacterium on those sweet – '

I hung up right away, sweating. Creaking was going on. The whole damned house was creaking. Door okay; key in lock. I reached for the bottle and had one. I had two. I had the impression she'd stood with a megaphone in Gower Street, roaring the good news to everyone.

Over the second drink I thought about the post office in the morning. I was too near my own flat in Russell Square to go looking for one in the vicinity. I'd have to call a cab to the house; and early, so that we could go to some outlying post office. Yes, and then have to get from this outlying post office, probably through outlying traffic jams, to the airport. Yes, quite. I poured myself another small one, as Hopcroft would say. I remembered his state of mind when he'd said it. He'd been frightening himself looking out the window at darkening and emptying streets.

Quite dark now – pitch black, in fact. I couldn't actually hear anybody in the street. Curtains well drawn; no light showing. Nobody knew I was here. Certain resemblances seemed to be showing up between Hopcroft's state of mind and mine. I pulled myself together.

To get to the airport at nine-thirty, I'd call a cab for eight-thirty – earlier if we were going looking for a post office. With the further point that who knew if post offices were open then? Very probably they weren't. Which meant running about at the airport looking for one. While panicking about the copy still sitting in the baggage office, which had to be got out of there and transferred to my case.

There were all the makings here of a fluid situation. And with what object? The object was to separate the copies. Rehovot didn't need two copies. I suddenly thought of another way of separating the copies.

I could leave one here.

It was such a sound thought that I nodded at it, and tiptoed over to the bottle again. I'd have to hide the thing away tonight, anyway, just in case . . .

Glass in hand, I inspected the flat. In the living room, a desk, a few chairs, ancient sofa, bookshelf. The only decorations were a steel engraving of the death of Nelson, which seemed to go with the place, and two small framed photos, one of Marx and the other of me at the age of ten in my Pioneer uniform.

I had a look in his desk: nothing except a few rubber bands, paper clips, a musty smell. He never left papers here, always a secretive man – perhaps the secret of his survival. No secret drawers, anyway, and I hardly knew why I was looking; a certain headiness coming on after three whiskies on an empty stomach.

I began to explore more earnestly: bathroom, kitchen, bedroom. Bedroom promising. A massive mahogany wardrobe stood in it, sunk deep in the carpet. It was possible to see, round its edge, the original colour of the carpet, which was mauve. The rest was now grey.

I had a look at the back. A long thin batten supported the rear panel, a good half-inch of dust on it. Yes. I tiptoed back and opened my case and returned with the envelope. I couldn't quite get a hand in the gap, poked the thing in sideways, and saw it cutting a groove in the dust. It sat securely enough, slanted against the wall; impossible to see unless you knew it was there.

I had another drink after this, considerably elated, and thought I should eat something. I found biscuits and cheese and had a cup of coffee. Then I made preparations for the morning. A taxi rank was listed in a little phone directory on the bookshelf. The alarm clock was in working order. I set it for seven o'clock. Just for the record, this was the night of Wednesday, April 17, 1974.

4

I was watching through the curtains in the morning when the cab arrived. Everything was now as I'd found it: bed made, ashtrays and dishes cleaned. I collected my case, unlocked the door, turned off the light, and went downstairs.

I'd only had coffee, unable to eat. I felt slightly sick and momentous. The everyday world, when I opened the door, had that somewhat crystallized look that it bears during moments of private stress or after a lengthy fast, its very humdrumness novel. Gower Street greyly reared, its long terraces distinctly mortared together. Early starters were pacing briskly along it on their way to work. The taxi shuddered slightly by the kerb, the driver's face a face of the utmost arehetypal cabbiness – all so ordinary on this extraordinary day.

'Was it you for the airport? ' he said soberly.

'That's right.'

I got in and we took off.

There wasn't anybody you could actually give a Nobel Prize to. Some muck had got into one of the retorts in a basement laboratory in Manchester seventy years ago. A refugee scientist had crazily diverged from his set task about thirty years after. A serious young man, intent on nourishing underfed Africans, had been sent packing for some piece of meretricious political nonsense. And an old marked Jew, life fast ending, had looked forward and backward.

Well, he couldn't have it. All the same, he had been the one to discern the fresh pattern, glimmering among the maze of patterns. Like Ziegler, the German, he had spotted what a bit of muck could do. But Ziegler's legacy was a world littered with polyethelene bags. Chaimchik's looked like bringing some changes in the stareh belts.

It was a busy time at the airport, loudspeakers steadily booming. 'TWA announces . . .' 'KLM announces . . .' I made a beeline through the crowds to the baggage office. The sick feeling hadn't left me. I kept the ticket in my pocket till it was my turn, and then handed it over. The grip had sat quietly there all night: no nonsense.

I took it right away to the toilets; found a lavatory, locked myself in, and took out the packet.

. . . & naphthylmagnesium bromide leading to *ortho*-(1-naph-thyl)-benzoic acid (CII) . . .

All present and correct. I licked my dry lips, transferred the packet to the executive case, and let myself out.

An El-Al flight was due to leave before mine, and I was glad I hadn't got it. The Israelis preferred their national carrier: the hijacking risk was less. Hundreds of them were in line for the security check.

I checked into mine. Even with the overflow from the Israeli plane there were only forty or fifty people travelling. I hung grimly on to the executive case, got to the check-point, and showed the grip.

'Is this going with luggage, sir?'

'Yes.'

'Please open it.'

A quick shuffle through.

'And is that your hand baggage?'

'Yes, nothing in it, just papers.'

They didn't make me open it. Then I was at the desk, and booked in, and the grip was gone. Only the case to hang on to now.

I passed through to the transit lounge, light-headed. I felt empty, but when I bought a cup of coffee, I couldn't drink it. The duty-free bays were a seething mass and I stayed well away.

Ten-thirty. Another half-hour.

A surprising amount of Hebrew was being spoken. The three million of Israel seemed constantly a-wing, inveterate travellers, keen smugglers. A good deal of swapping was going on, not for the benefit of the customs at the other end. At a quarter to eleven El-Al announced a delay in its flight. Only a small groan from the Israelis, and fresh hurried departures to the duty-free shops.

Eleven o'clock. Nothing.

Eleven-ten. A further delay from El-Al.

Eleven-fifteen. My flight. Gate 12.

I streamed bonelessly along to it. Flight card. A very long corridor.

An extra security check for flights to Israel, and further shuffling as overburdened Israelis reopened their luggage. They did it willingly, cheered by the precautions.

'What's in the case, sir?'

'Papers only.'

'Just walk through the light.'

I walked through it, into another check. A body frisk; a handheld detector. The detector came up with a ping.

'Carrying much metal, sir?'

'No. Only keys.' I handed over the keys. The detector still pinged.

'Please open the case.'

Damn it. I got my keys from him and opened it. He brushed aside the lab-book sheets and volume 15; fumbled, smiled. Razor.

'Right you are, sir.'

We were led to a long room with benches, again kept separate from other flights. A fresh delay here till everyone was in, and the door closed. Security men were about. The indefatigable Israelis were still swapping duty-free goods; one couple evidently had bought up half the world, Macy's, Selfridge's. The female of the two amply clad, had further clothing over her arm, and was trying to exchange perfume. Her mate was similarly overloaded. He managed to get rid of a bit here and there, then unfortunately saw me and addressed me in Hebrew.

I said, 'I'm sorry – '

'Oh.' The winning smile went, at this unpromising lack of Hebrew. Still. 'I see you don't carry your allowance of drinks. If it wouldn't be a trouble – '

'I'm afraid it would.'

'A single bottle?' He had four of them, Chivas Regal. 'My son is waiting at the airport. The moment we – '

'I'm sorry, I can't.'

He wasn't offended, and immediately off-loaded one on a rather indignant old lady a few places along the bench; his wife was doing a complicated perfume deal with a bearded man who had a problem with several bags of smoked salmon. Then we were moving, and with the strangest churned-up feeling I got up, and the perfume woman, now with a bag of smoked salmon, turned and almost immediately went full length over my feet. She fell heavily, smoked salmon and perfume skidding in all directions.

' Oh, I'm most terribly – '

'Elsa!' Her husband was there.

Several of us levered her up and got her onto the bench. She was practically speechless. They closed the exit doors again, and general pandemonium ensued for a few minutes. I picked up my case and hung on to it as the Israelis crowded round, giving advice. She tried to stand, wincing, and a nurse was brought in. We started moving during this, and I was in the first busload out to the plane.

Done it. Barring an attack by armed terrorists, I was practically there now. I hugged the thing all the way to the plane, went up the steps, strapped myself in, and sat with it somewhat tensely on my knee. The only thing needed was an engine failure. But no engine failure. The Israelis sorted out their luggage, doors were closed, jets howled, the plane lumbered to the takeoff position; and paused there, straining at the leash. A sudden increase in the howl, and we were moving again, faster, faster . . . Off.

I'd done it now. I'd really done it.

'Shall I take that case away, sir?'

'No, thanks.'

'It'll be in your way.'

'No, it won't,' I said, and ate a rather cramped meal, the little let-down table hard against the case, and the case hard against my knee; which was where it stayed.

I saw Connie as soon as I entered the airport building. She

was in the restricted immigration hall with a security man. The man took my passport and got it stamped right away; he also saw to it that the grip was first off. Ze'ev was waiting in the car, and we took off immediately.

We hadn't spoken much. Connie had given me a kiss, but the black butterfly eyes had noticed the strain. Barely twenty minutes later, we were turning in to the Institute gates, and driving directly to Meyer's.

He was actually on the doorstep, waiting. He'd heard the car pull up; white mane of hair, Red Indian face. 'Well, goddamn it,' he said. He had both hands out – I thought to shake mine, but it was to take the case.

'It's in here?'

'Yes.'

'How are you ? '

'Fine.'

'Goddamn it,' he said, and trotted into the house.

We followed him.

'You had no trouble?'

'No. Well, I had to be – '

'Tell me later. It's locked?'

'Yes.'

'*Nu?*'

I got out my keys and turned the lock. The damned thing had jammed.

'What the – What are you doing, torturing me?'

'It got – squashed – against my knee,' I said, screwing away.

'So break it – what? Give me a knife!' he yelled.

We got a knife, and then a screwdriver, and wrenched it open to find the *Daily Telegraph* and two packets of paper and the Bible. I stared at it and looked at the lid of the case. 'I.D.' My initials. Not my case, though. Somebody else had got my case, and the copy of the lab books and volume 15. I had got somebody else's, with the *Daily Telegraph* and two packets of paper and the Bible. Switched.

13

I went over to the San Martin in something like a state of shock. Connie went with me, and presently Ham looked in, and Marta, and a bit later Patel. The penthouse was occupied this time, and I'd got another room. It was the room next to Patel's. I was still almost speechless. I'd travelled two thousand miles with the wrong case.

I knew it hadn't been the wrong case when I'd gone into the departure room at London airport – the security man had just checked it. It had been the wrong one when I'd come out. The change had been made in that room – obviously when the woman had fallen over my feet and I'd momentarily put it down.

The unpleasant implications were not slow to sink in. Whoever had done it had known I'd be on that flight – indeed, to have got into the departure room, must have been booked on the flight himself. But who could have known? I hadn't known myself until last night. I had made only the single call to Rehovot. The information could have come only from Rehovot.

Even so, the operation had been conducted at mind-boggling speed. I'd rung Connie after ten. She'd had people with her. The people could have rung others. Between then and the morning, anyway, somebody had set arrangements in hand: booked tickets, duplicated the case, staged the elaborate ploy.

'Isn't it possible there's a quite normal explanation?' Patel said. 'You put your case down and someone picked up the wrong one – someone with a very similar case.'

'Very similar,' Ham said. 'With the same initials.'

'Possible, though.'

'Possible,' Ham said, and poured me another drop. He had brought the bottle. Marta hadn't spoken much, and she held her glass out, too, though she drank little. She said quietly, 'It's ghastly about your book, Igor. I'm so sorry.'

'Which book?' Patel said.

Marta told him about volume 15.

'What was it – a year's work?' Ham said.

'Almost.'

'Oh, that is dreadful,' Patel said. 'I am really – Perhaps I will have something to drink. Is there orange juice?'

There wasn't, so he went next door to get some of his own.

'Thank God you left the lab books at your father's,' Connie said.

'Yes.' It had slowly sunk in on me, amid other shocks, that I shouldn't have mentioned the lab books. I'd already told the other two, but it had obviously better go no further. I said so.

'Well, of course not,' Ham said. 'Couldn't they put a wiretap on the phones to try and catch this bastard?'

A rather unreal discussion on wiretapping was continuing when Patel returned, and he said indignantly that it was not only unethical but ridiculous.

'How could you tap all the phones in Rehovot? It would need a regiment of technicians. People would just not use the phone here.'

'True enough,' Ham admitted. 'And anyway, he wouldn't be calling his secret service – just some friend, with some kind of coded crap. You read about these things,' he said, nodding.

'If such a person exists here at all,' Patel said with a smile. 'Look, I am no expert, but another idea does occur. Didn't you say the plane was half empty, Igor, and that you booked in easily?'

'l did.'

'What was to prevent him doing the same? If you were being watched, and seen checking in, couldn't he have booked in after you?'

'Followed Igor to the airport?' Connie said.

'Certainly, from his home, why not?'

'Igor wasn't home last night,' Ham said.

I said, 'I was at a hotel.'

Three of those present knew that this wasn't the case, so a certain silence set in.

'That gives even another alternative,' Patel said. 'If you had, so to speak, disappeared, mightn't it have been supposed you were planning to fly to Israel? Someone might have been stationed at the airport. Not so? How prolific one becomes.'

'And the initials on the case?' Connie said.

'Prepared in advance. Igor uses such a case. Quite feasible, don't you think?'

It was; all feasible, as he said. My head swam as the talk went on. I was watching the smoked salmon and the little parcels of perfume skidding endlessly across the floor. A natural enough accident, and at the same time disarming; as Hopcroft had been disarmed on stepping out of the lift at Tancred Court. The same operation, even: the case snitched at the last moment when papers were expected to be in it. Except that this time they had been.

The theory that someone might have waited at the airport and booked in after me didn't survive the night.

The airline in London reported that no tickets had been sold or reservations made after eight in the morning; that was even before I'd left the flat, never mind arrived at the airport.

The overladen couple hadn't made the flight, though they had been booked in. The details they had supplied were false.

No; stage-managed from Rehovot, all of it.

Meyer wasn't shaved when I breakfasted with him in the morning. He'd had as little sleep as I. He said immediately, 'Did you tell anyone about the lab books in London?'

'Connie, Ham Wyke, Marta.'

'Who are they gabbing to?'

'They won't be.'

'You have to go and get the goddamn things.'

'Yes. I'd been worrying over this, too. 'Well, I won't be going,' I said. 'For one thing, I am being watched, so there is no point. For another, I'm not a hero.'

'What about this girl of yours there?'

'She hasn't got a key. Also she's probably being watched herself.' I didn't mention some other reservations.

'Would your father hand the papers to anyone else?'

'No.'

'Someone in authority, from the Embassy.'

'He knows about people in authority at embassies.'

'With a letter from you in your own handwriting.'

'He knows about letters from people in their own handwriting, too. He knows all the wrong things, my old dad. Anyway, do you want him to know what he's got sitting there?'

He thought about it. 'What, then – we hire burglars, agents, what?'

'Oh, for God's sake, Meyer!'

'I know, I know. At my time of life, cloak and dagger,' he said miserably.

'The question is, am I going to get to your time of life? There is this spy in the Institute, keeping an eye on things.'

'That I goddamn refuse to believe.'

'On me, in fact. I'm not moving anywhere till he's been sprung.'

He drank his coffee, gloomily watching me.

'Is a wiretap impossible?' I said.

He put his cup down rather sharply. 'Wiretaps. Where they play a recorder and listen in?'

'Wyke's idea, not mine.'

'Well, it stinks! What is this – the Kremlin?'

I got on with my breakfast.

'I feel old today,' he said.

'So do I. I live more here. I stay awake.'

'What useful things did you think of while awake?'

'Volume 15.'

'Screw volume 15.'

'With pleasure. I'm sorry I ever heard of it,' I said.

'You've surely got copies of that stuff.'

'Not of the last twenty or so footnotes. Complicated footnotes. I wrote them.'

'So you'll write them again.' He shook his head in bewilderment. 'A bastard sits here watching, reporting?'

'If it's any consolation, he can't have reported much. What's he got? Presumably not the batatas or Vava's process. The single reference in the letter to Haber, perhaps – that was bandied around enough. And Pickles's lab books. Well, the best of luck with those.'

'Say, wait a minute, 'Meyer said. He was looking at me rather queerly. 'Did Haber express further interest in that process?'

'He never expressed *any*.'

'Isn't that the period of volume 15?'

'Not exactly. Volume 15 only goes up to –'

'Well, it goddamn is!' he said. 'And he did express interest. He was *very* interested.'

'I see.'

'You do?'

'I will,' I said.

'Have a cup of coffee, Igor.' The salty look was back in his eye again. 'You know, already I feel younger.' He started telling me what it was that I ought to see.

*

It needed a pass to get into the special greenhouse, and the man on the door still had to check by phone, even though I was with Finster. It was hot outside, but a great deal hotter in. The geneticist working there was in shorts and sandals.

The plants due to change the world didn't take up too much room. The original lump had been duly forced into supplying ten cuttings, and these had recently been forced into supplying another ten each. The sprigs were growing away in individual small pots, eight dozen or so of them, a little stick supporting each skinny vine. The hulk of Uri's specimen was being grown on for experimental purposes; bits of it were going to Finster. It was a mass of greenery.

Since first struck, the plant had made almost ten pounds of tuber, as well as supplying the shoots. There was a wigwam of sticks around it. The thing seemed to wax a little more as I looked at it. Pale green tendrils delicately felt their way around the wigwam in the Turkish-bath air.

'This is some plant,' the geneticist said. He was looking at it quite affectionately as he wiped his streaming face with his hat. 'All it eats is the sun. A starch factory.'

He brushed away the soil at the base. A surly-looking hump, something between the colour of a tomato and a beet lurked dustily there. I thought I almost saw it move.

'How much?' he said to Finster.

'A hundred grams.'

The man produced a knife and sliced off a section with the dexterity of a butcher. He weighed it and puffed powder on the bleeding side of the tuber, while Finster placed the small steak in a plastic box.

It was quite cool in the blazing sun after the greenhouse; and upstairs in the Daniel Sieff cooler still. Finster locked his steak carefully away before showing me the results of his latest fermentation. The liquid dripping out of the fermenter was of an ominous beerlike shade. He uncapped the jar and inclined it towards me.

The rank smell was stronger than ever.

The yield from Vava's batatas, as I already knew, was something tremendous. So was the carotene. Finster inclined his own powerful nose over the vessel before gloomily recapping it. Then he wrote out what was required. Incurious as ever, he hadn't asked a single question. As Meyer had said, he'd be mute as a stone.

There wasn't anybody in the basement archives of the Wix, only Alizia. I sat in a corner and went through the boxes for October, 1933. The original of the letter to Haber was there, October 2nd. I recalled that there had been an exchange between them not long after, and hunted it down: yes, October 16th:

Im bezug zu Rutherford die momentane Position . . .

Rutherford was still trying. Approaches were still being made about the Nazi levy. More to the point, it was a one-pager: plenty of space for a PS. However, there was no PS.

I wrote the PS myself, in Meyer's study.

PS. You inquired after Vava's results. His bacterium and the proposed constituents for the *Ipomoea* . . .

I did it in German. The formula had been reduced to five simple lines, and Horowitz had made the few alterations that rendered it into intelligent nonsense. The formula itself gave no problem, but the required words in Weizmann's handwriting took some finding in his German correspondence. I copied them through tracing paper, and had several shots before assembling the PS into a coherent whole. After a few tries, letter and PS were both copied on a single sheet.

The effect was rather blurred and aged, curiously convincing. Large numbers of originals had been sent for safekeeping to Canada in the Second World War, and somewhat amateurishly photostated there. This looked very like one of them.

It was still not one o'clock when the manufactured copy

was back in the archives, and inserted in position, October 16, 1933. Trap set.

Meyer had a tea party in the afternoon. I wasn't at it, but at coffee at the Sassoons' in the evening, a couple of people came up and commented on the PS that had been found in the archives. They hadn't been at the tea party either. News travelled at Rehovot.

3

Events so soon became chaotic that it seems a good idea now to get the order of them right. It was Wednesday that I'd picked up the lab books from Miss Greatorex, Thursday that I'd flown to Israel without them, and Friday when the bogus PS went into the files.

I found I'd landed into a series of half-days and holidays. Friday was a half-day because it was the eve of the Sabbath. Saturday was the Sabbath. Tuesday was a half-day because it was the eve of Remembrance Day. Wednesday was Remembrance Day, followed by Thursday, which was Independence Day; followed once more by Friday, which was the eve of the Sabbath.

Because of this flurry of ceremonial days, President Katzir was tied up in Jerusalem being the President. He was still a professor on the Rehovot faculty, and liked to get down once a week to keep an eye on his scientific team. He had a house across the courtyard from Ham; a military guard post was on it since he'd assumed the Presidency of the State.

He had only a few hours available on Sunday this week. Meyer had been in touch with him about Kaplan's desire for a letter of appreciation, and had told me he might want to see me and to keep Sunday free.

Before Sunday, however, came Saturday (a rolling Saturday, spent in a now traditional manner in a former President's bed), and before that the busy Friday. That was the evening I was at the Sassoons' for coffee. I walked Marta back from there.

It was a delicious night, the scent of late orange blossom in the air, and a bit of moon lying on its back in the different sky of Israel. The tryst had already been arranged for the following day. All the same, moon and bloom were at work, and the place was deserted. She felt like a trip into the orange groves.

The groves were on private land and enclosed by chain-link fencing but her keen eye spotted a gap in it not far from the memorial plaza, so an entry was soon effected. Later on, we looked at the moon and strolled back to the Lunenfeld-Kunin. Among the subjects under review, however, one lingered later. Apropos volume 15, she told me something Patel had said to her.

'He said that whoever took your case couldn't be after your manuscript and it might easily turn up in the post. It's true enough, isn't it?'

'Yes.'

'He was thinking rather well last night, wasn't he?'

'Wasn't he?'

Patel had been thinking well. It struck me on reflection that if he thought volume 15 might turn up, it very easily might.

Whether it did or not, something had obviously to be done about it. For months a pain in the neck, volume 15 now rapidly became a major one. Though it was true that a copy of all the edited material was around, it was around in London. The burglars had left it in a mess, which hadn't properly been put right by the time I'd left. An early call to Caroline produced first a silence and then profanity.

'In *Israel*?' she said. 'You mean, you *got* the lab books?'

'Partially.'

'Partially! It was little old Kaplan, wasn't it?'

'What was?'

'He rang, genius. Yesterday. Out of the blue. Asking how you were.'

'Oh. Well, how was he?'

'Don't you trust me at all?' she said wearily.

I thought about this. The tone of surprise seemed genuine. On the other hand, whoever had stage-managed it from Rehovot had needed someone in London. It seemed as well to keep an open mind. 'Darling, what are you talking about?' I said. 'I was worried for you. Remember Hopcroft and poor Ettie.'

'Is that true? You really worried about me?'

'Well, what else?'

'You're a user. I cried last night.'

'Darling – '

'What do you want?' she said.

I told her. The pages of edited letters, though a head-ache, didn't add up to the mind-numbing kind provided by the footnotes. The uncopied ones had mainly been written in the last scrambled days at the PRO. However, the rough notes on which they were based ought to be kicking around somewhere. She said she'd look for them, and coldly rang off.

I made this call before going to the House on Saturday (rolling Saturday); I had my own key to the place again, and I was there on Sunday when Caroline rang back. Her disposition wasn't any more kindly, but it had not stopped her getting on with the job. She had expressed half the pages off to me, but parts of 1932 were still in confusion. 'I'm trying to put it together,' she said.

'Are you in the flat?'

'I've hardly left the pissy place. I was at it till midnight.'

'Darling – '

'Stuff that. I've been thinking. You could easily have said something to – well, I'll save it, too. How do they say "*au revoir*" out there?'

'*L'hitraot.*'

'That's it.' She hung up.

Sunday was trying, anyway. It brought the President, and the President an invitation to tea. Minutes later, Marie-Louise Wyke phoned to say they'd had one, too, and invited me to lunch. I was deep in 1932, but around one o'clock I biked there.

It was obvious at a glance how Ham had been spending his morning. A massive Scotch came my way from the bottle he held on greeting me. He was in high spirits. A friend had written him that a paper was soon to appear refuting the findings of his dreaded Japanese rival for the Prize. 'He's going to get the shit knocked out of him,' he said gleefully.

'It's a fine thing, the brotherhood of science.'

'Certainly is. Did you work yesterday, too?'

'Yes.' I'd worked with Marta yesterday.

'Dedication.'

'We have our disciplines.'

'Well, let's drink to them.'

'Oh, don't have another,' Marie-Louise moaned.

We did have another. Rather late, we rolled over to lunch. Marie-Louise prided herself on her cooking, and wasn't best pleased at the tough savory slab that her fancy veal had turned into. The dessert was a bigger success. It was her special, Southern strawberry fluff, and so stiff with cognac that Ham enthusiastically called for another, and insisted that I join him.

'Oh, I don't think I. . .'

'Bottoms up,' he said, and with bearish good humor 'poured' me one. The Southern strawberry fluff didn't pour, and his aim looked uncertain. I got my chair back a second late. The contents of the bowl smacked wetly in my lap.

In the small pause he said, 'Oh, Christ.'

'For God's sake!' Marie-Louise said. 'Igor!'

I was staring down at the stuff, now slithering through my legs. It looked as if a dreadful accident had happened to me.

'Jesus, I'm sorry,' Ham said.

Marie-Louise had run to get a cloth, but seemed reluctant to apply it. I dried myself. A large bloodlike stain had settled over my crotch.

'Oh, the lunatic!' Marie-Louise said. 'Take him to the bathroom. Take them off, Igor. I'll soak them.'

'I don't think you can wash these.'

'Put on a pair of Ham's.'

'Well, I – ' He obviously took several sizes larger. I suddenly recalled, with a sense of providence, the pair I'd bought in Manchester.

'He'll get them for you. Take him to the *bedroom* – are you completely mad?' she said to him.

Ham was terribly contrite; but when I took the trousers off in the bedroom and displayed what had happened to my shirt and underpants, he leaned against me and laughed feebly.

'Christ, Igor, you look like you had your – You'd better take a shower.'

I went and took one while he went to the San Martin. He'd evidently told Marie-Louise about the shirt and the underwear, because she called to me to throw them out so that she could wash them and put them in the dryer. When I did this, she put a fresh towel and a dressing gown through the door; I finished showering and went out.

She'd made coffee, and was in a long chair on the terrace, rather thoughtful.

'What is there to say?' she said.

'It's all right.'

'This drinking of his . . . His judgment has always been so good, but now – '

I groaned inwardly. A chat was on the way: the drink problem, the dropout son. However, it wasn't this. She said, 'He so hates gossip, but – Igor, how well do you know Ram Patel?'

'Patel?' I said, surprised. 'I hardly know him at all.'

'He seemed to know a lot about you. He dropped by

this morning. He mentioned something about – well, about Marta,' she said doggedly.

I didn't say anything.

'Stop me if you don't want me to go on. He said he'd seen you with Marta on some occasions – apparently leaving the Weizmann House last night, and earlier in the – in the orange groves, Igor. He takes exercise at night, apparently.'

'I see.'

'Believe me, after a lifetime of campus gossip – I mean, naturally Ham said the hell with it. But I don't know. He said a curious thing, Patel. He said you ought to be dissuaded from the relationship.'

The question of discreet Marta had to be considered, so I kept my mouth shut.

She looked at her watch. 'We have some time. I told Ham to pick up some things for me in the village . . . Igor, did you know Marta's husband was an oil engineer?'

'I knew he was an engineer.'

'An *oil* engineer, Patel says.'

I lit a cigarette.

'He asked if you had told Marta where these lab books were in London.'

I drew on the cigarette and thought about this. How came Patel to know of lab books in London? How did Marie-Louise herself know? Husbands and wives were a special case, of course, but still. Apparently Meyer was right: people did gab.

'Which lab books?' I said.

'I am telling you what *he* said. I know nothing of it.'

'What did Ham say?'

'He said he wasn't your keeper.'

I didn't say anything for a while. Marie-Louise watched me, troubled.

'Igor, I'm telling you this because – you saw how he behaved today. I'm not sure of his judgment lately. If this

233

is important, I thought you'd better know, however embarrassing.'

'Thanks.'

'We all love Marta, 'she said. Her eyes were still troubled. 'I discussed it with Ham, whether we ought to tell you, and he just said . . .'

I could imagine Ham's short reply. He returned just then, and not before time; we were due at the President's in a quarter of an hour. I heard the car pull up, and he came up the path fairly steadily, my trousers over his arm.

Marie-Louise glared at him. 'Take them in the bedroom.' He opened his mouth and closed it again, but meekly obeyed.

She said quietly, 'Don't mention this.'

'Of course not.'

A few minutes later, we were at the Presidential tea party.

It wasn't so very Presidential. Katzir was in a sports shirt, jovial, very friendly. I'd briefly met him once, but we had a lengthy chat this time. He seemed well up on the Pickles Effect, took down Kaplan's details himself, and promised a suitable letter would go off.

All through the tea party, with something of a delayed shock, I wondered about Marta's oil engineer, and about that man of many theories, Dr Patel, and his night exercises.

4

I wasn't clear what to do about it. Since Patel had been so explicit about the grounds for discouraging the relationship, he evidently intended me to know. Why hadn't he told me himself? He was certainly making himself scarce. All Monday and Tuesday I didn't see him. I heard him moving in his room, and wondered whether to beard him.

234

Far better to ask Marta. But not very wise, of course, if he was right . . .

I tried to remember all she'd told me about her husband. They'd met in Stockholm. He'd worked in foreign parts, Romania, Russia; last year in Norway. Hadn't there been an oil strike in Norway? There was oil, of course, in Russia and Romania . . . Well, it wasn't a crime to marry an oil engineer. Only why hadn't she told me? Perhaps because one engineer was very like another. She'd told me little more about any of her family. The family-mindedness hadn't actually run to many details. I'd put it down to reticence, a sense of propriety.

There was also the odd matter of Patel himself. Hadn't he been the one tying himself in knots to produce alternative theories, that it wasn't, needn't, be anyone at Rehovot? Why the sudden rethink?

I had a rethink: of the former ubiquity of this man. He'd approached me at breakfast the morning after I'd arrived in December – a very late breakfast. I remembered the long length of him, uncoiling like a python after the misplaced cucumber. After this, early or late, I'd scarcely moved without bumping into him: peering into the plant genetics lab, offering to accompany me to the Weizmann House, carefully reading the address on the back of Olga's letter. Now, all of a sudden, no Patel.

I'd been brooding for a couple of days, and it was now Tuesday evening. I hadn't told Meyer. There was the question of what to tell him. The extramural antics of a distinguished lady professor were a ticklish matter to set before the Chancellor. I heard a chair scrape next door and had a distinct impression of Patel thinking away in there, which suddenly decided me. I was waiting for a call from Caroline, but I picked up the phone and told them to put it through to Mr Weisgal's house, and went there.

He was looking rather glum, which had become familiar. He had the daily list of those who had visited the

235

archives. Only bona-fide researchers were on it (though anybody could go), and none had looked up 1933.

'Well, I don't know what you expected,' I said.

'Give him time. He'll try.'

'I wouldn't.'

'You don't know what you'd do in his spot. People behave strangely.'

'True,' I said, pouring myself a drop of his Scotch, and after some hesitation told him of other behaviour.

A rather stony look crossed his face at mention of the Weizmann House, but he didn't ask what we were doing there. He didn't ask anything at all.

'I'm sorry to have to tell you this, Meyer,' I said awkwardly.

'The man's a scandalmonger. Who asks him to go walking at night? People are human beings.'

'Quite,' I said, very relieved at his reaction.

'So what is it – an oil engineer,' he said mildly. He jotted himself a note and looked at it. 'Did you arrange to see her again?'

'Tonight, in fact, but that's – '

The phone rang. It was Caroline, from London, a good deal more cheerful. She'd put together the last of the pages. She had also managed to salvage almost half of my notes. Since this left over half missing, it didn't seem so cheering to me. However, she gave me one or two items of information. 'You should get everything by Thursday. I hurried,' she said. 'I'm going off for a few days.'

'Oh.'

'To a château or two on the Loire.'

'I see.'

'Yes, I expected this pent interest. You'll never guess who rang, of course.'

Châteaux on the Loire spelled Willie the wine merchant.

'No,' I said.

'There's nothing here that can't wait now, so I thought

what the hell. A little inspection of the vintage . . . Is it all right?' she said.

'Of course.'

'As I bloody thought . . . Burrowing away, are you?'

'Yes.'

'And missing me – a bit?'

'I miss you a lot, darling. I think of you.'

'I'll spit out the vintage and think of you, then. You *would* like me to call again, wouldn't you, even though the letters are away?'

'Of course. I want to hear you, darling.'

'All right, darling,' she said more warmly. 'I *will* reverse the charge.'

Meyer was looking at me, mouth a bit open, as I put the phone down. He studied his notes again.

'What's to be done?' I said.

'I'll think it over. Carry on with your own affairs.' He gave me another stony look. 'Casanova.'

Affairs weren't very lively that night. A pall of Remembrance-eve gloom hung over the place. Connie had invited us to a sober meal at Bat Yam. Ham picked Marta up first. The thing had been arranged before Patel's revelations, and as if to overcompensate, Marie-Louise sat in the front while I shared the back seat with Marta. I didn't know what to say to her. Perversely she began asking a series of probing questions about the discovery in the archives.

'I suppose they'll have improved the process since,' she said.

'Well, obviously.'

'But it would have been enough to go on, if you hadn't found the other papers?'

'Oh, yes.'

'Is the carotene thing so very important?'

'Apparently.'

'What luck you've got the originals in London.'

To me, every word she uttered was an absolute proof of

237

innocence, but from a slight stiffening of backs in the front it was painfully obvious that it wasn't so evident to all. Maddeningly, she wouldn't leave it alone.

'I don't understand how a letter as important as this could be overlooked, if he gives the whole process in it.'

'It wasn't overlooked. It's a known letter. I'm using it. It's just that the PS on it was never transferred to the carbon copy.'

'Do you work only with carbons?'

'No, I check with the originals if political points seem involved.'

'And they weren't here. It was just an ordinary little letter.'

'Exactly.'

'So now you'll be able to use the whole thing.'

'Oh. I don't know if – '

'But you'll have taken copies of the PS, naturally?'

'Isn't this the turnoff for Bat Yam?' Ham said, rather too loudly.

Marie-Louise switched the conversation, and we got there, and were greeted, and had our sober meal. It was very sober. Connie seemed to have been forewarned, and there wasn't much to drink, which made Ham restless.

Connie had managed at the last moment to get me a ticket for the Independence-eve concert the following night at Caesarea; a party was going from Rehovot. As a special effort after the punishing war, Menuhin, Barenboim, and Stern were appearing, with Zubin Mehta leading the Israeli Philharmonic and pitched choirs. The local Caesarea magnate, Foka Hirsch, whose party I'd been to at Christmas, was making his own special effort by throwing another party afterwards, and we were going to that, too.

There was some discussion about this. Ham asked me to look in and have a drink at six-thirty before setting off, and I said I'd probably be around and about by then.

'You're surely not working all tomorrow?' Connie said.

'No. I'm tired with it. I'll knock off early.'

We knocked off early that night, too, everyone a bit under par with the general gloom. The streets had been silent all evening.

Marie-Louise sat with Marta going back.

5

There was no Patel again at breakfast. He was either keeping me under observation or simply fasting. Well, damn him; I had my own breakfast, picked up a packet of sandwiches for lunch, and set off to the House. I left the bike in the shrubbery beyond the grave, crossed the lawn, and went up the three flights of steps.

I gave Chaimchik's bronze head a brief nod as I let myself in, and locked the door behind me. There was a fusty air about the place. With all the half-days and holidays, I'd had it to myself for days. I was beginning to dislike Verochka's dream house. There seemed something different about it today; some slight change in atmosphere that I couldn't quite place.

The curtains were still drawn in Chaimchik's room. I'd worked till dark the previous day. I opened them a slit. The sun was piercingly bright, too bright for the dim dead world awaiting disinterment here. Ah, well. Back to bloody 1933.

None of Caroline's material had turned up yet, and assembling the missing footnotes, not knowing which were missing, had proved such a hideous as well as baffling bore I'd been tempted once or twice to drop it, in the hope that Patel was right and the stuff would turn up. I was glad I hadn't now. With the information supplied by Caroline I had a pretty fair idea of what was needed, and had luckily laid hands on it; so I assembled my materials and buckled to once more.

I'd worked for an hour or two before the sense of unease brought me to a total halt. What the devil? *Something* was different. The massive Remembrance Day silence, perhaps? It was unpleasant, almost palpable, in the empty House; yet it didn't seem exactly that. Had someone been in – a security guard, perhaps – and made some slight change I'd subconsciously registered? Time for a cup of coffee, anyway. I thought I'd go below to have one and check at the same time.

I went down the marble staircase, whistling to keep my spirits up, and put the kettle on in the kitchen. Back door locked; kitchen and morning room windows locked. I went and checked the other rooms. Library, salon, dining room – all in order and keys turned in locks. The front door was as I'd left it. I stood there for a while, looking round the hall to see what could have disturbed me. The limed oak gleamed coldly back, everything else in place. The feeling was still strong, though, as strong as the day I'd gone into the room with the Christmas tree in it in Stockholm. But that had been an anticipatory feeling.

I had a sharp urge to leave it for the day. But tomorrow was Independence Day, and no one was coming in the day after, either . . . The sudden blast of a whistle sent me almost full length under the hall table. I collected myself, went and turned the kettle off, took the coffee upstairs, and returned doggedly to work.

Sir Montague Burton,
64, Kent Road,
Harrogate, Yorks.

My dear Sir Montague,
   You may know that our friend Israel Sieff has been building an Institute at Rehovot in memory of his boy Daniel. Last year when we were in Palestine, the foundation stone was laid on a little sandhill . . .

He was drumming up funds; and there was a missing footnote here from material gathered years later, 1950s. I went through to Connie's room and lugged the boxes back with me.

I worked on, with a break for sandwiches, till sometime after four when I stopped with a headache. Desk, floor, and bed were well scattered with files. It was early to knock off yet, so I shifted the files off the bed and stretched out there, with the notion that I'd put in another hour and sign off at six. I knew I wouldn't sleep, but the next thing was that bells were jangling, and I started up in alarm to find the room in semidarkness and all the phones ringing.

I chased them about the House until they stopped, and looked at my watch and saw with astonishment that it was half past six. I'd slept a couple of hours. It was probably Ham, anyway; time for the promised drink. So I returned to Chaimchik's room and switched on the desk lamp and began repacking papers. His death certificate fell out and I popped it back in again. In the last hour of work I'd drifted a bit – Hopcroft's old complaint – to pore reminiscently over the old lion's last winters of discontent. They had certainly been very bleak, all his triumphs well behind, the historic achievements over, and only the last bitter dregs left.

There were plenty of those, however. As a last kick, he had done some prodigious things: had swung American policy in a complete volte-face in favour of the establishment of the new State, had won for it the Negev and a loan of a hundred million dollars. While he'd done it, the new young lions had wisely let him get on with it and had played themselves in at home. By the time he rumbled what was going on and was homeward bound himself, he was too late: they had elected him President, stripped him of all political power, and made him, as he savagely said, 'the prisoner of Rehovot'.

Here were all his last rages, to the 'government of upstarts', of 'provincials': that they must surely have some use for his knowledge of affairs, his international reputation. But they hadn't; nor for the 'consultative capacity' he more humbly pleaded with them to use before arriving at decisions. To keep him quiet, Ben-Gurion sent the Cabinet secretary once a week to read him the list of decisions already reached. And so it passed for him, until the clock stopped at six, and the lifelong flow of papers stopped, too. *His* papers, anyway. After the death certificate came other papers, funeral arrangements, copies of the letters of tribute and condolence.

I stuffed them away in handfuls, came on other papers, and paused. Verochka's papers. I'd never seen them in order: only the ones I'd asked for. Here they were, following his death.

Time was ticking on, and I knew I should be going, but I sat down and looked at them, all the same.

She'd been stunned, evidently, for weeks: piles of unanswered letters, invitations. She'd accepted an invitation eventually, a memorial meeting in America (Chaimchik still, from his grassy plot, drumming up the funds). And here was her diary entry as she'd left.

What an ordeal to leave Chaimchik in his grave alone. I cannot get used to it I have already developed a double personality: the Verochka of the old days, proud and happy with her dearest one, and another who is lonely, desolate and forlorn. These two should never be allowed to meet.

But alas, they did. Not long after returning from the trip, she was going through the files and meeting herself when young (Verochka, Verunya, Verusenka, darling and joy), and also, in later boxes of correspondence, some other young. Life had kept a couple of things back for her, too; at about the time that I was seven.

I was musing over this when a door gently blew to below, evidently from a draught. I wondered idly where the draught came from, since no doors or windows were open, when another thought occurred. If no doors were open, how could they blow to?

Odd. A moment later, it got odder still, and without

knowing why I switched the desk lamp off and sat there, absolutely still, except for something throbbing in my throat, perhaps my heart. which seemed to have leaped there, because someone was moving below.

14

There were footsteps, evidently a man's, rather slow and cautious. He was walking about the hall. I heard a door tried, and the scrape of a key in the lock; then it was relocked and another door tried.

I sat with my heart thudding and thought over this. Through the slit in the curtains the sky was still luminous, a greenish-blue afterlight. Not much of it was getting into the room. With the lamp off, I could almost feel my pupils enlarging in the aquarium-like gloom. The sound, now I came to recollect it, had been the quiet snick of the front door. Who the devil had keys to it?

Meyer and Julian had, Harold, Connie, Nellie; perhaps Ze'ev. Could it be Ze'ev, come to see if I wanted a lift? But I hadn't heard the car or the clang of the lodge gates. Anyway, if he knew I was here, he'd have called to me. Whoever was below evidently didn't know I was here. The desk lamp would scarcely have shown up in the sharp afterlight. Intuition, or premonition, had been right. Or could it be a security man, checking that all was well?

I rose and tiptoed through to Nellie's room and peeped through the open door to the landing. Dark below. As I watched, a faint reflected glow flickered in the stairwell and turned away again. Flashlight. Someone was poking about with a flashlight there. Wouldn't a security man turn on the lights for a proper inspection?

The thudding of my heart unpleasantly increased. It was accompanied by a general shaking in every limb as another thought occurred. It might be that the person below did know that I was in the House. This alert person might have been watching the House; perhaps from the garden, or from a position where the bicycle, hidden in the shrubbery, was in view. There was no other way for me to leave. The gates were locked at the lodge.

But why should he come looking for me at the House? Perhaps he hadn't planned to meet me at the House but in the garden. Falling darkness and the possibility of missing me might have brought him here. But why should he want to meet me at all? Perhaps because he thought I had grounds for suspecting him, or to gather some information from me? Both possibilities carried such grave auguries of my subsequent unavailability for further information that I scuttled back into Chaimchik's room and stood there, my pupils enormous as an owl's, peering about in the deepening gloom.

What was needed was something in the nature of a hammer. There wasn't even a bottle. There was the small candlesnuffer and the desk lamp. Far better, altogether more inviting, there was the wardrobe, with dozens of suits to hide behind. Except that a certain doggedness in the researches below suggested that the wardrobe wouldn't go unchecked either. He seemed to be trying every door to see that it was locked from the outside. He would shortly be working upward.

It suddenly struck me that I shouldn't have run back in here but upstairs to Harold's lair. Apart from allowing more time, it had the advantage of opening onto the flat roof. I remembered the rain bouncing there when I'd run about looking for a heater in December. There must be some way off the roof – a drainpipe, at least, in some corner of the House.

I scampered immediately back to Nellie's room, and had got to the doorway when I saw the flashlight's beam, no longer reflected but coming steadily upstairs. Christ!

Back to Chaimchik's room, where I stood and wondered what to do. Put the lamp back on and jolly the whole thing out? 'Hello, old chap. How very nice to see you.' Yes . . . 'Broke in, did you? And what would you like to do, apart from murdering me?' He *might* be a security man, of course, the flashlight a badge of caste or profession. He hadn't broken in, anyway. He'd let himself in, with a key, through the front door.

While considering these niceties, I found that I was standing by the other door out of Chaimchik's room – the locked one that led out to the landing. It was the first door on the landing, facing the stairs. It was locked on the inside. Anyone familiar with the House would know this, and would either make for Nellie's room or start methodically from Julian's at the other end and work down. The thing to do was to let him enter Nellie's room, or pass it, and then unlock the door and get the hell out of it.

I felt for and found the key, while holding my other hand poised over the knob, and as I did this, it turned under my hand. The skin on my scalp crepitated as two thoughts surfaced. One was that he couldn't be a security man, and the other that I hadn't heard him, although I was only inches away and couldn't have been listening harder. He knew I was here.

He pushed the door very gently a couple of times, and then let the knob go. I felt it reverse under my palm, and kept my eye on the open door to Nellie's room, and saw the glow of the flashlight there, and very delicately, with my heart in my mouth, turned the key. Miraculously, it wasn't stuck, didn't creak, just solidly moved. I turned the knob, opened the door a few inches, and peered out. There was a dim glow, the reflection of his flashlight from Nellie's room. Not breathing at all, not even thinking any more, I slid out, closed the door behind me, and went tiptoeing down the stairs like a pantomime robber.

It was almost pitch black in the hall. The front door was over to the right, the area between well stuffed with *objets d'art*. I felt my way between them, arms out like a sleepwalker. I found the door, and the latch, opened it, and thank God was outside. I took an enormous breath of fresh air, and lit off round the House in the general direction of the bike.

Although a lifetime had passed, it couldn't have been more than four or five minutes since he'd entered the House. All the same, the greenish-blue afterlight had already turned to an unearthly mauve. Nothing was quite real in it, flowers and trees straining forward as though poised for some new experience in the approaching night. The bike was in the shrubbery beyond the sunken lawn below. I went down the three flights of rock steps to it, and almost immeditely realized that this was not such a good thing to do. The grave glimmered pallidly in the lawn below, easily visible from Chaimchik's window. So would I be. A quick look confirmed that this was the case. As I peered up, his face peered down through the slit in the curtains. I had an impression of a very tall figure hunched over the table in the dark. He saw me and immediately went. I had such a good idea where that I took the last flight in one jump and scuttled for the shrubbery.

I was in such a panic that I couldn't remember where I'd left the damned thing. It didn't seem to be where I thought I'd left it. No time for investigation now. I took to my heels again, and in the deepening violet light went haring down the straight approach lane from the grave to the plaza.

The enormous marble plaza was empty, except for the stark monument to the perished six million. I flew past it, to the long flight of ceremonial steps that led to the main avenue.

There was not a soul in sight. As I tore down the steps, I heard him pounding behind me, rubber shoes squeaking on the marble. There was something extraordinarily unnerving and desperate in the sound. He was intent on stopping me before I got to people. Breath sobbing, barely conscious of my legs, I took the steps without noticing, made the empty avenue, and decided to get off it fast.

There were trees on both sides. I suddenly remembered the hole in the chain-link fencing that bounded the orange grove to the right. At the same moment, the streetlighting came on, and I saw the hole, a ragged gap below a tree, and was through it, and had to slow in the blackness at the other side, and then had to slow a lot more, tall grass, old spreading trees.

Once I'd slowed, I had to stop, couldn't go on any longer, had never run faster in my life. I didn't seem able to take in enough air, breath painful and choked in my throat, my legs like lead. I stood in deep foliage and tried to control my breathing and wondered how I'd got into this insane situation. I should have left hours before, as soon as I'd felt the first tremor of alarm; have pedalled away in good broad daylight, instead of being caught here, in the dark, paralytic with fright.

I heard him suddenly, first some fumbling and then the swish of tall grass. He'd found the gap, had deduced what I'd done, knew I was here. This was a thinker, in a place that specialized in them. He came on for a moment, and abruptly stopped, realizing I'd stopped. He stood stock still and looked slowly round: a black indistinct figure, fifty yards away. Then he flashed his light, evidently had second thoughts, and put it off again.

Silence.

He did something strange. He went away, back to the fence. I heard him for a while, and then couldn't.

I was slowly realizing what an idiot I'd been. Beyond the fence, a network of lights now glimmered, a couple of hundred yards away, at the other side of the avenue. There was another development of faculty villas there. The Sassoons lived in it. A few minutes more of running would have taken me there. It suddenly struck me what he was up to. He had stationed himself between me and the villas, had put enough distance between us to spot any movement of mine back to the fence.

The last light had vanished from the sky; stars visible

now. The hard glossy leaves exhaled the scent of oranges in the warm night. The new crop hung tightly like marbles, a clutch of them against my sweating head. I looked at my watch and saw it dimly shining at a few minutes in seven. Ham would be wondering why I hadn't turned up. Just then a car came up the avenue, and I wondered if it was him, going to find out where I was. A moment later, in its headlights, I saw the man – at least where he was.

He was standing quite still against the fence, facing into the grove. The car turned in to the villas, and darkness fell again. I tried to remember the topography of the place. The next building on this side must be the Institute of Nuclear Science. It stood in a landscaped area, set well back off the avenue, with a network of paths behind. Was it possible to get at it by going into the grove?

Very cautiously, I got down and began to crawl, brushing the ground in front of me to avoid the crackle of twigs. There were various unpleasant messes from old rotted oranges. I passed several lines of trees and looked back. No movement. Away to my left now I could hear the soft thud of the heavy-water plant. Far enough. Time to turn.

I crawled for six or seven minutes before I heard the rustling, and immediately froze. It wasn't from behind. To the front and a bit to the left. Was he outflanking me?

I kept absolutely still, and listened, heart thudding. The rustling was rather deliberate and investigative. Suddenly I got the lot, all at once. A growl, a rush. A dog! It had scented me, was on to me, with a series of rushes, a little snarling thing. I heard a clattering, well behind, and knew he'd heard it, too, and at once rose and gave the little bastard a heartfelt booting before taking off.

On my feet, I could clearly see the upper storeys of the Nuclear Building, coolly and discreetly lit, and the return line of the fence silhouetted against it, not fifty yards away. As I neared it, I saw how the dog had got in. Building work was going on beyond the fence, and the bottom of the wire mesh had been cut and rolled back to facilitate the digging. I took a running dive underneath it, kicked the dog back to keep the approaching brain busy, and spent a few seconds pulling the rolled-up fence down. A couple of boulders helped with this, and then I was off.

A dangerously exposed road led to the frontage of the building on the avenue. It was quite empty. Service personnel might more reasonably be expected to be at the back – a prospect enhanced by a soft roar, evidently from a turbine house there.

I took off in that direction, and found the turbine house. Hot air was venting from exhaust grilles, and its steel doors were firmly closed. I ran past it into a lane of service sheds. There were armies of oxygen cylinders and steel bottles, a network of piping, the odd engine roaring away, lights blazing: not a soul in sight. I kept to what shadow there was, rounded the back of the Nuclear Science Institute and a complex of adjacent buildings. Still nobody.

There was presently a great gap of churned-up earth and a rocketlike structure surrounded by cranes and tractors. A lit-up poster on stilts showed what it was going to be: the Koffler Accelerator. It was the skeleton of an advanced atom-smasher that would go nineteen storeys high. Its roots were somewhere in an enormous hole. On all sides there were small mountains of spoil.

I paused awhile, breathing heavily, and peered about. There was no obvious way out of the place, once in it: it offered plenty of cover, though. I thought of something else as I panted into this desolation. I suddenly recalled having seen the tops of these mountains of spoil before, also the cranes at work on the accelerator tower: I'd seen them through the windows of the plant genetics lab. It couldn't be far away; and at the special greenhouse, at least, a guard was on duty day and night.

I looked for a way through the mess, and heard the dog yelping from the direction of the sheds; which was cheering. In giving him the dog and a reliable early-warning system, I'd shown thinking as fast as his – faster, probably, if he hadn't yet assassinated the dog, which would have been an early project of mine.

There didn't seem to be a way through the mess. The thing was simply an immense crater, rimmed for more than 180 degrees by the spoil. I took an uphill track between two mounds, sinking in the sandier soil, and reached the top drenched in sweat. I saw him from there; saw the dog, at least, snapping and jumping at an elusive shape in the shadow of a tractor. I sank down on my haunches and looked around.

The greenhouses were a couple of hundred yards away on an opposite hilltop, and streetlighting was shining right through them. In the valley between was a road, and a building that I vaguely remembered but couldn't identify. Puzzling over it, I thought of something else. The moment it occurred to him where I was trying to get to, he could easily run round by road and cut me off.

No time for reflection here. I rolled over on hands and knees right away and got moving. He couldn't have seen me, but earth must have tumbled down, because the next thing I heard was the dog yelping as it ran along the road I got to my feet and went pellmell down the hill, almost skiing, and in a flash, quite a flash, slammed into a boulder, and blacked out.

Everything black. There was earth in my mouth. I spat it out and tried to scramble to my feet but discovered that in some curious way I was stuck. I was in a pit. My feet were tangled in a cage. It took some scrambled moments to discover that I'd come to rest in some newly prepared foundations. A web of reinforcing iron was in them, ready for concrete-pouring, and my feet were jammed in. I tugged and wrenched them out, and one immediately twisted underneath me.

I leaned back against the mound of spoil and felt the foot ache quite sickeningly. All the rest of me was aching. I'd collected a solid thump on the head and a bruise was swelling above my eyes. Another thing was that I couldn't hear the dog.

Strange.

Stranger, now that the world was slowing, the unknown building was slowly turning itself into the back of the San Martin.

How the devil had I got to the back of the San Martin? I couldn't remember seeing it from this position. Ahead and a bit to the right were lit-up streets and buildings. My instinct was to go for them – to get away from the San Martin, anyway. Except that whatever I thought, wouldn't this fast thinker have out-thought me? I felt the hairs prickling all over my body. Away from here, anyway!

Resting on the good foot, I felt around and found a solid lump of rock with each hand, and at once began to hobble away from the San Martin. The damaged foot ached quite hideously, but it supported me. Towards the edge of the area of light, I paused and gradually began to orientate. Some of the buildings were definitely familiar. The Institute of Applied Science – wasn't it? Definitely the Institute of Pure Mathematics. Quite close by, the heavy-water plant was thumping and gurgling: a cloud of steam hung in the air.

Lit-up windows in the buildings, cars parked, air conditioners whirring. Safer here, surely, to stop skulking in shadow and come out into the light. There must be people about.

I took a breath and hobbled out into the road, into the middle of it, and actually began to trot, clutching firmly to the rock. Weirdly, there still wasn't a soul in sight. The whole Institute might have been hissing and clicking away like a robot installation on the moon. I had a distinct impression he was going to spring out at me from somewhere. I thought I'd send one rock through a lighted window and save the other for him. But nobody sprang and nobody appeared, and with a deepening sense of unreality I realized I wasn't destined to encounter another human being in this particular nightmare, until I looked to the left and saw one.

A cosy and familiar building sat at the end of a narrow lane, and a cosy and familiar figure was coming down the steps of it. With the nightmare knowledge that nothing would avail and nobody hear, I inflated my lungs and roared.

'Finster!'

He stopped as though shot, and after a pause began turning this way and that, powerful nose almost scenting.

'Finster!'

He saw me, and by this time could hardly help it. In the empty lane I was springing high in the air on the good foot, both arms semaphoring. He continued slowly down the steps of the Daniel Sieff and I hobbled rapidly towards him.

'Finster – I'm so glad to see you!'

'Ah.' He seemed pleased at this. 'You are taking some exercise?' he said.

I was in a fine lather all over, the breath fairly singing from my nostrils. 'Yes,' I said.

'Excellent. It is too easy to be lazy when the warm weather comes. What is it – specimens you have collected?' He was adjusting his spectacles to examine more closely the rocks in my hand.

I had a look, too, before throwing them away, and then back at Finster. He looked so real, so good. 'What are you doing here?' I said.

He smiled indulgently. 'A fermentation knows nothing of Remembrance Day. There are certain readings I must check ... But I understand well the urge to pick up a specimen or two, however worthless. It's hard to run, without an object. Although I understand Dr Patel does it. He runs also at night, I believe.'

'I know he does,' I said.

I recalled Marie-Louise's remarks about his night exercise, and at the same moment had a recollection from last

December, looking out the window at the rapid, jerky movement of a running man. Patel.

'It's a question of temperament,' Finster was saying. 'It's hard for a person of impatient temperament just to exercise. I myself use the stationary bicycle. One can take a reading at the same time.'

We walked amiably back to the avenue together, and he cited a further example or two to illustrate the impatience of his temperament. He walked me right up to the academic courtyard before wishing me a good night, and I hobbled briskly into it, giving the guard on Katzir's house a loud *shalom* to insure that he was awake and watching me as I made my way to Ham's and pressed the doorbell.

He answered it himself. He had a towel round his waist and a glass of Scotch in his hand. His mouth opened as he took in my dishevelled condition, and then a bit more as I took his Scotch from him and drank it.

'What the hell happened to you?' he said.

I let the Scotch go down.

'Ham, did you call me at the House?'

'Yes. I tried the San Martin, and they said – '

'About half past six?'

'No, two minutes ago. I thought maybe you'd fallen asleep, so – '

Not Ham, then. Patel had phoned, and received no answer . . . He hadn't known I was there. It had been surprise, shock, he'd shown when he'd hunched forward and seen me from the window.

'What is it?' Ham said.

I told him.

He didn't seem able to take it. He stood blinking at me. He said, 'But that's absolutely – Are you sure?'

'No doubt of it.'

'It's unbelievable . . . Oh, my God!' His face suddenly changed. 'We are expecting him. He's coming here. Marie-Louise thought it would be better if Marta and you didn't – if Marta went with the Sassoons. Now what the – '

The phone rang, and Marie-Louise answered it, apparently from upstairs. She shouted down presently that it was Patel to say we needn't wait. He was at the Sassoons', and not feeling well. If he went to the concert, he would go with them.

'Did Igor arrive yet?' she called.

'He's here now.'

'Oh. He asked. I didn't know. Hi, Igor! I'll be down in a minute.'

Ham poured another drink.

I was rapidly phoning Meyer; but he'd gone.

'Ham, what am I to do?'

'Well, goddamn it – look, don't alarm Marie-Louise.' There were hurried sounds of her collecting herself. 'Are you sure it was him?'

'It *was* him, damn it. It was.'

'Well, I suppose, the police, security . . . What do you tell them?'

'Well, I say . . . What do I say?'

'That a guy broke in, who looked like – who was of the physical *type* of – '

'He didn't break in. He had a key.'

'Well, he wouldn't have that now.'

'No.' We looked at each other. 'I can't just go to a concert,' I said.

'What is *he* going to do?'

'Run.'

'After you?'

'No, I meant – Well, maybe,' I said, worried.

'At the concert?'

'Well, he won't go to the concert.'

'Would he expect you to go?'

'No. Yes. Damn it, I don't know. What do you think?'

'I guessed he'd think, after everything that's happened, that you certainly wouldn't – I mean . . .'

'No. No.'

'So maybe it would be better if – I mean, not to stay where . . . God knows.'

'Yes.'

'Hello, Igor.' Marie-Louise was coming downstairs. 'Ham, aren't you dressed yet? . . . Igor?' She'd suddenly caught sight of my battle stains. 'What on earth have you done to yourself?'

'He fell over,' Ham said truthfully. 'Out there.'

'Oh, Igor! Those building sites. Are you hurt?'

'No, I – '

'And your trousers!' They were liberally bespattered with dirt, an orange stain on each knee. 'Well, thank goodness I got the others back. Come upstairs and wash up. I'll give you . . .'

In a couple of minutes I was washing up, and changing into the other trousers. I seemed to be changing trousers a good deal in this house. Just a few minutes later, still unclear about most issues, I was on the way to Caesarea.

I recovered a little on the way, and thought out the position: Patel's gumshoeing around and watching me, the careful sowing of suspicion about Marta. He had evidently wanted Marta out of the way. I stayed in the House longer when Marta was there. Remembrance Day must have seemed a good bet: nobody about if I didn't work late. He had telephoned first, had quietly and systematically tried all the doors. He must have got the shock of his life when he'd seen me watching him from below . . .

I recalled the desperate squeak of his shoes on the marble plaza Like a fool, I'd dived into the groves at the very place where he'd earlier spotted me with Marta. Well, he'd lost me, anyway. Perhaps I'd been knocked out longer than I thought. I hadn't appeared where he'd calculated I would appear. He had evidently figured that I must have found a way of getting to Ham's. He hadn't turned up there, anyway. But he had telephoned to see if I had. And

Marie-Louise had told him no. He must now be working out what I was up to.

I tried to work out what he was up to. At the Sassoons'. Deciding whether to go to the concert or not; trying to read my mind, as I was his. Either I'd recognized him or I hadn't. If I hadn't he must act quite naturally. He hadn't been acting naturally; he'd changed plans abruptly. But of course he'd been rattled. I looked at my watch. Unbelievably, it was still not quite half past seven. Less than an hour since I'd heard the quiet snick of the door from Chaimchik's room. But he would have pulled himself together by now.

How would pulled-together Patel read the situation? Somewhere in the rubbish heaps by the atom-smasher, he'd lost a very frightened I. Druyanov. I. Druyanov, whether he'd recognized him or not, would shortly after, from some haven, be raising hell and security men. Security men would by now be at the House. If Druyanov *had* recognized him, they would also be beaming in on Patel. He would by now be regretting that he'd gone to the Sassoons'; would be rapidly thinking up some reason why he was there instead of at the Wykes', where he was supposed to be. But from then on he'd do everything that he was supposed to do. What was he supposed to do? Go to the concert.

Yes. He'd go, certain to. I was suddenly sure of it. I'd be seeing Patel soon. He wouldn't expect to see me. Well, jolly good. In a way . . .

2

The amphitheatre at Caesarea was a splendid sight in the black night, but as I hobbled up the steep stone steps I was on the lookout for an even more splendid one. I saw it presently: white mane of hair, Red Indian face very grave as he peered down into the arena below. He was in the

VIP tier, some tiers below ours, and an aisle away. I couldn't stop or turn back in the file of late arrivals, but I marked the spot, and when we were seated marked it again.

He wasn't so far from the aisle. I was seated at the edge of mine, which was all to the good. I needed him. The first car park had been full of buses and we'd been signalled on to the secondary one beside the Crusader town. I'd thought out the position as we hurried back the few hundred yards to the amphitheatre.

We were scarcely seated on the stone benches (on cushions Marie-Louise had wisely brought) before the drums rolled. Everyone stood as Katzir arrived below. The national anthem was played, and then he took his seat and the whole place settled. In the general hubbub, even later arrivals were still scuttling up the stone steps.

I hadn't seen Connie, or Marta. I hadn't seen any of them. All around, the great rock bowl seethed, the tiers aglow with faces, like banks of flowers; there was the glint of jewellery, women's bare arms, petal-like. But now, as I sank back, I saw Connie waving, some distance along the row. She'd come with a party, and a block of vacant seats stretched between. It suddenly struck me why they were vacant as Felicia Sassoon came loping, pinkfaced, up the steps. She was followed by Marta, and by Michael, and by none other than Dr Ram Patel.

There was a very satisfactory double take out of him as he spotted me. I was standing to let them shuffle past, everything now ashuffle: choirs below shuffling onto long benches at the back of the brilliantly lit arena; musicians fiddling with their music stands; Zubin Mehta gently flexing inside his tail coat on the podium.

'So sorry . . . so sorry,' as they passed.

'I must speak to you!' Patel was gripping my arm, hissing in my ear.

'All right.'

'Most urgent. Do nothing until then.'

He had passed, and passed Marie-Louise and Ham and Felicia, was sinking furtively into place as the conductor's arms came up, and down, and the *Eroica* began.

I was in some turmoil as I listened to the sonorous opening chords. 'I must speak to you! . . . Do nothing until then.' He'd thought up something fast, then. I was in turmoil, anyway. There was something peculiarly apt and sonorous about all ceremonial events in Israel: a resonance of ages. Just now, in this place, there was an aptness so extraordinary that two thousand hearts seemed to catch, all around.

Beethoven had dedicated his symphony to Napoleon, and then had second thoughts on observing that the idol had feet of clay, a notion familiar in the area. But as the massive work proceeded with its hammer blows of fate, its lament for heroes and its funeral march, there was a spasm even more intimate and poignant from the audience. Between the last Independence eve and this, heroes had fallen here, some for good and all, others into political darkness. A whole sanguine society had been felled, was on hands and knees, still stunned; and not for the first time, or even for the first time in this place.

Twenty-five hundred participants of an earlier debacle had found themselves on hands and knees here; the Roman conqueror Titus had brought them, prisoners of war from Jerusalem, after destroying it, and matched them against lions in a lively season of sporting events.

The place had been built by Herod three generations earlier and dedicated to his patron, the Caesar Augustus, in 13 BC It had been the most magnificent town on the East Mediterranean, with a huge and splendid port and a colonnaded jetty for VIP arrivals from Rome. There'd been no economy out of Herod in the matter of local materials; his marble, prime stuff, had come from Italy, and I could see bits of it still strewn about the cliff top beyond the amphitheatre: broken columns, busts, sarcophagi.

This area was only a small part of Herod's town; to the north a kibbutz now sat on another section, and to the south, where we'd left the car, the Crusaders had built their town on another bit. It had even extended beyond that. Twinkling lights in the distance marked the country villas of Foka Hirsch and his affluent neighbours, and somewhere behind me Lord Rothschild had laid out a golf course on another of Herod's suburbs. In the years after the Arab conquest, Bedouin had come to squat in the tumbled magnificence. I could see the rough fishing jetty that had been cobbled out of one arm of the Crusader harbour. The tiny figures of tourists were ambling up and down it now, between the floodlit mosque and the fish restaurants and art galleries that were the most recent contributions to the scene.

As Beethoven thundered on below, I thought hard. Patel had evidently realized that I'd recognized him; must have, to have approached me so directly, this man who'd been staying away. 'Most urgent. Do nothing until then.' Why? Because he wanted to do something first. Explanation, entreaty, bribery – or something of a more active antipersonnel type?

I leaned forward slightly and looked along the row. His eyes reflected glassily in the lighting from below; there was greenish pallor about the face, which was glistening, mouth a bit slack. Something would be going on in the upper storey. Whatever it was, it boded no good. Definitely, Meyer first.

As the long work came to an end, to tumultuous and emotive applause, Marie-Louise said she had to spend a penny. The same emotional response seemed to be wrung from other ladies, some hundreds of whom sprang up on all sides. This was fortunate. Almost trampled underfoot by urgent matrons, going both down and up, I was immediately engulfed, but managed to shuffle sideways down. I didn't see what happened to Patel. When I looked back, only Ham and Michael Sassoon seemed to be left in the row.

Coffee bars were operating in the intermission in various parts, and Meyer was stretching his legs on his way to one. He was chatting to the American Ambassador, Keating. I kept my eyes on both white thatches and struggled through to them. He saw the look on my face and excused himself to Keating.

'Meyer, I've got to talk to you. Patel – '

'Okay, we'll talk about it later.'

'What do you mean, later? I – '

'How did *you* find out?' he said.

It took a moment to sort out this tangle. He'd had a phone call when on the point of leaving. The security guard on the Wix had come upon Patel rather peculiarly circling the building. He'd asked him what he wanted. Patel said he was looking for somebody. The man had told him the place was closed and that nobody was about. He'd phoned Meyer about it.

'Damn it, that isn't anything,' I said. I told him what was.

'He's here?' he said.

'Of course he is.' I looked frantically around in the mob. 'He's trying to find me.'

'So stay away from him. Is he going on to this party?'

'Well, he came *here*,' I said.

'So he'll find us both. I'll look in there.'

'But what shall I – '

'Nothing. Do nothing until then. What can he do now? We can't talk here. I'm sorry,' he said to Keating, who was drumming his heels, and turned away.

'Do nothing until then' from both of them. Definitely a fluid situation here. What was the matter with everybody? Couldn't they understand the terrible, the absolutely grotesque things that had happened to me this evening? Ham's principal concern had been that I shouldn't alarm Marie-Louise; Meyer's not to offend Keating. I had a look at my

261

watch. Still not nine o'clock: barely a couple of hours since the nightmare had begun. It showed no signs of abating. It had become that bit worse, in fact; was insidiously transforming itself into that more hideous type in which the awful things happened in a jolly carnival atmosphere with nobody apparently noticing, or caring if they did. *What could Patel do now?* He could do a lot. There were such things as knives, or needles. There were such things as huddled figures discovered after the throng had passed.

My mouth was dry and I needed a cup of coffee myself, but by the time I struggled to the bar, bells had begun to ring and the crowd to disperse. It seemed safest to disperse with them. I kept my eyes open on returning to the auditorium. I felt like a lost soul, an exceedingly panicky one, in this sea of drifting faces. The aisles were crowded, people shuffling back into place along the clifflike stone tiers. I saw him, miles up. He was coming *down*, with Marta and Connie; had evidently been to a coffee bar on top. He was looking about him. His eyes seemed to fix on Meyer, who was settling convivially back in place.

I shuttled swiftly back into the entry arch again and thought this out. Obvious enough that Meyer had been to a bar below; better if I hadn't been. I pattered rapidly-back through the bar, found the steps to the upper level and re-emerged into the amphitheatre with the last of the crowd from above. He was still looking all about, screwing round in his seat – except that he had changed his seat. He'd swapped with Felicia, was now sitting next to Ham, one nearer to me. He saw me coming down and his eyes hung rather sickly on mine. I dropped into my seat just as the choir all stood up and, after a trill-up or two from the orchestra, broke into the most tremendous hosanna.

The already good acoustics of Herod's amphitheatre had been rendered near perfect by a massive honeycomb-design baffle that deadened the slight hiss of the sea beyond. The sound level was quite extraordinary. My mind flooded instantly with climactic scenes from old movies in which mayhem had taken place under cover of similar blasts of cutural uproar. As Mehta wound up the orchestra to add to it, I felt myself shaking like a leaf.

But what could he do here, after all – blow a dart tipped with fatal curare? Yes, easily. He could do any damned thing he wanted, probably. He wasn't only fast in the upper section, but everywhere else – exceptionally nippy and dexterous in all directions. I recalled the unnerving speed with which he'd practically caught up with me after my flying start – only seconds in it, really. I'd won those seconds by leaving through one door as he entered another. The trick was to make every second count.

As the bellowing continued, I tried to do this. It was a question of identifying a critical situation ahead, of bringing some large magnification to bear on it; if only the pandemonium would let up below.

It did, mercifully. A brief cantata or two followed, and then the masters of keyboard and string took over, and Vivaldi began delicately to unravel. Much easier on the ears, and I leaned over and whispered, 'Marie-Louise, change places with Ham after this.'

Her eyes were moist and she seemed to come back from some distance, but she nodded, and I nodded, and gave more of an ear to Vivaldi. They were delicately unpicking him below. I began to unpick the next hour, looking for the vital seconds where the action was. In the busy brain along the row, the options would be under review. He'd missed me in the interval. Something funny could have happened in the interval. He wouldn't like anything funny to happen again. He'd stick like a leech; wouldn't want to delay whatever he'd got in mind till we got to the party. The difficult moments would come between here and the party; in practice between here and the car. These were the moments that called for the magnification.

Vivaldi ran out, and in the delighted applause Marie-Louise shuffled about with Ham, who presently shuffled down beside me.

'What is it?' he said.

'Stick tight when we leave here. Meyer wants me to keep away from Patel till we get to Hirsch's.'

'Well, that is going to be embarrassingly bloody difficult,' Ham said. Patel had already spoken to him; he'd changed seats to ask if he could come in the car. He had met friends of the Sassoons' in the coffee bar, who had come by bus, and who were also going to the party. His offer to give up his seat in the Sassoons' car had been gladly accepted.

I began to sweat very slightly. I was on to him, was reading him pretty clearly now. But his reactions were coming altogether too fast. I looked along the row at him, and found he was looking at me, face still glistening. I felt mine glistening more, with the sheer strain of trying to outthink him.

Barenboim, Menuhin, and Stern had taken their homage below, and with great good humour now embarked on something of a fugal nature. So did I. I had the glimmering of something as the piece ended and the orchestra limbered up for the last item (also well chosen, a final salute to the ship of state on its twenty-sixth year: Mendelssohn's *Calm Sea and Prosperous Voyage*), and was on my feet applauding with the rest of them as the concert ended.

'Let the air out of a tyre,' I said to Ham.

'Goddamn it, I can't do that.'

'I'm not going in that car with him.'

'But – '

'Do it, Ham. Please do it.'

Marie-Louise passed; then Patel. He took my arm urgently as he stood in the aisle. 'I must talk with you, Igor.'

'Of course,' I said, and opened my arms to Felicia and gave her a tremendous hug. I gave Marta one, too, and then Connie. Patel got himself bundled down the steps during this. He called, 'Igor!' His face was quite greenish. 'We will meet below?'

264

'Of course we will.'

No help for it; but I saw that I had an arm round both Connie and Marta as we did so. There was still a considerable scrum of people, but as we got into the lane numbers of them streamed off to the buses. In the lane, Ham didn't seem to know what was for the best. He started off in front with Marie-Louise, but then dropped uncertainly behind as he saw what Patel was doing. Patel was very weirdly running about there, unable to decide which end of the threesome to attach himself to.

'Igor, we must talk,' Patel said.

'All right.'

'Alone, please.'

'Ram, what is the big secret?' Connie said.

'Ah, men's talk!' Patel said, with a gruesome attempt at gaiety.

'But we're going in the same car,' I said.

'Ah, I had forgotten,' Patel said. He said it at about the moment that Ham, dropping behind, came into earshot.

Several hundred people were moving along the road to the car park, and we stood around in a loose cluster when we got there. Ham stood around, too, until I gave him a look and he wandered off.

He was away for what seemed a long time, which Connie fortunately filled in with illuminating comments on the Crusader town for the benefit of a couple of Americans in her party. We were standing just outside it, the massive walls floodlit from the dry moat below. Connie gave all the facts about Richard Lionheart and Saladin, and also about Louis IX, who had rebuilt the walls, and then Sultan Baybars I, who had finally stormed them in the Arab conquest of 1265. Not much had happened since until the Israelis had excavated and found it all still there, and had put it back in position again, together with a box office to greet tourists at the business end of Louis IX's moat.

Ham returned towards the end of the dissertation, and he was smiling. 'Aren't we going to a party?' he said.

The group split up, and I reluctantly let Connie and Marta go, and placed a protective arm round Marie-Louise instead as we went to the car.

'Well, goddamn it!' Ham said as we neared it.

'What is it?'

'Have I got a flat?'

'A flat?' I studiously examined the car. He had got it flat as a pancake. 'I do believe you have,' I said.

'Oh, no!' Marie-Louise said.

'Oh, yes.' He was down on his haunches. 'That's very flat.'

'You can't mend a flat,' Marie-Louise said.

'You don't have to mend the goddamn thing. You just change the wheel.'

'When did you change a wheel?'

'I can change a wheel,' I said.

'We'll both change it. You two go on with the others.'

'I will help,' Patel said.

'No, no. Hey, Connie!' Ham yelled.

The argy-bargy had gone on considerably too long; the Sassoons had already cruised by. Connie came slowly up, headlights on. 'Are you in trouble?' she said.

'A flat. Can Marie-Louise and Ram squeeze in?'

'Of course.'

'I will stay,' Patel said. His face had a drenched look in the headlights.

'We'd get in each other's way. Carry on.'

Connie and Marie-Louise saw that this happened, and Patel left with a rather despairing look; he was on somebody's knee as the car pulled out.

'You certainly have some cute ideas,' Ham said. 'Can you change a wheel?'

'Well, bugger the wheel!' I said. An enormous wave of relief was sweeping over me as I realized the strain I'd been under. I'd been under it for hours, with nobody apparently understanding. Ham still didn't seem to understand. In the massive silence, the floodlit walls exuded a healing calm.

'Ham, this is the most incredible thing,' I said.

'Well, it is. I didn't like to say it.'

I looked at him. 'You didn't believe me?'

'Well – *something* obviously happened. But – '

'Oh, for God's sake!' I told him of Meyer and the incident at the Wix.

His face creased up at this. 'What the hell was he going round and round the Wix for?'

'Well, there's no doubt it *was* him. He was after me.'

'At the Wix?'

'He must have thought I'd gone that way. It's not such a crazy idea. You can get out to the avenue there, people likely to be around. Anyway, that's what he did.'

'He went from the Wix,' Ham said, slowly working this out, 'and passed our house and went to the Sassoons'?'

'He must have thought I'd got to your place.'

'Why?'

'Well, he knew I was going there. He rang to ask if I'd arrived.'

'Marta must have told him. He didn't know earlier. He assumed you were going with her. He said so when he called in the morning to ask if he could come with us. He'd been chewing my ear about Marta, so I didn't bother to disillusion him – some nonsense you don't need to – '

'I do know. Marie-Louise told me.'

'Oh. Well,' he said.

We were walking, and I lit a cigarette. We had the night to ourselves. It was marvellous just to walk and think in it without pressure; except that Ham had become characteristically occupied with the logistical problems of the Wix and the Sassoons. Had I been so obtuse about Hopcroft's danger? Probably.

'I could have been killed!' I said.

'Oh, Igor, come on.'

'What else could he have wanted?'

'You said it wasn't you. You said that.'

'He'd have preferred me out of the place, it's true. He phoned to see . . . But where did he get the key? Help a bit, Ham.'

'Well, I don't know where he got the key.'

'And what was he after if not me?'

'God knows. Perhaps the letter?'

'The letter?' It was so long ago I'd almost forgotten it. 'There was no letter,' I said.

'There wasn't?'

'There was no PS. We made it up. The idea was to trap him.'

'Well, it looks as if it worked,' he said.

'But he was supposed to go to the archives for it.'

'Maybe that's why he didn't.'

'So why the House?'

'Well, goddamn it, I don't know. The copy, maybe?'

'What copy?'

My jitteriness was making him jittery. 'Any copy. Didn't Marta think there was a copy?'

I remembered it just as he said it; her questions in the car. Oh, my God, it couldn't be. 'You don't think – I mean Marta and . . . It's ridiculous.'

'Well, of course it is,' he said.

So it was, and I told myself how ridiculous it was, the idea of Marta and Patel, the one casting suspicion on the other, in order to distract attention from . . . Except. Except, I thought sickly, the key. Marta had often been in a position to extract my key, and have it copied, and handed over to . . . And attention then directed to her so that I wouldn't invite her on the chosen day . . . Nonsense, of course. Such nonsense that I changed the subject right away. I heard myself gabbling. 'He wasn't in the place two minutes. He must have come in and right away started working up – Damn it, he *was* after me!'

'Hey, now, Igor!'

'Ham, I'm not going there!' I'd suddenly remembered

the garden at Hirsch's. People would be drifting about it with drinks in this season: a shadowy subtropical place. He'd been taken off balance by the ploy with the tyre. But he knew I was evading him now. He knew. He wouldn't let it happen again. 'We'd better shoot right back to the security people!' I said.

'And make a public scandal before hearing what Meyer has to say? After all, no harm was – '

'He wanted to kill me!'

'Igor, calm down – '

'He knew I was there. He just didn't know where. He went hunting from room to room – '

'But if he phoned first – '

'I don't know that he did. Anybody could have phoned. Connie could have phoned.'

'Okay, she could. Forget the phone. It doesn't mean he was after you.'

'There's nothing else he can have – '

'The bloody copy!'

'There was no copy.'

'But he didn't know it.'

'So why didn't he look for it?'

'Maybe he did'

'I tell you he wasn't in there two minutes. He went in, and I wasn't there, and he came out after me!'

'Maybe you'd frightened him. Maybe he'd found you just had been there.'

'Ham, he knew it.'

'It doesn't follow. He could have gone looking for this goddamn letter, and discovered you weren't working with the period, but with 1952, and the desk lamp still warm, and realized – Well, God knows what he realized. Couldn't it have been like that?'

'Well, it could. It could,' I said. But I said it a bit late. With something very like a heart attack, I'd suddenly wondered how he knew all this about 1952 and desk lamps. In the brief pause, and a rapid review of all I'd told him, no desk lamps showed up. No 1952, either. I felt myself beginning to vibrate all over. Even my teeth began to chatter.

'Of course it could,' he agreed. But he agreed a bit late, too. There was a tone of somewhat ominous kindliness in his voice, as of a man who has also taken a point, and that it was all rather a pity. It certainly was.

I was grinding out my cigarette at that moment, which seemed to be an exceptionally long one. The next, I was halfway up the wall, having sprung there. I could hardly see for fright, and was by no means clear where I was going. If tonight's experience showed anything, though, it was that after discoveries of a certain kind it was as well to be elsewhere. The early moments tended to be the significant ones in getting there.

15

Louis IX had put it up and Baybars I had knocked it down and Igor the Quick went up what was left of it like a cat. I'd landed on a low wall, which ran up, via a long buttress, to a flight of crumbling steps. I scrambled up them in blind panic to a little parapet, and cocked a leg over, and saw solid footing and dropped down to it.

I was in a watchtower. I had a single petrified look over the parapet and saw Ham looking up at me, quite a long way below, with his mouth open. He was at the other side of the moat. I'd crossed the moat! I was in the Crusader town. He'd so soon be in it with me that I looked wildly round for another way out.

There was a slitlike hole in one wall of the watchtower, and I went through it, into an evil little chamber with a triangular embrasure and an arrow slit. I scurried through this one, too, into an opposite hole, with steps going down. Little men, medieval ones, even with their helmets on, and I ducked just in time. The place was like mine-workings; coffinlike passages, fetid smell. The cracked uneven steps descended into a corridor, very long and narrow. Bewilderingly, it was set high on the wall of a big stone hall. The hall was vaulted and arched, with stone tracery above and a stone floor below, a good thirty feet below. The corridor was a sentry walk, just about one man wide. I could see all this because bars of light were coming in. There were embrasures the length of the sentry walk, and the floodlight from outside was shining through the arrow slits.

The sentry walk was an open gallery that commanded

not only the scene outside but the hall below. Its open side was fenced by a sagging chain, and a notice above warned that the National Parks Authority wouldn't be responsible if anyone fell over.

I read the notice from the first embrasure, into which I'd immediatdy stuffed myself. I saw right away what I'd have to do. He'd come scrambling up behind me, and without allowing him the benefit of the brief survey I had made, I would shove him over the chain. Then I'd go below and see what could be done about him. He wouldn't be able to do much about me, not after alighting from thirty feet. That's what I would do, and I held my breath and waited for him to do his part of it.

He didn't do it, and I couldn't hear what he was doing. I couldn't hear him at all. I hadn't heard him when he'd been outside Chaimchik's room – just the squeak of his shoes on the marble plaza when he'd come after me, very fast.

What a fool I'd been! Not Patel following me. Ham had been following me. Patel had been following him; had probably come on the strange scene during his night exercise. When I'd vanished in the heaps of spoil, he'd probably continued following him, had gone round and round the Wix looking for him, until stopped by the security guard. He'd probably been trying to tell me so all evening. With consummate cunning I'd got rid of him, of everybody, had carefully manoeuvred Ham back into the position he'd been in shortly before losing me at the atomsmasher.

I heard him suddenly below. A stone snicked and I craned forward and saw him. He was walking in the hall. There wasn't a gate to the hall; simply an entry arch. He had come over the bridge and passed the box office and just walked in. He'd evidently been here before, knew the place. I didn't.

There was no other sound. He padded through the hall, peering upward to the far end. I suddenly realized, with some horror, that in craning forward I'd placed a large head of myself in the bar of light on the opposite wall, and froze in case he noticed.

He was peering at a flight of steps, now visible against the far wall, and evidently running down from the sentry walk. The walk didn't end at the wall but continued through a slit in it, probably along the battlements to the next watchtower. He was peering there, up the steps. Presently he began climbing them and went out of sight.

In much panic I immediately began tiptoeing out of the embrasure to go back the way I'd come. I tiptoed off on the right foot and nearly went over on my face as the left failed to follow. It was wedged in the arrow slit. I felt my head drench with sweat. I tugged, twisted, wrenched, without avail; and just as well because within seconds there was a movement below and he was there again, looking up. He looked right at me, without seeing me, a measuring glance, the length of the sentry walk, and then round again to the opposite wall. A curve of indigo showed another open arch there. He went rapidly through it.

I slipped my foot out of the shoe, and then bent and screwed the shoe out as well, and put it back on and wiped the sweat out of my eyes and wondered what to do. To get outside again wasn't such a magnificent option: big empty car park, long empty road. The road led into a far-flung web of other roads snaking through the sand dunes overlying Herod's suburbs. We'd got lost there in the dark at Christmas while trying to find Foka Hirsch's. He could easily appear on one of the roads moments after me, if not before. I remembered his turn of speed.

Still, I couldn't stay here. His wits were all away at the moment. When he'd got them back, he'd return for a proper check. He'd evidently calculated I hadn't run along the battlements. I made haste in that direction, and at the far end saw the flight of steps going down and the open arch, and saw why he'd guessed I'd gone out that way. It was the quickest way out. Experience had shown him that when pursued I ran. He wasn't to know that a more basic reaction was to hide myself somewhere. His return measuring glance was probably to see how far I could have run in the time. He'd certainly left the hall at the double himself.

I went cautiously through the slit and saw why he'd concluded I hadn't gone this way. It didn't go anywhere, ruined battlements, just a broken platform, evidently the remains of another watchtower, and a flight of exterior steps running down from it: they were badly deteriorated, more like a rocky track. I stepped carefully down them, and in a moment or two came out to a scene of considerable eeriness.

A bit of moon was up and a hazy glow, reflected from the floodlighting, hung like a luminous cloud above the town evacuated by the Crusaders. The excavators had removed the sand of centuries, and here it was, more or less as left, in a hurry, in 1265, after Baybars had sacked it. The Arabs hadn't altered it much. They hadn't done anything with it much. They'd just left it.

All about there was a large confusion of excavated streets, buildings, bases of things, bits of statues. It had been a garrison town, and the paving of the main street was scored and grooved to prevent the cavalry mounts slipping. The grooves glinted now in the electric radiance of another century. Some of the men who'd made it in the last dash down this street to the harbour now lay under slabs in English and European churches, and people took brass rubbings of their sedate effigies. Those little men would have found their way around this place, which was more than I could.

'Igor,' Ham said.

He said it from not far away. I couldn't tell how far or in which direction. I was in deep shadow in the lee of the hall, but I froze.

'Igor, stop this nonsense,' Ham said. 'Let's talk.'

There was a flatness about his voice. He wasn't talking in my direction.

'You aren't going anywhere, Igor,' Ham said. 'I can see you.'

He was a liar, because he couldn't.

I saw him. He was looking the other way.

He was one of the statues with a head on. He was standing about a couple of hundred yards away, on what seemed to be a street corner. He was standing on a plinth. I edged forward and looked where he was looking. A long way off, a good half-mile off, a cluster of lights twinkled. They were the lights of Foka Hirsch and his neighbours. I suddenly realized what he thought I was up to. You didn't have to lose yourself among the sand dunes. From here you could simply keep to the coast and turn inland at the lights.

I turned and looked the other way. The other way was good, too. The jetty was the other way. People were still walking up and down it; mosque floodlit, restaurants and galleries apparently open . . .

I began to move the other way, sideways, watching him. There was a basilisk quality about him as he stood on the plinth. I suddenly remembered this quality of stillness. He'd always been very economical in his movements; except that when he moved he moved fast. He only had to turn for an instant and he'd see me. A moving cat would have been visible enough in this dead city. He stood so still it was hard to keep an eye on him. I had to blink to see him. Presently I couldn't see him. The ground level seemed to be changing alarmingly. I was going downhill. This area was evidently only partly excavated; there were shafts about and newly dug holes. I shuffled cautiously about and skirted them. The glow of the floodlighting was no use here. It hadn't been much use, anyway, in revealing the ground, or more importantly the parts of it that had been removed.

I came quite suddenly on a part that had been removed.

My foot went in it, and fractionally later my behind, sharply, on a spike of rock – fortunately without sound. I was sitting in a long shelf that had been sliced out, and I remained there, watching and listening. Nothing. I waited a little longer and got moving again. Between me and the jetty I could see a low building. It gave the appearance of a solid huddle that one could hide in or about while investigating the scene further. As I drew nearer I saw excavation work had evidently been going on recently, the ground pitted with holes. There were planks across the deeper ones. I crossed a plank and looked in through the doorway of the building. It was roofless but inside was a maze of rooms; corridors, a flight of steps going down, plenty of window spaces to watch from. Not a good idea to be stuck in a building, though. I needed one good look to see that the coast was clear before sprinting for the jetty. It had to be a careful look; so I went out again, and took a bearing on the main street, and decided to get in the lee of the building to view it more thoroughly.

This meant crossing another plank, and then a larger one, a square sheet of wood with a large stone on the edge of it. I began to do this, except that the sheet wasn't of wood, and I didn't cross it. The sheet folded and fell with me and the stone, and a shower of smaller stones, down the shaft that it was covering.

I fell and fell, like Alice in Wonderland, and landed at the bottom, right way up, with a bonejarring thud. The large stone and the sheet of cardboard had landed ahead of me, but the smaller ones continued cascading down for some seconds afterward. The moon was shining brightly down the shaft, and my arms were weirdly raised to it as if in supplication. There was an open space ahead of me. I got my arms down and felt about in it, and then poked a foot out. There didn't seem to be any ground beyond. I must be on a platform of some kind. I looked up at the moon again, and found that my mouth was open, and closed it, and licked sand off my lips.

My wits were so scattered I remained looking at the moon for some moments, and then into the darkness round me; then slowly lowered myself to a sitting position, poked about further with my feet, and found ground. I didn't trust it too much after what had happened, so I put weight warily on it, and found more of it, and stood up and looked at the shaft again. In the moonlight the lower bit of it was streaked with soot. So was the platform I'd landed on.

I felt in my pocket for a lighter, flicked it, and looked about in the little flame. I seemed to be in somebody's kitchen, most probably a Crusader lady's, hurriedly vacated in 1265. The fireplace was set in the wall; it seemed to be the business section of a cooking range, and the stone platform was the rest of it. It extended for a few feet on either side.

In the flame of the lighter I saw that the backs of my hands were bleeding; I'd evidently held them up to slow the fall down the shaft. My hair was full of sand and grit. The cardboard had fallen on the ground, also right way up, and painted on it were the words 'DANGER — KEEP OFF'. The stone had been there to keep it down; I remembered the sound of it as it fell down the shaft, a bouncing and booming sound, with a double thump at the bottom. Accompanied by the percussion of my own arrival, it must have sounded like a landslide above.

Out of here, fast! I looked about to see how the ladies had managed in 1265. There was a corridor, with heaps of rubble in it, and a few openings off, all blocked by fallen masonry. The stairs weren't blocked, thank God, the rubble evidently cleared from them.

I looked up and saw a suggestion of chalky moonlight at the top. Then I looked more closely at the stairs to see that they were all there, put out the lighter, and went up.

I emerged into a small hall with an opening into a corridor and a maze of rooms; and with a little sigh I recognized the old place. It was the one I'd first looked in, that I didn't want to be caught in, and the flight of stairs I'd just come up had been the ones I'd seen going down. Ah, well, it seemed to have been intended that I should view the kitchen, even if by the shorter route – by no means an out-of-the-way route on this grotesque evening – so I gritted my teeth and gibbered a little and waggled sandy eyebrows, did all this in a northerly direction through the window opening there, while looking to see if anything was doing.

I looked just long enough to establish that something was definitely doing. A black object was bobbing and weaving in my direction. Still gibbering, I looked about and decided against the door and in favour of the opposite window, and exited through it. This brought me to the open shaft, and I spat in it before leaving it briskly behind. With the house solidly in between there was no need for concealment, so I made good speed, till my nerve ran out, and then I crouched and looked for him.

I couldn't see him. He wouldn't have reached the house yet. Panting quietly in the darkness, I suddenly realized that there was no reason why he should. Nothing to pinpoint where the sound had come from; only that it had come from near the jetty. It might have given him ideas about the jetty, of course; and this was quite right, because it had.

He showed up presently – not by the way he'd approached. He'd swung round the house. He was making no attempt at concealment. He was talking to himself, quite loudly, and flapping his arms. He was walking in an odd, stumping fashion, without particular haste.

There was an area of light before the jetty and he got to it and stood looking about. He was rubbing his face, rubbing it all over. He began patrolling up and down, covering the approach to the jetty. He came gradually out of the light, and stopped, to my relief.

He called, 'Igor! You are making a terrible mistake, Igor.'

There was a bleating quality to his voice as if he were giving an unaccustomed public address, and his arms were still flapping.

'Do you want to destroy a life, Igor? Do you want to do that?'

I looked about and wondered what to do if he came on. The immediate locality offered some leeway. A number of small walls and stumps stood about. It would be possible to crawl out of it, if one did it slowly: sideways, in the direction from which he had come, the direction of Foka Hirsch . . .

'If it not a life without merit, Igor. You don't have all the facts. Let me explain the facts, Igor. Only, for God's sake, I can't stand yelling here all night!' he said, with something like a return to normality. 'Look, you have had a shock. I understand that. You don't want to talk with me. But at least answer, so I know you are there.'

Quite. And so would he be, moments later.

I'd been outthinking the wrong man. This was no Patel, by no means so fertile or subtle in plan or suggestion. He rarely suggested anything. He waited for things to happen. I recalled Michael Sassoon telling me of a similar pattern in his career. There had been no flights of intuition – just slogging work and some luck. He had never predicted snags. As snags showed up, he had demolished them, and moved on to the next. His experimental initiatives had been similarly simple, with plenty of loopholes. When loopholes showed up, he had covered them.

As this evening: I remembered him opening the door to me. He'd had a towel on. Well, he'd just had a shower, and probably needed one after his cruise through the orange groves (and so did I; I could smell myself sweating in the unpleasantly humid night). He must have been as shaken as I, but he'd let me do all the work, blinking slowly as I came out with the heaven-sent scenario featuring Patel.

He'd gone on letting me do it. With only the slightest

nudge here and there, I'd convinced myself I'd be better off with him at the concert than running about Rehovot telling my story to security men. He'd let me cleverly box Patel out of the ring; had responded to all my initiatives calmly and cautiously, awaiting what God might send next. Except that the news of Patel at the Wix had shaken him. A very nasty loophole. I remembered him laboriously working out the implications. Patel had by-passed his house; had gone from the Wix to the Sassoons'; had seen him, then. Well, it was a loophole, and it needed covering. Perhaps it was while worrying how to do it that he had slipped into his rash disclosure.

And this was much worse. The Patel problem was capable of solution. (He could claim, after all, that he was doing what Patel was doing: following somebody who was following me – an insane enough spectacle but not impossible.) What he had told me offered no loophole. This was a cast-iron snag of the kind requiring obliteration.

I watched the strange tanklike figure flinging his arms as he continued to harangue me. 'Igor, please answer me. I know you'll regret it otherwise. I need your help. I need advice! How could I harm you? You surely know me well enough. Believe me Igor!'

It was hard to know what to believe. It was hard to believe that this enormously distinguished man could have got himself in such a mad position, anyway. But distinguished men were getting themselves in mad positions everywhere. President Nixon was in one at the moment. Willy Brandt, a wiser and better-conditioned man (they'd even given him a Nobel Prize for being so good and kind), was in another: a trusted adviser had turned out to be a spy. In a world where the wise so ludicrously stumbled and the beggars were buying the banks, it seemed as well to keep all options open. So I thought Ham had better tell me about his elsewhere. I was already moving elsewhere, past a low wall and a pedestal and a fallen pillar. After about fifty yards, I looked back and saw him still haranguing me in the darkness, and continued forward, on my stomach.

2

I crossed the main street at its darkest point and cut across to the north of the town. Plain sailing here: hardly anything excavated. I came to hummocky land that wasn't excavated at all, grass still bushy from the winter rains, and went briskly across it. There was a ruined watchtower on the skyline, which looked a useful observation point. I made for it.

A sickening but ovious enough fact hit me at the watchtower. The watchtower was set in the wall. The wall continued round, as did the moat. The Crusader town was enclosed on three sides; the sea was on the fourth, and the Crusaders had controlled the sea (which accounted for so many of them being under slabs in the West instead of the East). There was no way out in this direction.

I remembered Ham having said as much: 'You're not going anywhere Igor.' But wait. He'd been here and I hadn't; on the other hand, I was the historian and he wasn't. I knew enough to recall that Crusader strongholds had more than one gate. They had gates in all walls: postern gates at the least, for surprise sorties. I set out to look for one.

The watchtower was a shade to seaward; no need for sorties this way, so I beat to landward and, to my satisfaction, within minutes came on a finger post, which read clearly in the moonlight, 'TO NORTH POSTERN'. This was where the knowledge came in, and what put the historians that touch ahead at the post.

The finger post pointed further east, and I scurried along there, peering at the wall. Its character changed presently: the ground dipped away and the keying of the masonry altered to accommodate the arch and the steps down. At

281

the same moment, I saw another sign, fingering directly at it – also clear, but not quite so clear. This was because there were more words on it, and they were smaller. It took some time to decipher all the small words: 'NORTH POSTERN – NOTE SORTIE EXIT COMPLETELY BLOCKED, PROBABLY DURING ASSAULT OF BAYBARS I (1265)'.

Well, bugger Baybars, and also Louis IX, the bungling fool. He deserved to have lost, and I was glad he had. Getting his sortie exit blocked. He'd blocked me, anyway. It was true I wasn't going anywhere. Also, where the devil was Ham?

In the last excited minutes I hadn't thought about him, but he surely wouldn't still be haranguing me in the darkness. I came out of the dip in the ground and looked about. There was an arrow slit in the wall above the postern, and the remains of a little guard position; the rest of it was on the ground amid other debris from the wall.

I climbed up it, keeping in the shadow of the wall, and had a good look all round. Nothing was moving in the Crusader town. I watched for several minutes, perfectly still, and then inched cautiously higher and looked along the wall.

It sloped away several hundred yards towards the sea. Bits of it had broken off, and through the gaps I could glimpse the floodlit moat below – a good forty feet below, flat and dry and hardlooking. I couldn't see the end of the moat. I could see where the wall ended. A hump of masonry loomed distantly, evidently the remains of a tower. It took some moments of peering to see that it probably was in the water; a faint luminescence indicated foam in that direction.

Hope began to swell. Of course. The whole lot ended in the water: tower, wall, moat. All Louis's works ended in the water. The water didn't even seem far below. It ought to be possible to get to the tower and either clamber down or swim round to the beach on the other side – the Foka Hirsch side . . .

I came down off the wall and set off there briskly. I found I was going downhill, which made sense. Everything made sense now. I'd had to march uphill *to* the North Postern. From on top I'd seen the wall going downhill. It followed the lie of the land. It was possible that the whole thing sloped gently into the water, without cliffs or obstructions or further nonsense out of Louis; also without the need to climb anywhere. I'd done enough climbing for one night, also crawling, skiing and free-falling, not to speak of probably mile upon mile of steady running.

I came cautiously out to land's end and saw it didn't quite slope gently into the sea. There was a cliff of sorts, twenty feet or so, well-bouldered, nothing to a man of my experience. The beach looked trickier. It was boulder-studded, too. The boulders were set in a continuous drift of cobbles, huge ones, like giant sugared almonds, pale in the moonlight and dappled with tar; it was evidently on the tanker route from Ashkelon. Not easy to teeter, probably slither, along to where I could see lights twinkling from the Foka Hirsch belt to northward. It could take an hour. Where would he be in an hour?

Not continuing to harangue me in the darkness, anyway. Distraught he might be, but stupid he wasn't. It wouldn't take an age for him to review the options open to me. How long after that before he spied me delicately picking a way along this ankle-twisting and slimy beach?

Not a good idea. On the whole such a lousy one that I cudgelled my tired brains and tried to think of others. I could creep back the way I'd come, retracing my footsteps in the dark except that there was no way of telling precisely where he was in it. The basilisk could wait a long time. Time was not one of the things working for me. The night seemed to be getting lighter.

I was suddenly aware that it didn't only seem to be getting lighter. It *was* getting lighter. You could see more in it. The moon was coming into its own as other lights went off. Three went off simultaneously on the jetty, and I looked there. People and cars were still moving on it. Not so many now, of course. Still. The jetty. If he had given up the notion of the jetty . . .

In much confusion, not knowing if it made sense to be stuck on the beach, I began clambering down to it. I got there and waited a moment at the bottom, looking back in case he might be clambering down, too, and put myself behind a boulder twenty or thirty yards away. The journey there convinced me right away that the beach was out. The ankle I'd wrenched hours earlier – only *hours* earlier? – came signalling back strongly. I felt it grinding away as I crouched and looked about.

There was a mutter of water all around as it washed gently over the shingle. A calm swell, very calm – possible even for me to swim. I was a poor swimmer, had a horror of the sea, of getting swept out in it. I'd been swept out once at Sochi, on the Black Sea, had had to be dragged out. But it was no distance to the jetty: barely ten minutes. There was an obstruction on the way and I peered at it. A long line of stone columns, toppled over, were lying in the sea, glittering in the moon. The remains of Herod's VIP jetty – which had in some way offended Baybars?

I followed the line of it to the beach. There was a tiny crescent of white sand there, evidently a result of the breakwater effect of the fallen columns. Something moved on the sand, and my heart missed a beat. *Was* it moving? It was. While moving, it stayed in one place. A dog pawing at something? Prolonged peering revealed not a dog, but two people intent on becoming one. They became two presently, and kneeled, holding each other's shoulders and laughing: a girl and a boy. She gave him a quick kiss and angled herself into a bikini, and he into a pair of shorts, and I poised there, anxious to spread the good news of my presence but held back by a certain ticklishness in the situation. While I hesitated, they ran into the sea.

I watched them swim easily to the fallen pillars, and

heave themselves over, and swim on to the jetty. They didn't get out, but splashed round to a beach beyond.

Well, I could do that. It was visible, though. Of course, they hadn't tried to conceal themselves; they had laughed and called to each other in the water.

I slowly took my jacket and shirt off, and then my shoes and socks, and my trousers. I kept my underpants. The little bay flashed and glittered like silver in the moonlight. I teetered down the beach towards it. It only took a teeter or two to see that shoes were needed after all, so I returned and put them on again and crouched in a low shamble, and entered the water like that.

The sea was warm, scarcely cooler than the humid night, and I suddenly realized I was desperately thirsty. I'd drunk nothing since the glass of Scotch earlier in the evening. The water lapped limpidly about me as I went further out. It was shallow, still well-cobbled, so I shambled a good way, till the sea bed began to shelve, and then abruptly fell away, and I was levitating in it, my shoes suddenly like little rafts of lead.

The glitter all about was dazzling: totally unreal and hypnotic. I kept myself well down in it and turned and looked back. After the brilliance, the floodlighting was positively mellow, the Crusader town with its three walls open to the sea like an enormous theatrical set. I bobbed in the water and looked at the whole length of it, and wondered how the devil I'd got away with it, scurrying up and down there like a demented beetle. The whole area seemed fully exposed in bland hazy lighting. However, I knew it wasn't. There were plenty of pools of darkness there, and he was in one of them.

I'd drifted nearer the columns, and I paddled myself away. Even in the trancelike state induced by the glitter, I knew it wasn't a good idea to put a moving object near a fixed one. I would appear a small moving object, true, something the size of a football, a piece of flotsam, not very visible. Just then a piece of flotsam floated by, an old waterlogged basket. It actually touched me before I noticed it.

I put more distance between myself and the pillars, and began a majestic slow breaststroke. Going full out, it would take only minutes to reach the jetty. I wasn't going full out, and I wasn't going to the jetty, either. I headed slowly out into the moonstream, saw the end of the pillars drift past on my left, and began the wide circle that would carry me beyond the jetty to the little beach at the other side I'd spotted the couple making for.

The sea developed more body as it deepened, the unpredictable sinister lurch well remembered. Everything still very near, though. Music was coming off the end of the jetty, and a couple of waiters were having an argument there. They were doing it on an almost empty restaurant balcony, snapping at each other in Hebrew as they scraped leavings off the plates. The floodlighting went off suddenly at the mosque, and I looked round and saw it dying on the walls of the Crusader city, too. Midnight, evidently. The lion-coloured walls had turned ashen grey, all of a sudden terribly old and insubstantial in the moonlight. The harbour below came suddenly into its own, good nights ringing out, cars manoeuvring. One backed and turned, its two fingers of light swinging across the water. As they did so, I saw another piece of flotsam bobbing in the sparkle by the jetty.

I trod water and watched it. It didn't do anything, just bobbed there. I kept my eyes on it and changed direction slightly, towards the end of the jetty. It still didn't do anything. I watched so hard I could hardly see it, so I altered direction again, towards the shore.

The flotsam altered direction, too.

I thought, Oh, God no, and turned back again and put more steam into the breaststroke. The flotsam did, too. It seemed to be enlarging. All of a sudden there was no strength in my arms as I realized where I was, well out of my depth, floundering, everything suddenly not near but too far, much too far, and no help. Even the waiters had vanished from the balcony. And the flotsam had developed a pair of arms that came suddenly flailing up and down in a fast overarm.

I dropped the breaststroke and went into an overarm myself. But I'd never mastered it and couldn't now, panic rising, water slapping in my face. I took some in, and choked, and knew I had to relax now, take in air, float. But no time for it. He could simply be out to drown me, no violence, just an arm round my shoulders, down, down . . .

I could hardly keep my shoulders up as it was, everything heavy as lead, shoes heavy as lead. I tried to kick them off, but they couldn't come, so I threshed on, and saw a waiter appearing on the balcony again, and in a last effort raised myself in the water and shouted at him. But the shout, when it came, came more as a vomit, and he couldn't have seen the feeble signalling. He paid no attention, anyway, just pitched a bucket of something over the balcony and went back inside and switched the light off.

I saw I wasn't going to make it to the jetty, impossible to make it, so I ploughed heavily round in the water and began trying to thresh back to the pillars. I thought I might just do it, but as I turned he was barely thirty yards away and coming strong. He was fully dressed, jacket, shirt — tie, even. He must have waited till he'd seen me in the water; had watched and waited for me, had seen what I was up to. The clothing didn't seem to impede him. He came powerfully on, mouth in the shape of an O and water spewing expertly out of it. He got to me long before the pillars, his last stroke more in the nature of a lunge. It caught me a bat on the shoulder, and I went under right away.

I didn't take in water this time. I'd expected it, even nerved myself for it, but it didn't diminish the horror as I went down, all my worst fears now on me, the childish, irrational ones although nothing so irrational about it in

287

the case of one who'd had to be dragged out of it. I'd been told at the time that the thing to fear was the panic itself, which wasn't a great help then. It was some now.

In a curious way, fully engaged with my own horror, I felt myself detach from it. If this was the worst, I had to accept it in fact, make the best of it. He could swim better than I, it was obvious. Could he hold his breath better? Could he drown better? I kicked away from him under-water, and came up again, and was in some way behind him, and at once made a grab at his hair. I grabbed it with one hand, and then the other, actually managed to get both knees up and stuck well into his back.

He lumbered heavily round in the water, so surprised that he tried at first to get his arms up to release himself. He couldn't do it but he was still trying as we both went under, backwards. I'd taken several deep breaths while up on his back, and he was still taking one as we went under. I heard him spluttering, and concentrated simply on keeping him under, jackknifing myself over his head, and grimly counting the seconds, one thousand, two thousand . . .

He fought like a big cat in the water, twisting and writhing, trying to pry my fingers loose from his hair. He couldn't do it, and he scrabbled at my face, my nose, found my ears, and practically yanked them off before I had to let him go. I could feel his clothes fluttering away in the water, but a moment later he was trying to clutch me again.

He caught a leg, but his hand slid down it and he only managed to grasp the shoe, and it came off. I kicked out at him with the other, the right, pretty hard. It was a solid jolt, not apparently on clothing, and we lost contact. I came up gasping. I couldn't see him, but I saw the pillars and struck out for them. I heard him behind me but I didn't look round till I'd got there. He was just resting in the water, coughing and panting heavily.

Only a section of the pillars showed above water. There was a foundation below, forming a ledge, which was just as well. I could barely manage as it was. I got a foot on the ledge and a hand on the fluted marble, and levered myself up. The ledge was slimy, and the marble, too, covered in a kind of fungus; I slid onto it and lay there for a few moments, exhausted. He was swimming slowly towards me when I looked back, so I kneeled wearily up. His face was bleeding. It seemed to be his nose. He came right up to the pillars, and I got to my feet. I said, 'Keep away.'

He didn't say anything. He got a foot on the ledge. I said, 'Ham, I'm telling you!'

He just pulled himself heavily up, so I swung my right foot and kicked him hard in the face. His mouth was open and hanging loose and it caught him precisely under the chin. I heard his teeth click, saw his head snap back, then the rest of him, and he toppled back into the water. He floated there awhile, not trying to right himself. I saw him feeling his face. Then he came back again.

I said, 'Ham – please. Keep away.'

He didn't say a word.

'I don't want to keep doing it,' I said.

He just pulled himself out again, streaming water. I couldn't tell if he'd even heard. His face was dazed and bloody and he looked battered and dead beat. But he kept coming, so I waited till he was in position and did it again. He caught the foot in the air, casually, almost irritably, and hung on to it. For a moment we stood and looked at each other in a ludicrous *pas de deux*. Then I jerked the leg away and overbalanced, and he was left with another shoe in his hand and also overbalanced, and we went down together, in opposite directions.

I landed hard on my behind, tried to get up, and went skittering backwards on the slippery marble in a series of pacy little skating steps and tumbled off the other end. I tried to clutch the edge of the pillar as I fell, and did, taking it with me, the edge of it, into the water, and went under again.

I was coughing as I came up, and my only thought was not to let him get near me again. Thoroughly exhausted he might be – he undoubtedly was – but brain still ticked there. He learned. He'd only let me kick him once.

I still had the piece of marble in my hand. It was a jagged segment and I could feel the fluted surface; it seemed to weigh a couple of pounds. It had waited here a long time to be of further use.

He hadn't tumbled into the water himself. I saw him slowly picking himself up, like a mechanical man. He came to the edge of the pillars and looked down at me. There was a strange zombie-like expression on his face. He still hadn't said a word, and he didn't now. He just lowered himself slowly and sat on the edge of the pillars and held out his hand to me.

I said, 'Go away, Ham.'

Blood was pouring from his nose. He kept the hand outstretched.

'I am not coming out, Ham. Go away – please.'

His mouth was opening and shutting. He stepped down from the pillars to the ledge, evidently preparing to join me in the water; so in a panic I gave him a hand, the left one, and kept the other underwater.

There was no particular expression on his face as he pulled me out of the water; he just looked at me in a dazed sort of way. I let him pull me half out before bringing the other hand over in a tremendous haymaker. The thing caught him such a bloody thump on the forehead I actually said aloud, 'Oh, God, Ham, I'm sorry!' and put a hand on his shoulder.

The look on his face didn't change. His eyes didn't even shut. He just continued bending over, and folded on top of me, and we were both back in the water, and I was under again, scrambling and kicking away from him. I still had the stone as I came up and was already wondering – the moment of sympathy undergoing rapid sea change – if I'd hit him hard enough.

290

He was floating face down, so I backed off and let him float. He continued doing it, and I approached cautiously and tugged him with my left hand and slewed him round. He came round slowly, head still down, so I raised it, stone at the ready, but he was flat out, blood-tinged bubbles on his mouth.

I dropped the stone and turned him on his back. He wasn't breathing. I dragged him to the pillars and tried to roll him on the shelf, but he wouldn't stay there, so I got out myself and propped him in a sitting position till I could scramble onto the pillars and drag him up. His jacket rode up and he was a dead weight and kept slipping down through it, but I got half of him up, and then went down on the shelf and shoved his legs up, and got back and rolled him over on his face.

There was still no breath coming out of him. I pressed down on his back, but in my own exhaustion couldn't press hard enough, so I stood on him. Something spewed out of his mouth, and I did it again, and kept doing it till water pumped out, and a choking wheeze sounded, and he was evidently breathing.

He was still unconscious and in the most terrible mess. Blood was coming from his head as well as his nose, and mixing with the vomit and sea water he was spewing up. I didn't know what else to do for him, but he was alive at least, so I slid him out of the pool of vomit and laid him with his head over the edge of the pillars so that he couldn't choke in any further vomit.

I waited awhile, regaining my strength. There was no point in walking ashore along the pillars; apart from the slipperiness, they led only to the little sand beach, and beyond were cobbles again. The quickest way to the jetty was the sea way; so I lowered myself wearily once more into the warm water and slowly swam there, keeping to the shallows.

When I got to the jetty, I was too enfeebled to drag myself up the high wall, so, even beyond swearing now, I continued round to the little beach at the other side, and floundered ashore. My legs were as weak as a kitten's, but I got on the jetty with them and lurched along it in my streaming underpants and looked for the people. They'd all gone. There was just a spark of life in one of the galleries. A neon sign over it said 'GALERIE DELILAH', but even this went out as I approached, and so did a little light inside. The door opened and a small man with a big moustache and a valise came out. He looked at me a bit sharply as he turned to lock up.

I said, 'The police.'

'Eh?'

I could hardly speak. I could hardly even stand. I said, 'I've been attacked. There's someone down there.'

He couldn't at first understand my English, but when he got the idea – it turned out to be not an exact idea – he opened the door in a flash, shuttled me inside, locked it again, and reached for the phone, almost in the same movement. In about half a second he was telling the phone that there were terrorists on the beach, and in response to a quick gabble from it, we moved into an inner room, with the door also locked, and the lights off.

He didn't have any water in the inner room, and he wouldn't unlock the door again, but there was an opened bottle of warm lemonade; so we sat and drank lemonade, Delilah and I, while we waited.

16

It was a strange grey day, Independence Day. I felt strange and grey myself. I'd been booked on the 11 a.m. flight, which meant a hurried departure, but I went to see him first. He was up on a lot of pillows with an enormous bandage round his head. He didn't turn away from the wall as I entered the room. I thought for a moment he was dozing, but then noticed his eyes slowly blinking.

I said awkwardly, 'Well, Ham.'

'Of course, I'll have my name withdrawn,' he said.

'I'm sorry about my superhuman strength.'

'It's all I can do. I'll withdraw from everything.' He was still looking at the wall.

'You'll have to think that over,' I said.

'I've done that.'

He had. They had sedated him but he hadn't remained sedated. He had been talking all night. Marie-Louise's eyes had been red as she showed me in.

I said, 'You know what has been decided, Ham. You know all about that, don't you?'

'It seemed to me a moral obligation. I did what I could. And I am the chief sufferer.'

This seemed such an excessively cool remark, taking one thing with another, that I wondered if it was actually meant for me, and looked round to see if anyone else had slipped in. But there were only the two of us. 'I expect that will remain a matter of view,' I said.

'All I wanted was your goddamn view,' he said. 'That's what I wanted. A life was at stake.'

'That *was* my view,' I said.

He slowly shook his head, wincing. 'I'll have to explain it when we meet again.'

'We won't.'

'Igor – '

'All I want is to see you've got it right. Stick to the story, Ham. Maybe some of your harm can be undone.'

He was blinking slowly at me. 'That is a goddamn harsh remark,' he said. 'If you understand anything, it really is.'

Perhaps it was; it was certainly, in its latter reaches, somewhat overripe. However, I couldn't think of anything better to say, and all of a sudden didn't want to say anything more to him, so I just nodded and said, 'Get better,' and went.

Marie-Louise was outside. It was hard to tell if she'd been listening. It was hard to tell what this rare couple got up to. Her face had been closed in but composed enough when she'd let me in. It seemed to fall apart now. There was something so helpless about the blind and froglike look there that I unwisely put an arm round her, and she collapsed instantly against me in a gale of weeping.

I patted the warm and heaving shoulders for a while, and heard Ze'ev give a peep on the horn outside.

'Marie-Louise, I've really got to go.'

'I know.' She dragged herself away and made some repairs with a damp ball of hanky. She blew her nose in it. 'Would it be treacherous to say I didn't know?' she said.

'I'm not good on the finer points of treachery.'

'For your information, I didn't.'

'No reproaches, then.'

'What about Rod?' she said.

'I'm not good on the finer points of treachery.'

'I'm sorry, too.'

'Keep him to the story, Marie-Louise.'

The story wasn't doing so badly outside. 'That was certainly a brave thing he did,' Ze'ev said. 'How is he?'

'Bearing up.'

'No other news yet?'

'Not yet.'

'Don't worry. We'll get the bastard.' He asked me a good deal about the bastard on the way to the airport. It was the mysterious bastard from whom Ham had saved me.

London was strange and grey, too. I'd mainly dozed on the plane and hadn't taken the meal. I felt empty as I got out of the cab in Gower Street.

My father was coughing over one of his cigarettes and he looked up in surprise as I let myself in. 'Hello, my boy, what's this?' he said.

'How are you, Father?'

'Not so bad. I've been trying to phone you. You seem to have been out a lot lately.'

'Yes. How's Mama?'

'She has a cold again. They started taking the windows out since the weather improved. They'll get it right by next winter. Have some tea.'

'Thanks.'

He went into the kitchen and attended to the tea and I went into the bedroom and attended to the wardrobe. I examined the back of it for a minute or two. There were two grooves in the dust now. Only one before. That was all that there was in the dust. Ah, well. Not a lot to show for what had gone on. It had gone on quickly. Barely twenty-four hours since I'd sat and read Verochka's lament. Only Sunday that I'd got the Southern strawberry fluff in my lap. I remembered Ham walking back up the path before the Presidential tea party. He'd had the keys copied by then. The one to the House had been numbered and tagged, so he'd known which one to keep. He hadn't known which of the others was my father's, so he had sent the lot. With holidays in between, mail irregular, they couldn't have arrived before yesterday at the earliest. Perhaps they hadn't arrived until today.

'Igor?' My father had come into the bedroom. 'What are you doing here? Are you tired?'

'No. I only wondered if something of mine was here. It isn't,' I said sadly. I'd opened the wardrobe and now closed it. 'You look tired yourself, Father. Are you getting out enough lately?'

'I was never a fresh-air fanatic. Yes, I was out today. I gave a lecture, had lunch with the publisher afterwards. Do you know, I think I'm finished with that damned thing, my boy.'

'Well, that's marvellous,' I said. 'And did you manage to get out yesterday?'

'Yesterday, not. I stayed in yesterday. I did the finishing. It was only a matter of looking over a few things. But it's over now. I really think it is,' he said with satisfaction.

This morning, then. While I'd dozed in the sky, and my father haggled with his publisher, and Ham had looked at the wall, another hand had scribed another groove in the dust. Only a few hours in it, really . . .

I absorbed it, during tea. It was quite an animated tea, my father unusually gay. He hadn't haggled with the publisher. He didn't even know the terms. Definitely an act of expiation, then.

It wasn't till I let myself in at Russell Square that I realized there was nobody to tell. She was away with Willie the wine merchant. I stood with my bag and looked round the place. It had a rather forlorn and suspended look. I'd lost track of the various bodies who'd helped liven it up in the past. I'd have to get back on the track. No time like the present, in these matters. Still, I felt like a bath at present. I put my bag down and went in the bathroom and ran it. A few minutes later, I lay prone in it, hot water trickling, and thought over the situation.

I thought of the day I'd walked into this room and found Caroline where I now was, hot water also trickling.

She hadn't been able to hear me above the noise of the water. I'd been saying it was funny Hopcroft hadn't called.

That had been – when? – the latter half of December. Only four months ago? A lot had surely been packed into four months. The British three-day week had come and gone (the bleeding lockout prophesied by Ettie in that bygone era?). So had a British government, and several other governments. Scene-shifting on a large scale had gone on all over the planet's hoary old surface. I seemed to have done a bit of it myself. I felt flat as hell suddenly, and got up and poured myself a drink and took it back to the bath.

The scenery seemed to be in place now for a new kind of entertainment, an *Arabian Nights* one. The customers weren't exactly lapping it up, though they'd accommodated fast enough to the topsy-turvy new logic. Yet an alternative production had been waiting – perhaps still was – in the wings: less fanciful, more humdrum, definitely still in need of a final touch to bring it to the peak of perfection. A spot of new blood among the performers couldn't come amiss, either. Not all the old troupe, shuffling in the wings, had even known what they were performing in.

I got out of the bath and got another drink and got back in and thought over the old troupe: Chaimchik and Pickles, Vava and Olga, Kaplan and old Nancy, to name but a few, with a special guest appearance by the young man from Africa. I had another couple while thinking them over, then I pulled the plug and got out. I didn't feel like dressing. I got into a bathrobe instead and padded down the corridor to pour another. I was putting a bit of ice in, at the fridge, when the latchkey turned, and a few seconds later Caroline was in the doorway.

She said, startled, 'Igor?'

'Hello.'

'What on earth are you doing here?'

I had a distinct sense of *déjà vu*. Surely all this had happened before.

'You're supposed to be in Israel,' she said.

Just as she said it, I realized it *had* happened before, but in reverse order. She had been the one getting the drink after the bath before; I had been the one appearing unexpectedly with my bag in the doorway.

'How was the vintage?' I said.

'All right.' She was staring closely at me.

'Am I looking unusually saturnine?'

'Unusually pissed, I'd have said.'

She was looking different herself. I tried to think whether this was because of the condition in me she had referred to or whether it was because she was looking different. She was certainly calm – unusual after jaunts with Willie. There must have been more going for him than she'd thought.

'Is something wrong?' she said.

'Have a drink. Then you can stop interrogating me.'

We had the drinks in the living room.

I told her presently.

It didn't seem to me as complicated as the carbon cycle. Perhaps my condition made it complicated. Or perhaps the meeting of minds with Willie had rendered her less quick on the uptake this time. It took her a long time to make the connection between tar sand and cancer, and cancer and my trip to the Crusader lady's kitchen.

It had taken Ham a long time, too, to make all the right connections years before. He had been in charge of the tar-sand project for the oil company with which he had been a senior research chemist. There had been several proposals for the exploitation of the Athabasca sands, so all previous work on tars had been investigated. This included Weizmann's, from the still earlier dyestuffs era, whose derivatives of coal tar had apparently merited special scrutiny.

Ham had duplicated these experiments himself, and it had been his successful isolation of cancer cells (produced in mice by some of the derivatives) that had caused him to switch disciplines, to biology, subsequently immunology. A bit later, with the aid of a research grant, he had left the oil company to embark on a purely academic career.

As Michael Sassoon had told me, his work had been plodding, and he had plodded steadily on, producing a stream of useful but unspectacular papers, until towards the end of the 1960s he had suddenly produced a massive and quite spectacular one. It was a reinterpretation of all he had done, but with additional material unpublished from his earlier experiments. For the first time he was able to produce a sizeable chunk of jigsaw, with a strong hint of what the overall pattern was likely to be.

This major breakthrough won him immediate acclaim, several gold medals, and an excellent position in line for the Nobel Prize. Since then he'd moved steadily up the line, to the point when he was hotly tipped to get it this year. Except that, as was now apparent, the work hadn't all been his.

It hadn't sounded specially lurid when he'd maundered on about it last night, and it didn't now. An old colleague had phoned him one day, the senior research chemist (a junior one in the old days) of the oil company he had worked for. He said he had something of interest.

The company had long ago dropped work on the Athabasca sands, but proposed legislation to limit exhaust emissions from automobiles had made them review the work on tar again. One team, headed by a young computer expert, had worked on the 'medical' aspects.

This young man had spent weeks collating the last sixty years' work in the field, and had then fed it to the computer. The computer had come back with, among other things, something very like Ham's latest findings. He had been tickled by this and had fed these findings, too, into the computer, together with some wild flights of his own, until the game had got out of hand and it had been dropped.

The colleague had phoned because he had just read another paper of Ham's; it uncannily bore out the computer's predictions. He had read it, coincidentally, on reading that the young computer man had died in India.

When reading the computer print-outs (by this time some years old), Ham had said he felt as if he'd been 'punched in the gut'. The computer had been not only well up to the mark on his as yet unwritten work but also indicated where he had gone wrong in it.

'Goddamn it, I would have got it right. This happened to me fifty times. There are no easy answers. You have to struggle to all the dead ends. It's a part of the process.'

Whether it was or not, he hadn't had to struggle to these particular dead ends. The computer man, coming freshly to the problem and reading only what the computer told him, had been able to ask the machine some astute questions. The replies gave a wide survey, including many things that Ham had disregarded.

Ham had asked if he could have the work, and his ex-colleague had let him. It had only been a computer game, of no use to the company. However, it had provided the basis for the spectacular paper – and without acknowledgment, an omission made simple by the anonymity of scientific parlance ('it was observed that', 'subsequent investigation showed that'); and his live colleague had kept silent.

This lapse, if it was a lapse (for, after all, the young man had known little of cancer, and relations with the computer had been somewhat incestuous, Ham's own work having gone in it, and the results making sense only to him), had affected Ham badly. It had inclined him in the direction of the booze, with the uneasier effect of putting him in the debt of the former colleague.

The man had rung him up at Rehovot at about the time that Bergmann was in America spreading the tidings of

Vava's batatas, the tidings at that time unknown to me. He had asked Ham what was this new thing with fermented oil. The story was by then all over Rehovot and no secret; in fact it had become a talking point of every coffee party. Olga, as sibyl of the sacred rolls, had become one, too. Ham had seen no harm in telling his friend about it, and the friend had asked where Olga lived these days. Later he had told him more of the unfolding serial of Olga's marital troubles.

Obviously this friend, a distinguished enough man, had not gone about hitting people on the head; the thing had passed out of his hands. At some point, presumably, private detectives or better, or worse, had been employed by some department of the mammoth business. But when people did begin to get hit on the head, Ham had uneasily wondered if it could have anything to do with him. It was at this point that he could have spoken if he wanted, but he hadn't. Despite the booze, despite his easy ways, he was a figure of towering eminence in his field; there was the Prize in the offing. Anyway, he hadn't, and after that he couldn't.

And then his terrible son Rod had made a re-entry into affairs; for a long time I'd had my ears bored off with his misfortunes. There had even once been a suggestion that I could be of help to him: this had been in his Maoist period. (The suggestion had been Marie-Louise's, always a bit hazy on the political spectrum, and apparently had to do with my own early indoctrination in the workers' fight.) He had been kicked out of Berkeley, in itself no easy thing (nothing came easy with this boy), although it turned out that his expulsion had less to do with Mao than with heroin.

From then on, heroin was the word with regard to Rod. It was very like a Victorian tract on the wages of sin. He'd had to be pulled out of increasingly dire situations. Expensive legal work had got him off a charge of pushing the stuff, but his latest communiqué, of a few weeks before, was the most critical yet. He was in hiding, and frightened: a confused story to do with the takings of a pushing venture, of which he had been robbed. It had been a large sum of over a hundred thousand dollars, and little was left. He said that unless he repaid it, he would be found and killed, with or without police protection, and in or out of prison. The organization had a reputation to keep up in this respect. Alternatively, he wondered if his parents could get him to Israel, and what cover was available for him there.

This evil news sent Ham immediately to the bottle. Of the ideas canvassed, that of somehow raising the money seemed infinitely preferable, except that he had nothing like the sum. And then his colleague at the oil company rang up with a proposition. He said the company wished to commission a confidential and fully documented assessment of the Weizmann-Vava process. Though discreetly worded, it was plain that what the company really wanted was someone to dish the dirt, which it had failed to get.

Brooding on his problem, Ham had asked how much. His surprised colleague had named a large sum. Ham said he would let him know, and hit the bottle again. He sent his son a thousand dollars, told him to stay out of sight, and then wrote a cryptic note saying that he knew of someone for the job.

His idea, he had said, was to talk to me: he knew he could convince me of the moral duty of saving a life. Despite all evidence to the contrary, there was merit in this life. (It was this hard-to-define merit in Rod that he had been haranguing me about in Caesarea last night.) Over several bottles he had convinced himself of a couple of other things; he had brooded on my query of months before about the suppression of scientific knowledge. It seemed to him that if the process was economically viable there would be no need to suppress it; if it wasn't, it wouldn't matter if it was suppressed; a useful argument, not quite circular, which omitted a few mundane factors such as existing contracts, refineries, port installations in the wrong ports.

Anyway, he had supplied the information requested, principally about me and my movements. He had specifically demanded guarantees that I wouldn't be harmed, which was very good of him and as satisfying as his arguments on suppression. But to his dismay he had learned he would be paid by result. The copy of the lab books taken from me at the airport was worth only a few thousand dollars; the original, if he could substantiate that there were no other copies, would be worth much more. He'd only get the full sum for the full process.

By this time, realizing the odium of his position, he hadn't been able to 'talk to me'. He had come to the same conclusion that had later occurred to Marta on the car ride to Connie's, that copies of the PS ought to be in the House – the PS that apparently contained the details of the process – which had suggested to him what he had better do next. He had been alert enough not to go to the Wix. He had seen me shuffling about with keys. The Southern strawberry fluff, his suggestion for seconds on dessert, had followed . . .

He had been more or less continuously boozed at the time; though the line had lately been pretty fine with him, accounting for Marie-Louise's anxiety. Anyway, he had had the keys immediately out of my pocket and copied at a locksmith's in the village while I stood under the shower, thus making a bid for the original lab books sitting behind the wardrobe in Gower Street. Yesterday afternoon, after phoning the House and assuring himself that I wasn't there, he had gone for the full sum . . .

Thinking of the House standing in its glacial calm, the whole thing struck me suddenly as a hallucination: what had these absurdities to do with the real world, with the boxes upon boxes of letters, the bits and pieces from Christie's and Sotheby's standing where they had been put in the silent rooms, relics of the couple lying in the grass?

Or with the apartment canyons of Bat Yam, which had somehow resulted from the years and years of drudgery, committee meetings, fund drives, carefully arranged briefings of those temporarily in power – all that intelligent effort? It had more in common perhaps with a pogrom in distant Russia that had brought an excitable rally in Manchester, fortuitously attended by a young Liberal candidate. Or with an unlikely accident in an explosives works in Scotland that had resulted in a brisk train ride and a sudden glint of recognition between kindred spirits. There was a decidedly random quality about things as they happened. I looked into my glass and realized I'd been silent for a while and that she was asking me something.

'How did Dr Patel know about the lab books here?'

'Patel?' He'd cropped up somewhere along the line. 'He deduced it. He's a deductive fellow, Patel.'

'Have you told anyone yet that they aren't here?'

'Not yet.'

'Hadn't you better?'

'There doesn't seem such tearing urgency now.' There wasn't any comfort left in the glass. It had all gone. 'Why don't we just go to bed instead?' I said.

'Well, have you finished with all that? I mean, do you want to chat?'

'I feel chatty as hell.'

'I am sure this is going to be one of those major bombshells.'

'How's Willie?'

'I have consented to be Mrs Willie.'

'Well, congratulations,' I said.

'This isn't the time to explain. I will, though.'

'In bed.'

'That would be a bit damned inappropriate, wouldn't it? I came to collect my things.'

'Afterwards you can collect your things.'

'Igor, darling. It isn't on.'

'*Droit du seigneur?*'

'You aren't the *seigneur*. This isn't the first night.'

'We could anticipate,' I said.

We did, anyway, and Independence Day passed. It had been a long one – rather mixed, on the whole, like Remembrance Day.

2

April, that was. I had a lot of work. May, June, July, and so forth, followed. I was in the history, not the oil, business.

Batatas grew, Finster fermented, Professor and Mrs Wyke returned to America. Connie sent me a cutting from the Jerusalem *Post*, though I'd already seen it in *The Times*. It was headed 'THREE SHARE NOBEL PRIZE FOR HUMAN CELL RESEARCH'. 'Stockholm. An American, a Briton and a Belgian yesterday shared the 1974 Nobel Prize for their research on lysosomes. American George Emil Palade, British-born Christian du Duve and Belgian-born Albert Claude shared $124,000 for their work in "creating modern cell biology"; the "disposal of worn-out parts" and "defence against foreign organisms."'

Well, jolly good. The Jap had been spectacularly dished, as foretold by Ham's jubilant friend. Ham had been quietly dished by other agencies. Cancer wasn't on this year. Bully for Palade, du Duve, and Claude, then, and their disposal of worn-out parts and defence against foreign organisms. We all needed help there.

I knocked off volume 15 and attended to volume 16.

Caroline left me during this. There wasn't much for her to do, anyway, and it seemed to her safer.

Ettie left the service as well, for less complicated reasons. 'Things were going up.' She needed a fulltime job. The 'bleeding lockout' had proved not the peak but the foot-hills of problems. Things were getting steadily madder.

Everybody I'd started with had now left me: Hopcroft,

Caroline, Ettie. Still, I soldiered on. Friends gathered. The Sassoons turned up from Israel, Michael on a sabbatical to Cambridge. They filled me in on what had been left out by other sources. (There had been other sources: Meyer rang from time to time. So had Marta, once, on her way back to Finland, her sabbatical over. 'Perhaps we will meet again,' she said brightly, and we agreed it would be a very fine thing.)

With regard to Ham, the story had been kept up to the end, Patel nobly cooperating. He had been allowed to depart with dignity. He'd harmed the place, of course, might even have harmed millions; still the story hadn't been designed for his protection. It had been designed to give me some leeway in case the keys hadn't yet turned up in London and a collaborator was still around on the campus (impossible to check, all at once, if he had told all the truth, or if some sympathetic sick-visitor might yet gather he had been 'blown' and rapidly pass on the news). But the keys had arrived before me, and there had been no collaborator.

Vava's process had been costed out. It was quite workable. Spread out over enough million barrels, it could provide highgrade oil at a dollar or two under the current price. Finster had worked marvels but the 'unwanted substances' still proved the headache. A good deal of the cost went into getting rid of them. Trying out the stuff on a commercial scale, it seemed, would at once produce a graceful curve in the price of commercial oil to cope with the threat. It would have to come a good deal under the 'dollar or two' to be a workable alternative.

With the carotene converter it would certainly come dramatically under the dollar or two; but they didn't have a carotene converter. So the chaps in the starch belt might have to wait a bit longer. I took a bus to the Embankment one morning and walked for miles through Chelsea and Victoria, watching the sluggish Thames and thinking of the two young men beavering. away in the Manchester basement an unimaginable seventy years before. They had found a solution before the world knew it had a problem. There was a Yiddish proverb of Meyer's that seemed to cover situations like this: '*Gott shickt die refuah far der makke.*' God sends the remedy before the affliction. Well, maybe. Perhaps the affliction hadn't shaped up well enough yet. The remedy was around somewhere, though.

I tried to convey some of this to little Miss Margalit, the Pitman expert, who plodded along the Embankment with me. But she was an uncomplicated person and she made short work of such nonsense. Problems cropped up. One dealt with them.

She had cropped up, not long after the Sassoons. She had phoned me, strangely enough from the YWCA in Great Russell Street. She had come to England for a trip before her military reserve duty. She wondered if I knew of a job for her. I did, of course.

She did an excellent one on volume 16, and since, as she said, there was no sense in paying good money to the YWCA if other accommodation was available, she took up residence with me on the seventh floor. She was an economical and efficient body, only extravagant along the lines slightingly alluded to by Caroline as being to my taste in the long ago, and she fitted perfectly into the establishment. The departure of Ettie had been no disaster to her; she wondered why I'd needed anybody at all.

My father didn't think as highly of her as he had of Caroline, but then she didn't think much of him, either. Old revolutionary persons weren't so thin on the ground in her part of the world, and his defection had seemed to her a bit of a frost when I'd explained it. She was fantastically, marvellously ignorant. Every day was a new day. History had stopped two thousand years ago. Because of some events touched on in volumes 15 and 16, it had tended to start again in 1948. Listening to her explaining to my mother passages of everyday interest from the Bible, I wasn't sure it hadn't.

For all these reasons I was sorry about her and her martial duties. Still, they were some way off, and meanwhile we finished volume 16. I gave a final flick-through to the neatly typed pages, and paused a moment over one of them, comparing with the original. It was for October, 1933. It was October 2nd.

Was den guten Vava betrifft, er ist unverbesserlich. Er hat mit mir letztens . . .

As to the good Vava, he is of course incorrigible. He has been working with me lately . . .

Yes. Translation okay. Footnote key number in the right place, too. I followed it to the bottom of the page.

Vava. Dr Vladimir Kutcholsky: (1894–1962), chemist; a cousin of Mrs W. He collaborated with W. at the Featherstone Laboratory on the protein question.

I studied this for a moment, and after some reflection altered the full stop to a comma, and added 'and other questions.' Everything else about the chemistry of 1933 had shaped up pretty well, though.

LIONEL DAVIDSON

The Rose of Tibet

The Chinese rape of Tibet. A bad time and place to be. With witnesses definitely not wanted.

Hugh Whittington has gone missing, reported dead, while filming near Mount Everest. His brother Charles, determined to find him, embarks on a mission for information. It takes him to the forbidden monastery of Yamdring – and its abbess, a she-devil in her eighteenth incarnation. There Charles finds himself caught in a deadly struggle between the abbess and the invaders of her sacred kingdom. For the Chinese need the abbess and her historic treasure: the sacks of emeralds on which she must sleep with her long foretold visitor from the West . . .

'I hadn't realised how much I had missed the genuine adventure story until I read *The Rose of Tibet*'
Graham Greene

'An excellent and imaginative adventure story'
Observer

'A first-class piece of storytelling, well-plotted, convincing, suspenseful'
Sunday Telegraph

LIONEL DAVIDSON

Kolymsky Heights

Kolymsky Heights. A Siberian permafrost hell lost in endless night, the perfect setting for an underground Russian research station. One so secret it doesn't officially exist. Once there, scientists cannot leave. But someone has got a message out to the West – a message summoning the only man alive capable of achieving the impossible.

'A fabulous thriller . . . a red-hot adventure with a stunningly different hero'

Today

'Spectacular . . . a breathless story of fear and courage'

Daily Telegraph

'A tremendous thriller . . . warmth, love, heart-stopping action'

Observer

'A sustained cliffhanger – brilliantly imagined, thrilling, painfully plausible'

Literary Review

'The book is a triumph'

Sunday Times

LIONEL DAVIDSON

The Chelsea Murders

The young art student has been decapitated. The press dub her murderer 'the Chelsea maniac' – for the killer gives advance warning of each new victim in a campaign that is terrorising London's fashionable bohemia.

The police target three avant-garde film-makers. One of them is mocking the other two – and openly taunting the police as well. Their film itself shows clues. Indeed the murderer even shows himself – in a mask. But which of the three is it behind the mask? That's the problem.

Mary Mooney, an ambitious local reporter out for the big time, tries to solve it herself. In a tête-a-tête (so to speak) with the muderer . . .

'An entertainment. A puzzle. A black comedy. A pleasure through and through'

The Times

'Breathtakingly brilliant'

Spectator

**WINNER OF THE
GOLD DAGGER AWARD**

A List of Lionel Davidson Titles Available from Mandarin

While every effort is made to keep prices low, it is sometimes necessary to increase prices at short notice. Mandarin Paperbacks reserves the right to show new retail prices on covers which may differ from those previously advertised in the text or elsewhere.

The prices show below were correct at the time of going to press.

☐ 7493 1713 2	**Kolymsky Heights**	Lionel Davidson	£5.99
☐ 7493 1716 7	**The Rose of Tibet**	Lionel Davidson	£4.99
☐ 7493 1712 4	**The Night of Wenceslas**	Lionel Davidson	£4.99
☐ 7493 1717 5	**The Chelsea Murders**	Lionel Davidson	£5.99
☐ 7493 1718 3	**A Long Way to Shiloh**	Lionel Davidson	£5.99
☐ 7493 1714 0	**Making Good Again**	Lionel Davidson	£5.99
☐ 7493 1715 9	**The Sun Chemist**	Lionel Davidson	£5.99
☐ 7497 1719 1	**Smith's Gazelle**	Lionel Davidson	£5.99

All these books are available at your bookshop or newsagent, or can be ordered direct from the address below. Just tick the title you want and fill in the form below.

Cash Sales Department, PO Box 5, Rushden, Northants NN10 6YX.
Fax: 0933 414047 : Phone 0933 414000.

Please send cheque, payable to 'Reed Book Services Ltd', or postal order for purchase price quoted and allow the following for postage and packing:

£1.00 for the first book. 50p for the second; **FREE POSTAGE AND PACKING FOR THREE BOOKS OR MORE PER ORDER.**

NAME (Block letters) . . . .

ADDRESS . . . .

. . . .

☐ I enclose my remittance for . . . .

☐ I wish to pay by Access/Visa Card Number

Expiry Date

Signature . . . .

Please quote our reference: MAND